OFFSIDE TRAP

A MIAMI JONES CASE

AJ Stewart

Jacaranda Drive Publishing

Los Angeles, California

www.jacarandadrive.com

Cover artwork by Streetlight Graphics

ISBN-10: 0985945583

ISBN-13: 978-0-9859455-8-9

Books by AJ Stewart

Stiff Arm Steal
Offside Trap
High Lie
Dead Fast
Crash Tack

For Gareth Williamson,
in loving memory

CHAPTER ONE

A crime scene on a university campus attracts a crowd quicker than a Labrador to a dropped hot dog. Which made the scene I drove by as I swung in through the rear campus entrance all the more interesting. If not for the lack of students milling about, anything to avoid the three whole hours of class on their schedules, then certainly for the lack of crime scene tape. And police. I dropped down the gears on the Mustang and rolled by the baseball diamond that should have resembled a movie set but instead looked as quiet as a baseball diamond usually did in the off-season.

I pulled across the road and into the parking lot in front of the athletic center. Like much of the inner campus, the building was a mix of red bricks and white stucco. The red bricks hinted at a pedigree of Ivy institutions; the stucco hinted at the cost of red bricks. The result was less Harvard than Holiday Inn Suites. I slammed the car door shut but left the roof down, making me glance skyward. The sky was heavy for the first time in weeks and the air clung to my shirt.

I pushed through the double doors into the gym and was hit by a potpourri of dried sweat and cleaning solution. A fit young thing in a tight workout shirt and ponytail smiled and directed me to a set of stairs and I strode up two at a time and hit the second floor. The smell had gone and the easy care tiles gave way to gray industrial carpet. Each office door had a pane of marbled glass with a name or three stenciled on it. I reached the end of the corridor and found nothing but a women's bathroom. I turned tail and headed back along the row of doors. The room I wanted had one name and a title. *Kimberly Rose, Athletic Director*. I tapped the glass and stepped in. Beyond the door I found a small office. Another door sat off to the right. A young guy in a gold polo with a panther on the breast looked up from a computer monitor and smiled.

"Can I help?"

"Miami Jones," I said by way of explanation. The guy nodded, hit a button on a console and spoke into a small unit that was attached to his ear. He nodded several more times. I took in the office walls. They were covered in photos and posters of young people playing a variety of sports. Girls playing soccer, boys playing lacrosse. I noted there wasn't a football shot to be seen. There were team photos, basketball and baseball and field hockey. The shot of a girl serving in tennis. I thought I recognized her from somewhere. The guy at the desk looked up, smiled again and told me to go through.

The interior office was much bigger. There was a conference table in one corner under a massive whiteboard. A shelf of books flashed titles like *Leadership in Sports Management* and *Team Building*. Horizontal blinds were pulled all the way up offering a view of the road and an expanse of green sports fields. A counter-height desk without a paper on it took up most of the end of the room. Kim Rose stepped out from behind the desk, light on her feet. She wore slim khaki slacks and a blue polo with a panther on the breast. Her skin was pulled tight across her face. She had black hair cropped short and brown determined eyes that creased slightly in the corners as she smiled.

"How are you, Kim?"

"*The Miami Jones*," she said, opening her arms for a hug.

"In the flesh," I said. We wrapped arms around each other. Her waist was thin and she didn't carry an ounce of anything she didn't need. She slapped my back and then pulled out and held my shoulders like she was appraising a limited edition print.

"You're still alive," she said.

"Some days more than others."

"Well, it's great to see you. It's been too long." She gestured to a small sofa that sat below the window. I sat at one end. She faced me, her back to the armrest, and she crossed her legs like she was practicing yoga.

"How've you been, since college?" she said.

"Still alive, as you point out."

"I saw where you got pushed up to the majors. Oakland wasn't it?"

"Ancient history."

"What happened?"

"It didn't stick. And what about you? Olympics, World Cup?" I glanced around the room. "Where's the silverware? Or should I say gold?" It was then I noticed that the room contained nothing of a personal nature. No photos, no medals, no trophies.

"Ancient history." She smiled. "And now you're a detective?"

"I am."

"With that guy? The one you met while we were at UM?"

"Lenny Cox, yeah. But he's no longer with us."

"Rival company?"

"Dead."

She nodded the way people do when death rears its ugly head in a conversation. We sat in silence. I recalled how silence between us had once been so comfortable. Not so much now.

"So you called?" I said.

She took in a deep breath, in through the nose, out through the mouth. I recognized it well. She did it every time she stood in front of a penalty kick, every time she wanted to focus her mind on the task at hand. The last time I saw her do it I was watching the television in the bar at Longboard Kelly's, and she was shutting out the national anthem before a World Cup soccer final. Now her breath blew long and low and she looked at me. She laid her hands in her lap and tapped her fingertips lightly together. I don't think she noticed. She was focused on me.

"I need your help." She said it like she was requesting a kidney.

"Okay."

"I need you to investigate something for me."

I nodded. We had covered this much when she called my office, and it seemed we were tap dancing around a candle.

"Tell me your problem," I said.

"There are so many. Where do I begin?"

"At the end."

She tapped her fingertips. "One of our student-athletes overdosed."

"Yes. On what?"

"I don't know. Some new fancy thing."

"When?"

"They found him last night."

I nodded and looked at her. She was tanned but not too much. Like she spent a lot of time in the sun but always wore sunscreen. My hands looked like Naugahyde in comparison. She didn't take her eyes off mine. Most people would gaze away, at their lap or over my shoulder. Not Kim. When she gave you her attention, she was fully committed.

"Okay," I said. "Let's take a step backward. Who's the kid?"

"Which kid?"

"The one who OD'ed." I creased my forehead. It was reflex and contributed to the furrows on my well-weathered brow.

"His name is Jake Turner."

"Is? He's not dead?"

"No, God no. He's in the hospital."

"When you called, I assumed. So what's his condition?"

"Coma, I'm told."

I nodded. "What's his relationship to you?"

"He was on the lacrosse team."

"Any good?"

"The star player."

Kim unfolded her legs and stood. She strode to the front of her desk and leaned her back against the edge. It was one of those desks for people who liked to stand while they worked. Kim was one of those people. She never stopped moving. It explained why she was still so trim five years after having ceased playing any kind of professional soccer, and why I had to run six miles a day along City Beach just to stave off a muffin top. I didn't get up from the sofa.

"What aren't you telling me?"

Kim shifted her feet and looked at me again.

"The president of the university wants me out."

"Why?"

"He doesn't like sports."

"He wants you gone because he doesn't like sports?"

"No. He wants me gone because he wants all sports programs gone and therefore he has no need of an athletic director."

"The president wants to kill all sports programs?"

"Yes."

"He doesn't understand *salubre corpus, quod mens sana*?"

"I don't understand that."

"A healthy body, a healthy mind."

"No. He believes that sports takes money away from academic research."

"Does it?"

"What the hell has that got to do with anything?"

"It might explain his position."

"His position is moronic," she said, pushing away from the desk. She began pacing. "We're a Division II school. We don't have football so we don't bring in the big bucks. But our basketball team has won division titles, our lacrosse program is as good as any and our women's soccer team has produced two Olympians. That's not to mention Caroline Sandstitch."

When she said the name I remembered where I'd seen the girl playing tennis in the poster in the outer office. It had been at a tournament out on Key Biscayne. I got tickets from a grateful client and had been more interested in the hors d'oeuvres and champagne than the tennis, but I recalled her losing in straight sets.

"She top fifty?" I said.

"Top thirty now. And we have some good kids coming through. But it will be for nothing if he gets his way. It will be all gone. Basketball, baseball, crew, soccer. Everything, even golf."

"You have a golf team?"

"Of course, we're in the golf capital of the world. We have men's and women's teams, and we even offer a major in golf administration. Hell, he'll probably get rid of that too."

I paused for a moment and then asked Kim to come and sit down. She stopped pacing and sat, legs crossed, fingertips tapping.

"Tell me what all this has to do with the kid in hospital."

"He's a student-athlete, you see? Millet will try to link this to the athletics program. Use it to shut us down."

"Millet?"

"Dr. Stephen Millet, PhD. The university president."

"And does it have anything to do with the athletics program?"

"Of course not, Miami—come on. The kid took some designer drug. It happens. It's college after all. The fact he's an athlete is neither here nor there."

"Okay. So what is it you want me to do?"

"I need you to find out what the drug is and who's supplying it."

"I'm pretty sure the local police will do that."

"The local cops are all in Millet's pocket. I need you to find out the truth, not what Millet says, so I can show that this is not an athletic department issue."

"I see."

"And I need you to do it quietly. I can't have him know that you are doing this for me or he'll use it against me."

"That won't be easy."

"But you can do it, right? Discrete investigations, and all that?" She smiled her tight smile.

"With us, it's *relatively* discrete investigations. But I'll see what I can dig up for you."

She put her hand on mine. "I appreciate your help on this."

"You bet."

She stood and I followed. "I can get a few students together for you to talk to. A coach or two."

I shook my head. "I'll let you know if I need that, but for now, just tell me the kid, Jake Turner was it? He was found at the baseball diamond, right?"

"Yes, under the away team bleachers." Kim pointed out the window. "I'll have my assistant walk you over."

"Don't bother. I'll walk around a bit, get a feel for the place. I'll let you know if I need anything."

"Sure, whatever you want. And Miami, it's great to see you. I'm sorry it's been so long."

I nodded. I was going to wink but thought better of it. I smiled instead, and then I walked out.

CHAPTER TWO

The University sat on sprawling grounds west of Fort
Lauderdale-Hollywood International Airport, on the wrong side
of the turnpike. In the not too distant past there had been plenty
of land, so the campus had spread out rather than up. Then the
housing estates and strip malls leached westward until they
butted up against the Everglades. Now the college was
surrounded by suburbia, in one of those parts of the state that
baked in the summer to remind you that you were in Florida, but
was far enough away from the beach to make you forget why you
came.

Kim had described a gulf between her athletic department
and the academic side of the college. The gulf was literal too. A
thick expanse of blacktop, a road that severed the sports fields
from the main campus buildings. The only sports facility on the
campus side was the one I had just come from, which housed
the gym, the basketball center and the athletic department
offices. Across the road lay a speed hump that seemed much
larger than it needed to be. The far side of the road housed
several older buildings, tagged as offices for coaching staff,
physical fitness instructors and rehab. Beyond those lay the
green fields I had seen from Kim Rose's office. Fields for soccer
and lacrosse. There were no stands or bleachers, just what I
counted to be about ten playing fields.

Further along the road I wandered past a stand of Australian pines, which stood guard over the turnstiles to the baseball diamond. The structure was too small to be called a stadium. There were bleachers on either side of home plate, wood on the first base side, aluminum on the third base side. Either someone had started to renovate and quit halfway through, or they really wanted the away team's supporters to be uncomfortable. Aluminum seats in Florida summer were like sitting in a griddle pan. A green concrete ramp sloped up between the stands, right behind home plate. I ambled up to take in the ground. The main campus grounds were immaculate and the buildings new, clean and sterile. The baseball facility however, looked like it had been stolen from Asheville, North Carolina, circa 1950. Below me were ten rows of concrete slabs leading down to the plate. No ergonomic plastic seats. Seriously BYO cushions. The sideline bleachers above ran back just beyond the first and third bases respectively, each ending abruptly. Beyond the bleachers a chain-link fence looped along patchy grass, around the outfield and back again. The outfield was lush and long, recovering from a hot summer. The diamond itself was sharply marked on immaculately groomed red clay. Where the bases should have been there were only large divots, the bags themselves having been removed until spring training, lest the bases literally get stolen. The fractured gray sky served to throw a dull tint over the field, as if to say *closed for business*.

I noticed someone sitting in the bleachers on the home side, in the top corner as far from home plate as one could get without clambering off the structure and leaping onto the grass bank. The person was sitting alone with their thoughts, staring at the diamond. Bleachers are like that. Back when I played in the minor leagues I used to wander up into the stands along the baseline and think about my game or my life or nothing at all.

The person turned and I noticed a ponytail dropping from behind her head. She was wearing some kind of athletic training uniform: T-shirt; shorts and knee-high socks, all white. The sky made her hair look the color of straw. I didn't think she noticed me so I stepped back down the ramp. I ducked under the aluminum stand on the away side, where Jake Turner was found.

It was dark underneath, shards of light seeping between the gaps in the seats. The breeze tinkered with the hollow aluminum slats, making the whole area sound tinny. It looked the kind of place a student would go to take drugs. Secluded and dim. No one would have reason to go under there unless they shared the habit. The ground felt soft yet firm underfoot, like moist clay. I wandered back out to the green ramp and stepped across and under the bleachers on the other side. If anything the light was lower and the wooden benches served to absorb the sound, giving the space a silent, cave-like quality. This side was an altogether better place to partake in a drug habit, at least the kind that couldn't be consumed at a bar. It was a heavy and depressing area and I felt my back shiver as I moved about, light on my feet as if in a church. To my right the gloom seemed to shift, like a temporal displacement. I closed my eyes and then opened them and allowed them to adjust, and then I glanced sideways at where I thought I'd seen movement, and a hazy apparition appeared, ghostly white. It took a few moments to realize it was the girl I'd seen sitting up on the bleachers. She was hazy in my vision, but I could make out the uniform.

"Hi," I said. My voice was swallowed by the emptiness. I wasn't even sure I heard it myself. We stood for a moment looking at each other, like half-formed thoughts in our minds, and then bit by bit the white disappeared and the girl stepped slowly away from me and vanished. I didn't chase her. In fact I didn't move. I didn't see the point. I kicked around for a bit in the darkness, sweeping my foot across alternate patches of grass and dirt. I didn't expect to find anything, and nothing is exactly what I found. I made my way back to the green ramp. The dull day felt bright in comparison. I walked up the ramp to look at the bleachers again. The girl was gone. No one was sitting high in the stands contemplating life, physics, baseball or anything else. I wandered back down the ramp and away from the baseball field. I suddenly wished to be somewhere bright and cheery. Somewhere they served beer. I didn't get either wish.

CHAPTER THREE

I got about halfway back to the speed hump in the road when I noticed an old fiberboard building that looked something between a California bungalow and a portable classroom. It was a gritty cream color with green moss growing inches up from the ground. I stopped to look at a poster in the window. It was an angry cartoon panther holding what looked like a large fly swatter. Under the big cat were the words *Panther Lacrosse*. I stepped up a cracked path to a fly screen door. It creaked angrily when I opened it. I pushed open the wooden door behind it and stepped inside. The building was divided into four rooms of more or less the same size, with a tight corridor down the middle. Two rooms faced the baseball diamond, the other two faced the open playing fields. The space smelled of wet grass and sweat. It was more humid inside than out. I wandered past two doors with plastic nameplates that said they were coaching offices, one baseball, the other women's soccer. I kept walking to the door of the office I figured housed the Lacrosse poster. The door behind me had no nameplate; the door in front read *Coach McAllister, Lacrosse*. Having been a college athlete myself, I knew the drill. I knocked a quick double tap, and then waited for the call of *come*.

Coach McAllister's office was the same sort of chaos I'd seen in every coach's office, from my football and baseball

coaches at the University of Miami to every coach or manager
I'd played for in the minor leagues. It was just the quality of the
junk that changed. McAllister's desk was a bonfire in waiting. No
coach worth his salt liked the paperwork. In bigger programs
they had staff for the administrative stuff. Clearly Division II
lacrosse didn't qualify. The balding man behind the desk finished
what he was scribbling before he looked up. He was a thick man,
barrel-chested with lumberjack's arms covered in dense black fur.
His face had the topography and color of a walnut shell. I
couldn't have guessed his age, but he certainly wasn't young. He
looked up at me with expectation, like a stranger walking
through his door was a regular occurrence.

"Coach McAllister," I said.

He pulled at his polo shirt to show me the embroidery
under the Black Panther. In prosaic script it said just those
words.

"Miami Jones," I said.

"You're a little out of town, aren't you?"

"I live near West Palm, so I guess so."

"No, I meant Miami. You know. Forget it."

I already had. Standup wasn't this guy's gig. "I'm looking into
the Jake Turner thing."

He leaned back in his chair. He was wearing a whistle on a
lanyard around his neck.

"I know," he said. "Miss Rose said I might expect you."

I noticed a touch of New York in his accent, but there are
so many New York accents in Florida, *fugedaboudit* was like the
local vernacular.

"Where you from?" I asked.

"New Paltz," he said. "You?"

"Connecticut. How long you been down?"

"Five years. You?"

"Since college."

"You must like it."

"I do," I said. "It's home. You don't?"

"It's hot. But my wife hates the winters in New York, so here we are."

He hadn't offered me a seat, and I knew the program, but I figured he wasn't my coach so I helped myself to a chair.

"What can you tell me about Jake Turner?" I said.

He blew out a big breath and his lips vibrated. "Where do I start?"

"At the end," I said.

"Well, it's a shock, I'll tell ya that. Drugs. I never would've picked it."

"Why's that?"

"Jake was a good kid."

"He's not dead."

"Not far off it is what I hear. I went to the hospital but they only wanted family. I told 'em there weren't no family here but they didn't care. Now the family says they want no one from the school to visit."

"Tell me about him."

"Like I say, good kid." McAllister unrolled a mint and tossed one into his mouth. He offered me the pack and I shook my head. He took a couple of sucks before continuing. "He can sure play lacrosse. He's one of those kids, you know. Could play anything. Our best player. But a smart kid too. A leader. That's why I made him captain."

"Where's the family from?"

"New England. Massachusetts, I think. He had one of them accents, you know?"

"I do. So how do you think a star athlete winds up under the bleachers?"

McAllister shook his head. "No idea. Honestly. The wrong crowd I guess. It happens, don't it. Terrible waste though."

I let him ruminate on that for a bit—then, "Who did he hang out with? Teammates, friends? Girls?"

"The team mostly. I mean we're not Division I or anything, but we work plenty hard. Between practice, games and classes, not a lot of time for much else."

"Time to fall in with the wrong crowd."

McAllister nodded. "True enough. Look, I wasn't the kid's minder. He was popular, charismatic even. I guess there were parties and stuff, but I never heard of any trouble. None of my players have ever turned up drunk or drugged to practice. They know they'd be out if they did."

"Nothing in drug testing?"

"Never. I've never had a positive result."

"Neither did Lance Armstrong."

McAllister shrugged.

I stood and brushed my khaki trousers. I'd chosen a button-up shirt with vertical stripes that made me look even taller than I was. It seemed on this campus I should have worn a polo. Coach McAllister stood and shook my hand. I made it to the door before I turned around again.

"What do you make of your President Millet?"

McAllister shook his head. "No good. Wants to get rid of us all. I mean, what the hell is a college without sports?"

"What indeed. Thanks for your time."

"Anything I can do. He's a good kid."

I left McAllister to his bonfire preparation and wandered back out onto the road. The cloud showed no mood for breaking but the day had warmed up some. I got to my speed hump across the divide back to the main campus. A car crawled toward me. I turned away and kept walking until the car reached me. It was a police cruiser. Not campus cops, the local town variety. I wasn't sure what they were doing on campus, but it may have been a reaction to the Jake Turner situation. The cruiser slowed to walking pace and stayed beside me. I kept walking. There's nothing that a patrol cop loves more than being ignored. We continued for about twenty paces before the cop got sick of waiting for me to take the hint and gave me a bleep on his siren. I stopped. The cop kept going a few feet before noticing I wasn't alongside. He waited for me to walk up to the car until he figured I didn't get that hint either, and he threw it into reverse and rolled back until the passenger window was opposite me. The driver's door flung open, and the cop unfurled himself from the car. He was a hard-looking unit with a square head.

"You Miami Jones," he said.

"I am."

"Get in," he said. So I did. I am nothing if not a law-abiding citizen.

CHAPTER FOUR

The cop's car was a police spec Dodge Charger, a couple model years old but impressively clean inside. It smelled of Pine-Sol. The cop filled the driver's seat completely. He wore cologne and gave off a minty scent. I sat in the front with him. He didn't seem too fazed by it, so I assumed I wasn't in any kind of trouble. If a cop thinks you are in any kind of trouble, you sit in the back, no questions asked. We drove in silence around the campus, and then he cut in toward the center of a phalanx of buildings. We drove around the quad, modeled on Harvard Yard or Brown or some such, with concrete pathways cutting across the lawn, under the cover of trees. Only difference was instead of ancient oaks, the trees were palms, and offered next to no shade. But I liked it. There's something about the naked trunks and jaunty throngs of palms that makes me feel at home. The cop stopped his car outside a gleaming glass and concrete building that could have been a bank or an office for some technology firm. Concrete steps led to the large mirrored frontage. On one side of the steps a sign declared the building to be *Johnson House, Administration*. On the other side of the steps, a newer sign read *Office of the President*.

The cop got out of the car, so I followed. We walked up the steps to a revolving door. The cop stopped and ushered me in with a wave of his hand.

"You first," I said.

He shook his head. Not even a smile. I might not have been in any kind of trouble, but he wasn't going through a revolving door with anyone behind him. I stepped in and spun around. He waited until I got into the lobby before following. As he came through I got a look at his nameplate. Black letters on gold told me his name was Steele. That seemed about right. His jaw was all sharp lines and set firm. He walked me to the elevator. We waited in silence for the elevator to come. I rocked back and forth on my heels. Steele stood at attention. He was only a touch under six feet, so I looked down on him by an inch or two, but he was bigger in every other way. The elevator dinged and two young women got out. We waited for them, and then stepped in. The buttons gave a choice of one, two or three. Steele hit three. The door closed and the gears clunked and whirred and that silence that people observe in elevators descended upon us. Not that things had been particularly chatty up to that point.

"Any clues?" I said.

Steele turned his head slowly and stared at me. "Excuse me?"

"Where we going?"

He turned his head back to face the door.

"The president wants to see you."

I had to admit for a second, thoughts of CIA and international espionage flew across my mind. Then the elevator dinged again and the doors opened and I found myself in a large foyer. The floor tiles, furniture and lamps were all cream-colored. The walls were wood paneling, some expensive and nearly extinct hardwood from South America. In the middle of the space a huge hole opened up revealing the second floor below. An ornate balustrade encircled the hole in the floor, and above a stained glass dome filtered colored light across both floors. Offices fed off the balcony that ran around the atrium. On our right was a reception desk. Steele deposited me there.

"Mr Jones," he said to the receptionist. She was short and wore way too much makeup for someone not appearing in Japanese opera. She reminded me some of my own office manager, Lizzy.

"Thank you, officer," she said. Steele turned on his heel like he was changing the guard. He marched back to the elevator without a word.

"Would you like to take a seat?" said the receptionist, gesturing to some waiting chairs that looked like mini Swedish sofas.

"No," I said. I stood by her desk and watched her work for a couple of minutes. I generally find support staff hustle things along when they have someone hovering over them like a vulture. She picked up the phone three times to rouse the president. He must have been on the phone himself because it took a fourth try before she got through. She asked me to follow her. It wasn't a long journey to the door next to her desk, and I felt confident I could have made it on my own, but it seemed that pomp and ceremony were a thing around here. I wondered if a lone bugler played *taps* in the quad at sundown.

"Mr Jones, sir," said the receptionist, and she stood aside to let me pass. The room wasn't Florida at all. It wasn't even New England. It was old England. A twenty-foot ceiling allowed for two tiers of books to wrap around the room. I didn't see too many John Grishams in there. Just a lot of brown leather. A large round table sat to my left, under a window that looked out onto the quad. The table was burgundy-colored wood and looked like it would have been at home in Windsor Castle. Green leather upholstered chairs ringed it. A massive book lay open on the table. It looked as big as the King James Bible but could have been the Magna Carta for all I knew. A man stepped around a large dark desk that looked like it was once part of a city wall. The man smiled a butler's smile. He wore a beige cotton suit that clashed with the room. I expected pinstripes. He had a neat, close-trimmed gray beard that was as well manicured as the greens at Augusta National. His hair was cropped and the gray-white color of cigarette ash.

"Mr. Jones," he said, extending his hand. I didn't take it. I just kept looking around the office.

"I thought your office was an oval," I said.

He had a forehead as smooth as Formica, and it barely rippled as he frowned. Then the penny dropped, and he gave me the butler's smile, all form, no substance.

"I see, the Oval Office," he said. "And me being the president."

I smiled and put my hands in my pockets.

"So," he said, turning back to his desk. "I am Dr. Stephen Millet and I am president of this university. But you know that."

I love it when people with PhDs refer to themselves as doctor. It always feels so warm and friendly.

"Actually I didn't know that. Your name that is. Everyone around here just refers to you as *the president*."

"Universities can be such formal places," he said, sitting behind his desk and gesturing to a visitor's chair that looked like a museum piece. I wandered over to the wall of books. They were the kinds of books one didn't touch, lest one crease the spine. Call me old-fashioned, but if I'm going to bother buying a book, I figure I might as well give it a read.

"What can I do for you, Mr. Millet?"

"It's Dr. Millet. And I heard you were on campus, so I just wanted to let you know how horrified we are with what has happened."

"With what has happened."

"Yes. I can assure you that this university takes drugs in our student community very seriously, and we are doing our utmost to assist local law enforcement with their inquiries."

"You are."

"Of course. Now unfortunately I haven't been able to get to the hospital personally as yet, but I do hope you pass on our thoughts and prayers to Jacob's family."

"You a religious man, Mr. Millet?"

He coughed and rubbed his hands together like he was cold.

"Well, it's Dr. Millet, and please just pass on that we are thinking of him."

"I'm sure you are. Can you tell me why a town PD cruiser picked me up? Where are the campus cops?"

"We don't have a separate campus law enforcement department. Our size doesn't make it efficient."

"You mean it's cheaper," I said.

"Well no, it's just with our population, it works better for everyone if we contract that work out to the city."

"You pay the city to have their cops patrol your campus?"

"That is correct."

"What about security?"

He rubbed his hands more. I was going to be able to see my reflection if he continued much longer.

"We have our own security director."

"And who works for him?"

"Mostly the local law enforcement officers also help out with campus security. You know, when they are off duty. We find it to be an excellent system."

"Not so excellent for Jake Turner."

"Mr. Jones, I can assure you that this is an isolated instance, and we are moving heaven and earth to find out how this happened."

"Many other drug problems on campus?"

"Of course not. But we are looking at the relevant programs to ensure any bad apples are not allowed to poison the barrel, so to speak."

"What relevant programs?"

"Well, I can't say too much until the investigation has been completed, but sports programs often have such problems at other schools."

"Sports programs? Like lacrosse?"

"All sports programs. That's why the USADA exists. I can assure you there is no such body required to test our physics students."

"More's the pity. Someone should have tested the guy who came up with string theory, that's for sure."

"Be that as it may, we are looking into these programs, as are our law enforcement authorities. Now whilst I appreciate that Jacob's family want answers, and we will as such accommodate you and your inquiries, I do hope you appreciate that our authorities are best placed to investigate this matter, and will allow them to do so unfettered."

I wasn't completely sure what it was Millet had just said, but my babel fish was translating it something like *stay the hell out of our way*. Which wasn't going to do at all. I just didn't feel like saying that. What I wanted was to be away from this stuffed shirt of a man and on a comfy stool with a cool one in my hand.

"Understood," was what I said. I told him it was good to meet him, and he got up from his throne and walked me to the door.

"If there is anything I can do to help, or any news on Jacob, please call on me." He offered his hand and this time I took it. I was expecting it to be a cold, wet fish but was surprised to find it firm and warm-blooded.

"And please pass on our thoughts to Jacob's family."

"I surely will," I said, and I strode to the fire stairs and down into the quad. The sky looked brutal, like something was brewing up there. Despite the heavy day it was glaring out, so I donned my shades and wandered back to my car, thinking that I would indeed pass on the good doctor's wishes to Jake Turner's parents, just as soon as I tracked them down and met them myself.

CHAPTER FIVE

By the time I headed north out of Fort Lauderdale and got back to West Palm Beach the sky had thickened and fat dollops of rain were hitting the windshield and spreading out like pancake batter on a hot pan. I made the call to head straight to Longboard Kelly's. I could have gone to the office, but then I would have just disturbed Lizzy from getting on with whatever it was Lizzy got on with that kept LCI ticking as a viable entity. Business in the Palm Beaches was decent enough. There were plenty of rich nosy neighbors, jilted lovers and spouses, and annoyed insurance firms to keep us busy. But if it were up to Ron or me to keep focused on the business nitty-gritty, we would have been a sunk ship years ago. Lizzy held things together, and I think she more or less preferred it when I was out of the office, so I skirted downtown and pulled into the lot behind Longboard's.

It was as steamy as a crockpot when I got out of the Mustang, so I let the big raindrops hit me. It seemed I wasn't the only one with the evaporative cooler idea, because most everyone was standing in the courtyard, eyes closed, faces to the sky. Ron opened one eye, scoped me and smiled, and then closed his eyes again and turned his weather-beaten face to the heavens. A large splotch exploded in his gray hair and he laughed. Muriel the bartender had abandoned her station and stood arms outstretched, huge breasts pointed to the rain, mouth open to catch her fill. All the other patrons were out there with them. A visitor might have thought they had landed in the Oklahoma dust bowl, a year since the last rains. Truth was it had only been three weeks. But three weeks in the tropics feels like forever, as the heat rises from the ground and the humidity builds like a pressure cooker. People start doing crazy things. Standing out in the courtyard of a bar that sells cold beer, waiting for a raindrop to land on your tongue was the least of the craziness. I glanced at the courtyard bar, where my favorite stool sat waiting. It was under a thatched palapa that usually served to shade me from the beating sun. My stool faced across the bar and into the main barroom. Mick, the owner of Longboard's, stood behind the bar watching the lunatic rain catchers with an impassive face. Mick had no mind for such antics. He stood, tattooed arms crossed, wearing a tank top like Muriel but without the topography. I wandered over to him.

"What do you think of the weather?" I said.

"This too shall pass." It was a truism alright.

"Hard or soft?"

"Hard," he said. And he was right. We watched for barely a minute before the heavens cascaded down like Niagara Falls themselves. The crazies didn't run for shelter. It took no longer than five seconds for each of them to be drenched to the bone. That's the thing about tropical rain. It really gets about its business. And then there's only so wet you can get. Mick grabbed a dish towel and threw it across his shoulder, and then he nodded at me.

"Make yourself useful, Miami." He ambled back into the dark bar and I wandered around past the bathrooms and inside, and then I ducked under the counter and stood behind the beer taps. Ron was my first customer. I poured him a Yuengling, and he held it up in cheers and wandered back out into the rain. I served a few more beers, two white wines from a bottle with no

label and a couple of tequilas and lime. Everyone went back out
into the rain. It didn't matter. No one was catching a cold. It was
pelting down but still eighty-five degrees out. People
congregated around the plastic patio tables, each with a faded
beer labeled umbrella in the middle. Everyone held their drinks
under the umbrellas so they wouldn't be diluted by the rain. For
half an hour I acted barkeep and the rain pounded down. Then
as quickly as it began, it stopped. The sun didn't break through
the cloud, but the humidity wrapped itself around the bar and
everyone retreated, dripping and sodden, back to their seat or
stool. Ron took his stool at the outdoor bar, where I poured two
beers. Muriel swung in under the counter. Her skin was wet and
tan, and the drops of water ran across her arms like mercury.
She wrung her hair with her hands like a wet dish towel and
dripped all over the floor, and then she patted me on the
backside.

"Thank you, darlin'."

I skipped back under the counter and took my stool.

"So what's the news on campus?" said Ron, sipping his beer
and then running his hand through his wet mane.

"A student-athlete overdosed."

"Not good. On what?"

"As yet unknown."

"So no clues?"

"None at all."

"How's your friend? Kim, is it?"

I sipped my beer. "Odd. You ever been close to someone?
Someone who was like a brother or a sister, way back when. But
you drift apart. Then when you meet again, you feel like you
should know them, like you do know them. But you've both
lived another half a life. So now maybe you're working on bad
knowledge, false assumptions."

"You need several more drinks, my boy."

"That's why I'm here." I took a long pull on my beer. As I did I felt a pair of arms wrap around me and a pair of cool lips plant themselves on my cheek.

"Well, hello." I smiled and put my beer down, and turned on my stool. She was wearing a summer dress, yellow with blue flowers, thin straps. Her short brown hair was, like everyone else's, wet. The dress clung at her hips and thighs, and gave way to thin tanned legs.

"You're not wet," she said. Her lips were thin and her smile stopped traffic. At least when I was driving.

"Bar duty."

"Since you're offering." She took a seat and Muriel made her a vodka tonic. Muriel passed the drink across. "There you are, Danielle."

"How are you this fine, damp afternoon, Deputy Castle?" said Ron.

Danielle smiled. "Better now." She took a sip of her drink and turned to me. "And you? Campus tour?"

"Weird. Just telling Ron. They got some odd dynamics going on there. Can't make it out. But the upshot is they got a kid in hospital from a drug overdose."

"He okay?"

"That's the thing. No one really seems to know. It's like they're trying to put a lid on a situation rather than solving the problem."

Danielle sipped her vodka. "Wouldn't be the first time a college did something like that."

"Right enough. But here's another thing. They don't have campus cops. None. Local PD does it all."

Danielle shrugged. "Not uncommon."

"Really?"

"Sure. There are lots of smaller colleges—liberal arts, privates, career colleges—that don't have the size to justify a full police department of their own. So they subcontract to the town they are in. In many cases they're an important part of the town anyway."

"So why don't all colleges do it? Why does UM or Florida have their own cops?"

"In some cases politics, often logistics. A big school like University of Florida has what, fifty thousand students and staff? That's a decent-sized town right there. A town within a town, essentially. And they have unique issues, dealing with lots of underage kids, that sort of thing. So it really makes sense to have their own law enforcement unit. A school with a couple thousand population, not so much."

"Makes sense. But then the local cops moonlight as paid security on campus. That seems pretty cozy."

"It is," she said. "But still not unusual. Lots of cops have second jobs and many as security guards, doormen or bouncers."

"Guys do that in the Sheriff's Office?"

"Sure, some. There are rules about what you can do, but it's not outlawed. And that's how these things happen. Cover-ups occur in colleges just like towns. The colleges are hard though, because they have thousands of students and staff who are probably not so interested in keeping the secret and plenty of time on their hands, and these days they all have access to social media. News gets out."

I nodded and drained my beer.

"What's the next move?" asked Ron.

"The kid's parents are in town, down from New England somewhere. I guess I'll go and see how things are doing at the hospital."

"Which one?" said Danielle.

"Broward General."

"You want company?" said Ron.

"Don't think they'll be all that receptive to my visit."

"I been married twice. I'm pretty sure I can handle it." He smiled.

"Then meet me at the office at nine."

"Will do, boss."

I turned to Danielle. "Swim?"

"Actually these vodka tonics are going down pretty well, but I guess I better come in case I need to rescue your sorry carcass."

"You always say the most romantic things." I turned to Ron. "You cab it?"

He nodded, so I tossed him the keys to the Mustang.

"You two behave yourselves, you hear," said Ron. He didn't wait for an answer; he just swiveled back toward the bar and tossed the keys to Muriel. She poured him another beer. She would be the ultimate arbiter of whether Ron drove home tonight, or stopped by in the morning to retrieve the keys from a hiding spot in the courtyard that both Ron and Muriel would take to their graves.

CHAPTER SIX

When I woke the next morning the heavy cloud had vanished and the first hints of orange light shone across a cloudless sky. I lay for a moment, allowing my brain to drift into the day. Danielle lay with her back to me, all soft tan skin and brown hair. I slipped out of bed and threw some water on my face. When I came back into the bedroom Danielle was sitting up, bare-chested with sleep in her eyes.

"Going somewhere?" she whispered.

"Thinking about a run."

Danielle smiled and bounded out of bed. She was the only person I'd ever known who rejoiced at the thought of an early morning run. She was ready and bouncing up and down on her toes when I got to the front door. We walked briskly to warm up, from my little seventies rancher on the Intracoastal side across Singer Island to the beach. Real estate wisdom said you should buy the worst house on the best street. I was a disciple of that logic. My place was the worst on the whole island. It was the only one on the open water that hadn't been knocked over and rebuilt into a mini mansion. It was, like me, a seventies original, and I liked it that way. When we reached the sand we started running. We headed north to where the island thinned to a finger, past the apartment towers, and onto the empty stretch by MacArthur Beach State Park. I dropped in behind Danielle and kept her pace. It was convenient for both of us. She loved to lead, to set the pace and dance across the freshly washed sand. I liked to sit in behind and watch her. She was lithe and fluid. I could bounce a quarter off any part of her body. I wasn't a natural runner and found the view super motivating. Her shorts were tight and she had sprinter's legs. She took us up to where the park gave way to the homes that surrounded Lost Tree Golf Club, where she stopped, sucked in a deep breath, winked at me and then took off back south. By the time we got back to City Beach I was shot. Danielle stretched. We wandered back to the house, past the homes with pools in mosquito-proof cages, and showered. I went to the kitchen and pulled out the blender. I tossed in some flaxseed, kale, strawberries and pineapple, split a few dates and filled it up with ice. Two large glasses of smoothie were poured when Danielle came out of the bathroom. She was in her uniform, all starch and crisp lines, looking hard and serious but sexy as hell. We drank our smoothies as Danielle drove me downtown. Traffic was steady. She stopped outside the county courthouse building. It looked like something that belonged on the Mall in Washington DC. We kissed, and I got out and walked through the huge archway that separated the family courts from the criminal courts. The building was new but the revolving doors were old brass jobs, like something you might see in New York at the entrance to Bloomingdale's. I cut across the road and wandered through the parking lot beside our building. Ron was waiting for me, sitting in the Mustang with the air-con running, eating a bagel with peanut butter and sipping on a Dunkin' Donuts coffee. I opened the passenger door and slid in.

"You made it home," I said.

"Decided if I was visiting a hospital I didn't want to look like a patient. So I headed to the yacht club for dinner. Coffee?" he said, offering me his Styrofoam cup. I shook my head, so Ron dropped the coffee in the drink holder, punched the gearstick into first and headed out to I-95. We took an easy hour to hit the hospital. The sign on the building said Broward Health Medical Center, but everyone called it Broward General. It was a sprawling campus that from the outside looked like a large shopping mall, cream concrete and glass. Ron parked in the multistory parking structure, and we took the enclosed footbridge across to the hospital. Inside it wasn't like a mall. It was all hospital, cold and antiseptic. It took ten minutes and a couple of white lies to track down Jake Turner's whereabouts. We got to the duty nurse's desk. She was a fierce black woman in a pink uniform. She looked like she was at a pajama party but wasn't enjoying it very much.

"Jake Turner?" I said.

She glared at me like I was a bug and she was a boot. "You are?"

"I'm from his attorney's office." No one likes attorneys, but few people live in abject fear of them like medical professionals. She looked me up and down. I'd worn a plain shirt, no palm trees or surfboards, and tucked it into my chinos. The boat shoes didn't really fit the attorney story, but she couldn't see those.

"You're an attorney," she said, eyebrow raised.

"No, I'm from an attorney's office."

"Let me guess. Jimmy Buffett and Associates."

Normally I was cool with wardrobe comparisons to Jimmy Buffett, because normally that was spot on. But I was wearing my good shirt.

"No, ma'am. Croswitz and Allen. We specialize in medical negligence." It was harsh but half true. They were attorneys in my building. Allen had retired to Naples and Croswitz specialized in whatever cases he could get his crusty old hands on, mainly wills and personal injury.

"Is it casual Friday?"

"No, ma'am. I'm on vacation but was asked to come and speak with them because of the boy's grave condition."

The nurse gave me a good hard look. "You wanna chat? The boy's in a coma."

"I know. It's his parents I need to speak with. I understand they're here."

"Room eight," she said, nudging her head and then returning to her paperwork.

Jake Turner's room was opposite a small waiting area. A tight gathering of small-backed, uncomfortable-looking chairs sat on a square of industrial-strength green carpet. A man in a long-sleeve blue business shirt and purple tie was standing in the middle of the space, talking on a cell phone. He kept his voice down but his body language was angry. A young guy, maybe nineteen or twenty, sat on a chair against the wall. He wore a black hoodie with the hood over his head and a pair of burgundy basketball shorts. He watched me approach with a scowl of indifference. The man on the phone paid me no mind at all. I didn't knock because I didn't think Jake Turner would answer. We slipped into the room. It was a single room. Jake Turner lay on a bed, like he was asleep. He was flat on his back, a mask over his mouth, I assumed to assist with breathing. A small woman sat by the bed. She wore a long, blue dress, and pearls around her neck, as if she had just dropped by after church. She was facing the bed but looking at the window. Just staring at blue sky through tinted glass. Her body was in the hospital room, but her mind was a thousand miles and twenty years away. I figured that's what a mother would think about, sitting in front of her son who was lying in a coma. I walked to the end of the bed, but she didn't look at me. Ron hung back against the wall. The room was quiet but for the low-grade murmur of the building and the soft hiss of oxygen. The woman finally pegged my movement because she snapped out of her thoughts and looked at me, sleepy-eyed.

"Hello," she said. She didn't smile or not smile. Her face was neither here nor there, like the emotion button had been switched off.

"Ma'am," I said.

"Are you a doctor?" She seemed to consider it a possibility. But even in South Florida, doctors just in from eighteen holes at PGA National slipped a white coat on when they got to the hospital. It's a status thing. The people in the pajama suits do the work; the lab coats collect the cash.

"No, ma'am, I am investigating the circumstances of your son's incident." I picked up the slow cadence police talk from watching my part-time nemesis Detective Ronzoni on the job. It seemed appropriate.

"You're a policeman?"

"No, ma'am, I'm a private investigator. I'm told your son played lacrosse."

She nodded slowly. "He does. He's quite good. Captain, you know." Still she didn't smile, but there was a glimmer of pride in her eyes.

"I know." I smiled. "Did your son ever mention any trouble, any problems with school?"

"No. His grades were good. I think he could have done better, but a mother always does, don't you think?"

"I do. So you never heard anything about drugs?"

"Good Lord, no. He wouldn't do that. He's a smart boy."

I wanted to say he did do it, but I held my tongue. "Was Jacob on a scholarship?"

"Jake. Not Jacob," she almost whispered. "And yes, he had a tuition scholarship."

"How did he fund the rest?"

"We paid for it. That's what you do, isn't it?"

Not in my experience. "So his apartment, living expenses?"

"We paid for everything. His father handles the college fund. I don't know."

"Did Jake take any medications, vitamins, that sort of thing?"

She shook her head. "No, I don't know." She fiddled with her wedding band. Her hands were old, much older than the rest of her. "Well, there were some vitamins, I think. When he came home last Thanksgiving. He said they were for sports. Energy, that's what he said they were for."

"What did they look like, exactly?"

"What did what look like?" said a voice from the door. It was the guy with the tie and the cell phone. "Who are you? What are you doing here?" He looked from me to Ron and then back. Ron leaned into the wall like he was trying to make himself invisible.

"You must be Jake's dad."

"Who the hell are you?"

"Michael, language," said Jake's mother. Michael shot her a stinging look, and she retreated back into her shell.

"Sir, my name is Miami Jones. I am assisting inquiries into your son's incident."

"Miami Jones? What the hell kind of name is that?" Jake's mother gave him a look but said nothing. He glared at me.

"Outside." He barreled out of the room. I followed him. Ron didn't. Michael strode to the waiting area. The kid in the hoodie was gone.

"Who do you work for?" he spat.

"I'm afraid that's confidential."

"It's the college isn't it? That weasel, Millet. You tell him I'm going to sue him to kingdom come."

"I can assure you, nothing would please me more. I'm not working for Dr. Millet, Mr. Turner. The people I represent want the truth to come out." I wasn't completely sure about that, but I hoped it was the case.

"My son was not a drug addict."

"I don't think anyone's suggesting he was. But was he happy at school?"

"He played games and did a few hours of classes. What's not to be happy?"

"It is college. You went to college."

"I went to a real college. We were too busy for games."

"Which college?"

"Brown," he said. He puffed out his chest when he said it, like the word gave him superpowers. "Then my MBA at Harvard."

"You live in Massachusetts?"

"Yes."

"And you wanted Jake to go to school in Massachusetts?"

"I didn't care. Massachusetts, Rhode Island."

"You wanted him to go to Brown?"

"Of course. But Harvard would've done. Hell, he got an offer from UMass Amherst. He could've lived at home."

"But he chose to come here."

"He said they had a great lacrosse program. Harvard has a good lacrosse program. And he wanted to major in construction management. Whatever the blazes that is."

"But he was offered a scholarship here."

"Half. Half a scholarship."

"And you pay for the rest?"

"He had savings and a college fund. I believe in people paying their own way."

"Was there any unusual expenditure?"

Michael Turner frowned. He was maybe two inches shorter than me, but he stood tall. "What the hell are you getting at, pal?"

"I'm not getting at anything, sir. Just trying to piece things together to find out who was responsible."

"You are a dirtbag. There was no unusual expenditure, you maggot. You're trying to make my son look like a drug addict." The words were fierce but the voice measured.

"Have you considered the fact that people who are not drug addicts rarely overdose under bleachers?" I realized the lack of tact a split second too late.

"Get out," he said. He didn't yell, he just pointed toward the elevators and a vein in his neck bulged some. He was a cool customer. But I didn't need a scene, so I put my palms in the air and walked away. I winked at the nurse at the desk as I wandered by, and she returned the favor with a look that would have killed the Ebola virus. When I got to the elevator I smashed my butt against the wall and waited. Ron was only a minute behind. Evidently Mr. Turner had gone straight back into Jake's room and evicted Ron. He wore a cheesy grin.

"Making friends again?" he said.

"I might have made one marginally tactless remark." I hit the down button to the elevator. "Who knew the guy would be so touchy."

"Everyone but you?"

"Fair call." The elevator dinged. We got in with a striking blonde in a lab coat. She looked like a doctor if Michael Bay were doing the casting. Ron and I stood either side of her, which was a little creepy but she didn't give anything away. We rode down in silence. We're men, and as such we are only capable of performing one human function with total focus at a time. Our eyes were working overtime so talking was out. As were walking, thinking and eating. Breathing was a chore. The elevator hit our floor, and the woman stepped out and strode in the direction of a big sign that read *x-ray*. I ambled out and watched her walk away. Ron was glued to the back of the elevator. The door bumped closed and I lunged at the button to open it. The door eased open, revealing Ron's broad grin. Even in hospital lighting he looked tan and healthy, despite the well-worn face and splotches where a skin guy in Boca had removed a few melanomas.

"Man cannot live on yeast and malt alone," he said.

"You're old enough to be her father," I said as we headed across the foot bridge back to the parking structure.

"There's plenty of snap and crackle left in this pop."

"So how's Mrs. Turner?"

"You spoke to her."

"After I left with her darling husband, I mean."

"You are asking if I charmed a poor woman sitting at her unconscious son's bedside?"

I raised an eyebrow as I hit the key fob and unlocked the Mustang. We got in, and I pulled out of the huge structure and headed back toward West Palm.

"Well, since you asked," smiled Ron, "I did have a little chat with Elise."

"Elise. And?"

"And I'm not surprised the kid is where he is."

"How so?"

"It's a little bit Stepford. She's worried, about her son, I'm sure. But more so about what her neighbors will think about having a drug user son. She's trying to convince herself it was an accident."

"An accident? Under the bleachers?"

"Never let the facts get in the way of a good story," said Ron.

"You should run for office."

"You know, I've been thinking about that."

"Oh, what have I done."

"At the yacht club."

"Commodore Bennett? Save us. You wouldn't be put in charge of a vessel or anything, would you?"

"No." He laughed. "No one starts at Commodore."

"First mate?"

"There you go, that sounds about me."

"So what else did you glean from Jake's mother, First Mate?"

"She didn't seem very engaged. Like she was a bystander to the boy's life. She kept saying *Jake's father takes care of this* and *Jake's father takes care of that.* As if she deferred to him on everything."

"Sounds like New England old money to me."

"You're just bitter because you were New England no money."

"There is that. But how does this leave a kid under the bleachers at the ballpark?"

"You tell me," said Ron.

"What does that mean?"

"The kid grows up in New England, wants to get out, chooses a college in Florida. As far away as he can get. Sound familiar?"

"What's your point?"

"Point is you didn't just choose University of Miami because it had good football and baseball programs. You could've gone to Boston College—hell, you could've gone to UConn or even Yale. But you chose South Florida. So did Jake Turner. Why?"

I drove in silence for a while, letting the throb of the engine and the hum of tire on blacktop cocoon the Mustang. Why had Jake Turner gone so far from home? Why had I? Ron was right, I could have gone to UConn and stayed in Connecticut, or moved up to Boston. Yale wouldn't have had me, despite my dad having worked there. They don't offer athletic scholarships in the Ivy League, and my high school grades weren't Yale material. Perhaps Harvard wasn't an option for Jake. His grades might not have been Ivy League material either. Ron sat staring out at the horizon whizzing by, waiting for me to conclude the discussion in my head.

"The weather," I said. "The weather was a big part of it. I had enough football in sleet and snow."

"No argument from me. Why anyone lives up there is beyond me. But that's not your reason."

"No, it's not." I breathed in deeply, through the nose, held it, then out through the mouth. Like Kim Rose. She taught me that, back in college. I'd used it before every single pitch I'd thrown, from sophomore year until the day I hung up my cleats. It calmed me. For Kim it was all about focus. For me, it was about being relaxed, beating back the voices in my head and the shouts of the coaches and the taunts of the fans. People think the pitcher is too far from the crowd, out there on the mound, to hear the taunts and the catcalls. Even the encouragement. At Fenway it's probably true. But in the minor leagues, you hear everything. If you can't learn to shut it out, you're done before you even begin.

"I wanted to get away. Not because life was so bad. But it was stifling. New England's as old as this country gets. Its traditions are firm and true and it felt like there was no room to breathe, to explore. To be yourself. In New Hampshire they like to say *Live Free or Die*. In Connecticut it was more like *Conform or Perish*. Florida was like a new day. I came for a baseball carnival during high school, in Orlando."

"Orlando?" Ron made a face like he'd eaten a bad pickle.

"Yes, I know. The other Florida. The one for all the tourists. But it was a revelation. The sky was bright and the ballparks were new and the people smiled. I knew from that trip on I'd be coming here again. It was like a new frontier. Like people wanted to be here. To create their own traditions rather than be defined by them."

"And so it was for Jake Turner," said Ron.

"His father was an old school control freak, and mother was distant. Lots of families like that. But it's like boiling a frog. You get used to it. It might not be loving and caring and sitcom saccharin, but it's not bad either. So Jake wasn't running away. He was running to."

"Keep going."

"Running somewhere he could be himself. Express himself. Be what he wanted to be. Prove his worth on his terms."

Ron nodded. "And what about Jake?"

I smiled. "Jake. The question is, did getting out of that environment and into this one raise him up or push him down?"

"Gut?"

"Star player, according to the coach, good grades according to the president. Doesn't sound like a hard-core drug user. But evidence suggests otherwise. Gut is confused."

"What's the absolute best way to get a batter out in baseball?" asked Ron.

"Get in his head."

"So."

"So I gotta get in this kid's head. Get into his space."

Ron nodded.

"You are quite the piece of work, Ron Bennett."

He smiled. "And you are racking up quite the tab on the couch there, grasshopper."

"Can we start a payment plan?" I asked.

"Of course."

"You accept payment in amber liquid?"

"Is it cold?"

"Always."

"In a frosty goblet?"

"Will you take a frosty bottle? Don't think Mick does goblets."

"I will."

"Done. Let's get some lunch."

"Drive on, McDuff."

CHAPTER SEVEN

Ron was right. I needed to get my head in the game. To get into Jake Turner's world. I bought Ron lunch, turkey on wheat with a Miller Lite, and then spent the afternoon in the office. I didn't get anything done. Lizzy popped in a few times with things to sign, pouted at me with her vermilion lips, and then left me to my thoughts. There were none. I don't think well in the office. Usually I like to walk, down along the promenade on Flagler Drive or on the beach. Maybe it's the negative ions. I heard once that because negative attracts positive, negative ions attract positive thoughts. I heard it from a drunk in a bar, so it might have been complete baloney. Maybe people at the beach weren't happy because of negative ions; maybe they were happy simply because they weren't at work. This was the direction my thoughts were taking, so I slipped into my canvas boat shoes and headed out in the Mustang. It seemed I'd only just driven up on I-95, now I headed back. I needed some bleacher time.

Bleachers would have some tales if they could talk. They see the spectrum of life. The highs and lows of sports, cheering crowds, jeering crowds, silent disappointed crowds. They watch training, vacant and alone, then they fill with tapping feet and hoarse calls and dropped popcorn and hot dog wrappers. And they see the other side. Underneath. In the dark spaces, teens sneaking a cigarette. Forbidden lovers capturing a moment together. Needles and small flames and anguish and release.

I parked near the college fields and walked in the fading light to the ballpark. No lights were on, the season over. In the distance I could hear the calls and whistles of practice, the dull thud of boot on soccer ball. Empty bleachers eat up the sound like cathedrals. People speak in hushed tones. Perhaps for that reason they are good places to think. I walked up the ramp between the stands and glanced left under the away team bleacher. It was pitch black down there. There was nothing to see anyway. I glanced at home plate in the twilight, and then turned right and headed up the steps. The nearby offices threw enough light to see. I stopped three quarters of the way up and sat down at the end of the row. The home team side, wooden slats. I sat in the bleacher, listening to my breathing, the rhythm of it. Thinking about Jake Turner and me and New England and traditions and freedom. I felt the presence of another person long before I heard them. Not some sixth sense type of feeling. I literally felt them. The bleacher vibrated. I didn't see anyone come up from below, so the person was above me, and I thought to my right. Further down the baseline. There was probably a ladder or emergency stairs back there. I paid them no mind. It wouldn't be the first time two people shared a bleacher, separated by their thoughts. I continued my breathing and thinking until I was overcome by the sense of being watched. This one was of the sixth sense variety. I leaned forward, elbows on thighs and rubbed my hands together for a while. Then I leaned back, and as I did, I glanced over my shoulder with as little head movement as possible. Someone in white sat in the very last row, far top corner of the stand. White shirt, white shorts, white socks. Like the apparition I had seen underneath the bleacher the previous day. I resumed looking at the diamond. I couldn't see second base, shrouded in darkness. I sat for a few more minutes. Then I heard a voice.

"Mister. Hey mister." It was a spoken whisper that rippled down to me like a stone dropped in a pond. I glanced up at the white form high in the stand.

"Mister," it whispered again. It was a girl's voice. Not high, but not a post-pubescent boy.

"Yes," I said, as if addressing someone in the pew behind me.

"You the one checking out Jake?"

"What?"

"You checking out Jake?" she said slower this time, like it was comprehension, not volume, that was the problem.

"Yes."

She stood and shuffled along between the slats. I turned back toward the diamond. Felt the bleachers creak and moan as the girl scootched along the boards. She came down the steps as quiet as a ballerina, slipped into the row behind me, and sat off my right shoulder.

"You checking out Jake," she said again.

"Yes, I am," I said. I didn't take my eyes off the baseball field.

"Who you working for?"

"I can't tell you that."

"President Millet?"

"No."

She sat quietly for a moment. "Not Jake's parents."

"No. But I'm not going to keep saying no until you eliminate everyone."

"They're the only two that matter."

"Why's that?"

She paused again. Took a deep breath in through her nose, out through her mouth. I wondered if she had learned that in the same place I had.

"Millet wants us out and Jake's parents don't care."

"Who says Millet wants you out?"

"Director Rose. Everybody knows it."

"Why don't Jake's parents care?"

"Because he's an embarrassment."

I rotated my butt on the plank and put an arm along the back so I could face her. She was in white athletic wear and was shorter than I thought. I looked at her face. She still had the rounded cheeks of youth.

"Why is he an embarrassment?"

"He doesn't fit their mold. His dad's Ivy League. You know how that goes."

I nodded. "Sounds like you know him pretty well."

"More or less."

"They call me Miami. Miami Jones." I didn't offer a handshake.

"Miami? Seriously? Were you conceived there or something?"

It was as good a reason as any. "No." I smiled. "It's from college."

"UM?"

"That's right."

"So it's not very original then."

"Not really. You got a name?"

"Angela. Everybody calls me Angel."

"What do you prefer?"

She grinned out the side of her mouth. "Don't think anybody ever asked me that before. Angel, I guess."

"Then I'm pleased to meet you, Angel."

"You too. Have you seen Jake?"

"Briefly."

"His parents won't let anyone from college in. I sat in the waiting area for a few hours, but they wouldn't let me see him."

I recalled the brooding kid in the hoodie, waiting outside Jake's room. Perhaps he was a friend too.

"No, they don't seem too keen on it."

"How'd you get in?"

"I walked in. Tell me about Jake."

She leaned against the backrest and tapped her fingers on her knees.

"What's to tell. He's a good guy."

"Athlete?"

"Yeah. Lacrosse. Captain this year."

"What about you?"

"Soccer."

I looked her over again. She was the opposite of Kim Rose. Kim had short, dark hair. Angel's was long, blond but not really so, and in a ponytail. Kim was whippet thin and had body fat hovering as close to zero as a woman could get. Angel looked fit, but was rounder, fleshier, and had breasts that I imagined to be a burden on the soccer field.

"You know Director Rose, then?"

"Course. She's the reason I came to this school."

"She coach you?"

"Some. Not much. She's got a lot of admin crap to do, you know? Waste really. She'd be an awesome coach. She's done it all. Olympics, World Cup. Everything."

"That what you want to do?"

"Me? No. I'm not in that league. I finish college, that will be it for me."

"So why do it?"

She frowned like I'd asked a redundant question. "Because I love it."

I knew the feeling. For four years I hustled in the minors before I got a shot at The Show. Twenty-nine games and zero pitches later I was back in the minors. For another season I played believing I'd get back, get another shot. The last season I played because I loved the game, the locker rooms, the guys, while the fire dimmed inside, and then extinguished.

"How do you know Jake?"

"We practice on the same fields, take some classes together."

"You his girlfriend?"

"Me? Hell, no. We just talked, here and there."

"Does he have a girlfriend?"

"No."

"Is he gay?"

"Why would he be gay?"

"Why not? It's a possibility."

"No, he isn't gay. He had girlfriends. Nothing serious, though. He was too focused."

"On what?"

"Winning," she said, as if the answer were obvious. "Lacrosse. He was totally fixated on it. He wanted to be the best. Like he had something to prove."

I sat in silence for a while and looked over the diamond. Then I turned to Angel. I couldn't tell what color her eyes were. Maybe brown, maybe gray.

"Was Jake into drugs?"

"How do you mean?"

"Did he take drugs?"

"No."

"How do you know?"

"I just know. He wouldn't. For him, it was all about performance. He wouldn't take something that would hurt his performance. He just wouldn't."

"So how else can someone be into drugs?"

"What do you mean?"

"I asked if he was into drugs and you said *how do you mean.* So if he wasn't taking drugs how was he into them?"

She looked at her feet. I didn't take that as a good sign.

"You can't tell his parents."

I shook my head. "He was dealing," I said.

Her head shot up and her eyes burned. "No," she said. "It's not what you think."

"What do I think?" I frowned.

Angel shook her head. Her ponytail flopped onto her shoulder, and she brushed it away.

"He would never touch that stuff."

"What stuff?"

"You know, the hard stuff. Maxx and all that."

"Who's Max?"

"Not who, what. M-A-X-X. Where have you been?"

"Listening to Jimmy Buffett. So what's this Maxx?"

"It's the in thing. Meth. But what I'm telling you is Jake wouldn't touch that stuff."

"How can you be so sure?"

"Trust me, I know. Jake, he was all about performance. He hardly even drank."

"So, Angel, how did he end up unconscious under the bleachers?"

The whistling from the playing fields grew loud and impatient. Angel looked toward it and stood. She was holding a pair of soccer cleats, white with three pink stripes.

"I gotta go. I'm late for practice." She stepped out of the row in one swift move and took off down the steps, ponytail flopping from side to side. She turned and ran down the ramp and out of sight without looking back.

I watched her go and then looked back to the baseball diamond. Put myself in Jake's cleats. What would he do to focus on his performance. What, in four years of college and six years of pro baseball, had I tried? What hadn't I tried? I still drank smoothies for breakfast because of the desire to stay healthy and on the park. I still ran, even when Danielle wasn't there. I took weekly massages because I learned the value of staying supple. But smoothies, jogs and massages didn't get you overdosed under the bleachers. Then it hit me. The one thing I'd done that led to the slippery slope. The sort of slippery slope that ended under the bleachers, fighting for your life. And the word flashed in my mind, like a giant neon sign on Forty-Second Street.

Performance.

CHAPTER EIGHT

I wandered back along the road that divided the sports facilities from the main campus. The playing fields were alive under floodlights, athletes running up and down, doing drills and sprints. There was more than one team, in fact more than one sport. The coaches' offices were darkened. I assumed they were on the field, whistles in mouths. On the other side of the road the main campus offered a quiet glow. I noted the gym and Kim's office were on that side of the road. I wasn't sure whether that meant something or nothing. I took out my cell phone and punched a contact. The phone rang and I looked at the gym building.

"Kimberly Rose," she answered. Evidently the assistant got paid by the hour.

"Kim, Miami."

"Hey there." Her voice softened. "Getting anywhere?"

"Early days. Listen, you free for a drink?"

"Sure. When?"

"How about now? I'm on campus."

"Not here. I know a great place. Let's say thirty minutes?"

I parked in a lot just off East Las Olas Boulevard. It was fully dark, and the beach chairs from the resorts had been pulled in. All the tourists and business types were in bars or restaurants, or in their rooms getting ready. A soft breeze blew in off the

Atlantic, pushing the whitecaps up onto the sand. The glow of waterfront hotels and restaurants glimmered in the breaking waves. I sucked in a couple lungfuls of ocean air, and then headed down the beach to meet Kim.

The restaurant was in a chain hotel with a million-dollar view of the beach, at least during the day. I have a theory, developed through years of studious research, about restaurants with million-dollar views. The food is usually not worth a nickel. And a modest bar tab will give you a coronary. I wondered how much athletic directors were paid. Kim arrived during my second beer. She looked fantastic. She wore a simple black dress that accentuated her firm legs and arms, and drew attention away from her flat chest. A designer had put a great deal of thought into it. She got a few glances and glares as she sauntered through the room. Kim was not what you would call conventionally beautiful. Her hair was black and short, more about management than style. She was angular rather than curvaceous, and her cheekbones and jaw were strong, almost masculine. But she wore that glow that only the truly fit and healthy possess.

"Look who grew up," I said.

Kim smiled. "You look good."

"I look like the dog's breakfast two days later. You look stunning."

"This old thing?" she said, sitting opposite me. The waiter appeared and Kim ordered a martini. She leaned toward me as if we were about to discuss treason.

"I never get to wear it. I'm usually at home with ESPN and a yogurt." Her drink arrived and she took a sip. "So how's it all going?"

"Meeting some interesting people."

"Well, that's the main thing," she said, eyebrow raised. We turned our attention to the menus. The waiter reappeared and told us that the specials were Blue Point oysters, beef tenderloin and a white fish ceviche. I'm from Connecticut, so I know that Blue Points are about the only good thing to come out of that state. But the thing about bivalves is this: they live inside shells. They're not designed for travel. If I'm in the Panhandle I'll be sure to do a stopover in Apalachicola for some excellent oysters. Otherwise in Florida, I steer clear. I also have another rule: don't eat seafood in Vegas or beef in the Bahamas. I went with the ceviche. Kim ordered the oysters and a heritage beet salad, which made the beets sound like they had been around in Lincoln's day.

"So what have you been doing for the last decade or so?" Kim said, sipping her drink. She took it dry, no olives.

"A bit of ball, out in Cali first, then down here. Became apparent I wasn't going to go big, so I took a masters in criminology and joined Lenny."

"I'm sorry."

I smiled. People always said stuff like that. Especially people like Kim. "I'm not. Life is what life is."

"You don't believe that. Life is what you make it."

"Sure, to a point. You got to make things happen. But unexpected stuff comes up. Life throws a curve. You deal with it and move on."

"But you've got to regret it. I mean they sent you up and never gave you a shot."

"No regret. I didn't understand then, but I do now." I took a gulp of beer. I just couldn't get used to drinking beer from a something that resembled a champagne flute. "You won a World Cup final, right?" Kim nodded but didn't smile.

"So there were some girls on the squad who didn't play. Who weren't selected for the final. Why weren't they selected?"

"They weren't good enough."

"Exactly. But should they regret that? That they got as far as they could go, tried as hard as they could, played a game they loved, but weren't quite as good as the very best in the world?"

"*If* they tried as hard as they could." Kim looked at me. Hard. When her focus was on something, it was totally on it. Her eyes held the gaze of a tiger summing up its lunch.

"You think they didn't work hard enough?" I said.

"I never left anything on the field. Every game, every practice, every gym session, every meal I ate. Anything less, maybe I don't play a World Cup final. But I did."

I nodded. I had nothing to say. Harsh but true. I sipped my beer. Kim's oysters arrived. They were Blue Points all right. It isn't always the case, but with oysters, size isn't everything. An oyster shouldn't feel like you've just swallowed a pound of phlegm. Kim offered me one and I gulped it down. Despite having traveled the length of the country it was better than I expected it to be. I smacked my lips and took some beer.

"So let me ask you something. When you were playing soccer, college and the pros, how did you keep yourself on the park?"

"I looked after myself. I stretched for an hour every day after practice, I ate right, stayed fit in the off-season."

"But it's a pretty rough game. I mean tackles, leg injuries, all that."

"I never got injured."

"Never?"

"Not badly. Bruises and scrapes, sure. Every game. But I kept my nose clean and stayed out of trouble."

"What about teammates? They must've gotten injured."

She wrinkled her brow. "Sure, there were always injuries with some girls. What are you getting at?"

"Did any girls use alternative methods to overcome injury?"

"You mean like acupuncture?"

"I mean like performance enhancers."

She leaned across the table toward me again.

"You mean drugs?" she whispered.

I nodded.

"I never had anything to do with anything like that. Ever. I could run through the midfield all day because I worked my ass off. I didn't get injured because I looked after myself. Not because of some pill." The tiger eyes had turned into shark pupils.

"It's usually a jab in the thigh or the butt, actually. But what about other girls?"

"Are you saying the US women's soccer team took performance-enhancing drugs?" She practically just mouthed the last three words.

"I wouldn't know. I wasn't there. But I did play professional sport. I know what it's like to be hurt, to want to be on the field. The pressure to be better than your best."

"Did you ever take drugs?" she spat.

I leaned back in my chair and put my beer down. "Yes."

Kim followed my lead and leaned back in her chair. Her mouth dropped open like a drawbridge.

"Really?" she said. "You really did?"

I nodded. "For a while. Guys were doing it. Guys were getting big. Big hitters, big throwers. It felt necessary to compete."

"Did you get tested?"

"Yeah, but back then it wasn't so sophisticated, and the big names hadn't come out. Canseco, Rodriguez, Maguire. BALCO hadn't happened. There really was no policy. You had to be suspected of something before they could test you."

"What did you take?"

"Steroids, HGH."

"Human growth hormone," she said to herself. She shuddered. "So what happened?"

"I got lucky. I had a pitching coach. Good guy. He knew it was going on but said guys needed to make their own decisions. But he taught me something important. Not that the drugs were bad, even though they were. Not that they wouldn't work, because they did. I guess he knew guys didn't want to hear those arguments."

"So what did he say?"

"He showed me tape. Video of great players, great pitchers. He showed me that great pitching wasn't just about arm strength. It was in the mechanics. Your form. And he showed me that bulking up could actually interfere with your mechanics and make you pitch slower. You could lose your form, and lose your curveball. He sold me on it. So I stopped. Looked for every other way, healthy way, to stay on the field."

"I have to say I'm shocked." Her eyes softened with something bordering on pity. I took a long gulp of my drink.

"You never saw anything like that?"

"No. My job was to prepare myself as best I could. What other girls did to prepare themselves was their business. Not mine. Just as long as they were ready to go for the team, on the day."

"What about now?"

"I don't play anymore."

"I mean at the university."

"No," she said. The shark eyes were back. "There are no performance-enhancing drugs on my campus. Why would you say such a thing?"

"Lots of young, impressionable athletes, trying to be the best, win NCAA titles."

"I run a clean program, Miami."

"How do you know? I mean, I've been there. It's not that hard to hide if no one's looking."

"But people are looking, Miami. The NCAA, the USADA. They're looking. Our student-athletes get tested. In and out of season. People are most certainly looking. And they have my full cooperation."

"Okay," I said. We both sipped our drinks. Then our food came. The beet salad looked fresh. My ceviche was decent without being outstanding. The silence was awkward. Again I was reminded how it never used to feel like that. We could sit in my dorm or hers, or on the bleachers at Mark Light Field. We could read or not read. Do stretching or do some study. Our chats, when they came, were always long and deep and focused on the future. Now it seemed all we had to talk about was the past, and it wasn't such good conversation fodder.

"What happened to Jake Turner wasn't about that," said Kim. "He was a good kid who fell in with the wrong crowd. I need you to understand. I need you to find that crowd, so we can make sure this doesn't happen again to another athlete."

"Okay."

"This is why I called you, Miami. President Millet will try to make the same argument, that something systemic has caused this. But that's not right. What happened to Jake wasn't anything to do with the athletic program. He got into something bad, and I need you to find out what and how and who, so I can stop Millet from blaming this on me." She spiked a beet and ate it. I said nothing.

"Can you do that for me, Miami? I really need you on my team."

"Of course," I said, forcing a smile. The what, I thought I knew. I'd clarify that for sure in the morning. How and who, those were questions I needed to answer.

CHAPTER NINE

What I needed was a frequent user card for I-95 between West Palm and Miami. Drive ten times and get a free car wash. But knowing the way the Florida legislature worked, I'd drive ten times and have to wash some other guy's car. I sped down the freeway, steering with my knees, egg and bacon sandwich in one hand, coffee in the other. Ron's treat. He sat next to me, smiling like a midway clown, top down on the Mustang. Ron was the poster boy for Florida living. Both the good and the bad. He was tan and fit, but wrinkled and spotted with removed skin cancers. He loved the heat, humidity, sun and torrential summer rain, but had survived Hurricane Andrew inside a refrigerator. His father had been a US diplomat and Ron had been born in Jamaica, so he was American through and through but could never be president. He was okay with that. He wasn't completely convinced Florida belonged in the union, but he kept that view to himself except when he had a belly full of Crown Royal. But I don't think Ron loved anything more than cruising along the freeway on a cloudless Florida day. I always expected him to put his head out the window and stick his tongue out.

Our stop was Broward Memorial. I wanted to confirm exactly what it was Jake Turner had inside his body. Hospitals are like airports. They have their busy times, but even at the slow times, there's always plenty going on. We parked near the foot bridge and headed back toward Jake's room. We had timed our arrival before visiting hours so as to avoid the parents. I figured someone who looked like they had just come from church wasn't sleeping in a cot next to her son. We got the elevator up and stepped to the corner of the corridor near the ward nurse's desk. I couldn't help thinking we would have looked less conspicuous in lab coats. I wore a white linen shirt and chinos; Ron was in a red short-sleeved shirt and blue trousers. We looked like escapees from a beach party. The nurse at the ward desk was a large, stern woman with pink cheeks and a mouth like a slit envelope. She looked about as closed as Santa's workshop on December twenty-sixth.

"Bait and switch?" I said.

Ron frowned. He wasn't convinced. Neither was I. He could distract her all right, but Jake's room was just down the hall from the desk, so he'd practically have to get her in the back room for me to sneak past unseen. We were assessing our options when the door to Jake's room opened. A white lab coat came out. In the white lab coat was the gorgeous blonde we'd seen in the elevator the previous day. She stopped at the ward desk and signed some papers. She gave the nurse a cute but officious smile that was not returned. If the nurses thought the male doctors were overpaid and oversexed buffoons, then a stunning woman doctor was positively the spawn of Satan. I looked at Ron. Now he was grinning. I was about to speak when Ron pulled me back around the corner.

"She's coming," he said. I looked back toward the elevators. Just beyond was a door marked fire stairs. We hit the stairs at pace and danced down two at a time. We broke out onto the floor we had come in on, where the lovely doctor had headed off to x-ray on our last visit. We watched the elevators. One was going up. The other down. It hit our floor and didn't stop. There was only the ground floor below us, so we hit the concrete stairs for one more flight. The elevator was closing as we launched out of the staircase. We were in a large lobby area, like the entrance to a mid-range business hotel. I spotted our good doctor heading down a corridor. We followed, as casual as could be. Two guys clearly not hospital staff, not quite sick-looking enough to be patients, casually wandering the halls. If I had seen us from the outside I would have pegged us for serial killers.

The doctor went into a cafeteria. It was the bland, industrial space that hospitals like to serve food in. In college I read somewhere that Hippocrates believed that fresh food was the greatest medicine. In hospitals it had to be a revenue generator with a shelf life that could outlast a nuclear winter. The doctor got in line.

"I'm going in," I said.

"Bottle of Zinfandel says you crash and burn."

"Done."

"California Zinfandel. Not that rubbish you passed off last time."

"California. Done."

I joined the line behind the doctor. She had long hair that shone like a showroom Ferrari, and she smelled fantastic. I waited as we shuffled past prefab sandwiches and something resembling Jell-O, for the good doc to glance my way. She didn't. I went to Plan B and bumped her with my hip. She looked at me. Like I'd just driven a monster truck over a baby.

"I'm sorry," I said.

"Really."

"Too focused on these delicious-looking Caesar wraps."

"Aha." She turned away. That's the thing about stunningly beautiful people. They perfect the art of the dismissal. I guess they get accosted a lot. Not usually by me. I have a stunning girlfriend, one who is proficient with most types of firearms, and she had to ask me out. But perhaps that's how it goes. I wouldn't know. It's not that I look like the hind end of a puffer fish. I'm fit and I look as normal as the next guy. But I wouldn't know about people who look like fine art. I couldn't do the hip bump again, so I went to plan C.

"You're a doctor, right?" It was as original as any movie with the number four at the end of the title, but I was under pressure.

"You think?" she said over her shoulder.

"I think you're looking after a friend of mine."

"Yeah? Well, he's in good hands."

I couldn't have agreed more. "Yeah, Jake Turner."

"Aha."

"How is he?"

"I believe he's stable. Beyond that I don't know. I haven't done rounds yet."

She had me there. I could hardly call her out and say, that's garbage, I just spotted you up there. I'd look like a peeping Tom.

"What did he take? It's so unlike him."

"I tell you what." She turned and looked at me. I sucked a gulp of air against my will. It gave me hiccups. She was stunning. Like goddess-stunning. Both sides of her face were perfectly symmetrical.

"You come up when visiting hours start in"—she looked at her watch—"two hours, and I'll go through his chart with you." She smiled a perfect smile and turned to the cashier.

"Chamomile tea, please, Rhonda."

Rhonda handed over a tea bag and a stainless pot of hot water.

"Seventy-five cents, darlin'." The doctor handed over a dollar, got change and dropped the quarter in a bucket labeled *Toys for Tots*. I ordered a coffee and watched the good doctor saunter over to a table by the window and sit. I took my coffee and shuffled back to Ron. He was smiling like we were still driving on the freeway.

"She's a tough nut. We're not going to get anywhere there."

"I was thinking I'd like to try something from Lodi. Ancient vine."

"Let's not get delusions of grandeur here, pal. A California Zin is a California Zin."

"Double or nothing. My choice of bottle. Anything from Cali."

I looked at the doctor sipping her tea, and then back at Ron.

"You don't want to do that to yourself."

"Wait here."

I almost couldn't watch. It was like reality television. A train wreck in the making. Ron ambled over and leaned his hands on the chair opposite her. She looked up. He spoke. She listened. He spoke again. She spoke. He spoke again. She brushed her hair back behind her ear. Then she smiled. She pointed to the chair opposite. Ron sat down. If I'd heard the story in a bar I wouldn't have believed a word of it. I was fairly certain I hadn't been exposed to any class A drugs that would make me hallucinate. Ron and the doctor chatted for a good ten minutes. She pulled a napkin out from a steel holder on the table and wrote something on it, and then pushed the napkin over to Ron. Then I finished my coffee. It was tepid and burned but I didn't care. I watched Ron hand the napkin back to the doctor, and she wrote something more, before returning it to him. Ron finally stood up, shook hands, and walked away. I slipped back into the corridor so she didn't see me standing there. Ron came around the corner, looking like the Cheshire cat. He slapped my back and kept walking.

"I changed my mind," he said. "I'm thinking Napa. Opus One." He kept walking so I followed.

"How, what?"

"She says he overdosed on methamphetamine. A new designer drug doing the rounds."

"Do they know what the drug is?"

"She said the street name was Maxx. With two x's."

It was the same drug Angel had mentioned. Ron read off his napkin as we walked back to the car.

"Also, she wrote down this. Y hydroxybutyric acid."

"Which is?"

"She said was something to do with increased growth hormone. She said it was at an unusually elevated level in Jake's body, but that it might be normal as we all produce it but some more than others."

We reached the car, and I looked across the roof at Ron.

"Or he could have been taking human growth hormones to make him a better lacrosse player. But the question is, how did that lead to taking Maxx under the bleachers."

CHAPTER TEN

I pulled out of the hospital and headed toward the university campus. Ron was smiling but he wasn't telling. I waited for him to fess up but nothing came. I caved as I pulled onto the road between the main campus and the playing fields.

"You cannot leave me hanging like this," I said.

"Hanging?" Ron grinned.

"How did you get anything out of the doctor."

"Shaughnessy."

"Doctor Shaughnessy."

"Doctor Morgan, actually. Her first name is Shaughnessy."

"Jeez, that's a hell of a moniker to wear."

"Look who's talking."

"Fair enough. So how?"

"I saw her last night at the club. Turns out she's taking sailing lessons."

"You're kidding me."

"Nope. So I offered to take her out sometime with a group of us."

"You don't own a yacht."

"Yachts are easy to find, my friend. Lots of old crusties in Palm Beach who like sipping Chardonnay on the deck of their boat, but hate the thought of yanking on a sheet. Want someone to do it for them."

I wasn't all that keen on the sound of yanking on a sheet either, so I just shook my head and grinned at Ron sitting there talking about old crusties. He'd played me. I wasn't sure what he wanted more—to see me make a fool of myself, or a bottle of good red wine. We passed a sign stuck in the grass near the fields, directing away teams to the parking lot near the gym. I followed it and took a spot in the shadow of Kim Rose's office. I walked Ron down to see the bleachers where Jake Turner was found. He stepped under the shadow of the stand and looked around at nothing. When he came out he was quiet. We walked back along the sidewalk, by the road. We were headed for the sports fields. We didn't get there. Not straight away. I didn't see the black pickup roll up from behind. It pulled level with us, but on the opposite side of the road. The driver's-side window came down. Officer Squarehead was at the wheel.

"Quick word." It didn't come out like a question. Ron and I waited for a minivan hauling a cargo of away team players for some sort of sport, and then ambled across the road. Officer Squarehead put his flashers on and got out. He came around the front of his truck at a slow march. He wore Wranglers and a black T-shirt that rippled across his taut chest.

"Officer Steele."

"Mr. Jones."

"I hadn't pegged President Millet as a work on the weekends kind of guy."

"This isn't about President Millet."

"Oh?"

"Who's this?" he said, looking at Ron.

"This is my associate, Ron Bennett."

Ron offered his hand. "Pleased to meet you, Officer."

Steele remain standing ramrod straight. Ron dropped the hand.

"What can we do for you, Roger?" I said.

"Excuse me?"

"Ramjet."

"What?"

"The chin? Forget it. What's up?"

"I know you are investigating Jake Turner."

"You're right on top of things, aren't you."

"And President Millet says you're working for the family."

"He does."

"But you and I both know that's not the case."

"That so?"

"I spoke with Jake's father last night. He doesn't think much of you."

"He doesn't think much of anything not wrapped in Ivy."

"Says he didn't hire you. Something about hell freezing over."

"I really didn't give him credit for such a vivid turn of phrase."

"So who are you working for?"

"That would be telling."

"Gotta ask. Don't matter."

"This the bit where you tell me to keep the hell out of your investigation?"

"No. This is where I tell you I want you on my investigation."

I hadn't seen that coming. I traded surprised Muppet faces with Ron.

"I thought you said *on* your investigation."

"These kids smell a cop at a thousand paces. After the Turner OD, lips are closing. We can't get any momentum."

"You think I can?"

"You're not one of them, but you're not one of us. They might open up to you."

"You really have donut."

"I'm a blink away from raiding every party in a twenty-block radius of this campus."

"President Millet won't like that."

"I don't work for President Millet. I work for the city."

"That why you're on campus, out of uniform, on a Saturday?"

"I do campus security. Most of the PD boys do. That's got nothing to do with the investigation."

"I'm sure President Millet doesn't see it that way."

Steele stood at ease and said nothing.

"So I have to ask myself, why would I bother sharing anything? I have a client. I don't work for the city and, as you point out, I sure as hell don't work for Millet."

"Let's try it this way," said Steele. "You don't share intel with me, I will tell President Millet and he will have me remove you from campus and have you charged with trespass if you return. Then your client, whoever that is, can read about the case in the newspaper."

I curled my lip and nodded my head. "Checkmate," I said. "Let's see what I can find out."

"Right," said Steele. He chinked his chin to me, and then Ron. I thought he was about to salute. But he spun on his heel, marched around the massive grille of his pickup and slid in. The shocks groaned at his mass. He was one big, strong unit. The black truck peeled away and headed around the campus, obeying the 15 mph speed limit.

Ron looked at me. "You always bring the best out in folks."

"I'm a people person. Let's go watch some sports."

CHAPTER ELEVEN

The playing fields were a mass of a human activity. There were teams in various sports, some warming up, some playing, some waiting to play. There were coaches and support staff and a handful of spectators. There were no bleachers or stands, just white lines on massive expanses of green. Everyone stood along the sidelines. It was my childhood writ large, minus the overcoats and scarves. It took a while to locate the match I wanted. I heard Coach McAllister before I saw him. That solid New York accent should have felt out of place in the mild morning sunshine, but didn't. Ron and I ambled to the opposite sideline from McAllister. The away team sideline. I'd never watched a game of lacrosse before. It was fast and physical. Someone had once described it to me as being like field hockey with no regard for where you put your stick. I found it closer to rugby with weapons. There was more blood in the half we watched than in a season of college football. The premise seemed to be that goals were scored at either end, like soccer, with sticks like hockey, but the sticks had little nets at the end, which allowed players to pick up the ball and run with it, and then fling it with daunting power to a teammate or at the goal. And they flung their bodies at each other with blatant disregard for their health or lack of padding. I started to wonder if Jake Turner hadn't wound up unconscious under the bleachers as a result of playing lacrosse.

When the game finished the players were spent. Physical contact is way more draining than people imagine. In football there was a lot of contact but a lot of stoppages. There were also offensive and defensive teams, so there was recovery time. And while lacrosse was more random crashing than full-on tackles, the game was played at a continuity and pace that the average person couldn't comprehend, let alone perform. I wondered how even athletes of this caliber could do it. At least unaided. The players shook hands. From what I could tell, the home team had won. There was no scoreboard. This was Division II lacrosse. In parts of Texas they have better facilities for Pop Warner football. The players gathered their stuff and ambled to a change shed to shower. They grabbed a variety of colored sports drinks from a plastic picnic table as they headed inside. Each player seemed to have his preferred bottle. Coach McAllister went into the shed, I guess to give a rah-rah speech and hand someone an MVP. He paid us no attention. I was okay with that. I was hoping to speak to one of the players.

Ron and I milled about the abandoned sport drinks table. We watched from a distance a women's soccer match. They all looked like girls to me. I looked for Angel but couldn't see her, until I noticed a blond girl running from defense through the midfield. I was looking for a white uniform, but her match day kit was dark blue from head to toe. She had a low center of gravity and good ball control. Although she didn't look Kim fit, she didn't seem to drop off the pace at all.

After a time the lacrosse players began wandering out in dribs and drabs. I wasn't sure who was from which team. They were all now in civvies. Some wore letter jackets. Most did not. Then I saw the hoodie. Black. Hood up despite the warm day. Mopey face hiding underneath. The kid from the waiting area outside Jake's hospital room. So he was a teammate. Ron and I approached as he walked away from the change rooms toward the main campus. He saw us coming but pretended he didn't.

"Hey," I said. "I know you, don't I?"

"I doubt it," mumbled the kid.

"Sure I do. You're the guy who let his buddy OD under the bleachers and then left him there to die."

The kid turned to me in a flash. "The hell I did."

"Then who did?"

The kid frowned at me from inside his hood like the evil emperor from Star Wars.

"You're that guy. The one at the hospital."

"See, I told you we were acquainted."

"I can't talk to you, man."

"Sure you can."

"No, seriously." He began walking away.

"You want to do it somewhere quiet, or you want me to drop in on every class you have for the rest of semester and call you out?"

He stopped and looked at Ron.

"Who's the granddad?"

"He's with me. He's cool."

The kid looked around. "This ain't a quiet place."

"It's your campus. You tell us where."

Where turned out to look like a tavern in a barrio. The building was exposed cinderblock. The front was open to the elements. Latino music and charred meats wafted out onto the street. We walked in, following the kid's lead. In the back was a small lawn, surrounded on all sides by more gray cinderblock. The rush of the turnpike provided the backdrop to the Latin rhythms. A Latina with curves like the Monaco Grand Prix track came out to us.

"Cerveza?" We all nodded. She disappeared and then quickly returned with three cans of Tecate, and a wooden box. She dropped the three beers on the plastic green table we sat at and opened the box. Inside was an assortment of cigars. The kid and I shook our heads. Ron twiddled his fingers in the air, and then selected one that was the width of a pickle. The woman smiled. The gold tooth was a nice touch. Ron popped the cigar in his shirt pocket.

"For laters."

We all took a slug from our beers. They were icy cold. Cold beers, no view and an ID policy that consisted of being able to order beers *en espanol*. This was my kind of place.

"So, kid," I said. "What's your name?"

"Christian."

"You want to lose the hood, Christian? It's hot out here."

"I'm good."

"There's prison-quality cinderblock on all four sides. No one will see you. Your fashion cred is safe."

Christian pulled the hood back off his head. He needed a decent haircut, but he looked an okay kid.

"So tell us about Jake."

"Where do I start?"

"At the end."

Christian frowned, and then sipped his beer. "Okay, so he OD'ed."

"How?"

"Took too much of something."

"What?"

"You don't know?"

"Pretend I don't."

"I don't know," he said, sipping and sliding his eyes to Ron.

"Pretend I'm not an idiot," I said.

"I don't know."

"Pretend I'm not an idiot with a license to carry a concealed weapon."

He went to take another sip but stopped halfway to his mouth.

"You have a gun?"

"Let's keep on point, Christian." The truth was I did not have a gun on me. I did have a license to carry, however. My gun was in a safe in my office. I don't like guns. I carry them as infrequently as possible. Despite what the NRA says, people don't kill people. People with guns kill people. I can count the number of fistfight deaths I've seen on one finger.

"Okay, so I don't know, for sure. But I'm guessing it was Maxx."

"What's that?" I played dumb and ignorant better than Olivier.

"It's meth, dude. A party drug. It's all the rage."

"And Jake was a user?"

"You don't use Maxx. It's a party drug."

"What does that mean?"

"It means you take it at parties."

"But it's addictive."

"You drink beer?"

"Even Ron here can't drink enough beer in a sitting to OD."

"It's true," said Ron. "It takes years. Decades even."

"So was Jake a user?"

Christian sucked on his beer.

"Permit to carry, remember," I said.

"No. He wasn't."

"How do you know?"

"You don't know Jake, do you?"

"I'm getting an impression."

"Jake would never do hard drugs."

"Why?"

"Cause that stuff will kill your game. Jake was all about lacrosse, dude. Like, obsessive. He was a great player, but he was more than that. He lived it. He was a perfectionist. Trained like a dog. He'd never take something that would hurt his game. Never."

I took a sip of my beer. "So you said he'd never take a hard drug. What kind of drug would he take?"

"Dude, you're not listening. He wasn't into drugs. He was all about performance." There was that word again.

"Some drugs enhance performance, don't they, Christian?"

His eyes went as wide as hubcaps. I'd have loved to have played him in poker. In ten years time, when he actually had some money.

"Did Jake take any performance-enhancing drugs?"

"What? No!" It was about as convincing as the acting in *I dream of Jeannie.*

"Let me ask a completely different question than that. Have you ever taken performance enhancing drugs, Christian?"

"What? No!"

"Are you sure? And if you say 'what, no,' one more time I will exercise my right under Florida stand-your-ground laws and shoot you."

"What? No! I mean, hell. No. I mean don't shoot me, dude please." I put my hand on my hip.

"Oh, no. Please, no. Seriously, Jake never used. Never. He sold the stuff but he never used."

I took my hand from my hip and sipped my beer.

"Oh, man, please don't turn me into the NCAA. My mom will kill me."

"I'm not going to tell your mom, Christian. Just tell me about the drugs."

He chugged the rest of his can of beer.

"Is there another one going?" he said. Ron nodded and went into the bar.

"You can't tell anyone, okay?"

"I'm a private investigator. This is privileged information." I didn't bother telling him there was no real PI privilege under Florida law, and if there was, he wasn't my client so he wouldn't be covered.

"That's true? Really? Okay. So Jake was the guy, you know. The leader. The captain. The best player. But he was a machine. He was like, driven. I think his old man messed him up good. But no one could keep up with him. Guys nearly died trying. We're a Division II team at a Division II school. Jake, he was Division I. He would've been a star at Syracuse. Anywhere. We couldn't keep up with him."

Ron returned with three fresh beers. Christian took a long slug. "It drove him a little nuts. He should have been at a better school, but he wouldn't leave. So he found a way to be better. For us all to be better."

"Go on."

Another slug of beer. "PEDs, dude. Like you said. First it was guys who were DL. You know, disabled list."

"I know DL."

"So Jake, he turns up with this stuff to help them heal faster. Then guys are getting bounced, like they get run into and knocked down in the tackle. Jake comes in with something to make them stronger, bigger. Then most of us just can't keep the pace, so he turns up with blood to improve our endurance. Blood, dude. Like a vampire."

"Where did he get this stuff?"

"I don't know. And please don't shoot me, 'cause I'm serious. I don't know."

"What about the coaches? What did they say?"

"Nothing."

"But you must've been swimming in drugs."

"No, dude. It was all on the QT. The quiet."

"I know QT." The kid must have read Elmore Leonard for American lit.

"Each player was tailored. Get just what he needed. Nothing more. Jake was serious about that. It wasn't for fun. It was for the team."

"But you're telling me the coaching staff knew nothing?"

"Of course not. We were winning."

I nodded. I sipped my beer. Then I sipped again. Killing time. Avoiding the question I had to ask. I put my beer down.

"So what about Director Rose? She didn't know?"

"You hear what I'm saying? Nobody knew. Nobody wanted to. We won a regional title last year. Never been done before at this school. This year, we're going for the big one. NCAA."

"So how did you avoid detection? The USADA, the NCAA? You must have been tested."

"You think if they can't catch Tour de France cyclists they're going to catch Division II lacrosse? No one cares, dude. We're not on TV. There's no money. No one cares."

"The NCAA cares."

"You think? I don't know, maybe they do. But I never been tested. That's all I'm saying."

"Never? Not once?"

"Never."

"What did you take?"

He sipped his beer and looked at Ron again.

"Doesn't leave this bar, Christian."

"HGH mainly. I was too small. Needed to bulk up."

"I know that drug well. You know what that drug does to you?"

"Nothing proven."

"You happy being the guinea pig?"

He shrugged.

"Here's what I don't get. You good enough to go pro?"

Christian laughed.

"What? You're not?"

"No. I'm not. But who'd want to?"

"Why wouldn't you? There is a pro league. I've seen it on ESPN 3 or something."

"Jake could make Major League Lacrosse. But you know what the best player in the league earns? The LeBron James, the Peyton Manning?"

"No."

"About eighteen thousand a year. That's one-eight. You earn more at Starbucks."

"Seriously? That's it?"

"That's it."

"So why do it? Why train and work so hard? Why take drugs, for crying out loud?" I got it in major sports. The money in baseball, football, basketball. Huge sums of money made guys desperate. But I didn't understand why anyone would do it for zero payoff. Christian sucked on his beer.

"I'm serious, Christian. Why do drugs?"

He put the beer down and looked me in the eyes for the first time since we'd arrived.

"To win." We looked at each other for a long moment. I understood but found it insane at the same time.

"To win? Who taught you such a cockamamie idea?"

"Director Rose," he said. I felt my cheeks flush. Then a sound bellowed from Christian's pocket. A screaming, humorless noise: *Yo Fa Momma, Yo Fa Momma, Yo Fa Momma, Yo*. He tussled with his trousers until he pulled the phone from his pocket. It was massive. Mobile phones had started huge, gotten tiny, and then gotten huge again.

"This is Christian," he said into the device that looked like the television set in my grandmother's living room.

"What? When?" He listened, and then, "Okay." He hung up. He looked at the phone. He looked at Ron. He looked at me. Then he spoke.

"Jake's dead."

CHAPTER TWELVE

The memorial service was held in the main quad of the college on Monday evening. Evidently Jake Turner had been a big man on campus because the quad was full of students. The previous days had seen a field's worth of flowers, cards and notes left in tribute at the base of the bleachers where Jake had been found. Word was that President Millet wasn't keen on the memorial service being held on campus grounds. What he was keen to do was distance the university from the words *drugs* and *death*. But there was no stopping a thousand college students with a single purpose of mind. Someone appropriated a lectern; someone delivered a microphone and outdoor speakers. And that was that. Social media took care of the rest.

Millet didn't appear, but wisely he didn't shut the event down. A ring of security guys, no doubt all local PD, stood on the periphery of the crowd. Officer Steele was near the steps to the administration building. He was in uniform, his squarehead and sidearm serving to ensure no one got any ideas about turning the memorial into a protest against anything. The lectern had been placed at the base of the steps, right below President Millet's office window. I wasn't sure if that meant anything, and I wondered if he was up in his office, watching.

A kid I didn't recognize got up to the microphone and gave it the *testing, one, two*, which seemed out of place given the circumstances but served to turn every head in his direction. He started proceedings by talking about how terrible he felt and how everybody felt. He rambled on with that topic for longer than was necessary. I sat with my back against a palm tree, three quarters of the way across the quad. The kid lost his train of thought and stopped talking, and then he asked someone else to speak. Another kid, this one I remembered from the lacrosse match, took the podium and spoke of the team and the sorrow they felt but how it would unite them as a team to become stronger. Someone sitting within my earshot remarked that without Turner they were toast. A third person took the spotlight. A girl who looked like a cheerleader on her day off. She spoke about Jake. I was glad someone finally did. She talked of his commitment, his dedication to the team, to the school and to winning an NCAA title. She said they had taken him too young, and she'd miss him. Then she started crying. It wasn't very convincing, but she gave it a shot.

A procession of kids came and went from the microphone, saying pretty much the same thing. Sad, wrong, waste, miss him, tears. The tears increased until most everyone on the lawn was sniffing. I had to check myself to see if my heart had turned to stone. I wasn't feeling it. I decided it wasn't me. I'd cried before and I'd probably cry again. But teenage emotion was just so earnest and affected. It didn't look real. Like they were trying to out-emotion each other, in case a reality TV crew happened along. Perhaps I was being harsh. But I didn't think so.

The speeches petered themselves out, and people began standing. The guy who had supplied the loudspeaker came and unplugged it. Perhaps he had a gig to get to. Students and a few staff stepped forward and deposited more flowers, cards, a lacrosse stick. An old basketball. I wasn't sure about that one. Then the crowd slowly started drifting away, for a few quiet drinks and stories about a fallen friend, or to study, or to catch

the latest *American Idol*. I noted that Jake's parents had not made
an appearance. Ron said they were still in town, waiting for the
body to be released, which was due to happen the next morning.
Funeral arrangements had been made in Massachusetts for
Friday. A notice was in the *Boston Globe*. I understood why they
hadn't shown, why the funeral was in Boston. But I couldn't help
feeling they had missed something here that would have offered
comfort once the raw harshness of events wore away. Not every
kid gets a thousand self-interested college students to their
memorial service.

I watched Officer Steele watch the crowd disperse. His team
was good. Their presence was obvious but understated. Very few
uniforms but plenty of personnel. Enough show to deter
trouble, not so much as to cause it. I stood and brushed my
trousers off, and then wandered across the quad toward the gym
parking lot where I had left my car. Officer Steele saw me and
gave a small nod. I returned the favor and kept walking. The sun
was offering a final burst across the horizon. The playing fields
were dark and abandoned. Perhaps in honor of Jake. Perhaps
Monday was a recovery day. I pulled my keys out and spun the
ring around on my finger. Then I put the keys back in my pocket
when I saw Angel sitting on the hood of my car.

CHAPTER THIRTEEN

Angel had been crying. Not the limited tears I saw at the service. Her eyes were swollen, and her cheeks were red from the effort. She was a puffy-looking girl to begin with. Now she looked like she had an allergic reaction and might go into anaphylactic shock.

"You okay?" I said. I had a zinger like that for almost every occasion. Angel rubbed her nose with her sweater sleeve. She looked at me with liquid eyes, and then looked away, at nothing in particular. I couldn't think of anything to say that would match what I already said, so I stayed quiet. Angel took shallow breaths, like her lungs were in her throat. Then she wiped her eyes with her sleeve. Her hair wasn't in a ponytail, and it flapped around her face. Her red day pack was scrunched in her lap. She held it like it contained the map to King Solomon's mines.

"Take me somewhere," she said.

"Where do you need to go?"

She snorted to herself. "Need? I don't know. Take me to a bar."

I took her to Johnny Rockets. Burgers, fries, malts. And bright lighting. Of all the places in the world I was not taking an emotionally fragile, underage girl, a bar was at the top of the list. Bars pretty much were the list. I heard my assistant Lizzy in my head, telling me it was sexist to worry about that, having done the same thing with Jake's former teammate, Christian. I heard myself tell Lizzy that when the *Palm Beach Post* started treating those two events as equal, then I would. I ordered two malted shakes.

"Not quite what I was thinking," said Angel.

"You twenty-one?"

"What are you, my granddad?"

"I was thinking more about the bartender checking ID."

"Yeah, 'cause that's what they do."

"Drink your malted."

We sucked hard on straws that weren't designed for the task. It was like sucking a football through two-inch PVC pipe.

"Better?" I said.

"A vodka would've been better."

"Only today. Not tomorrow."

She sucked on her straw. "You want to split some fries?"

"Sure," I said. "You want a burger or something?"

She shook her head. "Vodka doesn't add pounds. Burgers do."

I stood and ordered some fries. I waited at the counter for them. A guy in a paper hat and white apron cooked them up fresh. I watched Angel as I waited. She hunched over and sucked at her drink, like a child. I wondered how a child like that comes to be wanting vodka. I shook my head at the notion, and of what I was doing when I was at college. That, and more. I dropped the paper bowl of fries on the table. Angel gobbled a couple down. She waved at her mouth.

"Hot," she said, slurping at her drink.

"You said you weren't Jake's girlfriend."

"I wasn't," she said, stuffing some more fries in her mouth.

"You seemed pretty upset. More than most."

She looked at me with doe eyes for a moment, and then renewed her attack on the fries.

"You wouldn't understand."

"Try me."

She shook her head.

"Why?" I said. "Because I've never been twenty? Never lost friends?"

She glanced at me. "Okay. We were friends. Close. We spent time together. Hanging out. We never dated or anything."

"But you would've liked to."

"Doesn't matter. He's gone."

"It matters to you."

She stuffed more fries in, perhaps to avoid answering. I said nothing. She finished her mouthful and considered putting more in, but didn't.

"We were friends. Nothing more. But in some ways, there isn't more. Having sex doesn't make you know someone better." *From the mouths of babes.*

"We just liked each other's company. We had stuff in common. I listened to him, about his parents and stuff, and he listened to me." She looked at the fries and played with one, knocking it around the bowl.

"Sometimes we didn't even have to talk. You know?"

I nodded. I knew. I thought of Kim Rose, and the times we did just that at college. I thought of Danielle, and how sitting on my patio in silence with her was among the best times I could have. I thought of the relationships that didn't work, like Beccy Williams, gorgeous and vivacious and sex in a bottle. Five minutes silence between us had been an eternity. Now she was in Connecticut, giving the sports updates on ESPN, fitting lots of words in between plays in college football. Angel was more on the money than her tender years let her know.

"Did you see him the night he OD'ed?"

Her eyes moistened again and she nodded.

"We hung out on the bleachers for a while. It's where we liked to go after practice. To you know, decompress."

I nodded. "How was he?"

"Distracted. And worn out."

"Worn out how?"

"We only stayed a little while. I had to get home and he was tired."

"Tired of what?"

"From practice, I guess. Some days hit you harder than others. He was kind of out of it, clumsy even, which wasn't him at all. When he knocked his Gatorade over he giggled at it and said he was beat. Said he'd catch me the next day." She gazed at the fries. "But he didn't. He didn't catch me the next day."

"I'm sorry," I said.

"For what?"

"For Jake. For your loss."

She dropped her head like she was in prayer. "Thanks."

"So tell me, why were you sitting on my Mustang?"

She looked up. "I've been meaning to say. That car doesn't seem very inconspicuous, for a private eye."

"I've been thinking that."

"I saw it from across the lot. Figured you'd come back to it after the service."

"So?"

"So you wanted to know what Jake was into? Parties and stuff?"

"Sure."

"I can get you into that scene."

"How so?"

"Everyone's been pretty low-key since we heard about Jake on Saturday. People will go easy tonight cause of the service, then tomorrow out of respect. By Wednesday there'll be a party. Everyone will have steam to blow off. You can come with me."

"What about Saturday?"

"What about it?"

"No one will wait until the weekend?"

"This is college. I thought you said you were young once?"

"I'm starting to wonder. So where's this party?"

"Dunno yet. I'll know on Wednesday. Why don't you call me?"

Angel took a pen from her day pack. She grabbed my hand and opened my palm and wrote the number on my skin. Then she half-smiled and put the pen away.

"So Wednesday, you think?" I said, looking at the blue ink on my hand.

"Def."

We finished our malts in silence. Not the comfortable kind. The slurping the bottom of a milkshake kind.

"Can I drop you home?" I said.

"You want to hang out?"

"No, I can't hang out. I have a previous engagement."

"A date?"

"What it is, is of no relevance to you. You wanna ride?"

"No thanks, I'll walk. I gotta work off these fries." She didn't seem put out by my rebuff, which stung a little more than it should have. Angel flicked her hair, slipped her day pack onto her shoulder, and led me out of the burger joint.

"Later," she said, wandering hands in pockets toward the campus. I turned back to the parking lot, headed for my car, looking for an explanation and hopefully a better understanding of the female side of our species. I feared I was in for disappointment.

CHAPTER FOURTEEN

"And she wrote the number on your hand?"

Danielle was twisting the top off a bottle of Sauvignon Blanc and looking at me with a scrunched brow.

"Exactly. What's with that?" I had a mini blender full of chickpeas, lemon juice, tahini and water. I sprinkled some salt in and a dollop of olive oil and hit the button. Danielle poured two glasses of wine and sauntered out to the patio. I could watch her walk on video loop. For hours. She had one of those bodies that looks so good in motion. Like a cheetah looks impressive enough just lying about in the grass, but in motion, it looks like physiological perfection. I released the button, scooped out the hummus into a bowl and placed the bowl in the middle of a plate of pita crisps. When I got out to the patio Danielle had lit a candle that smelled of vanilla. I put the plate on the table between our two lounger chairs. She was taking in the view of lights shining from Riviera Beach, as they were bounced and tossed across the ripples on the Intracoastal waterway.

"Cheers," I said.

Danielle smiled in the candlelight. "Cheers." We both sipped our wine.

"So?" I said.

"Hmmm? Oh, the girl?"

" Aha," I said, nibbling on some hummus.

"Be careful."

"What does that mean? Be careful."

"She just lost her buddy—who she liked a lot more than she's telling, I'm just saying—and now the mysterious, older man has swept in to save the day."

"You think I'm mysterious? Like dark and handsome, mysterious?"

"You're blonde. You look like a retired beach bum."

"Well, just handsome mysterious," I said.

"I was thinking more Loch Ness monster mysterious."

"Ouch."

"Just watch yourself is all I'm saying. She's looking for something. And it isn't you, but she might mistake you for it."

"I think I've been pretty upfront."

"Before or after she wrote on your hand?"

"Touché."

"Be brutal. Young girls' self-denial is matched only by that of older men."

"Thanks. You available for therapy sessions? Cause I reckon you could do wonders for my self-esteem."

"I'll work on your self-esteem later tonight." She sipped her wine and winked. I gulped and dove in for some more hummus.

"So that's my women troubles for the day," I said. "How about you?"

"No women troubles."

"Shame."

"Did go out for lunch today."

"Ooh, Sheriff goes out for lunch. Exciting. Let me guess. Donuts?"

"That's police, you goose."

"Right. Danish?"

"Seafood, actually. Crunchy grouper."

"Proper food? What was the occasion?"

"I got invited."

"Okay, you're going to make me drag it out of you. Invited by whom?"

"Eric."

"Eric?"

"Edwards."

"Eric Edwards. Your ex-husband Eric Edwards?"

"That's the one."

"And what did the state attorney for the Fifteenth Judicial Circuit want?"

"Lunch."

I looked at her as though I was looking over reading spectacles, which I don't own. The effect was to give her a face full of wrinkled forehead. She shrugged.

"What can I tell you? He called and asked me if I was busy for lunch. I wasn't so I went. I don't think I have to hate him forever, do I?"

"Nope."

"So I asked him what was up, and he said nothing. I told him to cut the crap, and he said that he just wanted to have lunch. He said we were law enforcement colleagues despite everything and he just wanted to catch up."

"He taking any other Palm Beach sheriff's deputies out for crunchy grouper?"

"No. I think he's just trying to move on."

"He still seeing his bit of fluff?"

"I didn't think it appropriate to ask. But I haven't heard anything, so I assume she's still in his office."

I sipped my wine and looked at the city lights.

"What?" said Danielle. "You've got something to say."

"Be careful."

"Oh, Miami. I was married to the man. I'd know if he was up to something. I really think he figures we're going to bump into each other professionally, so why not get along?"

"If you say so. But a wise woman once said, the only thing more self-delusional than a young girl is an older man."

"Touché."

Danielle nodded and sipped her wine. We watched the lights play across the water, and we descended into a long, comfortable silence that wasn't even broken when Danielle's glass ran dry. She waved the empty vessel before me. I smiled at her, and she at me, and I padded into the house to get refills, thinking to myself: Miami Jones, how did you ever get so damn lucky?

CHAPTER FIFTEEN

I woke up thinking about Hollywood. California, not Florida. About those movies where the rogue CIA director and his personal unit of flag-bearing patriots commit all manner of sins in the name of country. But then they don't tell the president, either for plausible deniability, or because they think he won't get what they are doing. Either way POTUS is left in the dark. I suppose in such a large organization it is possible that the people at the top don't know what the troops are really up to. But in my experience, the actions of any organization aren't driven by what the leadership knows, but by the culture the leadership creates. Hire a bunch of clean-cuts with Midwest work ethics and you'll get different actions than if you hire a team of fast-talking leather jackets from the Jersey shore. It was a pretty deep train of thought for first thing in the morning, and it was only interrupted by Danielle waking up, rolling over and laying a warm, moist kiss on me. To hell with deep and meaningful.

Post shower and smoothie I found myself on I-95, zipping back down to Lauderdale. I'd resolved that if I wanted to understand the culture of a movie studio, I was wasting my time asking the producer. I needed to take a walk on the studio floor. As I pulled the Mustang into the gym parking lot I also resolved that I had taken my Hollywood metaphor further than it was designed to go.

Across the speed hump on the dividing road, there was
activity on the fields. Some kids were running drills. Most should
have been in class. But the buzz was back around campus. The
mourning was over. I ambled up to the portable office that
housed the coaching staff. The Lacrosse poster hung in the
window like a reminder. I went straight in and knocked on
Coach McAllister's door. No *come in*. So I turned the knob. It was
locked. Perhaps Coach didn't keep office hours. Perhaps he was
on the field, watching over drills. I turned to head out and heard
noise from the office opposite. It was the only one of the four
that had no name on the door. I knocked on it. Heard a muffled
come in. Coach McAllister was laid back in a tatty old sofa with a
Dr. Pepper in one hand, pen in the other and clipboard
balancing on his belly. A television remote lay on the clipboard.
He was facing an old television on a rack with casters, the kind I
hadn't seen since elementary school. He looked up from the
screen for a moment.

"What do you want?"

"Morning to you too. Bad news about Jake."

"You don't need to tell me that," he said, not taking his eyes
off the screen.

"What are you watching?"

"Film."

I stepped into the room and closed the door. "You watch
film?"

"Of course I watch film. You think this is Hicksville? That
only Division I football coaches watch film?"

I hadn't really thought about it. At University of Miami we
had used coaches' film in football to analyze both our own game
and our opponents'. Although the games were televised,
coaches' film generally showed a static angle, known as the
all-22, which was like watching the game from the clouds. It

allowed coaches and players to analyze setups, pre-snap movements and the plays themselves. In baseball film was used less, but still helped to analyze players, especially batters, and which type of pitches they liked or disliked. I never considered it for lacrosse.

"How do you get it?"

"We have someone on the sideline with a camera. Then we swap tapes with our next opponent. It's not the NFL, but it tells us a little about their players, their structure." He picked up the remote and paused the game on screen.

"You come here to talk about film?"

"No. I came to talk about Jake."

"It's sad. It's a waste. But I got a game on Saturday. Jake was a pro. He'd want us to play to win."

"Can you win? Without him?"

McAllister sipped his Dr. Pepper. He was wearing his whistle around his neck. "We're a team. We'll do our best."

"I heard you were a shot at the NCAA title."

"Still are."

"Without your best player?"

"Is there a point you're making or are you just trying to rub me the wrong way?"

"I was wondering where the team got their HGH, steroids and that sort of thing."

He curled his lip at me. "Why don't you get the hell out."

"You really want to be left holding the bag on that one?"

"There's no bag, there's no drugs. Jake took some kind of meth, I heard."

"I'm not talking about what he OD'ed on. I'm talking about what he dealt."

"You're crazy, fella. Jake was our best player, but it wasn't 'cause of no drugs."

"But the rest of the team wasn't quite as good, were they? Needed some help. To get bigger, faster."

"I'm not going to ask you to leave again."

"Good, because it's really boring. I'll leave once you tell me the truth."

"I don't know anything."

"Ah, the Oliver North defense. Not buying it Coach. I know for fact that PEDs were being used by your team, and that Jake Turner was the source of those drugs."

"Looks like you've got the case sewn up."

"Not quite. I don't know where Jake got the drugs from, or how and why a kid so committed to enhancing his performance ended up overdosing under the bleachers."

"Like I say, I don't know anything about that."

I took a breath, in through the nose, out through the mouth. Then I glanced at the television. A kid in lacrosse kit was mid-stride. His cheeks were puffed out, straining for oxygen.

"You really are that stupid, aren't you," I said.

"You are seriously asking for a smack in the mouth." He had forearms like Popeye and would do some damage if he landed a punch. But it was the landing part he wasn't going to be able to do.

"I'd like to see you try and get your pudgy ass out of that sofa, let alone lay a punch." He didn't move. "I didn't think so. You've lost a player on your watch, and you're sitting here looking at tape, oblivious to the fact that when the fit hits the shan you're going to be the one they hang out to dry. You've got scapegoat tattooed on your forehead so you can't see it."

McAllister looked like he was going to puke. The color washed from his face, and he pushed himself forward in the sofa and put his head between his knees. The clipboard and remote dropped onto the government-issue industrial carpet. Then he threw up. It was unpleasant. The sound of throwing up doesn't make me nauseated, especially when it's coming from someone I don't care a lick about. But that don't make it pleasant.

Normally I wouldn't stick around for such a display, but McAllister had more to say, and I wanted to hear it. He must have had a hearty breakfast. After a minute and a few dry retches, he gained control of himself. I didn't offer to help. McAllister ripped a sheet from the clipboard and wiped his mouth. He looked terrible. Puffy and pale and red. He was out of breath. Vomiting takes a lot of effort. He looked up at me. The eyes he gave me weren't so much puppy dog as smacked cow.

"My wife loves it here."

"No reason she can't stay."

"You think so?"

"Sure. You'll be the one going to prison, not her." That brought more dry retching. It was like watching a 250 pound cat hack up a fur ball. He wiped his mouth with his bare arm. The hairs glistened with spittle.

"I'm not going down for this. I've done nothing wrong."

"You think."

"I didn't give anyone drugs. Not ever."

"But you knew it was happening."

"Everyone knew." He took a gulp of Dr. Pepper, washed it around in his mouth and then swallowed.

"Who's everyone?"

"Everyone. The players, the coaches, the administrators."

"You mean it's happening in other sports?"

"Of course. Everyone's doing it. Jake, he had stuff for everyone."

"Why? You're a Division II school. No major sports outside of basketball, and none of those guys will make the NBA. Why?"

"Winning. It's all about winning. That's all Jake cared about. Winning. Team. That was what the administration demanded. Do it for the team. For the school. For your teammates."

"Which administrators? Millet?"

"Are you kidding? Not Millet. He wants sports out. If he knew about drugs, he'd make it public. Use it against us."

"So who?"

"Director Rose. Kimberly is all about winning. Doing everything for the team. Winning at any cost."

"But why?"

"It's in her DNA. Besides, Division II athletic directors don't want to stay in Division II schools forever. And they don't go to Division I without winning."

"It's political?"

"Isn't everything?" He wiped his face with his palms, and then left his hands over his face.

"What about drug testing? How could you avoid USADA on every test?"

"I don't know. There are ways. Jake knew when they were coming. He'd pay other kids, non-jocks, to provide urine samples, and sometimes blood. Or the USADA reps would do legit tests on clean players only. Random, but not that random."

"So there were clean players? What did they think?"

"How would I know? If they were good enough not to need drugs, they were still in the program, I guess. They'd turn a blind eye like everyone else."

"Like you."

He looked at me again. "I'm not a bad guy."

"No. You're a prince among men. Parents all over the country send their kids into your care. And you turn a blind eye."

I turned to the door. I'd had enough of the stench.

"What are you going to do?" he said. His voice shook.

"I'm going to find out why Jake Turner died. Then I'm going to find out who did it. Then I'm going to turn a mirror on the lot of you, and watch you burn."

CHAPTER SIXTEEN

I leaped out of the coaches portable and dashed across the road. What I should have done was walk over to the baseball field, stand on the pitcher's mound and take some deep breaths. But the red mist had descended. I was being used, and that had my hackles up big time. I marched straight by my car into the gym building. Ignored the pretty little thing behind the gym desk and strode upstairs three at a time. Down the hall and pushed open the door marked *Athletic Director*. The kid in the polo was behind his desk. He looked up and watched me cross the room.

"Excuse me, sir."

I didn't bother to respond. I punched the door to the inner office. I marched to the middle of the room before I noticed the office was empty. I looked around and could practically hear the echo of crows calling.

"She's not here," said the assistant from the doorway.

"Where is she?"

"Gone for a run. She'll be back in a little while. Would you like to wait?" He stepped aside to open up the doorway. I sat down on the sofa in Kim's office.

"I'm sorry, I meant out here in the waiting room." He smiled.

"I'm good."

"I can't let you stay in here, I'm afraid." He lost the smile.

I glared at him. "What you can't do is stop me."

"Well, I'll have to stay in here with you."

"Do what you gotta do, kid."

I sat on the sofa and took the breaths I should have taken on the pitcher's mound. I didn't want to. I wanted to be angry. To let my emotions do the talking and not be dissuaded from my words. The kid leaned from toe to toe, fidgeting. He was bored, he had work to do and he was too young to know how to wait.

"I'm going to do some work," he said. "I'll leave the door open." I just raised my eyebrows. I waited ten minutes. Every tick of the clock lowered my heart rate. By the time I heard the outer office door open I was positively Zen.

"He's in there," I heard the kid say.

Kim Rose breezed into the room. She smelled like her name. Her short hair was freshly washed. She wore body-hugging tan trousers and the obligatory polo with a panther on it. She glanced and smiled at me as she strode to her desk.

"Miami, hi. I wasn't expecting you."

"No," I said by way of witty retort.

She stopped behind her desk and dropped her gym bag. "I hate to run out on you but I have a boosters meeting. How can I help?" She tapped at her computer.

"Tell me again about performance-enhancing drug use on campus?"

She ceased her tapping and looked at me. Then she strode back across the room and closed the door.

"Didn't we have this conversation?"

"We did, sort of. But there's a problem."

"What's that?"

"You lied to me."

She put her hands on her hips. "Excuse me? I've never lied to you in my life."

"Then you're lying to yourself."

"I don't know where you think you're going with this, but I don't like it." She marched back to her desk. I stood and wandered over to face her.

"Jake Turner was providing performance-enhancing drugs to teammates. Let's start there."

"You need to tread carefully with comments like that."

"I'm quite comfortable dancing in a minefield with comments like that. Unless I start getting some straight answers."

"I don't know what you're talking about."

"That line seems to be the university motto. So let me fill you in. Your star lacrosse player provided steroids, HGH and goodness knows what to make his teammates as good as him. NCAA title good. He also supplied athletes in other sports, and the coaching staff know about it. And a win-at-all-costs culture like that doesn't create itself. It comes from the top."

Kim picked up a leather folio and came around the desk.

"Miami, I need to get to a meeting, but I can assure you this is news to me. You know me. I don't abide drug use. If what you say is true, then I will see that the perpetrators are called to account, be they students, coaches or administrators." She put her hand on my arm and walked toward the door. If I were a sheep, I might enjoy being shepherded, but last time I checked I wasn't that woolly.

"What's important now is that we find out who was responsible for what happened to Jake. But the need for discretion hasn't changed. A lot of people could get hurt unfairly if Millet gets his hands on it."

"A lot of people are getting hurt right now."

"So get to the bottom of it, Miami. I know you can do that for us." She dropped her hand from my arm. "I'm at an AD's conference for the next couple of days. We'll talk when I get back. I promise," she said, and then she turned to her assistant.

"They're in the conference room," he said. She nodded to him, then turned and nodded my way. I watched her disappear in a flash of burgundy and tan. The kid smiled at me, and then focused on his computer screen. I wandered out. I wanted a pithy departing remark, but one didn't come. I was too busy thinking about Kim. Maybe I was wrong. Maybe she didn't know. Maybe McAllister was the problem and he was trying to lay the blame. Maybe, maybe, maybe. I ambled down the stairs to the gym and past a wall of mirrors. I stopped and looked at myself. I looked tired. My eyes moved across my reflection, head to toe, and then back. Checking to see if my body had formed a bow to it. Because despite everything, I couldn't help feeling that someone was playing me like a fiddle.

CHAPTER SEVENTEEN

It had been a long time since I'd been to a college party. I found myself listless during the afternoon, so I went home, showered and put on my favorite palm tree print shirt. By the time I got down to Lauderdale I was still way too early, so I went for a drink instead. I drove back to the cinderblock Latino bar that Jake's teammate Christian had taken us to. The shutters were up as they had been and the small bar was open to the mild afternoon. A couple of Mexican guys were at the bar, smoking. The same woman who served us last time was inside the horseshoe bar. She was staring up at a television that sat on top of a refrigerator. Mexican soap opera. The smell of charred meat wafted through the space as it had before. I felt my stomach growl like an angry bear as I sat at the bar. The woman turned from her soaps.

"*Cerveza?*" she said, with a glint of the gold tooth.

"*Sí,*" I answered. She opened a can of Tecate, apparently the house beer. I nodded at the two guys on the other side of the bar. They were digging into plates of tacos. I looked at the woman.

"*Lo que esta en los tacos,*" I said in my broken Spanish.

"*Carne asada,*" she said, pointing to the smoking grill sitting on the sidewalk beside the bar.

"*Me gustaría alguna,*" I said, hoping I hadn't just asked for the right to marry her favorite goat. She smiled, nodded, took some

meat from the grill and disappeared into another room. When
she came back she carried a plate of soft tacos, with shredded
onion, lettuce and salsa. The tacos were sensational. I had a
second beer. When the sun started to go down the woman
flicked the television over to Mexican football and muted the
excited commentary, and then turned on a stereo with Latin
rhythms. More people arrived. Most were surprised but not
disappointed to see a gringo at the bar. I chatted with two young
guys who worked as plumbers for a company that managed
apartment rentals. Apparently there was no end to the amusing
stuff that got stuck in toilets. Everything from false teeth to
Barry Manilow CDs. The guys' girlfriends arrived. Both girls
spoke flawless English. An impressive achievement, given they
were both products of the Florida state school system. I enjoyed
their company very much and didn't want to leave. But I had
another party to get to.

I drove back to the campus and called Angel on the way. She
directed me to a residence hall on the opposite side of campus
from the sports fields. The building was a couple of years old
and done in a Spanish style, with white walls and faux terracotta
roof. I found Angel's room. There were four twin-share rooms
facing out onto a common kitchen/lounge area. Angel answered
the door in black trousers and bra over ample breasts.

"That's what you're wearing?" she said. I didn't understand
people who looked down on palm trees on shirts.

"Right back at ya."

"Just give me a minute. Come in."

"I'll wait out here." I sat on a microfiber sofa that was in
desperate need of a vacuum or a Labrador. A few minutes
turned out to be twenty. Angel came out looking just as she had
twenty minutes before, with the addition of a white silk shirt
that did almost nothing to hide the bra beneath.

The party house was a two-story minimansion in Country Estates off 818, where civilization butted up against the Everglades. The lots were large and the houses well apart. We parked down the street, at the end of a procession of pickups and sports cars. There was a large concrete circular driveway, where an impromptu game of three-on-three hoops was taking place under harsh white spotlights. The entryway was two-story, marble tile. A chandelier hung from the ceiling. The house was buzzing. People were everywhere. I was the oldest person in the place by a disturbing margin. The home seemed to have built-in speakers, because the same drone-like so-called music was blaring from every wall. Clumps of people were bouncing up and down in a living room. All the furniture had been pushed to the walls.

Angel led me through to the kitchen, where two guys were tapping a fresh keg. There was a burst of foam into a bucket, and then one of the guys started pouring heady beers into red Solo cups, using a gun attached to a hose, like he was watering the house plants. Angel passed me a beer, and then proceeded to a bar in the dining room to pour herself a vodka tonic, heavy on the vodka. We wandered through the party to say hi to people. The music was too monotonous to allow for conversation. Angel paraded me around like a trophy wife. I started out feeling like any woman who has ever gone out on the arm of Donald Trump. I ended up feeling like Michael Jackson's chimpanzee.

A group of girls were drinking on the back patio and lunged inside to recruit Angel to their gaggle. She clawed at me to join them. I pointed at my red cup like I wanted to refill and winked. I walked through the kitchen without bothering to get more warm beer, and then around through the dancing to the entry foyer. In my experience, anything that should not be happening at a party will be happening upstairs.

I wandered up the staircase, stepping over a brace of couples necking on the steps. The first bedroom I came to was closed. I pushed the door open. A group was in a tangle on the bed. I counted five bodies, but I could have been wrong. The room was dark and the mass of bodies fluid. They paid me no mind, so I left them to their business. The second bedroom was open. A half dozen kids lay around smoking joints. A sweet fog hung in the air.

"Hey, man," said a kid with a scraggly beard, sitting on a child's size rocking chair. He offered me his joint. I stepped into the room and sat on my haunches, taking the joint. I took a drag, and then handed it back.

"Good stuff," I said.

"Mmm," said scraggly beard.

"You know where I can get some?"

He held his joint out to me again.

"Some more," I said.

The guy took a slow drag, blew out a small cloud of smoke, and then pointed in the general direction of the window.

"Jo Jo," he said.

I nodded. "Thanks, man." I left the room, looking for Jo Jo. At the end of the walkway that overlooked the marble foyer was a double door. I ambled past the chandelier. There was no dust on it. A professional job. I got to the double doors to what I guessed would be the master bedroom. I put my hand on the lever and pushed down. The door flung open, revealing a tall, dark man with a smooth head, pink gums and yellow teeth. His eyes glowed in the dimly lit room, and he wore a leather vest over his hairless, ebony chest. He eyed me up the way a Rottweiler eyes up a juicy bone. He must have had a little over six inches on me, which put him at a disconcerting six-eight.

"What?" he said with a tuneless baritone voice.

"Jo Jo," I said.

He looked at me some more. I did not want to play poker with this unit. He could have been watching a sitcom or considering an ax murder—it was impossible to tell. I tensed my body, ready to punch or run, or maybe both, as needs demanded. The big man stepped back a half a pace and nodded his head toward the depths of the room. I edged past him, and picked up a hint of tobacco as I did. The room was lit by a solitary bedside lamp. It was a massive room. Bigger than most New York apartments. The focal point was a California king bed. A tall boy and an armoire that each looked the weight of a baby elephant were pressed against the wall. There was a lounge suite, with a sofa and two chairs, near the window. Even then there was enough space left in the room to play eighteen holes of mini golf. French doors led to a large balcony. The doors were open. So I walked through. At a teak outdoor table sat a sporty-looking kid in a yellow polo shirt. He had perfectly coiffed hair and pale skin, and the collar of his polo was flicked up at the back.

"Dude," said the kid. "Who did your wardrobe? Tommy Bahama?" He gave a smug grin and looked about, as if his posse were nodding in admiration of his zinger. But there was no one else on the balcony.

"Bang on," I said with a smile. "Love Tommy B. I can't get enough of it. Who did yours? Ralph Lauren's dad?"

He lost the grin. "What you want, old man?"

"What you got, Joseph?"

The kid's eyes narrowed. "How you know my name was Joseph? You a cop?"

"Nope. But looking at you there in your preppy little threads, you sure as hell ain't no Jo Jo."

"Why don't you take a hike."

"'Cause we got some business."

"I don't got no bidness witch you, pal."

"Don't got no *bidness witch me*? What is that? Russell Crowe doing Brooklyn mobster?"

"Who the hell is Russell Crowe?"

"Where'd you grow up? Westchester?"

"Long Island. Look, who the hell are you, man?"

I kicked open a seat opposite Joseph and sat down.

"Where's the other guy?"

"What guy?"

"The guy who normally does the selling?"

"I'm the guy."

I shook my head.

"The other guy resigned. Now I'm the guy. So you wanna deal, or you want me to get Carlos to throw you off this balcony?"

I nodded my head back to the bedroom. "Carlos?"

The kid nodded. "He's Haitian."

"So what you got?"

"What you want?"

I rubbed my chin like I was considering this very seriously. "You got Maxx?"

Joseph smiled his best Tom Cruise. "I am Maxx."

I suspect I was supposed to be impressed by this, so I stared at him, stone-faced.

He dropped the smile. "How much you want?"

"One."

"One bag?" he grinned.

"One tablet."

Again the grin disappeared. His face was the veritable emotional roller coaster.

"Come on," he said. "Snappy dresser like you? Just one tab?"

"Call it a trial."

Joseph went fishing in his backpack and came out with a single white tablet in a freezer baggy. He placed it on the table between us.

"A hundred," he said. Now his face was emotionless.

"Pretty steep," I said, reaching for my wallet.

"Trial price. Volume discounts are available."

I took out two fifties and pushed them across the teak table, and then I picked up the bag. The pill was small, but large enough for me to clearly see the letters M, A, X, X. Branding is everything in pharmaceuticals. I put the bag in my pocket and stood.

"You want something for the lady?" he said.

"What lady?"

"It's a party, dude. I got Rohypnol."

"The date rape drug?"

"That's ugly, man. I prefer mood enhancer."

I preferred throwing Jo Jo off the balcony. But I didn't want to make a scene. The only person that would hurt was Angel. Plus there was the little matter of Carlos the Haitian. As I reached the patio doors I turned back to the kid.

"Where'd you find this guy?" I said, jabbing my thumb in the direction of Carlos.

"He's an international exchange student. I kid you not."

I shrugged and wandered back downstairs. There were more people now. It was like a shopping mall on Christmas Eve. The music sounded something like that used to torture the Viet Cong. I bumped and felt my way through the house until I found Angel. She was on a sofa with three other girls. She saw me and smiled like I was a long-lost puppy, then she wrapped her arms around my neck and tried to pull me down into the sofa. She was strong, but not that strong. The vodka was setting in. I unlooped myself, and she fell back into the sofa with a giggle.

I yelled at her like I was a drunk at the ballpark. "I'm going to go."

She shook her head. "The party's just starting."

I shook my head, smiled and walked away. I find such situations are only complicated by long conversations, and I'm a big believer that the best way to avoid long conversations is to not be in the room anymore. I strolled out to my car. My ears were ringing like a flash bang had just gone off next to my head. I wasn't thinking about the case. The ear ringing was causing vertigo. I focused on keeping the Mustang in the lane all the way back to Singer Island. I got home, poured myself a scotch and fell asleep on the sofa, dreaming of young girls, massive Haitians and guys who had resigned.

CHAPTER EIGHTEEN

Fishing is to sitting on your butt what golf is to walking in a park. I know a few guys who like to head offshore and catch sea beasts the size of Korean cars, but that just seems to me something best left to the burly lads on *Deadliest Catch*. Personally, I don't get up to go fishing before the dawn, I don't raise a sweat using a rod that I wouldn't have raised drinking a beer, and I don't leave sight of good, solid land. Which is why I found myself sitting in a Boston Whaler, sipping a cold one under the midday sun. A gentle breeze kept things cool and pleasant. The boat was anchored on the island side of the Intracoastal, just out of the channel south of Peanut Island. We had two Ugly Sticks in the water, but a bite would have been more a bother than a bonus. I sat in a swivel chair next to Sally. He was smoking a cigar the size of a rocket launcher, and it was putting off the same amount of smoke. The smell didn't bother me. I don't smoke and I never have, but Sally's cigar smoke was being picked up on the breeze and sent to Grand Bahama.

I had known Sal Mondavi a long time. Sally had watched me pitch for St. Lucie, and had passed me notes in the dugout about my form. He had become a mentor and a friend. The breeze kept blowing strands of hair across his face. I could count the hairs on his head using my fingers. But Sally grew what was there and spent his afternoon pushing them back into place. He didn't seem bothered by it.

"How's your son?" I said.

Sally took a puff. "Doing good. Still in the Windy City. Girls are in school. They got a nice house near the lake. He emailed me photos."

"You do email now?"

"He wanted to buy a computer for me." Sally cackled a laugh that sounded like a gurgling drain. "Me. I own a pawn shop, for chrissakes."

"You should've called. I could have helped set it up."

"I got a kid from the community college." He butted ash overboard. "How 'bout you? How's that lady deputy of yours?"

"Well. It's all good. She's busy, upholding the law and all that."

"Glad to hear it. You should make an honest woman of her."

"Plenty of time, Sally."

He grunted like a bull. "Don't take time for granted, boy."

"Spoken like an old man."

"Spoken by an old man." He took a long drag on the cigar. "So I know what I'm talking about."

"You always do. You wanna beer?" I dove into the cooler of ice.

"No. You get old, the high ain't as high, but the low is lower."

I opened another and took a long pull. There were tiny shards of ice in it.

"Speaking of my lovely lady, you had any trouble with her ex-husband lately? Or can't we say?"

"Turn on the engine."

"I think they call it a motor on a boat," I said, grinning as I leaned over and pushed the red start button. The motor roared to life.

"Okay, smart guy. In the duffel there. Grab that radio thing."

I opened Sally's duffel, a cheap sports bag, and found a device that looked like a high-tech walkie-talkie. I handed it to him and he switched it on. Sally played with a couple of knobs and then took the strap on the device and looped it through the frame of the Bimini top on the boat. The device hung in the air as if Sally was going to listen to the ponies from Gulfstream Park. But the device made no sound.

"Care to share?" I said, frowning.

Sally smiled his nicotine grin. "Sound jammer. Interferes with any listening device our friends from the FBI or Florida Department of Law Enforcement might care to try."

"That's very James Bond of you, Sally."

"My kid from the community college. Boy's got promise."

I smiled. "So anything from the state attorney for the Fifteenth Judicial Circuit?"

"Nothing I can't handle. I get my visits, bit of good cop, bad cop. Every now and then they'll put a car on the store, but nothing happens so they get skittish about their budgets."

"They don't get rough or anything?"

"You think I can't handle myself?"

"I think you can handle anything, Sally."

"Believe it. I like to mess with them. I got that from you— you're a bad influence. I like to see if I can make the good cop laugh and the bad cop lose his rag."

I laughed. "How do you go?"

"Like feeding a baby to get 'em grumpy. Makin' 'em laugh ain't easy though. Buggers don't got much sense of humor. I'm probably batting about .200."

"Good for you. Just let me know if they get a bit warm."

"They're okay. Thirty years ago they might have got something on me. But I'm an old man now, Miami. I don't get up to much these days. And the people I move stuff for got the connections to not get caught."

We both turned to the side of the boat where one of the fishing rods was bobbling. The tip bounced up and down like a tease, and then the rod bent right over. I stuck my foot out just in time to wedge the rod and stop it flipping over the side.

"What the hell is that?" said Sally.

"That's called fishing, Sal. When we put little morsels of food on hooks and drop them into the water, we are supposed to wait for the fish to bite."

"Just pull it in, smart guy."

I grabbed the rod and started reeling in the line. I knew there was some kind of technique, letting the fish run and then winding in a bit. I couldn't be bothered. I just wound the little handle as fast as I could. The rod bent more as I did. The fish was heavier than I thought it would be. I wished Ron were with us. He was the nautical one. I wound fast, and before I could stop, the end of the line came flying out of the water and into the bright blue sky. My catch launched up over our heads, like a slow-motion replay, spinning like a football, and then landing with a hollow thud on the deck of our boat.

"What in the name of Babe Ruth is that," said Sally, jumping back into his seat. It took me longer to figure it out than it should have.

"It's a stone crab." The brown-red beast flashed its massive claw at us and tickled the fiberglass floor with its tiny feet. The feet kept clacking like it was on speed. It thrust a nipper at Sally, and he recoiled further up his seat.

"Look at the claws on that thing," he yelled. "Well, claw. It's only got one."

"No, it's got two, but one is much bigger."

"Did it eat the hook?"

"I think it was just hanging on." I bounced the rod in the air a few times and pulled the crab upwards like a puppet. After several yanks the hook came away from the crab's claw and it fell to the deck. It didn't look happy, but I'm not sure what a happy crab would look like.

"What do we do with it."

"There used to be a guy who drank at Longboard's, Pat McGinnis. He used to catch them." The crab must have understood English because it turned at me and thrust its claw like a drunk in a knife fight.

"Pat always said their claws come off and grow back. It's a defense thing. He used to bring the claws into the bar, and throw the crabs back." We both stared at the alien-looking crustacean.

"You want to try ripping that thing off, is that what you're telling me?" Sally looked at me like I had suggested we pool our credit card limits and buy the Yankees.

"No, I am not saying that."

"Good, because I'm sorry, Miami, but you take that thing on, you are on your own." I looked at Sally. He'd seen enough scary stuff in his lifetime to keep Stephen King in material for the rest of his.

"I think we need to get it back in the water," I said.

"We?"

I shook my head at him, and then I picked up the rod again and dangled the hook about the crab's claw. It didn't seem remotely interested. I gently angled the barb down between the pincers. The crab closed its claw and I lifted up. Then it opened its claw and dropped back to the deck.

"He fell for that already," said Sally. "Ain't buying it again."

"Sounds like the Jets' pass defense."

"Hey. You'll leave the Jets out of this, if you know what's good for you."

"Any thoughts here?"

"I'm from Jersey. I don't do seafood."

"You ever hear of the Jersey shore?"

"You go to the Jersey shore for hot dogs."

"Well, thanks for your stellar advice."

"You want some advice? Man up."

I thought that was pretty rich coming from a guy who was marooned on a vinyl swivel chair, like an elephant escaping a mouse in a children's book. I'd seen guys holding lobsters when I was a kid in New England, and the key seemed to be to get at them in a way that didn't involve the nippers. The crab had gone quiet. I wasn't sure if he was suffocating or sleeping, but I took my shot. I waved one hand in front of its eyes while I came at it from behind with the other hand. The waving had no effect. Picking it up did. I grabbed it from the backside and it was like putting voltage through a cartoon character. The crab flapped every limb it had. Its little legs, its mini-claw, its eyes. The big claw waved and snapped maniacally, and with an audible crunch. I didn't wait to find out if it could reach around to scratch its back. I swiveled and launched the crab out into the water. The crustacean skipped across the surface like a bouncing stone, then dropped into the water, gone. I nodded to myself and brushed my hands together. Sally slid back into a normal seated position.

"That's how we do things where I'm from," I said.

"You're from Connecticut. The scariest thing they got in Connecticut is oysters. More people die in Connecticut of boredom than heart disease."

"Can I interest you in that beer now?"

"Most certainly."

I didn't put the line back into the water. We drank our beers, and when we were done, removed the other line, pulled up anchor and motored our way to the boat shed. On the cruise in I remembered I had a question for Sally that didn't involve seafood.

"Sally, you heard of a drug called Maxx?"

He shook his head and tapped his mouth with his forefinger.

"I don't like drugs, Miami. So many better ways to make a living."

"I'm not asking if you're moving them."

"Max, you say?"

"M-A-X-X."

He nodded. "What is it? Meth? Heroin?"

"I'm not sure. We think an amphetamine. What I know is it's a tablet and it's already killed a kid."

"Bad news. I don't like drugs, and I don't have much time for those who deal in that business." He tapped his lips again. Then he started nodding like he remembered something.

"You see Buzz Weeks about those lessons yet?"

"Not yet. Been kind of busy."

"Never too busy for cultural enrichment."

Sally had given me a saxophone from his pawn shop and directed me to a local jazz player for some tips on playing it. I hadn't gone because my solitary attempt at blowing the thing sounded like a wounded rhino.

"You go down to the Funky Biscuit, see Buzz Weeks. I'll call him, tell him you're coming. He'll sort you out with the horn, and he'll know something about your Maxx stuff."

"He uses that sort of thing?" I said, pulling the boat into the dock.

"Buzz? No. Nothing more than secondhand smoke and rye whiskey for Buzz. But he plays a lot of smoky rooms, you know. Such things pass through rooms like that."

CHAPTER NINETEEN

The Funky Biscuit was in a small Mediterranean-style mall on Mizner. From the outside it looked like a dentist's office. Inside was dark and clean. Stylish chrome chairs faced a polished stone bar, backlit by muted spotlights of pinks and oranges. The stage was lit in red. Canned jazz was playing over the speakers. Given the location I expected it to be Kenny G, but it had a whole lot more cred than that. The bar was full, the tables about half. A guy in a black T-shirt and black jeans was setting up some equipment on the stage. I asked at the host desk for Buzz Weeks. A very cute little thing with perfect teeth called someone on her desk phone.

"You are?" she asked me.

"Sal Mondavi sent me." She repeated that, nodded, and then directed me to the stage. I sat on the stage and waited. Before long a rake-thin black man appeared from backstage. He was dressed in a black T-shirt, black trousers and a herringbone sports jacket. He wore a thin string noose around his neck, with a small hook at the bottom of it. He looked timeless, with a high forehead but no hair loss. His skin said he was thirty, but he had the eyes of a sixty-year-old.

"Buzz Weeks?" I said.

He nodded and shook my hand.

"Miami Jones," I said.

"You know Sally?" he said, sitting next to me on the edge of the stage.

"I do. He suggested I come see you."

"How do you know him?"

"You could say he saved my life. You?"

"Same. What can I do for you, sir?"

"Couple things. Sally gave me a saxophone, said you'd be the guy to talk to about it."

He nodded. "What sort of saxophone?"

I raised my eyebrows.

Buzz shook his head. He pushed himself up and stepped onto the stage. The lights made him glow purple. He picked up a shiny saxophone from the stand. He brought it to me.

"Does it have a curved neck like this one, or a straight neck?"

"Straight."

"So an alto. This here's a tenor sax."

"Okay."

"The reeds I have for alto will be too stiff for you. Go to Leonard's Music. You know Leonard's?"

"I do."

"Tell 'em I sent you. Tell 'em to set you up with a starter pack for alto sax."

"Okay."

Buzz slipped the saxophone back into its stand. He sat back down on the stage with an audible harrumph.

"What's the other thing?"

"Sally thought you might be able to point me in the right direction on something." I looked around the room. People were drinking and eating, keeping to themselves. But I felt exposed on the stage.

"Perhaps somewhere more private?" I said. "Your dressing room?"

"Dressing room? This is a jazz club, not Carnegie Hall."

I shrugged.

"Come on," he said, leading me out the door near the stage. We walked through a corridor, past the kitchen and outside into a small, dark space between the buildings. Two black dudes were pressed against the wall, smoking. Buzz nodded at them, and they returned the favor. Buzz turned to me.

"So what's your problem?"

"You tell me anything about this?" I pulled out the freezer baggie with the Maxx tablet inside. Buzz took it and held it up to his eyes, and then he threw the bag at me.

"What the hell you think I am?"

"A jazz player, and a very good one, from what I understand."

"You don't understand nothing. You think it's cool to come here and accuse me of pushing this, this . . ." He finished the thought with a throw of his hands.

"No, Buzz, you've got it wrong. I'm not saying you're into this garbage. But Sally thought you work in these clubs, maybe you see things."

"I see plenty."

"I'm sure you do. And a kid died because of this stuff. I don't want a second one dead."

Buzz shuffled his feet. I noticed he was wearing wingtips. They were good quality. Leather soles, not rubber, and they tapped against the pavement.

"You ain't gonna find nothing here," he said.

"Come on, Buzz. Help me out."

"I'm serious. I don't see that stuff here. This is Boca, man. You get it? This is white man's jazz. This crowd be killing themselves with cigars and bourbon. This ain't your crowd."

"So where's my crowd."

He put his hands in his pockets like the sixty-five degree air was turning his hands blue, and he shuffled some more.

"Nothing gets back to you, Buzz. I swear."

"It always gets back, brother. Look, you get your sax stuff, and you come to a club called Ted's. It's in Lauderhill. You got a pen?"

"No," I said, pulling out my phone. "Just tell me." He gave me the address, and the directions.

"You come by Sunday night. Bring your sax, I show you some moves. And maybe there be a guy there who can help you with your questions."

CHAPTER TWENTY

I woke late on Friday. I had decided to stay on at the Funky Biscuit and see Buzz Weeks play. And play he did. He renewed my desire to learn to play the saxophone. It never ceased to amaze how the professionals could make the near impossible look like shelling peas. As I sat in the dark club, sipping a single malt, I remembered when I got picked up by the Oakland A's for twenty-nine days. They had a roster of guys who could do things with the ball that defied physics. I saw Barry Zito hit a soup can off the top of a barstool with a baseball, from forty feet. Throwing fast balls. Down the aisle of a moving bus. He hit the can twenty-seven times in a row. We got to Camden Yards to play the Orioles before he ever missed. We might have been there all night waiting. At his best Zito had that kind of ungodly control. I've set that same game up at Longboard Kelly's. Most people struggle to hit the stool, let alone the can. Let alone twenty-seven times. Now I'm not saying it's brain surgery or anything, but what it was was the perfect confluence of gift and work ethic. And so it was with Buzz Weeks. He and his band could take a piece of bent brass tube and make your soul cry, like it was the instrument rather than the man that had its heart broken.

I made a smoothie from kale, Valencia oranges, dates and pineapple for brunch, then slipped into the Mustang and cruised down the freeway. The worker bee traffic in Fort Lauderdale was done, and it was an easy drive. I felt good. Wisps of clouds painted the sky and gave the birds something to look at. I wanted to chat with Angel, ask her some questions about Maxx and the preppy guy selling it. I parked near the gym even though it was the wrong side of campus. It's the ten-minute walks I do when I park away from stuff, rather than the morning runs, that keep the muffin tops at bay. And with a girlfriend who beats me in sit-ups, keeping the muffin tops at bay is important. I knocked at Angel's door, and one of her roommates told me I'd missed her. She had just left with the soccer team. Tampa. Due back Sunday night. I thanked the roommate and got a perfunctory whatever for my trouble.

I was heading back toward the quad when I heard the low rumble. The Crown Vic and the Dodge Charger both have it, but the Charger is more throaty, like Pavarotti with a cold. I was in such a good mood I considered sprinting across the quad to see if they would get out and run, but thought the better of yanking the chains of guys with guns. I stopped walking. The police cruiser pulled up beside me. The window came down. The cop inside looked like he'd been sprayed into the car through the window and then expanded on impact. Like that foam they used in insulation, or dairy whip. He was altogether too big for his seat, for the car and for his uniform. I should have run for it. There was no way this guy was getting out the same day. Stepping out of his vehicle looked like a weekend project.

"You Jones?" he said. He spoke through his nose, like a Texan without the accent. I nodded.

"Steele wants a word."

"I'll be sure to drop by the station house sometime."

"He's on campus. In the security office." The cop may have jinked his head to the back seat, or it may have wobbled under the weight of keeping it upright. "Get in."

"I'm good. I'll walk."

"I wasn't asking."

"Good. 'Cause I wasn't listening."

A pudgy hand appeared from the darkness of the cabin and grabbed the radio handset.

"He won't get in the car."

A voice came crackling back. "Make him."

"He says he's gonna walk." Words of more than two syllables left him breathless.

"He doesn't know where we are."

The cop swiveled his head like Jabba the Hutt. "You don't know where it is," he said to me.

"I might not be related to Columbus, but I can read a map." I turned and walked away. It was true—I didn't know where the security office was. So I could have been headed for the New World. I strolled over to the quad where some bright city planning major had placed a campus map. The spot on the map where I was had been rubbed away by a thousand pointed fingers. I never understood the need to touch the position on a map, like you weren't really there until you pressed yourself into being on the chart. An enterprising soul had scribbled in a sharpie pen, *vous etes ici*, on the rubbed away circle. I found the campus security office in a cluster of green buildings marked *Life Sciences*. I wasn't sure if there was meaning in that, but it was the sort of thing a philosophy major could spend weeks thinking about. I continued my stroll and found the campus security building without incident. It had a big blue light out front. It was more of the same white concrete with brick veneer at the base. The fat cop sat in his car out front. He watched me approach. I wondered how he passed any kind of fitness test at the Academy. When I got level with the car he wound the window down again.

"He's waiting." It was incredibly useful information, and I wanted to thank him for it.

"Don't pull the string to inflate your life vest until you leave the plane." He frowned and I walked inside. The campus security office looked like the cashier's window at the DMV. If the signage was anything to go by, its main function was to issue parking permits and collect payments for parking fines. Four kids were in line for one or the other. It seemed fleecing students was a growth business. There was a solitary door to the interior so I went through it. The guy issuing the fines gave me a sideways glance, but I didn't stop to measure his level of displeasure. Steele was sitting at a desk in the rear of the office. He was in uniform, but not a cop's uniform. That was blue—this was khaki.

"What's up?" I said as I reached his desk.

"Have a seat," he said.

"I'm good." I stayed standing. Steele wasn't that tall, but he sat as erect as he stood. He looked up at me from his boxy head. He might have had a haircut. It was hard to say. It was like trying to guess whether they'd cut the greens on a golf course.

"You been busy," he said.

"I don't get paid if I sit around on my backside."

He stared at some papers on his desk like he was reading the evening news.

"Chatting with coaching staff, chatting with students, visiting the hospital, attending memorial services, going to parties." He looked up at me. "You been meeting lots of folks."

"It's part of the college experience, don't you think?"

"Didn't you already have your college experience?"

"I've got my second wind."

"But what you haven't done is chat with me. I thought we had a deal. You get to stay on my campus, you share what you learn."

"I haven't learned much."

"Then tell me what you think."

"I think your officer outside needs to cut out the donuts."

"Tell me something I don't know."

"I can hit a pitching wedge about a hundred ten yards."

He frowned. "Meaning?"

"Meaning I could pitch a golf ball from this office to where Jake Turner overdosed."

"So?"

"So that's right in your backyard. Hell, it's practically your living room."

"So?"

"So, embarrassing for you, I think."

"I don't care. You think I care?"

"No, I don't think you do. If you did care, you'd actually be doing something to solve this crime."

"I'm doing plenty, pal."

"You're sitting in this office in your natty little rent-a-cop uniform, doing nothing but sending the doughboy out on rounds."

"You think you know what's going on here?"

"Let me see. You don't know anything. You're not doing anything to learn anything. You give the only guy actually investigating this thing, namely yours truly, some hogwash about not being able to get inside, so you can share my information. Seriously? This is how you guys investigate? Can I assume you've given up on any drug-related crime in the city, or is it just here on campus? Oh, that's right, President Millet doesn't hold any sway off campus. I thought you were just inept when you said you couldn't get tapped into the party scene. Until I went to a party, and it took me half an hour to find the same drugs that killed Jake, even though I was the oldest person at the party by an uncomfortably large margin. So I'm thinking, why can I do this if you can't?"

"I don't know where you're going with this."

"You know where I'm going—you just don't like it. You're throwing the game, you're sandbagging. You want to know what I know, not so you can use it to investigate, but so you can cover it up."

His face was a blank. He looked like a furry cardboard box. He didn't take his eyes off me. He reached out and picked up his phone. Hit a button and put the handset to his ear. Eyes still on me.

"It's Steele. Get him." He waited, then: "He's here. He's got nothing to say." He listened for a moment, and then put the phone down without another word. He stood, checking his belt, shifting the weight of his weapon so it sat right. Then he picked up his keys, and they clinked in his hand.

"Let's go see the president."

CHAPTER TWENTY–ONE

Steele headed for an electric vehicle that looked like a golf buggy on steroids. I walked past and headed for the quad.

"Get in," he said.

"You could do with the walk." He was a big guy, but not fat. But I didn't care.

"You want me to arrest you?"

I smiled over my shoulder. "Yeah, that's the thing you want to do right now."

I kept walking toward the quad. I heard the footsteps behind, and then Steele dropped in beside me. He marched. Literally. Hands beside, eyes front. There was cadence to it. I found myself dropping into step with him, the way you walk to a beat when you listen to music. I tried to keep out of step just to make a point, but couldn't. It was hypnotic. I guess that was the point. Armies marching hundreds of miles did best when the troops weren't thinking about how far they were walking. We strode across the quad, under the palms as they cast dollops of shade on the grass. Up the steps and in through the glass front of the administration building. Steele hit the button for the elevator and then stood back, ramrod straight. We came out the elevator into the wood paneling and glass dome. The receptionist gestured that we go in.

President Millet was sitting behind his desk, attempting to look busy. Like he hadn't been waiting since Steele's call. I bet he'd been pacing. He was that sort of guy. He looked up as if we'd interrupted his train of thought.

"Ah, Steele," he said. "And Mr. Jones. Take a seat."

I sat. Steele didn't. Millet steepled his fingers and put them to his lips. Then he gave me a knowing smile.

"You misled me, Mr. Jones," he said, like I was a three-year-old with my hand in the cookie jar. I didn't speak.

"You told me you worked for the Turner family."

"I did no such thing."

He dropped the steeple but not the smile. "You allowed me to believe that you worked for the family."

"What you believe is none of my concern." I could feel the university-speak creeping back into my vocabulary. I needed to spend some time at Longboard's.

"Well, now we know you do not represent the family. So the question is, whom do you represent?"

I didn't speak.

"Mr. Jones?"

"Yes?"

"Whom do you represent?"

"Who I work for is none of your business, Mr. Millet."

"It's Dr. Millet."

"You perform any surgery today, Dr. Millet?"

The grin faded and then reappeared. He was like a used car salesman. Or a politician. Yes, a politician. The thought of which sent me off in a whole other direction.

"You well know, Mr. Jones, that I am not a medical doctor. But I can assure you, I worked just as hard to achieve my PhD."

"Coal miners work hard. PhDs get cardigans to ward off the chill in the library."

"I see," he said, steepling his fingers again. It was like watching a puppy who had learned a new trick. "Well, given your reticence to divulge your purpose on this campus or to assist Officer Steele in his inquiries, I am afraid I can no longer tolerate your unauthorized presence on campus. I have students' welfare to think about. So I must ask Officer Steele to escort you from the grounds, and that you not return, lest you be charged with trespass."

I held his eyes. They didn't waver. Millet was a cool piece of work.

"I understand why you'd want to cover up Jake Turner's death. Even if that is a stupid and pointless thing to do. But what I don't get is why you want so badly to kill off athletics."

He smiled. "I don't want to kill athletics, Mr. Jones."

"All evidence to the contrary. There isn't a single person I've spoken to who doesn't see you culling the athletics program. Even the crucial ones."

He scrunched his brow. "Which ones would be the crucial ones, Mr. Jones?"

"You don't think any of them are?"

"Quality research institutions are not built on sports." He said sports like he'd eaten a moldy olive.

"You're hardly MIT."

He stiffened, like a small jolt had shocked his body. "We punch above our weight. And I intend to see us do more. This part of the world is screaming out for a world-class research institution. I intend to make us that institution. The Caltech of the Southeast."

"And sports has no part in that?"

"No."

"Caltech has an athletics program. So does MIT and Harvard. Doesn't seem to do them any harm."

"But does it do them any good?" he said, standing. I didn't move.

"Officer Steele will see you out."

I stood. The whole office was starting to feel like the Seafood Bar at The Breakers. Something very fishy was going on. I walked to the door with Steele.

"One question, Mr. Jones," said Millet. "Why the interest in sports? Whom do you represent that is so interested in the athletics program?"

I turned to him. He was standing behind his desk like it was a fortress.

"My client is interested in the death of Jake Turner. A star student-athlete. And you've got me wondering if him being an athlete isn't the salient point."

"I hardly think so. Good day, Mr. Jones." He dismissed us with a wave of his hand. Being dismissed like I was the hired help always endeared me to a person. Steele walked me back to my car. As I unlocked the Mustang he spoke.

"You think there is a link to Jake Turner being an athlete?"

"You actually think I'm gonna share anything with you?"

He didn't move. He was like a flagpole. Then his face broke, in the tiniest way. The way a face looks different in the sunshine than when a cloud drifts across the sky. Less color to it. Softer around the edges. It was so fleeting that I had to consider that I hadn't seen it at all.

"If you come back on campus, I will have no option but to arrest you."

I got in my car and started it up. Steele turned his eyes down but stayed at attention.

"The kid died on my watch. Despite what you might think, I do take that seriously."

I punched the transmission into drive. "Not seriously enough," I said, hitting the gas and heading off campus.

I was sure I'd be back.

CHAPTER TWENTY—TWO

The Palm Beach County judicial facility takes up three city blocks north of the main drag in West Palm. It dwarfs anything else in that part of town. It is the kind of massive edifice that, were it a library, would convince a visitor of the sophistication and intellect of the townsfolk who lived there. But it wasn't a library—it was a courthouse. I parked in the lot next to my office and walked up Banyan in the late afternoon sun. My stomach tightened and reminded me that I hadn't eaten since my smoothie for brunch. Or maybe it was the person I was about to see. But I wasn't buying that. The state attorney's office was in the building between Third and Fourth Streets. I made my way through security and was issued my visitor tag. I got to the office for State Attorney Eric Edwards. His secretary must have gotten a call from downstairs because she was waiting for me. She said he was on the phone but wouldn't be long and offered me something to drink. I figured she didn't mean an ice-cold beer, so I declined. She smiled and went back to her work. Either she was very professional, or she liked me. There needs to be a high level of friendliness and professionalism in the support staff of people who get elected to their jobs, so maybe that was it. But I thought I saw that little extra glint in her eye that suggested she liked me, or she didn't like her boss. Either way, I was only seated about a minute before she told me I could go in.

The state attorney for the Fifteenth Judicial Circuit had a cracking view of the parking lot. His office was government model, sufficiently up the totem to demand decent furnishings. A small conference table, a large desk, plenty of bookshelves. Flags behind the desk for the United States and the state of Florida. The shelves and walls dotted with pictures of Eric Edwards with the famous and infamous. The governor, at least one Supreme Court justice, a bunch of men in suits and women in evening gowns, whom I recognized from the society pages of the *Palm Beach Post*. Donors, I guessed.

Eric came out from behind his desk. The desk was covered in papers, but the papers were all in orderly stacks. Eric looked as trim and vibrant as ever. The state attorneys are hardly on the breadline but they don't make anything like their colleagues in private practice. Even so, Eric Edwards always dressed immaculately. He wore a charcoal pinstripe suit, which only served to make him look taller and thinner. And he was marathon runner-thin. He had cheekbones a supermodel would kill for, with dark features and a permanent three o'clock shadow. As he put out his hand I caught a whiff of something fruity, possibly Calvin Klein.

"Miami, good to see you. Come in, take a seat." He gave my hand a good pump and grinned his perfect orthodontic work. It was disconcerting to say the least. I rifled through my brain files for motive. Perhaps he was hard up for votes and decided he needed every last one in the next election, even mine. I dismissed it as unlikely. He looked handsome and well spoken on camera, and was in with the rich red-voting set in Palm Beach who bankrolled his campaign. He might have decided to take a new tack in dealing with people like me, who are essentially on the same side, purveyors of justice, if you will. I suspected Eric still had FDLE guys tailing Sally, so I wasn't ready to accept that Eric had overlooked my relationship to Sal. I wondered if he had finally forgiven me for sleeping with his ex-wife, but put in his shoes I wouldn't have, so I dismissed that out of hand. The final idea I came up with was that Eric was up to something. I chose to keep that thought close at hand.

"I'm good, Eric. You?"

"Fighting the good fight," he said. It was like a tagline from an SNL character. "What can I do you for?" he said as he sat back behind his desk. He smoothed his pink tie with his hand.

"I'm working on something down in Lauderdale. You heard of a guy called Dr. Stephen Millet?"

"Rings a bell. Enlighten me."

I told him about Jake Turner and President Millet. I didn't mention the sandbagging job by Steele or who hired me.

"So your summation is that something's fishy. Is that right?"

"Pretty much."

"And what would you have me spend the taxpayers' money on, based on this fishy sensation?"

"There's more to it. Millet seems to have grand ideas about becoming the next Caltech, or something. He's not even close right now, so it begs the question, how? Something that big, must have some state involvement, someone backing the project."

"Nothing illegal about Millet backing an education development. Some might even argue it's necessary."

"When was the last time a big state project happened with zero media fanfare?"

Eric rubbed his stubble. "Could be nothing. Could be early stages."

"I'm not saying launch a full-scale investigation, Eric. I know that you know how to ask these questions quietly. That's all I'm saying. Ask around."

"I don't know, Jones. Could upset a lot of people based on very little."

"What could the uncovering of fraud worth tens, maybe hundreds of millions of taxpayer dollars do for your reelection campaign?"

He sat back and smoothed his tie again. It saved on ironing. He was a crafty operator, I knew that. He'd be weighing the pros and cons, assessing the angles. He smiled at me again. This nice guy Eric was giving me the willies.

"Okay, Jones. I'll help you out. I'll ask around, see if there's anything in it." He stood. The meeting was over. Which was fine with me. I wanted something to eat, and an early dinner with Eric Edwards was not on my menu. We walked to the door.

"You hear anything that could help my inquiries, you call, okay?" he said.

"Will do."

He slapped my back. "I'll be in touch. You take care."

I left Eric's office feeling like he'd done everything short of pinning a campaign button on me. Asking him for help left me uneasy. Him giving it with a smile left me feeling like I'd completely skipped a chapter. I was trying to figure out what I'd missed when my phone rang. One look at the screen and the tumblers all clicked into place.

"Hello, sweetheart," I said.

"Sweetheart? Wow, you must be in a good mood," said Danielle.

"All the better for hearing your voice, believe me."

"I'm coming off shift. Plans for dinner or you have a frat party to get to?"

"I was just heading to Longboard's."

"See you in thirty?"

"Sold," I said. I smiled as I put the phone in my pocket. Eric Edwards was playing all nice with me, while having lunch with my girlfriend, his ex-wife. The fact that I had come to Eric had thrown him. He figured I didn't know, that Danielle had kept their lunch date to herself. So he was playing nice as a diversion. That was fine with me. I could use the help. But it left one nagging question. What the hell did Eric Edwards think he was up to?

CHAPTER TWENTY—THREE

I stopped by the office to kick Lizzy out. The sun was heading for the horizon and the town had a Friday evening buzz going. Lizzy was at her desk, punching keys.

"Evening, Miss Lizzy."

She looked up at me. During my whitebread Connecticut upbringing I would have called her gothic. With a few miles on my clock I'd say just a little overdone. Her thick red lipstick was accentuated by her jet-black hair.

"Good day?" she said.

"Eventful and ponderous," I said. "Quittin' time, I's thinks."

"Soon." She handed me some messages. "The guy from Third Fire and Casualty called. He's got another job."

"I'll mention it to Ron."

"And that nasty piece of work from the restaurant, Pepper, is it? He called."

"Message?"

"I told him if he wanted to leave a message with me he should reassess his attitude and call back when he felt he could act in a civil manner."

I smiled. "Fine. Now out with you."

"Just a few things to clean up."

"Nothing that won't wait until Monday."

She shrugged her shoulders and packed her things away. I locked the office and walked Lizzy to her car.

"Ron's at Longboard Kelly's," she said as she fumbled for her keys.

"Of course."

She opened the door of her Ford Focus. "Don't drink too much."

I shook my head. "I'm having dinner with Danielle."

"I'm praying for you two."

"Any feedback from the big guy?"

She slipped into the car. "I keep telling you, He works in mysterious ways, even for you." She started the car. "But I'm sure He wouldn't mind you taking care of business yourself."

"I'll take it under advisement."

I stood and watched her pull around the lot and out onto the street, then I got in my Mustang and put it on autopilot. When I got there Longboard Kelly's was humming. Ron was on his stool at the outdoor bar, holding court with two ladies of a certain age who looked like they just bounced off the tennis court. They were hanging off his every word. Which in itself wasn't surprising. Ron could tell a tale in a way that Samuel Clemens would have been jealous of. Ron finished his story to glorious laughter as I reached the bar. He looked at me with ruddy cheeks and a smile.

"My lord and master." He turned to the bar, and Muriel passed him a beer, which he grabbed by the neck and handed to me.

"May I introduce Miss Hannah and Miss Margaret." Each of the women was closing in on sixty but looked ten years younger. They had thin legs and the healthy glow of those with sufficient leisure time and disposable income. They enjoyed being referred to as Miss.

"I hope we're not in your spot," said one of them—Hannah I thought.

"You are, but my spot has never looked so good." I got a girlish smile and wondered if I was spending too much time around Ron.

"We were thinking about the yacht club for a spot of dinner," said Ron. "Care to join?"

"I have a previous engagement, but thanks."

"Ron, we're just going to freshen up," said the other lady, Margaret.

The women slipped off their stools and headed into the barroom.

"How was your day?" said Ron.

"Eventful and ponderous."

"Ponderous?"

"I met with Eric Edwards. He's helping me out."

"He's helping you? What's he want?"

"Didn't ask for anything."

"He's up to something. What's he helping with?"

"Doing some digging around about our friend Stephen Millet. Which is the eventful part of the day. President Millet kicked me off campus."

"Do tell."

I gave Ron a rundown on my adventures with Steele and Millet, and Millet's notion of developing the Caltech of the Southeast.

"Well that sort of makes sense," he said, sipping his beer.

"How so? What did you find?"

"Our Doctor Millet grew up in Michigan but was obviously not a fan of those Ann Arbor winters. I mean, who could blame him? He left to go to college at Berkeley. Stayed in the Bay Area after he finished at Cal, and he did his master's and PhD at Stanford."

"Nice," I said, waving to Muriel for another beer.

"There's more. While doing his doctorate in electrical engineering, he had a rival."

"Ooh, the plot thickens." I sipped my beer. It was a poor substitute for real food, and my stomach grumbled at it.

"Indeed. Seems candidate Millet was a constant second fiddle to one of his contemporaries, a fellow by the name of Remus Leavensong."

"Remus. Nice."

"Yes, old Remus got the grades, the fellowships, the research dollars. And from my calls to California, the girl."

"And the plot solidifies. So what happened?"

"After getting his PhD, Millet left the shadow of Leavensong and headed east, to Princeton, where it seems he did good, but not extraordinary research."

"And Leavensong?"

"Stayed at Stanford. Won the Draper prize, which I'm told is like the Nobel prize for engineering."

"Ouch."

"Yep." He finished his beer and put it on the bar. "He was then headhunted by MIT, and currently serves as provost."

"Which is what exactly?"

"They tell me provost is head of academic affairs, whereas president is head of the university. Either way, the folks at MIT suggested that Leavensong would be the next president."

"So Millet's nemesis wins the Nobel prize—"

"Draper prize."

"Whatever—then he becomes heir apparent as president of MIT."

"Right. And at the same time, Millet apparently applies to come back to Stanford as dean of the school of engineering."

"But?"

"They chose someone else. I spoke to a woman in administration who said it wasn't so much that he is a bad guy, but he is, and I quote, *a bit of an ass*."

I smiled and concurred. "So what happened?"

"It seems he got the chance to jump a rung or two, and become a president of a small private university in Florida, rather than be humiliated by the Ivy League."

"Stanford and MIT aren't Ivy League."

"How would you know?"

"Stanford are Pac 12. MIT are Division III I think."

"So whatever sports conference, they're good schools."

"That they are."

Ron's eyes bounced over my shoulder, and I turned to see his lady friends coming out of the bar.

"My ride," he said, eyebrows raised. He patted my shoulder and walked away. I took a stool and sipped my beer. Then I felt a hand on my shoulder again. Danielle stood behind me in a white T-shirt and Levi's.

"Hi, mister." She didn't wait for an answer, she just kissed me. She was cool and moist, like the first day of spring training. She pulled away with a killer smile.

"Right back at ya," I said. I was ready to forget food and cut straight to the chase. But I figured I should offer her a beverage after her long shift.

"Drink?" I said, turning to the bar.

"Actually, I'm starving. What are your thoughts on dinner?"

"Thoughts? Couple pounds of peel and eats, and a bucket of beers."

She smiled. "Can we get a salad with that?"

I finished my beer and waved bye to Muriel. As we wandered out the back courtyard to the parking lot Danielle took my hand, weaving her fingers between mine. She was warm and comfortable.

"You'll never guess what I heard today," she said.

"Go on."

"I heard on the vine that Eric's bit of fluff has gone home."

"The paralegal? The one he slept with?"

"Uh-huh."

"I thought they were a bit of an item."

"No more. Word is she's gone back to the Northeast."

We got to the car, and I faced her and took her other hand.

"How do you feel about that?"

"I think she dodged a bullet, so to speak."

"And he took you to lunch."

She looked me right in the eyes. Hers were full and brown and like laser beams.

"That makes me realize how lucky I am." She leaned in and kissed me again. It was long and soft and deep. When she came back up she wore a puzzled grin.

"It also makes me wonder what the heck he's up to."

I nodded to myself. There seemed to be a bit of that train of thought going around.

CHAPTER TWENTY-FOUR

We slept late and woke easy. I made omelets with mushrooms, peppers and tomatoes, topped with a sprinkling of Parmesan cheese. Danielle squeezed juice from a bag of Florida oranges. We ate on the patio as the pelicans and cranes played on the Intracoastal. My house was a relic of Florida past, a low ranch that I picked up at a tax lien auction at the bottom of the market. Palm Beach Isles had plenty of similar homes along the channels of the estate, but all the properties on the Intracoastal had been razed and replaced with mini mansions. My next-door neighbor lived in a giant Greek wedding cake. I suspected he didn't think much of my place. But it suited me just fine. We read the papers—nothing about goings-on at the university, but then few folks on the Palm Beaches cared much for news from Lauderdale. Danielle took a shower and got dressed in her uniform.

I smiled. "You do all kinds of things for khaki."

"This is green, sweetheart."

"Khaki's a kind of green."

"No, khaki is khaki. This is darker. Green." She kissed me and picked up her bag. "So tomorrow night. Jazz, you say?"

"Yeah, gotta see a guy about a dog. Thought we might catch the show after."

"Count me in." She dashed out the door to save the world. I, on the other hand, wandered down to a sports bar near City

Beach Park, settled in with a Dos Equis and corn chips, and
watched the Hurricanes take on Duke in Durham. By the time
the game was over the sun was dropping behind Riviera Beach,
and I was bloated from beers and chips. I had just walked back
over the bridge onto my part of Singer Island when my phone
rang.

"Miami? It's Kim Rose."

"Kim. What can I do for you?"

"I was hoping we could talk."

"Okay. I have a couple of minutes." I walked toward the orb
of flame on the horizon.

"I mean in person."

"Sure, I guess. Not sure I'm mister popular on campus right
now, though. Let me call you tomorrow."

"What about now?"

I put my hand on my stomach and felt the hops and corn
sloshing about. "Sorry Kim, I'm not going anywhere tonight."

"I could come to you. You're in West Palm, right?"

"I live in Riviera Beach."

"Oh. Well, I could come there."

I didn't want the company and I didn't care for the chat, but
I just didn't have the bother to argue.

"Okay, Kim." I gave her the address and directions, and she
said she'd be there in an hour or so. I got home, kicked off my
deck shoes and headed for the shower. I let cold water run to
sober up a little. Then I wrapped myself in a towel and poured
some leftover orange juice. By the time there was a knock on the
fly screen door I was dressed in a Tommy Bahamas shirt and
khaki shorts, *sans* shoes.

"Come in," I yelled.

Kim strode in. She was dressed in a tight yellow T-shirt
made of that material that wicks away sweat, and tight black

yoga pants. She looked healthy and vibrant and alive. She always had. Kim came bearing wine. I needed another bottle in front of me like a frontal lobotomy, but I didn't want to get the conversation off the wrong way. I wanted to hear what she had to say. My mouth was drying out, so I figured I could do with the drink. It was a screw top, a genius of an idea. Sauvignon Blanc from Marlborough, New Zealand. Pretty much the only white wine I drank. I poured two glasses.

"Nice place," she said.

"Thanks. I like it."

"Is that a shag rug?"

"Seventies original. Hurricane orange." We sat on the sofa.

"So, you had something to say?"

She smiled and raised her eyebrows. "You cut to the chase."

"So did you, as I recall."

"I guess. All that social stuff was never my strong suit."

"Must be a big part of your job now, though."

"It is." She sipped her wine. "I gotta psych myself for it. Boosters, donors, the board. Not the side of my job I love."

"What is the part you love?"

She looked out toward the night lights dotting the shoreline across the water.

"I guess the sports. Being out there. Part of it. Listening to the whistles and boots on ball and the effort."

"So why not coach?"

"You know how much a coach earns?"

I shook my head.

"Every job has its pros and cons. Even playing soccer did."

"But you loved to play."

"Mostly. I loved winning."

"And you're not winning now?"

She finished her wine and shook her head. I filled her glass.

"You wouldn't believe the pressure," she said, sipping. "You know how many female athletic directors there are in NCAA schools?"

I shook my head.

"Not many. It's an old boys' club. And the pressure to succeed, to win, for the guys is intense. For the women it's unbearable."

"You won a World Cup, Olympic gold. I don't think you're any stranger to pressure."

"That was different. I was harder on myself then than anyone else could be. And any external pressure was shared across the team. Now I don't have a team."

"What about the coaches?"

She smiled. It wasn't a happy one. "Half the coaches want my job, the other half just don't think I can do it because I'm a woman. I don't get any support from the other administrators because they see what President Millet is up to, and they're choosing sides."

"What about students? They seem to think highly of you."

"There are some good kids there, Miami. Some real winners. But they don't factor into this. They can't help me." She sipped more wine. "Besides, I don't get to spend as much time on the fields as I'd like to."

"Well, I know a lot of them look to you as inspiration."

"I should do. I'm an example of what they can achieve with a lot of hard work and determination. But I'm also a warning. Especially for the girls. That there really isn't much career path in women's sports. The pay is poor, but the work is hard. One or two of the prettier girls get endorsement deals, but most barely make a living. It's the same for the boys in a lot of our sports—field hockey, lacrosse. Even our basketball team. If they were pro material they'd be playing in Division I. There's not much future there."

"So why do it? Why fight for it? Maybe Millet is right to shut it down."

"He's not right. He's a moron. We do it because there's more to it. Because for these kids, going pro isn't an option, or at least not a profitable one. So for most, this is the pinnacle of their sports career. This is it. The time they'll look back on. Glory days. And they will look back as winners, or as losers. That's the harsh reality of our world, Miami. There are winners and losers. Not my decision, but that's how it is. And now schools teaching this garbage where nobody wins and nobody loses? Just setting kids up for a fall. This is their last chance before the big world swallows them. To choose to be winners, or losers."

"Not every team wins gold," I said. "Doesn't mean all the others are losers."

She sipped her drink and put it down, and then took a deep breath.

"You misunderstand. For these kids, it's not about medals, trophies. Sure, shooting for those things is crucial, but in any given sport they are not the pick of the crop. Not the pro material, or the Olympians. You don't play lower division sports if you are good enough to go pro. So for these kids, winning or losing, it isn't so much in the trophies, as in the mindset. If they leave here believing they are winners, understanding the hard work, the sacrifice that is required to win, then they win. They can take that mindset and apply it to anything. Talent for sport, any sport, is fleeting. But that mindset is for life."

I nodded. I had to admit there was something in what she said. I played college football knowing I would never be good enough to make the draft. But I learned to face down hard work like I was in jail and it held the key. I was drafted by the A's and played six years of minor-league baseball, and I didn't throw a pitch in the majors. But I developed a work ethic that still served me well. I learned how to stay on the field, stay healthy. To analyze people, to solve problems. I never threw a pitch in The Show. Winner? Loser? I was comfortable with where I was.

"So you think if Millet kills sports, those kids will lose the chance to develop those skills."

"Not just those kids. All kids. These are not big dumb jocks who can't do anything but block or tackle. Stats show that successful athletes at lower divisions are also better students. They know how to win. It's transferable."

"You're turning them into A-type personalities."

"People always say that with a snigger. *Oh yeah, she's an A-type.* But they snigger because they're not, and it's the A-types who work harder, it's the A-types who win."

"You're saying win at all costs?"

"Yes. No. Not all costs. Every game has rules. Even life. But those who work hardest, those who ask more of themselves are the winners. In sports. In life."

"What if they push too far, cross boundaries?"

"You mean performance-enhancing drugs?" In my home, with half a bottle of Sav Blanc under her belt, she didn't whisper it. I nodded.

"I was wrong before. I shouldn't have said there was no PED use on the campus. You're right, I can't know that. There might be some bad apples. But I'm confident there is no systematic program of drug use. You can understand why you might hear otherwise. Coaches, staff, they're just saying what they think Millet wants to hear."

I wasn't convinced on that front yet, but decided to let it slide until I knew more.

"Why would Millet want to hear that? Drug use on campus is not a great selling point for him. He's actively trying to cover up Jake Turner's death."

"Jake's death wasn't sports-related. Yes he was an athlete, but he got into something else. The drug that killed him wasn't a PED, right?"

"No, it wasn't."

"So that does look bad for Millet's recruitment pitch. But framing a systematic performance-enhancing drug program? That's just ammunition to kill off the athletics program."

"But why? In this whole thing, I don't get why."

"He wants to focus on academics."

"I know that," I said. "He wants to be the Caltech of the Southeast. His words. But here's the thing. Even Caltech has an athletics program. They're called the Beavers. NCAA Division III. So there's no athletic scholarships. The athletes have to gain admission to the school first, and then they can play sports. Lots of schools are like that. Hell, all the Ivy League is like that. So what I don't get is why Millet doesn't do that. Drop down to Division III, no scholarships for athletics. No need to get rid of athletics."

"They're a financial drain he doesn't want."

"Everything in a not-for-profit college is a financial drain. The courses don't make money, the lectures don't make money. Sports either. It's about providing a well-rounded package, so you get the best students. The best students produce the best research, which leads to research dollars. Athletics isn't core, but it is part of the puzzle. And if you're not offering scholarships, or big-budget sports, how much money do you really save by killing off athletics altogether?"

"Maybe he hates sports."

"I think we can take that as read. The man's about as athletic as Pee Wee Herman," I said. "But have you ever seen a sporty-looking college president? Me either. Yet they're not all trying to kill athletics. Just Millet, and I don't get why."

Kim smiled. "But you're going to find out, aren't you?"

"I am."

"Thank you."

"Don't thank me yet. You don't know what I'll find."

"Doesn't matter. You've just proven my point, is all. You're one of the winners. You don't give up. That's why I came to you. And I'm glad I did." She finished her wine and smiled. Then she slapped her hands on her tight thighs.

"Well, if I have another glass of wine I won't be able to drive." She stood and I walked her out. The old wooden door was open, letting the breeze blow through the house. She put her hands on my shoulders, and I thought she was going to kiss me. But she didn't. She gave me a hug that felt like something you might get from a business associate. I felt her balled fist pump my back.

"Thanks for everything. Really." She flashed a smile and then strode to her car. I closed the door as she pulled away, then I took what was left of the wine out to the patio and watched the lights play on the water until I fell asleep.

CHAPTER TWENTY—FIVE

Ted's Jazz and Social Club was behind a strip mall off West Sunrise Boulevard in Lauderhill. The area was like landing in Jamaica. The green, yellow and black of the Jamaican flag hung from every surface. A street sign pointed to a cricket ground. I could smell jerk chicken on the air as I parked in front of a nameless convenience store. A dark alley split the convenience store from a nail salon and the rest of the stores in the strip mall. As directed by Buzz, we walked down the alley until we reached the building with the sofa sitting outside it. Two old guys with matching white hair and brown faces sat in the sofa. They both broke out into huge toothy grins. They weren't smiling at me. Danielle stood beside me making a million dollars look like a buck and a half. She wore a tight black dress that ended mid-thigh and showed every curve mother nature gave her. While the old guys smiled their approval, I checked a piece of rusted iron that hung on the stucco wall. It read *Ted's Jazz and Social Club*, as Buzz Weeks had said it would. I looked at one of the old guys.

"Buzz Weeks?" I said.

He smiled. "Inside, son. Inside."

We stepped into the dark room. A big guy who I recognized as a former linebacker for University of Miami sat just inside the door, next to a cash tray. He looked me up and down. I wore a blue shirt with surfboards and station wagons on it, and chinos.

Danielle felt a fedora was going to be a touch too much. The big guy looked at the saxophone case in my hand.

"Buzz be in the back," he said.

The interior was dimly lit and simple. A dark painted stage that swallowed light like a black hole. Plain, round pine tables that sat up to four. Further from the stage a couple rows of plastic folding chairs. Behind that a small crowd of people laughed and yammered over the recorded music. They flocked around a small bar. No neon, no lava lamps. Beers and rum and lemonade. The whole space was the size of a large living room, but the thirty or so people seemed intimate rather than squeezed. We were the only white people in the room. Hell, we were probably the only white people in the suburb. A woman in a blue dress with large white polka-dots and an immaculate hairdo like something out of a 1920s speakeasy saw us and swept over. I noted that everyone was just as well dressed, as if they had all left their church clothes on. The woman spoke to Danielle.

"Darlin', you are looking fine."

"Thank you," said Danielle.

"Come, Martell is mixing the most amazing fruit daiquiris. You must try one."

Danielle smiled. "Count me in." The two women locked arms and walked away, leaving me standing there like a dandelion in the wind. The woman looked back over her shoulder.

"Buzz is in the back, honey." I watched them saunter to the bar, where they were consumed by the gathering. I took the hint and walked away. Two young guys, in shirts and neckties, smiled and nodded. I reciprocated and headed for the stage.

A door to the right of the stage was the only way to go. I walked down a short hallway to another door. Behind the second door was a dressing room. It was my ideal of a jazz club green room. There were ten men in the room, sitting on a mishmash of sofas, lawn chairs and bar stools. Musical instruments were positioned around the room. Saxes, trumpets, trombones, guitars, drums. A double bass leaned against a refrigerator. A fog of cigarette smoke clung to the ceiling and the smell of reefer hung in the air like perfume. Every eye in the room turned to the white guy. The faces were neither welcoming nor hostile, as if an alien had just landed and they were waiting to see if they were dealing with *ET* or *Mars Attacks*. A guy in a black shirt and white tie spoke from deep in a sofa.

"What the hell you wearing?"

"This is classic sixties social surf wear."

"You got some balls, brother."

I smiled. "Good taste is eternal. Me, I wear a black shirt and white tie if I want to go to Halloween dressed as a freeway."

Buzz Weeks popped up from the refrigerator.

"He's cool," said Buzz.

"If you say so," said the guy in the sofa, laughing and slapping high fives to the guys around him.

"Miami Jones, meet the band. Band, meet Miami Jones." I nodded to the gaggle of hey's and hi's. Buzz waved me over and sat me on a stool next to his chair.

"Let's see it," he said. I put the case on the arm of the sofa and clicked it open. I was aware that every eye was on me.

"You don't got a machine gun in there, do you, man?" More laughs.

I took out a sling from a small compartment and put it around my neck. I was thankful I had watched a video online about how to put the saxophone together. I took the main section out and clipped it to the sling.

"Now don't hurt yourself there, son."

"Hurt hisself? Forget him. Don't you hurt that fine-looking horn." More laughs. I put the neck into the main section, and then tightened the wing nut that held it together. Then I took out the mouthpiece. The sax was gleaming bronze, the mouthpiece black Bakelite.

"You go to Leonard's?" said Buzz.

"Yep." I pulled a plastic box from the compartment and handed it to Buzz. He flipped open a section of the plastic lid like a tackle box. From it he took a small piece of wood. It looked like shaved bamboo. He turned it over and nodded.

"Number two, okay." He looked at me. Everyone else looked at me.

"This is the reed. You put this on the mouthpiece and when you blow, it vibrates and makes the sound that travels through the horn."

"Okay, sounds simple enough."

"It ain't. You see, the heavier the reed, the sweeter the sound. But a heavy reed is also harder to play. So we start with this one. It's a number two."

"Okay."

Buzz took the mouthpiece and strapped the reed to it. Then he pushed the mouthpiece onto the corked end of the neck.

"Now, the most important thing with any horn, woodwind or brass, is the embouchure. That's how your mouth is positioned around the mouthpiece."

"You can't play with teeny white boy lips like that," came a call from across the room. Buzz ignored it. I smiled. These guys could talk some smack, but this was a picnic compared to a football field. Buzz continued.

"You need to practice keeping your mouth tight around the piece. If it's not tight enough, air will escape and the horn won't play right."

"Like skinning cats, brother," said a guy blowing spit out the end of a trumpet.

"But you hold it too tight, you gonna get cramps in your mouth."

"Like a cat's backside," said the guy in the white tie.

Buzz looked at me. "Well, go on. Play." I put my hands on the instrument.

"Don't touch nothing with your hands. Just blow."

I put the plastic piece in my mouth. I blew. Nothing happened but the sound of air rushing through pipes. It must have been funnier than Carson because the room broke out like hyenas.

"Don't mind them," said Buzz. "Moisten the reed. Lay your tongue on it for a bit. Soften it up. Then try again." I followed his direction and felt the wood soften on my tongue. Then I blew again. More air. More laughs.

"Tighten your embouchure—don't let the air escape." I clamped my lips down and blew. A sound! Something like the screech of a vampire bat, but a sound nevertheless.

"There goes them cats."

I tried again. More cats. Then, out of nowhere, the screeching stopped and for a scarce second, a sound almost musical in nature. No laughter.

"Now, on your top hand here, put your three fingers down." Buzz placed my fingers on three mother-of-pearl pads.

"That's the position for G. The note you mostly tune an alto with. You try it."

I blew through my lips to relax, and then took the mouthpiece. Tightened my mouth, but not too tight. My fingers down. I don't know why but I closed my eyes. And blew. The sound that came out was as if it emanated from somewhere else, someone else. Like the perfect fairway iron, where thought is banished and swing is natural and harmonious and the connection so pure that you don't feel it, you just lift your eyes to watch the ball fly long and straight and true and onto the green, as if hit by Tiger himself. I blew a note that was low and tender, a sound full of melancholy and history, as if the sax were telling its life story, exposing its soul, explaining its *raison d'être*. It was a singular note, nothing spectacular. Not Coltrane or Charlie Parker. Yet something very special. Audible tenderness. I let the air die and the sound fade. There was a hollowness to the silence that enveloped the room. I opened my eyes. No laughs. Every head in the room was nodding. Most had knowing smiles. The guy in the black shirt and white tie stood and crossed to me. He put his hand on my shoulder. I waited for the less than witty retort.

"Mmm," was what he said.

Everyone began collecting their instruments. Cleaning, constructing and tuning. Buzz Weeks showed me fingerings for the eight notes of the mid-octave in the key of C. I played it. Eight notes, three musical, five high-pitched squeaks. No laughs. The musicians were getting busy for the show, but they still had ears. It was as if I had crossed the line, been offered associate membership in the fraternity. Buzz handed me a workbook he said belonged to his uncle. Told me to read it, practice it. Scales and arpeggios. Boring, he said, but focus on the sounds, not the repetition. He left me blowing bad notes and picked up his own saxophone. It was bigger than mine. Tenor sax, if I recalled. He ripped a few riffs to get his head in the game, and then the band shuffled out, one by one. I packed my instrument away and heard the crowd clapping as the band made their way on stage. By the time I walked out, they were into it. They reminded me of baseball players. All jokes and pranks in the dugout but dead serious on the field. I found Danielle at a four cover, with the woman in the polka-dot dress and her man. I was introduced to him but didn't catch his name over the music. Danielle handed me a beer, which she must have ordered as the band came out because it was still moist on the bottle and snowflake cold. The band played. Mostly upbeat, lots of free styling. The crowd tapped along and drank their drinks and listened to master craftsmen ply their trade. The set lasted forty-five minutes and two beers. When they took their break they didn't return to the green room sanctuary, rather mingling with the audience and accepting drinks and cigarettes. Buzz Weeks came over to me with a rye whiskey in his hand.

"You wanna meet a guy?" he said into my ear. I nodded and told Danielle I'd be a moment. She was keeping company with a large, red fruity drink. Buzz led me back into the green room. A big guy, who looked just like the linebacker on the door except this one had no hair, was standing guard. He let us in. The only guy inside wore a short ponytail and a suit. It was my understanding that the seventies were big all over again, and this guy had embraced the trend wholeheartedly. His suit was pure burgundy velvet, and the white puffy shirt underneath looked to have been previously owned by a pirate. He wore a scraggly goatee that looked like the garden of someone recently deceased.

"What the hell are you, honky? The Beach Brothers?" Clearly his vocabulary had also been borrowed from the seventies.

"The Beach Boys," I said.

"What?"

"Forget it."

"Is that surfboards on there?" He swayed as he spoke, as if there was a rhythm in his head.

"Does the Scarlet Pimpernel know you raid his wardrobe?"

"What?"

"Forget it."

"What you bringing me here, Buzz?"

"He's okay, Cool-aid."

"He ain't okay."

"Cool-aid? Really?"

"Yeah, man. You got it. What's yo name? Bruce?"

"Miami Jones."

"Say what?"

I pulled the baggy with the Maxx tab in it from my pocket and threw it to Cool-aid. He caught better than he dressed. He scrunched his brow as he surveyed it, which made him look like a peanut shell.

"What the hell is this, man?"

"That's what I want to know."

He glared at Buzz and waved the bag in the air. "What the hell you thinking, bringing this clown onto my turf with this stuff?"

"Hey pal, I just want to know —"

"You a cop?"

"Do I look like a cop?"

"Bad shirt, bad attitude. Yo, I think you do."

Touché.

"I'm not a cop. I'm a PI."

"You bring this trash onto my turf, and you think you just gonna walk out of here?"

"Listen, Tang."

"It's Cool-aid."

"Whatever. I'm not here to mess you around. But I need to know about that tablet."

"What, I look like Wikipedia." And so into the twenty-first century we jumped.

"No. You look like Shaggy from Starsky and Hutch. But I don't care. You see, I know a kid. Good kid. Took some of that stuff. Now he's dead. I know it's not your stuff. And I don't bring it here to disrespect you. But I need to know whose stuff it is."

Cool-aid stared me down. He wasn't good at it. He didn't have the attention span for it. But I was under no illusion that he was a nasty piece of work who would kill me and bury me under the cricket ground down the road, before I could hum the *Hawaii Five-O* theme.

"What makes you think I give a damn, man."

"Because here's how it is. I know people. People from New York type people. Italian. I have been tasked with one job, and that job has one word. Payback. Someone is going down. And to be clear, when I say down, I mean all the way. Their business, their house, the whole enchilada. If I don't finish the job, if for example, I don't take out the house, someone else will take my place until the house is gone. You see what I'm saying? It never ends. So the only question is who goes down? The guy who is responsible for this junk, or the guy currently holding it." I gave him my impassive pitcher staring down the batter face. I'm told it's pretty effective. I breathed deep to hold my form. Cool-aid looked at me, assessing my story and running it through his BS meter. In the end he must have figured there was lots of downside in not talking, and lots of upside in telling me what I wanted to know. He shrugged like he didn't care either way.

"Whatever, man. Stuff's called Maxx. I know it. The white kids love it. It belongs to a cat called Pistachio."

"Pistachio? Jesus, where do you get these names?"

"He got a fancy office on Brickell," he said, ignoring me.

"Brickell?"

"That's what I said."

"Thanks." I put my hands out and he threw the baggy back to me. I nodded to Buzz and we headed for the door.

"Hey, man," said Cool-aid. I turned to him.

"You don't want to mess with Pistachio. The man, he be mean. I talking real mean. Those things you said you'd do? He'll actually do them."

"I appreciate the heads up."

"And, man? You a PI. I helped you out. Maybe someday you do something for me." I took a card out of my wallet, and tossed it on the chair next to me, and then I walked out. Bedfellows are often strange. We stepped into the small corridor and the linebacker stepped into the room. Buzz fell back against the wall. He took a sip of his rye whiskey.

"Brother, I was seconds away from soiling my good trousers." He took a long breath. "You really work for the Mafia?"

"No," I said.

"But you know some."

"Not really. Just Sally."

Buzz smiled. In the dim corridor I could see his mouth full of teeth.

"Man, you made that stuff up?" He let out a low whistle. "You are one cool cat."

I leaned across the corridor and grabbed the half glass of rye from Buzz's grip. I threw it back in one gulp.

"Yeah, I'm a regular iceman. Let me buy you another one."

As we walked back to the bar, I noticed the band making their way back toward the stage. Buzz held up two fingers to the bartender.

"Cool-aid do a lot of business here?"

Buzz shook his head. "No, man. This crowd ain't into that. Cool-aid comes here for the cred. Like white folks go to the opera." The bartender gave us a rye whiskey each, and Buzz headed back on stage. I returned to my lovely lady, who was into a daiquiri the color of a tree frog. She sniffed my drink.

"Rye?" She frowned.

I don't like rye whiskey. I don't like the taste of NyQuil either, but I still take it when necessary. The band played two more sets and Danielle got as jolly as a fat man in a red suit. The vibe was grand and the mood was easy. I slowed up on the drinks to ensure safe passage home. I wasn't the only one. These were smart, happy people, and I enjoyed them immensely. After the final set I thanked Buzz and he told me to practice my scales. Danielle got a hug from every woman in the place. The men had the good grace to be furtive in their looks at her. I didn't. I couldn't take my eyes off that dress. We walked to the car and as I fished out my keys she leaned into me and gave me a wet, fruity kiss. I helped her in the car and then slipped in myself.

"Home, James," she giggled.

Then my phone rang. It was Angel.

"Miami? Sorry, I know it's late."

"What can I do for you, Angel?"

"My roommate said you came by Friday."

"I did."

"I need to talk to you."

"I'll drop by tomorrow."

"I really need to see you. Can you come over now?"

"Like you said, it's late."

"Please, Miami? It's a matter of life or death."

CHAPTER TWENTY—SIX

We were at Angel's dorm in ten minutes. Danielle said she would wait in the car, and I didn't dissuade her. I knocked on Angel's door, and she answered wearing a gray Panthers soccer T-shirt and tight red shorts. She had a Bud in her hand.

"Hi." She smiled.

"Are you okay?"

"Sure, come in." She brushed my arm with her hand and turned back into her dorm. I closed the door. The living area was empty. Perhaps her roommates were in bed. It was late and bed was where I wanted to be.

"You said it was life or death."

"Isn't it? Can I get you a beer?"

"No, thanks." She didn't listen and grabbed me a Bud from the communal fridge. She handed it to me with a smile and a flick of the hair, like an Andalusian tossing its mane after performing a particularly difficult trick. I put the beer on a side table.

"Isn't it against dorm rules to have beer on campus? You are underage."

"You want to come in my room." It wasn't a question. I treated it as such.

"No," I said. "Angel, why did you call me?"

She stood in her bedroom doorway, pressed her back against the jamb. She tilted her head back. Perhaps she'd seen it in a magazine, or a Victoria's Secret catalog. She was no Victoria's Secret model. Her breasts were large enough, but everything else was out of proportion. Or perhaps she was perfectly proportioned and the models were out of whack. That one was going to keep me up nights. Either way, she was a girl, a kid, throwing pitches her body wasn't capable of handling yet, so they were coming out all wrong and dropping short of the plate. A thirsty teenage boy might have taken a swing. But a lifetime in the game teaches us that patience is the most important quality at the plate. Knowing that it's okay to see off pitches, to leave the inside fastball or the slider low and away. Because what you really want is a heater down the middle, a fastball over the plate that you recognize the moment it leaves the hand, and patience has you waiting and watching so when it comes you are ready, feet dug in deep, hips solid, grip firm. And you know that one hit, the perfect connection and the sound of pine on leather and then watching the ball sail high and long, over the outfielders, chins held skyward, as it plunges into the bleachers, smack into the cheap seats. You know the waiting was worth everything, and the aimless swinging of youth was merely the expulsion of excess energy.

"Angel," I said again. "Why did you call me?"

"You came by."

"I did. Two days ago. What is it that couldn't wait until tomorrow?"

"Tonight," she said, turning to me. "Tonight couldn't wait." She strode over to me and threw her arms around my neck. It was a stretch so she went up on tippy toes, and she kissed me. Her lips were soft and fat and clumsy. She tasted like beer and bubblegum. Her breasts squashed hard against my chest as she pushed herself into me. I took hold of her by the elbows and she pushed in deeper. I pulled her away. She stared into my eyes, and then she moved to go in for more. My arms stayed straight, so she couldn't get within a foot and a half.

"What are you doing?" I said.

"What?" She smiled, but the assurance was gone.

"What do you think is going on here, Angel?"

"You came over." Her face suddenly looked as fragile as a butterfly.

"I did. I am investigating a death. Your friend's death."

"But I thought you liked me."

I stood on the precipice, watching the ghosts of conversations past thrashing in the broken water below. A choice to be made. The easy way or the hard way. But it was a trick, always a trick. The easy way inevitably grew thorny, and the hard way was an illusion, like the reflection of a stone wall in a pond, daunting and impenetrable to the eye, but easily broken through by those with the courage to dive in and find salvation just below.

"I don't," I said. It sounded hard and mean and rattled around the dorm room for a while. I knew it would. But the other option was a sitcom of misunderstanding and Chinese whispers. *I do, just not like that*, was softer, but left hope when none should remain.

Her face was a kaleidoscope of confusion and anger and embarrassment.

"I need to go," I said. "I'll call you later." I turned and walked away, into the corridor, toward the exit.

"Why?" she yelled. "Why the hell would you call later?" I didn't stop walking, but I heard her heading down the corridor after me.

"Why?" she said again as I reached the door. I put my hand on it and opened it a crack.

"I told you. I am investigating a death. I may need your help."

"Why are you doing this?" Her voice was thin.

"For Jake." I pushed the door open and walked out into the crisp night air. Fall had arrived and brought what Floridians thought of as a chill. The mercury was ready to dive below fifty. I strode along the path toward the parking lot where my Mustang sat. I heard Angel running, bare feet slapping on pavement. I turned as she launched herself into me, arms flailing, fists slapping like windmills. She beat into my chest until she lost momentum and I'd had enough, and then I pulled her away again.

"Why?" she said again. Any answer was short change, unsatisfactory. But I gave her my hollow excuse again anyway.

"For Jake," I repeated.

She bawled like a child, rapturous and exhausting. I didn't console her. I dropped my hands from her elbows.

"Jake?" she sobbed. "What use is he to me now, huh? What good."

"I'm sorry." I was. Very sorry. Sorry she was young and slowly spoiling, sorry she thought she had found what she was looking for but didn't know she had a lot of living to do before she even knew what *it* was. Sorry she was searching in all the wrong places, like Jake Turner and Miami Jones.

"You're—" She spat the first word and choked on the second. She stared over my shoulder, mouth agape, the words and sobs sucked from her. I turned to see what had captured her attention so completely, half expecting to see Jake Turner. I didn't. What I saw was worse. Far worse. Danielle stood by the hood of the Mustang. The commotion had pulled her from the car. The door was open and the interior light gave her a soft glow. On another day, in another time, Angel might have seen the ghost of Christmas future, the potential, the opportunity. Everything that time and a healthy diet and a few miles on the clock could provide. Angel would never have Danielle's genetics, but that was to a large extent moot. Kim Rose was by no means classically beautiful, but she radiated an attractiveness, a confidence born of experience and a truly fit body. Angel was all that and more. Or could be. And perhaps, had Kim Rose been standing by the Mustang, that is what Angel would have seen. But Kim Rose wasn't standing there. Danielle, tousled hair, easy manner of a few daiquiris, in that black dress. She looked coy and playful, but had the confidence of an athlete and the coiled readiness of a law enforcement officer. Her puppy fat had long ago melted and with it the uncertainty. She looked stunning. She was every bit the woman to Angel's girl. Angel took it all in, imprinted onto her memory, chiseled into her brain. Then she turned and ran, feet slapping, back into the dorm. I watched her go and considered chasing, but thought of sitcoms and Chinese whispers. I turned to Danielle. She came to me, moving like a ghost. She took my hand, kissed me and led me back to the car.

CHAPTER TWENTY—SEVEN

The morning brought dark thunderheads over the Bahamas. The clouds hung offshore, a mass of potential energy, like a football team in the locker room, anxious to take the field, cleats tapping on concrete, bodies crashing in preparation. It was cool out so we ate breakfast at the orange Formica counter. Danielle prepped so as to ward off a smoothie. Such things do nothing for a daiquiri hangover. She toasted bagels and fried eggs and bacon, and we ate sandwiches with coffee.

"You had a good night," I said.

She smiled. "What does that mean?"

"It means you seemed to enjoy yourself."

"I did." She bit into her bagel. "Nice people."

"Very. And one hell of a band."

"For sure. You get what you wanted?"

I sipped my coffee. It was black and bitter and suited my mood. "Got something. Whether it's what I wanted is yet to be determined."

We ate in silence for a while, until I noticed Danielle watching me.

"What?"

"What?" she said. "What do you think, what."

"Angel?"

She nodded and chomped into her bagel. I enjoyed watching her eat. It was all about quality, not quantity, and she ate with an intensity most people reserved for chess.

"I don't know," I said. "Sometimes we hitch our wagons to the wrong train."

"Very nice, oh wise one."

"Hey, what do you want from me?" I bit into my breakfast, salt and hickory.

"Did you lead her on?"

I swallowed and it hurt. "Give me some credit."

"You have been known to use your charms as means to an end."

"That's Ron's department."

She raised an eyebrow.

"No," I said. "I didn't lead her on. She's a kid."

"She's not a kid. She's just not a woman yet."

"So she's young and she overthought things. Assumed facts not in evidence."

"Don't need to be young to make that mistake." She sipped her coffee.

"So what do you think I should do?"

"What do you think you should do?"

"Leave her alone. I don't want to send mixed signals."

"That's one plan."

"You don't agree?" I got up and poured us more coffee.

"Of course not. It's a terrible idea."

"Why?"

"She's hurting. It might not be your fault, but you're the reason. That and the death of her friend. But he can't console her, can he?"

"I don't think I should be consoling her right now."

"I'm not saying lead her on, you knucklehead. You need to tell her what you are doing and why. Explain you are in a relationship and your dealings with her are professional. You can tell her she'll get over Jake but it will take a long time, and that's okay."

"You think that'll make it better?"

"No, it won't make it better. She's heartbroken. You can't fix that. But leaving her in the dark means when she comes out the other end, she's just as confused. At least if you talk to her, she'll have some knowledge for later."

"I just don't want to give her the wrong impression."

"Then don't."

"And you're okay with that?"

"Why wouldn't I be?"

"Don't know. I don't want you to feel threatened by her."

Danielle grinned. "I can handle anything any college girl's got. Besides which, I have a sheriff's issue weapon and the training to shoot off any superfluous bits of you from twenty yards."

I crossed my legs. "Point taken."

She sipped her coffee and looked at me over the mug. "It's this other woman I'm concerned about. The athletic director."

"Kim Rose."

Danielle nodded. "What was the deal with you two?"

"We knew each other in college."

"How well?"

"Pretty well. Nothing sexual, if that's what you're asking. But we were good friends."

"Why nothing sexual?"

"Why does a relationship have to be sexual?"

"It doesn't. But this was college, right?"

"Yes, but I didn't sleep with everyone I met at college."

"But you spent more time with this woman than most, yes?"

"Well, she wasn't really a woman then. More a girl."

"Is that why nothing happened?"

I had to grin. "No. If I had wanted to, that would've been irrelevant."

"So you didn't want to?"

"You keep putting words in my mouth—have you noticed that?"

She smiled and raised her eyebrows.

"We were friends. That was it. We were comfortable in each other's company and liked spending time together. But there was no physical attraction there. Well, not from my side. Maybe hers, but I never got that impression. Now that I think about it, there just wasn't much physical anything. Touching, hugging, anything. I'm not sure she was all that comfortable with being too physical, being touched. I mean on the soccer field sure, but not in an intimate way." I shrugged my shoulders.

"You never thought about it?" Her face told me she wasn't buying a word of it.

"I'm not saying that. I thought about it. Like you say, I was in college, for crying out loud. But it never felt right."

"So why did you spend so much time together?"

"We were both student-athletes. We appreciated how much effort that took. Games, practice, classes, study. We were both trying to succeed on all levels, and build sporting careers. We had a lot in common then."

"What about now?" She got up and cleared away the breakfast dishes.

"Now, I don't know what we have in common. There's a big gap there. We've had lives since then. Both been pro athletes, and now we're not. So everything we have in common, maybe it's behind us." I looked out toward the water. The sky was still bright and clear to the west, but the humidity was creeping up, foretelling of the activity offshore. "What exactly are you saying?" I said, looking back at her.

"I'm saying that maybe you don't know her like you once did. Maybe, and this is just maybe, she's using your past relationship to get what she wants. And despite what she has pleaded, maybe her reasons are more self-serving."

"I don't know."

"Neither do I." She ambled behind me and rubbed my shoulders. "I don't want you to think I'm poisoning you against her, or saying your friendship wasn't special. But you said it, there's been a decade and a half of life since you knew her, and you're an investigator. So maybe you should investigate those years. You aren't the same person you were back then. Maybe she's not either."

I sat at the counter while Danielle took a shower. I resolved that there were too many women in my life at the moment. Life was a complex patchwork on a good day. All these women were making it an unnavigable torrent. I further resolved that Danielle was a lot smarter than me and I must listen to her. I didn't feel it in my best interest to let her know of this resolution, so I resolved to keep it to myself. Which led me to my final resolutions. First, that I needed to talk with Angel and mend fences if possible, for her sanity as well as the likelihood that I would need her assistance again. And second, I needed to know more about Kim Rose and the years I'd missed. Somewhere in those years lay the key to unlocking whatever the hell was going down on that campus.

CHAPTER TWENTY—EIGHT

There was an accident on I-95 in Lake Worth, so I dropped Danielle at home and cut across to the turnpike. First stop was Angel's dorm. I figured the best time to catch a college student in dorms was first thing in the morning. Especially one who had probably spent the night drowning her sorrows. I parked in the same slot I had a few hours previously. This time I backed in, and didn't hit the fob. I didn't fancy someone stealing my Mustang, but if Officer Steele or the donut patrol happened by I didn't want to be fumbling around in making my getaway. I left the car and hit up Angel's dorm. My knock was met with a resounding echo of silence. I hesitated a moment, and then turned to leave. As I did I saw a shadow shoot across the bottom of the door. I stopped and waited for the door to open. It didn't. I knocked again, hard but with suitable restraint. No dice. Someone was inside, but they weren't playing ball. I strode back down to the parking lot and looked to the east. The sky was bursting dark and gray, playtime over and the weather ready for business. I figured I had a couple of hours before the rains came. I walked over to the playing fields rather than drive. I thought I might catch Angel on the practice field, if it wasn't her hiding in the dorm. I didn't find her. I didn't find anyone. The fields were vacant, open spaces waiting for something to happen. It seemed such a waste. I crossed over the speed hump toward the gym. The lot was half full. Gym junkies like to get their licks in early, even in college. I strode up the stairs and went into Kim's office without knocking. I figured if the kid was doing something in the office that he shouldn't have been, he needed the lesson. He wasn't. He was behind his desk, wearing a fresh polo with a panther on the breast, playing solitaire or entering the launch codes or something equally mundane. He stared at the screen, his face as animated as white china. He looked up. I didn't parade across to Kim's office this time. I wasn't in so much of a hurry. The kid looked up.

"She's not in." He looked at Kim's office door. "You wanna wait?"

"You expect her?"

"Not for a while. She's in budget meetings over at admin."

"Sounds like a hoot."

"She won't be in a good mood when she gets back."

"Just tell her I dropped by."

I skipped back down the stairs and headed across the campus. I called Ron and got his voicemail, so I left him a message asking him to do some sniffing around about Kim and President Millet. The clouds were gathering like dark phantoms, and I revised my early estimate of the dumping by noon. It was coming. The moisture in the air made the grass on the quad stand to attention. I wandered back toward my car. It seemed no one wanted to chat with me today. I considered giving Angel's door another try. As I stepped past the Mustang I felt something amiss. One of those things your eye sees so quickly that your brain processes it as a feeling rather than a visual. I stepped back to the car and bent down. The door wasn't closed all the way. It sat out an inch from the rest of the body, like a wrinkle. I stood and looked around me, about the parking lot. Nothing moved and I saw no one. I looked back at the door, and then I pulled it open. The seatbelt hadn't collected fully in, and the buckle had fallen in the door well blocking the door from closing. Which was all reasonable and easily explained, except for one thing. It was the passenger side door. I ran my mental fingers through the filing cabinet in my brain until I was convinced that I had not driven all the way from Danielle's home, along the turnpike, cruising at a breezy eighty, with a slightly ajar door. I was pretty sure the Mustang had a warning light or a buzzer or something for that. Regardless, it would have made a hell of a noise.

I opened the door all the way and crouched. Lay my hand on the floor mat and looked under the seat. I had no idea what I was looking for. A bomb seemed way too James Bond for a sedate college campus, but it was the kind of thought that caught like wildfire on a hot summer day. Someone had been in my car. I had nothing worth stealing in it, other than the car itself. I opened the caddy between the seats and found tissues and a beer cozy from the Tiki Bar in Fort Pierce. I flipped down the sun visors and found nothing but a warning about the airbag. I half sat on the seat and pushed the button to drop the glove compartment open. Then I found something. Someone had left a little gift. I pulled a plastic bag out and held it up. It was full of Maxx tablets. There must have been five hundred or more. I glanced around the lot and gave myself a moment to process. I felt an undeniable urge to go to the bathroom.

Then I moved. I jumped across the center console into the driver's seat, pulling the passenger door closed as I did. I hit the gas before the first piston roared to life. Floored it and screamed out onto the road. I was thankful it was early Monday morning. Not much foot traffic, no one making their way to or from the playing fields. My tires gave a squeal as I spun into the gym parking lot. I hit my spot and lunged out. This time I slammed the door and hit the fob as I ran. Into the gym and up the stairs. Past Kim's office. I recalled the women's bathroom at the end of her corridor. I assumed there would be a men's as well. I reached the end of the corridor and hit the fire escape. I was wrong, no men's room. Probably at the other end of the building. Or on another floor. To hell with it, I decided, standing there with ten to life's worth of class A drugs. Going into the ladies' bathroom was certainly the lesser of two evils. I burst in.

It looked pretty much like a mens' room, just more stalls and fewer urinals. Dropping to the floor I saw no feet, so assumed I was alone. I lunged into a stall and tipped the bag of drugs into the bowl. I hit the lever and watched the pills circle around the bowl, mocking me, refusing to leave. Then they were sucked away. As the cistern refilled I tore the bag into pieces and then I flushed them as well. When I was happy nothing was going to swim back out for an encore, I went to the sink and washed my hands like I was shooting for employee of the month at McDonald's. Then I dried myself and looked in the mirror. I was sweating at the brow. My eyes looked hollow and dark. I needed some sleep, beer, and a vacation in Mexico. Not necessarily in that order. I sucked in a deep breath through the nose, held it, and out through the mouth. Then repeated it twice. My heart rate slowed. After splashing my face and wiping it, I wandered back downstairs.

I wondered if I had overreacted. I had next to no explanation as to why or how the Maxx had been deposited in my car, but I felt good about not having it around should I run into Officer Steele. It was nothing more than gut instinct, but I recalled a three-two pitch when I was in college, playing for Miami at the College World Series in Omaha. My catcher had signaled twice for a slider, to a guy who would be expecting a slider but loved the inside fastball. I waved the catcher off a third time. He threw his hands up as if to say, *hell it's your career*. Bases were loaded, the tying run on third, the leading run on second. I threw the heater. It was gut. The batter ate them for dinner so every man and his dog knew the safe pitch was the slider. My fastball hit the catcher's mitt with a thud, and we went to the CWS final. Sometimes you go with your gut. My gut had also been hit out of the park on numerous occasions since. You win some, you lose some. I went with the Omaha memory.

My gut was spot on. I stepped out into the purple light, the storm clouds swirling overhead. Officer Steele, this time the police officer version, was standing next to my car. His patrol unit, the Dodge Charger, was parked askew across the roadway. His rotund partner was leaning against the fender. He covered the part that said *911*. And half of the rest of the car. I walked up to Steele. He looked awfully smug for a man with a square head.

"Mr. Jones, I believe you are trespassing."

"You want to make a second mistake?"

"Second mistake?" he said. His eyes narrowed.

"You did choose that haircut, right?"

"You're under arrest. Harris, put the cuffs on." The big guy pushed away from the fender and the car groaned.

"You're kidding, right?" I said. "You're not in your sexy little security uniform right now. You're a cop today."

"That's why I can place you under arrest." The fat cop bobbled over to me. He walked like a buoy in rough seas. They were playing a game and playing it badly. Steele thought he knew what he was doing, but he was wrong. Too much time on an insular college campus had caused him to think that the real world wasn't looking anymore. My old mentor, Lenny Cox, once told me that a university should be a tributary to society, not a sanctuary from it. He'd have laughed his red head off at these clowns. I put my hands out in front to accept the cuffs. At this point it didn't matter that they were wrong and illegal in their approach. Resisting would have made things worse for me, not better. But I wasn't letting Dumpy cuff me behind my back, which is exactly how he should have done it, if he weren't sloppy. But he was. He clicked the cuffs around my outstretched wrists. I could hear him wheezing with the effort. I was certain I knew which of those two kept the patrol car spotless.

"Get his keys," said Steele.

"Why?" I asked.

"I need to search your car."

"You must be joking," I said. "First false arrest for a non-trespass, then you search my car, illegally."

"I can search a vehicle."

"Geez, did you start at the Academy yesterday? You don't have probable cause."

"We have a credible witness."

"Let me guess, an anonymous tip-off."

"His keys."

The donut muncher fumbled in my chinos for my car keys. I winked at him. His expression didn't change. He permanently looked like he been slapped and didn't know why. He came out with my keys, and then waddled them over to his partner. Steele started in the front. Repeated what I'd done. Under seats, lifted floor mats, the center console. He checked the ashtray. It had an emergency fifty stuffed in it. He didn't take the fifty, just pushed the tray closed. So he was a little bent but not completely dishonest. He rummaged around the rear, and then checked the trunk. His partner, Harris, perched the edge of his butt on the side of the passenger seat. It was like watching a circus elephant sit on a dining chair. He couldn't twist his body around so he flipped the glove compartment open and stuffed his hand in. He wasn't able to see from his angle, so he blindly lifted registration papers, the car's manual and repair log, a notepad. I wished I had left a mousetrap in there. He fumbled about for a few seconds and then flipped the compartment shut. He levered himself up like a champagne cork out of a bottle. There was a wheeze but no pop.

Steele came around from the trunk, avoiding eye contact with me. He could see his day, which had started with such promise, going down the gurgler like month-old buttermilk. He looked at Harris, who shrugged. Steele stood back at attention and surveyed the car. There were lots of places less obvious to hide drugs, but his intel source hadn't said they'd be hidden. They were supposed to be easy to find. Some might have suggested I was poking the bear but I found myself smiling like I just won the grand prize in Powerball. I wondered if Steele would follow through on his trespass story, or give up altogether. The two of them stood looking at the car like tourists arriving in Key West expecting to find sandy beaches.

"It's in the glove compartment, you loser." The yell came from the direction of the quad. We all turned and saw Angel.

"Young lady, go back to your dorm," said Steele.

She crossed her arms in defiance.

"This just keeps getting better for you, Steele."

He shot me the kind of look that a batter gave when I walked him by heaving a fastball into his forearm and we both knew I'd done it on purpose. Steele turned to his round partner.

"Did you check the glove compartment?"

"Yeah," Harris said, uncertainty etched across his face. Steele didn't buy it. I wouldn't have either. He marched to the door and sat in the seat. He pulled everything out of the glove compartment and placed it all on his lap. He went through it methodically, checking the pockets in the owner's manual. He found nothing and set aside the documents. Then he reached deep into the compartment. I figured he was looking for a secret stash or hidy-hole. He was disappointed. Steele sat up, ramrod straight, and looked out the windshield. I didn't know if he was tossing around places I could have hidden the drugs he knew to have been planted there, or if he was playing through the demise of his career in his mind. He swiveled out and planted his feet, then stood to attention and marched over to me.

"Let me see your hands," he said. I knew where he was going with it. We both knew the drugs were gone, and we both knew I had gotten rid of them. He was hoping to find drug residue on my hands. He must have thought I'd worn my *I'm with stupid* T-shirt, the one with the arrow pointing up, under my shirt, if he figured I'd fall for that. I held up my hands. He didn't touch them; rather he bent at the waist, putting his face right down to them, like he was Lord Squarehead introducing himself to the fair maiden with a kiss of the hand. But he didn't kiss. He sniffed. Long and hard so his back rose up toward me. He wouldn't have smelled fresher hands in a dentist's office. He stood up and looked at me. His face was still impassive, like he was on the parade ground, but his eyes betrayed him. He was deeply unhappy.

"I still have you on trespass," he said.

I laughed. I probably shouldn't have, and I knew I really was poking the bear now, but when something is so moronically funny, it's involuntary. All these guys needed was to bump into each other and they'd be the Keystone Kops. The laughing didn't improve his mood. His eyes narrowed and his chest heaved, and I readied myself for a sucker punch to the guts.

"Mr. Jones?" came the voice from behind me. Steele flicked his eyes over my shoulder. I glanced around. Kim Rose's assistant stood behind me. I made a mental note to learn the kid's name.

"What do you want?" barked Steele.

"Ms. Rose wanted to let Mr. Jones know she was running late for their meeting."

It was like the coyote had dropped an anvil on Steele's head. The color, such as it was, washed from his face.

"What are you talking about?" Steele said.

"Mr. Jones has a meeting with the athletic director."

Steele frowned. "What for?"

"I don't know, sir. I just fill the calendar. I don't sit in on the meetings."

A tsunami of thoughts must have crashed around inside Steele's head. I knew the feeling. Those days when you just knew the gods were against you. When you pitched it to a guy who could never hit a curve and was batting .005 for the season, and you throw the perfect curve, on the outside half of the plate, tantalizing in its trajectory, then at the last, dipping, sinking like the Titanic, and your batter, with no clue and no hope, sneezes as he brings the bat forward, and head down, eyes closed, hands flailing wildly, makes perfect contact with the ball and sends it out of the park along the first base line. Yes, I've had days like that. So I knew the look on Steele's face. Whether to barrel on, a small band of hardy souls in a battle against the mighty army, for a famous victory; or beat a hasty retreat, lick wounds and live to fight another day. He looked at Harris.

"Let him go." Harris bobbled forward and unlocked the cuffs. I had to give Steele his credit. He'd been beat, embarrassed and made to look like Millet's pet corgi, but he still stood at attention, took my gaze and held it. When Harris was done I rubbed my wrists like I'd been cast in a dungeon for ten years, and Steele stepped forward.

"Some days it just doesn't pay to get out of bed," I said.

"Do your meeting, then get off my campus."

"Nothing would give me more pleasure." I stepped back next to Kim's assistant and watched the cops head for the car.

"That's it? You're leaving?" said Angel.

"Young lady, go back to your dorm now, before I arrest you."

She gave him a face that was supposed to say something like *moron*, and Steele got in his Charger and pulled away.

"Thanks for that," I said to Kim's guy.

"Don't thank me. I saw you out here so I texted Director Rose. She told me what to do."

"Well, thanks anyway. You got a name?"

"Brian."

"Thanks, Brian."

"You bet." He pointed at the gym. "I got work to do."

"Sure. Me too." He walked back into the building, and I walked over to the stand of pines where Angel stood moping.

"That wasn't very smart," I said.

She said nothing, kicking at the fallen pine needles.

"I'm sorry about last night," I said. "You caught me off guard." More pine needles. She hit topsoil and kept going.

"You're a swell girl. And you're going to do great things and meet all kinds of great people. But I'm not part of your adventure. You've been a great help, and I appreciate it. I'm glad we met. But I have my own adventure. You see?"

She kicked at the dirt with less enthusiasm. She didn't look up.

"Swell?" she said.

I smiled. I find it effective in situations where I want to sound old and crusty and thoroughly undesirable to use words that my father favored.

"Yeah. But this morning's actions were not quite so cool."

She stopped kicking.

"You realize that I could have gone to jail if they found those drugs in my car?"

"How did you know they were there?"

"I wasn't born yesterday."

She started kicking pine needles with the other foot.

"I'm gonna need them back."

I laughed. It wasn't a rib-busting roar. More a mildly amused tee-hee. But I wished I hadn't.

"Seriously? You plant drugs in my car, and when I don't get caught, you want them back? That's not how this works."

"I need them."

"Where did you get them?"

"Doesn't matter."

"It matters a lot, Angel. A stash like that comes with strings."

She said nothing.

"Jake would want you to tell me."

It was her turn to give an ironic laugh. "Jake would want it? What the hell do you know?"

"I know that."

"You don't know jack. The stash was Jake's."

"The drugs were Jake's? How did you get them?"

"When he was in the hospital. I thought the cops might search his room. So I went over and took them. He was keeping them in a trunk under his bed. I knew where."

"And you didn't think to mention that before."

"I didn't want him to get into trouble."

"He's dead, Angel. Trouble doesn't get much worse."

She shrugged.

"So he was a dealer?"

"No. He wasn't."

"But he happened to have a huge stash of expensive designer pills."

"You don't get it. It was supposed to be just the sports stuff."

"Sports stuff? You mean performance-enhancing drugs?"

She nodded. "I didn't know. Then last semester one of my teammates got injured and asked me if I could get something for her, since I was friends with Jake. I asked him about it. He said it wasn't a big deal. He said he was just helping athletes perform at their best. I didn't think it was that great, but we never really talked about it much after that." She shuffled in the pine needles, and kicked a pinecone with her instep. "Then over the summer it changed."

"What happened?"

"I don't know. I went home for summer."

"Jake didn't?"

"No. He never went home. He got a summer internship."

"Where?"

"Some property developer. Jake was majoring in construction management."

"So what changed?"

"When I got back, he was quiet. Moody. He seemed to be darker. I asked him and all he said was there was bad stuff going on. He said, I remember him repeating it, that it was about making people better, athletes better, the program better. Not putting poison into people's bodies. He said they'd given him some bad stuff, but he wasn't having anything to do with it."

"So who sent him the bad stuff?"

She shook her head. "I don't know. The same guys who got him the other stuff, I think. But you just need to give it back now."

"I can't give it back, Angel. You planted it in my car and called the cops. I flushed it."

For the first time she looked at me. She didn't look good. She was puffy and tired. Her young eyes carried the baggage of a middle-aged bank executive. She shook her head more.

"That's not good. He wants it back."

"Who wants it? Pistachio?"

Her mouth fell full open. "How do you know . . ."

"That's what I do."

"He wants it back."

"Ain't gonna happen. What did you think would happen if they found it? It would've become evidence."

"I don't—I didn't."

"Where will I find this guy?"

"I don't know. Really. But you don't want to find him."

"Oh, I do."

"No," she said, stepping away from me. "And stay away from me. He'll think you've got it. So stay away from me." She turned and ran toward the quad, and her dorm beyond. I let her go. She was right. If this guy Pistachio was responsible for Jake's death, and he was firming as favorite, and he was looking for me, then she shouldn't be anywhere near me. I ambled over and leaned against my car. The clouds that had come in from the Bahamas began to leak misty rain, like a brush-free car wash. I jumped into my car and watched the tiny drops cover the windshield. I wondered how Jake Turner had gotten in so deep, and whether his refusal to play ball was the reason for his death. I was trying to figure out my next step when my phone rang.

"Jones, it's Eric Edwards. We need to meet."

"Okay. I'm in Lauderdale. I'll be back later today."

"No, I'm in Miami today. Meet me down here."

CHAPTER TWENTY—NINE

I met Eric Edwards in a small restaurant in Little Havana. He was in a booth at the back and looked like a skinny gangster. He wore a double-breasted suit and autumnal orange tie. His stubble had reached five o'clock by noon. I slid in opposite but didn't shake hands. He was drinking ice water, and a short Cuban guy brought me one, along with the menu.

"What's good here?" I asked.

"Cuban sandwiches are excellent."

I looked at the menu. It was entirely in Spanish. Not a single conversation in the restaurant was in English, except ours.

"Wouldn't they just call them sandwiches?"

"Probably." He really had undergone a humor bypass. I ordered *Bistec de Palomilla*, which sounded like grilled horse but was actually a thin cutlet of steak with sautéed onions. Eric got the *Ensalada de la Casa*.

"So you called?" I said.

"What exactly are you into?" He sipped his water and tapped his moist lips with the cloth napkin.

"How do you mean?"

"I mean, there are all kinds of red flags going up on this one."

"That so? Like what?"

Eric looked around the restaurant like he was about to spill the beans on Jimmy Hoffa's resting place. Not only was no one in the place interested, most would have struggled to comprehend what was their second or third language.

"So I put in a few calls," he said. "I spoke on the quiet to a junior staffer I know in Tallahassee. Guess who called back. Senator Lawry."

"State Senator Lawry? *Boondoggle* Lawry?"

"The very same."

"What did he say?"

"He wanted to know how my campaign was going. If I needed any help."

"Generous."

"Very. He's known to be very good to his friends."

"And not so good to his enemies."

"Exactly. He said I was doing sterling work and he saw a bright future for me, maybe even in Tallahassee."

"Tallahassee. Everyone's dream."

"You can mock all you like, Jones. But some of us aspire to public service, and some aspire to self-service." It was smug beyond belief, and I was dying to stick in a crack about aspiring to nail your paralegals, but I didn't think it would help my cause.

"And some, like Boondoggle Lawry, aspire to both. So are you getting frightened off there, Eric? Seeing your political future flash before your eyes?"

"You won't believe me, and I don't care either way, but I will do my job as state attorney as best I can, consequences be damned. But what I won't do is shoot myself in the foot for no reason."

"For what reason would you shoot yourself in the foot?"

Our food arrived and we both leaned back as it landed on the table. Eric rubbed his hand down his tie as if the steam coming off my lunch might help press it smooth.

"What do you have, Jones?"

"Beef and onions?"

"On Millet."

I cut the thin steak. "Not much more than hunches. A dead kid, a connection to a drug organization, and an unnatural predilection against athletes."

"What's the drug angle?"

"I don't know. Seems to be headed by some character calls himself Pistachio."

"Pistachio? Where do they get these names?"

I ate some beef and onions. It was typically overseasoned, but delicious.

"Search me. You know him?"

"No. Where is he based?" Eric leaned over his salad and ate with one hand, using the other to hold back his tie. It made the whole thing look like too much work. I resolved that should I ever buy him a Christmas gift it would be a tie clip.

"I'm told he has an office here in Miami. So what do you know about Millet?"

"City planner tells me there are provisional plans for a new biotech facility, and a research center."

"Provisional?"

"It's big. Think four or five box stores. The size of a decent hospital."

"So?"

"So city ordinance doesn't permit that kind of development in what is now essentially a residential area. Basically anywhere east of the Everglades."

"Okay," I said, pausing to swallow. The salt was making me thirsty. "How do you overcome that?"

"State override. But that's a long process."

"Things can happen with a bit of motivation. Even in Tallahassee."

"There's something else. Because the university is private, any state funding has to go through considerable oversight. Unless."

"Unless?"

"Unless someone is motivated to fast-track it."

"Someone like Boondoggle Lawry?"

Eric shrugged and stuffed some lettuce in his mouth.

"So the college is paying him off."

He shook his head. "Hard for a private university to give large sums of money to politicians."

"So who? Who's motivated?"

He ate and watched me, waiting for me to put it together myself. Who had the most to gain from a huge research facility, other than the college itself? I tossed around what was involved. The planning, the money, the infrastructure.

"The developer," I said. Eric raised his eyebrows.

"Who is?" I asked.

"Rinti Developments."

I sat back in the booth.

"You're familiar with them?" he said.

"I've had cause to be involved with old man Rinti once or twice. It was called Rinti Construction then."

"Now it's Rinti Junior. He changed the name. I hear the old man's got the big C."

"Couldn't happen to a nicer fellow. What's the word on the son?"

"Cut from the same cloth, just meaner."

"Oh, joy." I finished my steak. I had eaten so much sodium that I thought I might have a stroke in the booth.

"It explains how things might get expedited," I said.

"And why I don't want to dance this dance unless I'm damn sure."

"Fair point. Any connection between Lawry and Rinti?"

"I'm looking into it. But prelim, Lawry's nephew was one of three kids from the college who did a summer internship with Rinti."

"Internship?"

"Yeah, why?"

"Nothing. Just processing."

"Well, process this. There's nothing I can find regarding the land. A project this big would take a lot of space. The university is in a built-up area, so that's not it. But I can't find where they're planning to put all this."

"Five big box stores, you say?"

"Yes, a lot. Maybe ten football fields. Possibly more."

"How big is a football field compared to soccer?"

"Not sure. Roughly the same, give or take. Why?"

It was my turn to give the pious look as Eric played catch-up. The borders of the puzzle were beginning to fill in. Things were far from clear, but I could feel some momentum picking up. I watched the idea plant itself in Eric's brain.

"The sports fields at the university. Are they big enough?" he said.

"Close, I'm guessing. And if you don't have sports fields, you don't need coaching offices, admin, that sort of thing. Might free up a bit of extra room."

"A college with no sports?"

"My point exactly. But *El Presidente* Millet is hell-bent on getting rid of the athletics programs."

"And now we know why."

The check came, and Eric pushed it toward me. "You're not going to make the people of Florida pay for lunch."

"The favor I'm about to do the people of Florida, they owe me more than a Cuban steak lunch. But no, it's not on them.

You're picking this one up. We both know what this could do for the corruption-fighting politician in waiting."

"I don't know what you're talking about," he said, snatching up the check.

We walked out into a break in the rain. Eric told me to tread carefully and not use his name, and then dashed to his car. Fat drops fell on my head and the wet pavement. The sky prepared to peel open again. I got in the Mustang and took out my phone. I had an itch I needed to scratch.

"Yes?" she said. Her voice was robotic, from her mood and the heavy atmosphere.

"Angel, it's Miami. Where did Jake do his internship?"

"I told you, at a construction company."

"Do you know the name?"

"Off the top of my head, no."

"Does Rinti Developments ring a bell?" It was leading the witness, but I'd worry about that if I ever went to law school.

"Rinti? Yeah, that sounds right. What about it?"

"Where was the job?"

"Brickell Avenue."

"Thanks, Angel."

I wanted to know more about the internship and what role it played in Jake Turner's demise, so I called Kim to get me the names and addresses for the Lawry nephew and the third intern. She was in a meeting, but her ever helpful boy-servant Brian said he'd pass the request on. I hung up and watched the splatters on my windshield turn into dinner plates, and waited for the heavy stuff to end before I paid a visit to *El Presidente*.

CHAPTER THIRTY

I thought I'd be cunning and park somewhere different, so I took a visitors' space outside the university administration building. The glass facade reflected the dreary sky and made the building look like it had a veneer of sheet metal. I made my way up to the executive floor. The stained glass atrium threw a cathedralesque light across the space, somber and gothic. Water streaks on the windows were shadowed on the wood-paneled walls, making it look like the room was weeping. I strode up to the reception desk. The receptionist who had attended me on my last visit was typing into her computer and took her time to look up with a perfunctory smile. The smile dropped when she realized who I was, and that I had no intention of stopping for a chat.

"He's expecting me." I smiled as I dashed by.

"But, sir, you can't—"

I punched open the double doors to Millet's vast office. Even though I had been in it before, I was impressed all over again. It was more a small but grand library than an office. Millet's desk could easily have been a reading table. The space was everything a wood-paneled, leather-bound library should be. Opulent, elitist and pretentious as hell, and I have no doubt if I had the money I would get one in a New York minute. Millet was sitting at his desk, reading through half glasses. He looked over the top of them at the commotion, and in a well-practiced move snapped them off his face as he stood.

"You can't come in here like this. You can't even be on this campus." I kept marching toward him. "I'm going to call security. Genevieve!"

So that was her name. It suited her well. He came around the desk, calling for his secretary. I grabbed him by the lapels of his beige suit. The material was sumptuous, perhaps Egyptian cotton. I wrenched him around and threw him into a wingback leather reading chair. He hit the leather with a crumpled pftt, the bravado knocked out of him. Physical confrontation does that to a lot of people.

"I tell you what, you call security, I'll call the *Miami Herald*, and we'll all sit down and have a nice chat about dead lacrosse players and Rinti Developments."

Millet wasn't a physical man, but he was smart and he processed information quickly. He waved a shaking hand at Genevieve and told her to give us a moment alone. She retreated from the office, pulling the double doors closed.

"Tell me about the research facility. Tell me about your involvement with the Rintis."

"Do you mind if I get a scotch?"

"Yes, I do."

"You're welcome to one, of course."

"I don't like cheap scotch."

"Thirty-year-old Islay single malt is not cheap." He gave me a face like I just called his suit a polyester blend.

"Fair enough. Where is it?"

"On the bar over there."

I walked over to a crystal decanter and poured two shots of amber liquid into heavy crystal glasses. It smelled of burned oak and peat. I handed one to Millet, and I sat in the second wingback chair with the other. We were at an obtuse angle to each other so I had to push myself into one corner of the chair to face him. He didn't care about facing me; he just sipped his scotch with two hands like he was drinking hot soup on a frigid day.

"So tell me about you and Bruno Rinti."

"Who?"

"If you're going to be like that, I'll have to throw this glass at your face."

He took a quick sideways glance. "That's not the name of the person I know."

"Who do you know."

He sipped. "Gino was the gentleman I have dealt with."

"Gentleman?"

"More or less."

"And what was your business with Gino Rinti?"

"I'm not at liberty to say."

"This is fine scotch, Mr. Millet. It would be such a waste to have to dump it on you."

"It's Dr. Millet, but do what you must with your beverage. I cannot discuss confidential business dealings."

It would have been a waste. Good scotch is the product of the one thing no man can buy. Time. It would have left me with an empty feeling inside to have wasted even a single drop. So I gulped it down and threw the empty glass at Millet's chair. It was good-quality lead crystal, heavy and dense. I was pleased to know that the university wasn't paying for their administrators to drink ancient whiskey from cheap glassware. I aimed at the chair wing, behind Millet's head. The crystal flew past Millet's nose and hit the chair right on the wing and bounced back into the side of his head. I was glad to know I still had decent control. A direct crack in the head, even if I took the pace off, might have killed him, or least left a difficult-to-explain bruise. As it was, he recoiled against the opposite wing of his chair and spilled his scotch on his lovely beige trousers, as my glass bounced across an expensive-looking rug before spinning to rest under Millet's hefty desk. He was more shocked than hurt. He screeched like he was auditioning for the Vienna boys' choir but said nothing more. He checked the spot for blood, and not finding any, gave me a withered look, the sort a child might give in anticipation of the evil character coming on screen in a Disney movie.

"What is Rinti doing?"

"Building," he yelped. "He's a builder, he's building."

"Building what?"

"I told you but you didn't listen. He's going to build me the Caltech of the Southeast. A state-of-the-art research facility focusing on biotechnology, the physical sciences and engineering." He was almost getting into sales pitch mode.

"Why not be MIT?"

"MIT? Ha! This is bigger than MIT."

The look on his face suggested he actually believed it.

"You do realize that the Rintis have connections to organized crime."

"So says you. Every hard-working construction company suffers that label."

I stood and poured myself a fresh scotch. I left the thrown glass under the desk.

"So all these facilities, these buildings of Rinti's. I imagine they are going to take up a great deal of space."

"What do you mean?"

"You know what I mean. Unless you're planning on opening a campus in Port Saint Lucie, you don't have the space."

He watched the remains of his scotch in his glass but said nothing.

"Unless," I added.

Millet glanced at me. "What?"

"That does seem to be an awful lot of space out there on those sporting fields."

"What is it you think you know, Mr. Jones?"

"What I think I know I'll keep to myself. It's what I definitely know that concerns you. Shall we connect the dots? An athletic department who thinks you don't like them, your professed distaste for funding non-academic ventures, a big chunk of land used for sports, your desire to build stuff on a big chunk of land, a developer with connections to get things pushed through before the media makes a big noise, and you. With your history of being second fiddle and your hard-on over your nemesis, one Remus Levensong, PhD."

"I am second fiddle to no one. Nor is my university."

"What I heard was, he got the funding, the publication, the prestige and the girl. Oh, and he's now president in waiting of where? That's right, MIT."

"You think that makes him so much better?" spat Millet.

"On pretty much every measurable scale."

Millet's face flushed crimson. I didn't think it was the scotch.

"There are people who follow a path trodden by others, and there are those who blaze a new path." He looked away into middle distance, like the speech was more for his benefit than mine. "History remembers the pioneers."

"I'm sure the college's student-athletes will remember you."

"Oh, will you get your head out of the sand? You're fixated on athletics."

"You've never heard of healthy body, healthy mind."

"Please. We're not talking about getting rid of the basketball gym or the pool. These are facilities that all students can use. But sports programs are just rah-rah activities to get the undergraduates all full of school pride. Grad students are too busy to care. They've got research to do and papers to write and panels to sit on. The government and corporations with the research funding don't care about sports. Undergraduates are cash cows, Mr. Jones, nothing more. And sports are just an unnecessary marketing exercise to make them feel good about their choice of school. But within ten years the academic standard will be so high here that no undergraduate will have the time or inclination for your athletics programs."

"But MIT has athletics. So does Caltech."

"An historical aberration, sir. If they had it to do over, I'm sure they wouldn't. But as you point out, it's a luxury I cannot afford."

"I don't see why it's such a financial drain."

"You don't get it at all, do you? It's not money—it's space. We need the space for more research facilities. The sports fields and associated ramshackle offices are on that space."

"So why not build somewhere else?"

"You can't be a hub of academic and research excellence if your constituent parts are diversified far and wide. Name a great university that doesn't have its core on one unified campus. There aren't any. A campus needs that academic buzz, the free expression of ideas. Departments need to cross-pollinate. A singular campus is what makes a great university great."

"So you brought in an athletic director who would be easy to move on when the time came."

He shook his head. "I misjudged Ms. Rose. I thought she'd see a Division II school as a stepping stone to somewhere better. That she'd be keen to move on. But she actually gives a damn. All this team first, go Panthers malarkey. She believes it."

"So was Jake Turner's overdose a convenient accident that you could pin on the athletics department, or did you make it happen?"

"Make it happen? What are you talking about? I had nothing to do with that."

"So it's a coincidence that Jake did an internship with Rinti Developments this summer gone."

I watched his face, but he gave nothing away. Maybe he couldn't go any pinker. He rubbed his trimmed gray beard with his hand. I couldn't say what that meant one way or the other. He may just have been a beard rubber.

"I didn't know that," he said. "But I don't see its relevance."

"You don't? Let's try two birds, one stone. You have an athletic department you want gone. And a top student-athlete who happens to work for your secret development partner, alongside the nephew of a state senator who happens to be in a position to fast-track your project. What if Jake Turner heard something that he shouldn't have, something that could kill the project? Silencing his big mouth and laying the blame for his overdose on Kimberly Rose's athletic department would be a neat little tie-up. Don't you think?"

More beard rubbing. I was coming to the conclusion it was a nervous tick and Dr. Millet was feeling uncomfortable.

"I had nothing to do with Jake Turner's death. And any attempt by you to imply such, against me or this university, will cost you dearly."

"That a threat, Mr. Millet?"

"A promise. And it's Dr. Millet." His face was purple, and I was sure the tips of his gray beard were going pink with anger. Perhaps it was the light. I finished my drink and put the glass in the middle of Millet's desk.

"Thanks for the drink."

He flicked his eyes at me but said nothing. I made to leave, and then stopped.

"Do you know State Attorney Eric Edwards?" I said, in violation of Eric's direction to not use his name.

"No." He frowned.

"You will." I grinned and strode out of his office.

CHAPTER THIRTY—ONE

By the time I got back to West Palm Beach the sun had fallen behind Lake Okeechobee. I parked in the lot beside my building. The courthouse quadrant was a patchwork of old buildings of character and new buildings like ours with the charm of hospital bed sheets, interspersed with parking lots and vacant plots. I saw the light on up in my office. Lizzy hard at work. I glanced at my watch and figured it would be fifty-fifty whether Ron had left for Longboard Kelly's. As I looked up from my timepiece I saw two big guys step out from the shadows and amble toward me. They weren't looking for a car. Guys looking for a car do just that. They look around, or if they spot their car, they chat, or look where they're walking, or fumble for keys. These guys didn't take their eyes off me. Their hands were by their sides, but not relaxed. I stopped and let them come to me. I was no sprinter, but both these guys carried a lot more weight than I did, so if it came to a footrace to my office, I wanted the run to be longer rather than shorter.

They looked like nightclub bouncers. But they weren't from around here. Even in the yellow lights of the lot, they looked pale. Both had shaved heads, but not recently. One was my height and lean, the other a couple inches shorter and turning to flab. The smaller guy looked like one of those guys. The ones that act like little yap dogs, all bark and anger and bravado, to compensate for something they thought they didn't have. The taller guy looked calmer, and walked with a rounded hip movement that I'd seen before but he probably didn't even know he had. The tall one spoke.

"You Miami Jones?" he said in a voice like something off Masterpiece Theater.

"Where you from?" I said.

"Miami."

"No, I mean originally."

"England. So are you Jones?"

"It's him," said the stocky one in a similar accent. "Vat's his car." He nodded at the Mustang. I was reminded again that a red Mustang might not be the best choice of vehicle for someone in my line of work.

The tall one spoke again. "You have something what belongs to us."

I shook my head. "We won independence fair and square. Kicked your limey butts good and proper, if elementary school memory serves me."

"I'm talking about the Maxx."

I said nothing. The big guy glared at me. The stocky guy pulsed like a pit bull on a chain.

"Our drugs, right? We want 'em back."

"You work for Pistachio?"

"Mr. Pistachio to you."

"Seriously? Mr. Pistachio?" I shook my head. "The police searched my car and found nothing. You wanna look too?"

"We know you removed them. Now we want them. And we want you to stop sniffing around about the kid. That's done. Leave it."

"Kid's dead. It's not done. Not by a long shot."

The shorter guy took a pace toward me. We were striking distance apart. He had a round, bloated face and bad teeth, and puffy boxer's eyes.

"Just give us the drugs, you maggot," he snarled.

"I don't have them."

"Where are they?" said the taller guy.

"Somewhere in the sewer system below the university campus."

The tall guy tensed his jaw. "Bad for you, mate."

I leaned back on my left foot and put my hands in my pockets, and thought of the late, great Lenny Cox. Lenny had gotten me into the business, had been my mentor and had taught me more than a thing or two. One of Lenny's favorite sayings was *go hard or go home*. He applied it loosely and liberally to life. Drinking, dancing, fighting, loving. When confronted by the likes of the two knuckle monkeys before me he would have said: don't start fights. Fights aren't groovy. But when you know for sure the other guy is going to hit you, don't wait around for him to do it. Get your licks in first. And go hard or go home.

What Lenny didn't teach me was about injuries. When you play pro sports, even college sports, you see more injuries than most people have vodka tonics. And I noticed the walk on the tall guy straight away. Given his accent I was guessing a soccer injury, the way those guys slide into tackles, cleats up. But people also do their anterior cruciate ligament slipping in the bath. This guy had done his and done it bad. He had been through physical therapy and had regained the strength in the knee, but not in his mind. He favored the leg, so slightly he probably didn't even notice, but it caused him to rotate his hurt side in an unnatural fashion, which put stress on the opposite hip. I bet he went to bed nights with an aching hip and blamed his shoes. The sum of it all was that he stood at the ready with his weight on his good leg. The other leg was on the ground and made him feel balanced, but it may as well have been tucked up like a flamingo.

I took my hand from my pocket, my keys balled up inside my fist, with a house key protruding through between my index and middle fingers. The stocky guy was closer so he was first. His boxing background might have given him some skills, but he wasn't going to get to use them, because his boxing had also left the flesh above his eyes puffy and soft. I hit him with a glancing blow, not trying to knock him down but rather run my house key across his brow like a fillet knife. The skin above his left eye burst like a bloody piñata. It was dirty pool, but I wasn't trying to become an Eagle Scout. As the blood splattered into his eye, I pivoted and cracked my heel into the inside of the tall guy's good knee. The knee gave a sickening pop as the cap slipped out of place and his leg twisted and buckled. He thudded to the tarmac, gripping his knee and screaming. ACL injuries on both knees was really going to put a crimp in his gymnastics career.

I spun back to the other guy who had one hand trying to stop the geyser coming from his eyebrow. He came at me with one eye and one arm. The one arm swung like a Louisville Slugger, but I easily stepped out the way, because the one eye meant his depth perception was completely messed up. As his momentum took his club of an arm away from me, I strode forward and put a punter's special into his crotch. It wasn't full-blooded. That might have broken my toes. But it dropped him to his knees, where I kicked my heel into his nose. This had no effect on his face as his nose was nothing more than folds of skin and pliable cartilage. It did, however, knock him backwards onto the black asphalt, where his head released a dull crack and he unfolded like a tent, unconscious. The blood was pushing its way through me at close to two hundred BPM, and I felt light-headed, so I took a few long, deep breaths. Then I put my shoe into the shoulder of the tall guy, who lay writhing in pain.

"You're a dead man," he cried.

"Tell Pistachio I think he's nuts, and I'm coming to crack him." I pushed the guy away and marched toward my car, thinking that I really did have a future in the corny but pithy retort department.

CHAPTER THIRTY–TWO

My fingertips were shooting little bolts of lightning by the time I reached Longboard's. My heart rate had dropped to close to normal, but there was still plenty of adrenaline coursing around my system and I was as jittery as all hell. I strode into the courtyard and straight to the bar. Muriel frowned as she watched me come in.

"You look like hell," she said. She looked the same as always. A little more tanned than natural, tank top, explosion of cleavage.

"I was going for that."

"You look like you've been in a fight or had incredible sex."

"What do you think?"

"The look on your face says, if it was sex it was with a guy, so I'll go with a fight."

"I look that bad? They didn't actually get a hand on me."

"It's not that. You just look, I don't know, feral," she said, smiling like it was a compliment. She grabbed a shot glass, poured a generous tequila, and slammed it down in front of me with a lime wedge.

"For medicinal purposes," she said. "Now quick, before Mick sees. You know how he feels about freebies." She looked over her shoulder to see if her boss was around.

"Something about hell and a chilly cold front." I slammed the tequila back. It was rotten. The lime took nasty to a new level, but the net effect was calming as the alcohol went to work on the adrenaline.

"You wanna talk about it?" she said, wiping the bar.

"You being a barkeep?"

"You being a smart guy?"

I put my hand up to apologize. She poured a beer and put it on a paper map.

"That one's on your tab."

I smiled. "Thanks."

"So what's the other guy look like?" she said.

"Guys, plural. And they're not going to be happy. I got the jump on them this time. Doesn't usually happen twice."

"They know you come here?"

"You worried?"

She stood up and put her hands on her tight hips, puffed out her chest.

"Please. I'm just thinking if they know you come here then you might want to be somewhere you don't normally go."

"I never knew you cared."

"I care all right. Mick would kill me for sending you somewhere else, but he would kill me twice if I let you get hurt. You guys are his pension plan."

"Well, I don't want to be responsible for Mick retiring to the poorhouse, but I think I'll hang tight. In my experience trouble is like the IRS. They'll find you wherever you hide, so you might as well stay at home and tackle them on your own turf."

She smiled and shrugged and wandered into the bar. I took my phone out and called the office and told Ron where I was. Ron moves faster toward a drink than most people do away from a hungry lion. He walked into the courtyard with his arms out.

"You're leaving me in the office, dry as Death Valley, while you wet your whistle down here?"

I handed him a frosty glass, which brought a grin, and told him about my adventures in the office car park.

"You need something stronger," he said, nodding to my beer.

"Muriel obliged."

He raised an eyebrow.

"That doesn't become you."

"Merely suggesting she'd be a good nurse."

My phone beeped and I found a text message from Kim Rose's assistant, with the names and addresses of the two students who interned with Jake at Rinti Developments.

"News?" said Ron.

"The two other interns. Lawry's nephew goes by the name of Sean, and an Alice Chang. We should pay them a visit tomorrow."

"Sounds like a plan."

"How about you?" I said, pocketing my phone. "Did you learn anything about our nutty friend?"

Ron took his stool and a long slug on his beer. "A bit, but not much of it makes sense to me."

"Do tell."

"I tracked down the address you got from your guy, what's his name?"

"Cool-aid."

"Yeah," laughed Ron. "He should trademark that. Anyway, the deal is, the building in question is home to some of South Florida's most upstanding citizens. Personal injury lawyers, hedge funds, offshore banking offices. And all manner of import-export businesses."

"Gotta love a good import-export business."

"Indeed. Covers all manner of sins. So anyway, I get no hits on a pistachio. No pistachio companies or directors called Pistachio."

"So what doesn't make sense?" I said, signaling Muriel for two more beers.

"With all this import-export action I thought I'd check any shipments into the port of Miami from businesses at that address. Especially from our friends to the south."

"Elementary, my dear Bennett."

"I drew a big, fat donut."

"Damn."

"From South America."

"I feel a *but* coming on," I said as Muriel put down two more cold ones and gave me a look.

"I didn't mean your butt," I said.

She frowned.

"Not that it's not a great butt."

"How is Deputy Castle these days?"

I turned to Ron.

"So you found nothing from South America."

"But," noted Ron, as Muriel winked and walked away. "There was something from Turkey."

"Carpets?"

"Good guess, but no. Apart from carpets, Turkey is the world's third largest producer of pistachios."

"You don't say."

"I do. But the real question is why one would import pistachios into the US, given we are the second largest producer of pistachios in the world."

"A real brain teaser. Perhaps nuts weren't the only thing in the shipment?"

"Exactly my thinking. But why Turkey? They don't make designer drugs in the US?"

"Designer drugs, yes. But when I was playing ball all the best performance-enhancing drugs came from labs in Eastern

Europe. And the best port in that part of the world was a US ally."

"Turkey."

"The same. Maybe things have changed, maybe not. The question is, who's importing these pistachios?"

"This is where it doesn't make a lot of sense. The company is an S corporation, single director by the name of Alexander Montgomery. A quick Google search says the guy is a British national, worked in the oil biz, in Scotland, then Texas, then for a certain British oil company in South America. Real high flyer. Then he dumps the career and starts his business in Miami."

"And who did he meet in South America?"

"I think it's safe to assume an expat with money met anyone and everyone worth meeting. But if he made connections in South America, why is he getting shipments from Europe?"

"Is it possible he's getting PEDs from Europe and harder stuff care of South America?"

"Possible, if it's our guy."

"Oh, it's our guy."

"How do you know?"

I smiled and clinked glasses with Ron. "I got two limeys lying in our office parking lot says Alexander Montgomery is our guy."

"So what do you propose?" said Ron, finishing his beer.

"Well, I might do like any good Lord of the British Manor would do. I'll go grouse hunting."

"How in Zinfandel's name do you hunt grouse?"

"You beat the bushes with a stick and see what comes flying out."

CHAPTER THIRTY—THREE

Sean Lawry was bunking down in a three-bedroom new-build townhouse in Pembroke Pines off I-75. It wasn't your typical student digs, coming with HOA-supplied gardeners and golf cart paths to the rec center and pool. It was of little surprise that the entry gate welcomed visitors to *Another prestige Rinti development.*

Lawry the younger answered the door in khaki chinos and a white linen shirt. I knew it was him because he shared his uncle's massive chin that jutted out like a banana with a butt crack in it. I glanced at Ron, and he gave me an eyebrow raise that told me he thought the kid dressed better than I did.

"Sean Lawry?" I said.

"Who's asking?"

"Miami Jones. I am assisting with inquiries into the death of Jake Turner."

Lawry stuck his chin out. "Turner?"

"He was a classmate of yours?"

"No."

"No? You didn't go to college with Jake Turner?"

Lawry pushed his lower mandible out further like he had false teeth and frowned, giving him a rather simian look.

"We went to the same school, but we weren't classmates."

"Do you mind if we come in?"

"What for?"

"One of your colleagues has died. You might be able to help figure out why."

Lawry shrugged and said, "I don't see how I can help," but he stepped aside and let us in. The townhouse had brand spanking new cherrywood floors and marble counters. Certainly not builder's standard. There were upgrades galore.

"Nice pad," I said.

"Thanks," said Lawry like he owned it. He walked into the open kitchen and gestured for Ron and me to take the stools at the marble-topped island.

"Just you?" I said.

"Ah, no. I got a roommate."

"Your uncle's place?"

Lawry frowned again. He was going to have a forehead like Saharan dunes before he was thirty if he kept that up.

"No, it's my dad's."

"So you don't have anything to do with your uncle, then?"

"We're family, of course I do. We talk all the time."

"Your dad a buddy of Gino Rinti too?"

"Who did you say you worked for?"

"You're majoring in construction management, right?" said Ron, taking the tag.

Sean turned his focus to Ron and I noticed crow's feet at his eyes. He wasn't quite as young as I expected a college kid to be.

"Yeah, so?"

"So was Jake. But you didn't know him?" said Ron.

"Sure, I knew him. He was a sporto. Everyone knew him. But he was a senior, and I'm a junior, so we didn't have the same classes."

I looked at Ron as if to say, if this kid is a junior, he must have redshirted for five years.

"If you're a junior, how did you come to be doing an internship at Rinti Developments?" I said.

"How did you know about that?"

"It's what I do. So?"

"Yeah, so I did. So what. I'm good at what I do."

"Which is what, exactly?"

He turned from us to the stainless steel fridge and cracked open a Fiji water. He didn't offer it around.

"Look, I know what you think. That my uncle got me the job because of his so-called connections. Well you're wrong. I don't ride no man's coat sleeves. I got that job myself."

"Coattails, not coat sleeves."

"Whatever, *Roget*. I don't need anyone's help."

"You pay rent here?" I said. It was a low blow, but the kid was yanking my chain and I wasn't in any kind of mood for it. I knew he was young and wanted to make his mark on the world, and that couldn't be easy in the shadow of one of the greatest grafters the fine state of Florida had ever known. But he didn't have to be such a jerk about it. One might have argued that I was being a jerk too, and that at my age I should know better, but if testosterone serves one purpose it is to make us remember our glory days when our old bones ache while forgetting the hard knocks that others are yet to feel.

"What is it you want, man?"

"To know anything about Jake Turner that might explain why he got killed."

"Got killed? I heard he OD'ed."

"That's what they say, but I'm not convinced. You ever see him take drugs or act like he was on something?"

"Drugs? Not my area. I got a Porsche. I don't need to get high. But Jake? He was about to finish the best four years of his life, so who knows."

"Why the best four years?"

Sean grinned a wide, lipless smile. "He was a big man on campus 'cause he played lacrosse. Where do you think he was gonna go from there? He was next year's nobody."

"So you didn't get on."

"Like I said, I hardly knew the guy. I saw him a few times around the office over summer, but that's it. Look, I don't want to speak ill of the dead, but we didn't move in the same circles. He just wasn't in the same class. He was never going to be the developer, he was the foreman. Maybe he couldn't handle that." Sean shrugged and sipped his water.

"Did Jake know about the Rinti project at the college?" said Ron.

"No. What project at the college?" He sipped his water.

I didn't have anything further for the kid. I thought about giving him a business card, but Sean Lawry wasn't going to bother remembering anything so I skipped it. Ron seemed to have nothing, so I slapped my hands on the cold marble counter.

"We'll see ourselves out."

Ron and I left Sean Lawry standing behind his island and he made no move to show us out. I got to the door when I decided to do my Columbo.

"One more thing. Where were you the night Jake OD'ed?"

"Here."

"Anyone verify that?"

"My roommate." He turned to the stairs that led up to the bedrooms and yelled. "Elissa!"

A moment later a girl came halfway down the stairs. She was maybe eighteen, pretty with soft blond hair and thin jeans. She was wiping her hands with a chamois, as if she were polishing a car up there. I repeated my question to her.

"We were here," she said.

"All evening?"

"Yep," she said. "Is that all? I need to get finished." She retreated back up the stairs, and I looked at Sean, who raised his eyebrows and smiled.

We were in the car before Ron spoke.

"Pretentious so-and-so," he said.

"I'll say."

"Doesn't make him wrong, though. Jake Turner was in his glory days. He wasn't going to make a living in lacrosse. Who knows what else lay in front of him. Maybe he couldn't handle that."

"I don't buy it."

"Or you don't want to."

"Angela painted a compelling picture. So did the coaches, his team mates. They all suggested he was destined for greater things."

"Maybe Jake knew better, or at least feared it. Means, motive and opportunity. Applies not just to homicide but suicide too. He had the means and opportunity. Maybe a summer full of nepotism and backroom deals told him what he didn't want to know, and gave him his motive."

I took a deep breath and tried to process Ron's mental dump. My mind lacked sharpness and longed for some REM sleep.

"Then why is Pistachio so keen for me to stay away from the case?"

"Maybe he just doesn't want the attention on his business," said Ron. "Let's not jump to any conclusions. Let's see what the other intern says. What was the name again?"

"Alice Chang," I said, as I pulled away from Pembroke Pines and back toward the campus.

If Sean Lawry's residence was the antithesis of student digs, Alice Chang's was the thesis. She lived in the same sort of quad-share dorm that Angela Cassidy lived in, two buildings down from Angel's. Alice's building looked original to the campus, a pebble-encrusted utilitarian box compared to Angel's Spanish architecture. It looked every bit the budget-conscious choice. The girl who answered the door was a golf tee short of five feet tall and wore a Panthers hoodie that might have been stolen from the wardrobe of Active Barbie. Her round face contrasted the square glasses she wore.

"Alice Chang?"

She seemed to shrink an inch or two. "What has happened?"

"Nothing's happened. We just wanted to ask some questions about Jake Turner."

Her eyes opened like saucers and she took half a step back into her dorm.

"I don't know anything."

"You did an internship with him over summer?"

"No. Well, yes, but no."

"Can we talk inside?" I suggested, nodding toward the communal living room. Alice pulled the door tighter against her finch-like frame.

"No, sir, not here." She clicked the door closed on us, and we waited, looking at each other for long enough to think that she wasn't coming back. Then the door opened and Alice stuck her face out.

"You have ID?"

Ron and I both pulled our PI ID cards out of our wallets. They were rarely sighted and in pristine condition. People never asked for ID.

"You're not the police?" said Alice.

"No, ma'am, we're private investigators, assisting with inquiries. We just have a few questions you might be able to answer. We already spoke to the other intern, Sean Lawry." Alice looked at me without blinking or it seemed even breathing for a time, and then took photos of our IDs with her cell phone. She stepped back inside, and then came out with a courier's satchel over her shoulder and a long whistle around her neck.

She led us to the campus library. The building was attempting to mimic the Library of Congress, lots of steps and columns. I expected the interior was more utilitarian than the original in DC, but we never got that far. Alice stopped at the base of the steps.

"What is your question?" she said. She was rather to the point, so I reciprocated.

"You did an internship with Rinti Construction?"

"Rinti Developments."

"Okay. And you're a construction management major?"

"No."

"No? Why did you intern with Rinti?"

"I am studying to become a civil engineer."

"Okay. But you worked with Jake Turner and Sean Lawry over the summer?"

Alice frowned and said, "No."

"No? They did internships this summer too. We know that."

"Yes, they did. In a different area than me."

"So you had no interaction with them at all?"

"I don't associate with those sorts of people."

"What sorts of people? People with drugs? Sporty people?"

She shrugged. "Either of them."

"So you never saw them at Rinti? I didn't think it was that big a place."

"I never said I didn't see them. You asked if I had interactions. I did not."

Pedantic wasn't the word. But I cut her a break, because I assumed that pedantic was a good character trait in a person who would ensure the structural integrity of buildings and bridges. I smiled. Alice did not.

"What did you observe of them?"

"Hubris," she said.

I could see that. Jake Turner was a student-athlete who dealt performance-enhancing drugs to his teammates, and Sean Lawry was a Lawry.

"Did you ever hear anything about a Rinti project here on campus?"

"At the university? There are no current building projects on campus."

"Perhaps a proposed development?"

"No, I don't . . ." She was shaking her head and she stopped. "What?"

"There was a gathering." She paused and blinked hard. It was like listening to Jackie Chan do a reading of Charles Dickens's collected works.

"A gathering?"

"Yes. Post-work on a Friday. Some of the employees and interns gathered for an informal get-together."

"After work drinks," I said.

"If you like."

"And what happened?"

"There was an altercation."

"A fight?"

"Not physically but yes, verbally."

"Who?"

"Turner and Lawry. Well, Lawry, actually. He did most of the yelling."

"Saying what?"

"That Jake was, what's the saying? Out of his league? He said Jake didn't know who he was dealing with, and . . ."

"And?"

"And who is that?" She looked between us across the quad. I turned to see Officer Steele's rotund partner Harris huffing his way across the grass toward us. He pointed at me, but it affected his balance so he dropped his hand and marched onward. I turned to Alice.

"What did Sean say?"

Alice looked at me as if she'd just completed a Rubik's cube in two seconds. Or I had.

"You inquired after a project. That's it, isn't it? Sean said that the project would go ahead despite Jake. He said Jake couldn't and wouldn't stop it. They were both most irritated."

Ron was still facing the quad and he said, "It might be time to think about leaving." I didn't turn to look at Harris. I figured he would be slowing down as he marched across the quad. It was a long, arduous trek across flat grass for him.

"What happened, Alice? After the argument?"

"Neither was prepared to step down, but one of the Rinti employees told them to calm themselves, *chill out* was the phrase he used, and some beer was passed around. I don't partake of alcohol and my ride had arrived, so I left."

"And that was the only interaction you had?"

"Jake was into sports and I don't care for it, so we had nothing in common. I did hear that Rinti Developments was making him a job offer. He seemed as popular there as he was here." She shrugged and rubbed at the whistle around her neck. "And since Sean arrived at the university, well he is the kind of person I avoid." I could hardly blame her for that, and I had just spent five minutes with the kid.

"What do you mean, since he arrived at the university?"

"This is his first year here. He transferred from somewhere in Georgia. I heard there was an incident involving drugs—liquid ecstasy was the rumor. There was a kerfuffle, and his uncle arranged for him to come here."

"Time to go," said Ron. I could hear the wheezing breath of Officer Harris in the background.

"And I must study," said Alice, turning on her heel and heading up the library steps.

Ron and I took off. We didn't run. That was unnecessary. Harris wasn't going to shoot us in the middle of the campus, and he couldn't catch us if we were walking on our hands. We rounded the back side of the library and I glanced back to see the officer leaning against a lamppost, huffing and watching us walk away. We looped around another nameless building and backtracked toward the car.

"So Jake knew," said Ron.

"It would seem."

"And Sean knew he knew. So we can assume he told Rinti."

"Or he told his uncle. Looks like there was a little coattail riding going on after all. Maybe he told his uncle to get in his good books. Either way, Rinti knew."

We got in the Mustang, and I pulled out toward the freeway. Ron did the talking.

"So in addition to Montgomery, who is sending his hoods after you and clearly has a link to Jake, now Rinti does too. Right?"

"Right."

"So we're further behind than we were this morning."

"That's one way of looking at it."

"What's the other way?"

"That's pretty much the only way."

I got onto I-95 and pointed north. "I think we need to mull this one over a beer. To Longboard Kelly's?"

"I'm actually expected at the yacht club," said Ron.

"Someone I know?"

Ron shook his head. "Interview for the position of vice commodore."

"You're serious about that."

"Some members put my name forward. I'd hate to disappoint them."

"In that case," I said, "I'll drop you at the clubhouse, and I'll take care of the ruminating myself tomorrow on my little sojourn upstate."

CHAPTER THIRTY–FOUR

In the morning I put on a sweater and dropped the top on the Mustang and cruised up to St. Augustine in the cool fall air. Although I was still in Florida, St. Augustine marked the beginning of the South for me. The Spanish moss hung low from ancient live oaks. The old town spread like spider's legs from Castillo de San Marcos. I passed the imposing stone fort that had been occupied in one form or another since the Spanish arrived 450 years earlier. The downtown area was walkable and open, so I parked my car a few blocks from the fort and took off on foot. The dominant structure in town was Flagler College. Henry Flagler conceived the grand Spanish renaissance complex as the Ponce de Leon Hotel in the 1800s, as the starting point for his railway to Miami. Seemed he owned a great deal in the spots anyone might like to get off the train too. But now the grand building was a college named in his honor. I wasn't sure if Dr. Millet would have loved it or hated it. There was truckloads of that old world charm his office cum library told me he pined for. And its town center locale meant there was no room for sports fields. They were a few miles away on the outskirts of town. But the location also meant there was no room for expansion to create Millet's mega-campus. It would be tough to house biotech facilities in heritage listed buildings.

I looped around and ambled across the fine West lawn before the school, easy under patchy skies. Emily Getz stood waiting for me beside Kenan Hall. She had shoulder-length curly hair that reminded me of an osprey nest, and although fit like Kim Rose, Emily was broader, stronger. A Clydesdale to Kim's thoroughbred. She gave me a polite if guarded smile as we shook hands. She directed me back to Valencia and onto Cordova Street. We made our way to a small restaurant called The Floridian, and sat in a small room with a rowboat pinned to the ceiling. It was one of those places that used local producers and charged a premium for it, which always worried the hell out of me. Emily ordered a shrimp salad and I had something called a chipwich, which was a chicken sandwich with tomato, blue cheese and arugula, and potato chips smashed into it. First bite was dry, like they'd seasoned the chicken but forgot the mayo. The second bite put me into taste heaven. I had my eyes closed as I chewed when Emily spoke.

"So you went to college with Kim."

I opened my eyes. "How do you know that?"

"After you called, I called her."

"Cautious."

"Forgive me if I don't take some stranger at his word."

"Fair enough," I said through chip-crusted lips.

"You guys were close?"

"Back in the day."

"She never mentioned you."

"She ever mention anybody?" I said.

Emily looked at me with steel-gray eyes and the same intensity as Kim. I took a bite of my sandwich and let her size me up.

"Kim was a bit confused as to why you would want to talk to me," she said, stabbing a shrimp.

"Overview," I mumbled. "Just trying to understand the playing field."

"To mix a metaphor."

I smiled. "I do that."

"So what do you want to know?"

I sipped on some iced tea and wondered exactly what it was I wanted from Emily. I really didn't know.

"You played together."

"Olympics and World Cup."

"What position did you play?"

"Center back."

"You head the ball a lot?"

Emily frowned. "Plenty. You asking if I've got brain damage?"

"I can see you don't have brain damage. I just wondered if it hurt, heading a soccer ball like that."

"Almost every time, but you get used to it."

"Not sure I would," I said, taking another bite.

"Kim said you played football at college."

I nodded.

"You ever get tackled?"

"In practice."

"It never hurt?"

"Sure."

"But you got used to it, right?"

"I learned to live with it."

"Close enough," she said, eating some salad greens. "But that's not what you really want to know."

I brushed my mouth with a paper napkin and leaned on the table. Emily wasn't just wary, she was shrewd and smart and could read me with her eyes closed.

"Do you use performance-enhancing drugs in your soccer program?"

"No," she said. Her eyes didn't waver.

"How can you be sure?"

"Because I test. I removed a student-athlete from my roster two years ago for breaches."

"That's college policy?"

"That's my policy. And the college agrees, yes. Mr. Jones, we're not here just to teach athletes to win, but to win the right way."

"So you follow USADA guidelines."

"And then some. This is not about keeping the school out of trouble. This is about keeping the bad apples out of the school."

I studied her face and found no trace of irony.

"How hard would it be for a student-athlete to cheat the system if you were just doing the bare minimum?"

"It would go from impossible to possible, but not easy."

"And if you weren't doing the bare minimum?"

"What's your point?"

"Did you ever see any PED use when you played soccer?"

"I'm not going to answer that."

"So yes. What about Kim Rose? Did you ever see her do PEDs?"

"Do you even know Kim?"

"I did, a long time ago."

"And do you think she'd cheat like that?"

"People do all sorts of things under pressure."

"Not Kim. She was gifted, but she also worked hard."

"Sometimes hard work isn't enough."

"Besides which, Kim was a natural athlete. She hardly ever got injured and she could run all day."

"They used to say the same thing about Lance Armstrong."

"But his teammates knew, as it turns out. Didn't they? I knew Kim—I played, trained, traveled and lived with her for the better part of a decade. She's clean." She glared at me. "I'm surprised you don't think so."

"I do think so. But I don't think everyone in the program was. Law of averages."

The waiter arrived and bussed our table and refilled our iced tea. The interruption allowed an uncomfortable silence to descend on the conversation. I like uncomfortable silences because I rarely find them as uncomfortable as the other person. Most people try to wait, then they squirm, and fight the compulsion to fill the dirty void, and then the compulsion wins. Kim Rose never felt uncomfortable with silence, back in the day. I was hoping that not all female footballers were the same. They weren't.

"So let's say hypothetically, that some girls flirted with the rules on drugs, what of it today?"

"Let's say hypothetically you knew they were doing it. Would you tell?"

"I told you already, I expelled a player for it."

"That's now. I'm talking ten hypothetical years ago."

Emily went quiet and stared into her iced tea.

"Let's say, for argument's sake, you didn't tell anyone. Why wouldn't you then but would now?" I said.

"Hypothetically, you might not have thought it was right, but you didn't feel like you had the power to stop it. It might have kept you up at night, so you might've convinced yourself it wasn't so wrong or so bad. That it was more like medicine than a bad thing. And now you might know better. And you might be in a position to do something about it."

"And what about Kim?"

She sipped her tea and frowned.

"How well did you know Kim?"

"As well as anyone I met at college. Better maybe."

"You date?"

"No."

Emily gave me a knowing grin. "Why?"

"It never really came up. We had our common ground, and there was no impetus to go further."

"And that's the thing. Kim was a great teammate but a lousy friend. Everything revolved around the team and the team's performance. If she knew of someone doping, she wouldn't have thought about it more than it was just that teammate preparing the best she could; doing the best for the team. To think more would be to think like a friend, and that was never Kim's strong suit."

I took a long, slow sip on my iced tea and thought back to my time with Kim. Emily's words seeped into me like cheap wine on a linen tablecloth.

I paid for lunch, and we wandered back to the college. A bank of clouds hovered offshore, and I suspected I might have to put the roof up on the way home. I offered Emily a ride, but she had her car nearby and needed to get back to her office out near the sports fields.

"You staying in town?" she said.

"Gotta get back to West Palm."

"Long drive just for lunch."

"It was an enlightening meal." I shook her hand and left her by Kenan Hall and wandered back to my car. I dropped the top, slipped in some Kenny Chesney and headed out toward I-95 with the feeling that I had all the puzzle pieces in hand, but no idea yet how they fit together.

CHAPTER THIRTY-FIVE

The sun had set by the time I got home, and the Mustang's headlights played across the black Mercedes parked in my driveway. I pulled in behind the Merc and left the lights on it. The license plate was Florida, something about saving manatees. I couldn't see anyone in the vehicle. I cut the engine and slid out of my car, and let my eyes adjust to the dark. The Mercedes was a big four-door sedan, like a German version of the Lincoln town car. There was no movement in it, or around my yard, save the palm trees swaying in a breeze that was yet to bring rain but smelled as if it surely would. I stepped between the cars and across my lawn, keeping off the path to the front door. Once I got in view of the door I could see a heavy-set guy in a leather jacket leaning against it. He was smoking a cigarette that was blowing away toward the Intracoastal, and making no attempt to hide himself. He nodded toward me and dropped the cigarette and crushed it with his shoe. I took a couple steps toward him. My feet sank into my lawn, and I wondered when the gardener was due. As I got closer I noted that this guy was different from the limeys in the office parking lot. He was olive-skinned and tanned further, and had heavy eyebrows. Perhaps one of Pistachio's local crew.

"Where you bin? We bin waiting," he said. So local was out. The accent was old Brooklyn. Perhaps a transplant, one of those guys who loves the Florida sun but refuses to give up the leather coat regardless.

"I can't be too hard to find. You did it."

He grinned. "I heard you was a wise guy."

"Funny, I heard the same thing about you."

He pointed his finger at me, like a gun. "That's a good one. Wiseguy. I get it." He nodded and grinned again. Then something exploded across my shoulders, and I rocketed face first into the lawn. Pain seared across my back and shot up my neck, and breath came in short raspy stabs. I felt like I'd been smashed across the back with a club. The grass was soft and moist, and it felt like I was breathing it in instead of air. I was losing control, panicking. I rolled onto my side to escape the grass and then lost the ability to breathe completely. Now I knew I was either drowning or I was winded, so I got on my hands and knees and tried to relax. Danielle had taken me to a yoga class once, and I recalled the position being called downward-facing dog. I felt like a mutt that had just received a serving of the owner's boot, but my chest relaxed and my breathing kicked back in. My vision was blurred, and I blinked several times hard. It didn't clear things much, but enough to see the second guy step into view. He was as dark as the first guy, but wore a large Florida Panthers NHL jersey. He tapped a black hockey stick into his beefy palm. It hurt to talk, but I did it anyway.

"You hit like a girl." I was pretty certain I was concussed, and I was going to use that as my excuse for such a lame comment. For trash talk it was edible rice paper. And Danielle could hit a fast-pitch softball into tomorrow, so it wasn't even accurate. Plus, it didn't endear me to the guy. He swung the stick at me again. I saw it coming so I dropped away, but the blade glanced off my shoulder and splayed me out like a Portuguese chicken. Then he kicked me in the side of the stomach. It must have been the side my lunch was residing on because stabbing pain and chip sandwich launched its way up and out onto my lawn. When I finished I rolled over wearing a mask of vomit like a woman's face cream. The two guys stood over me. The guy who hit me had the stick resting across his shoulders, like he was stretching on the bench. The guy in the coat got on his haunches.

"You gotta learn to leave well enough alone, *capiche*?"

I blinked like an animatronic robot at Disney.

"*Capiche*? You guys really say that?"

The guy grinned again. "I like you. You got spunk." He stood up and nodded at his buddy, who lifted the hockey stick off his shoulders. The pain receptors in my brain cursed my stupid tongue and tensed for more impact. But the guy walked away. It hurt like hell, but I sat up and watched him get into my Mustang, fire it up and peel out my driveway backward, tires screeching for mercy.

"You're stealing my car? This is how Pistachio works?"

He grinned again. "I surely don't know what you're talking about." He looked up and turned his eyes to the street. I heard the rumble of the engine before I saw the headlights. It sounded a lot more impressive from the outside, and was one of the reasons I had bought the car. The lights grew bigger as the Mustang sped down my dark street, the placid homes of Singer Island looking on. My house was at the end of the cul-de-sac, on the edge of the Intracoastal. The car sped right at me, and then at the last second turned away toward the huge royal palm in my front yard.

"Are you kidding me?" was all I could think of to say. The Mustang hit the palm tree at full throttle. There was a sickening crunch of steel and fibrous wood as the tree gave way some and the car gave way a whole lot. The hood caved in to a huge Vshape, and the inside of the vehicle exploded in white as the airbags deployed. Steam and the hiss of hydraulics rose from the crushed vehicle. For a moment the night was still with the sound of frogs, cicadas and weeping oil, and then the occupant of the car began thrashing at the airbags until the door cracked open. The guy kicked at the broken door until it yielded. He unfurled himself from the wreck and strode toward me with a smile like it was his first day out on parole. He walked easily, as if he had been bouncing on a trampoline rather than totaling a car against a tree, and I got the creeping feeling that this wasn't his first time. He turned toward the driveway and bent down to retrieve the hockey stick that he must have dropped before getting into my car. I had to give him credit for not taking the weighty projectile into the vehicle with him, given what he was planning to do. He spun and carried the stick back to the car, where he smashed every window that wasn't yet in pieces, then he started in on the rear of the car which looked completely undamaged.

"Are you kidding me?" I said more for myself than the audience. The guy in the coat came around in front of me.

"Forget the college. Don't ever go there again. They open a hospital on campus and you have a heart attack, make sure they take you someplace else. You ever have a kid goes to college, send him to Harvard. You got it?"

I just looked at the guy. I had nothing to say. The guy turned, and we watched his pal finish off the rear panels, and then take a switchblade to the canvas roof and tires. When he was satisfied, the guy in the coat whistled and the roof ripper stopped, looked up and then came forward like a Labrador. They both got in the Mercedes and pulled out of the driveway. I noted pointlessly that the guy in the coat was driving. I felt bile and anger in my throat as the Merc did a gentle K turn in the cul-de-sac. I stood up like a newborn lamb, stumbled to the rock garden beneath the wounded royal palm and picked up a baseball-sized piece of quartz. The Mercedes pulled away and I flung the rock with everything I had, which wasn't much. My vision blurred and nausea rose with the effort. But even in my incapacitated state I still had some stuff. The rock flew into the night and hit the rear taillight, smashing it. The driver didn't miss a beat, and the Merc pulled away into nothing. I collapsed back on the grass, spent. I thought I could hear distant sirens, and I closed my eyes as the heavens decided to do what they had promised to do all day, and the rain fell down on me in sheets.

CHAPTER THIRTY-SIX

I spent the next thirty-six hours in bed, drinking green tea and munching Vicodin. The Riviera Beach cops had arrived promptly and upon seeing the house, the car and me on the lawn, had called the sheriff's office and Danielle arrived shortly thereafter. The cops figured I was drunk and had smashed my own car, but had the good grace to wait for Danielle before they did anything about it. She backed my assertion that I had not had a drop of alcohol, and the cops said I'd need to prove that if I hoped to make an insurance claim, so I gave them a breath test and surprised everyone with a negative result. I explained the story of Pistachio and his hoods, but I left out most of the details about the college and Jake Turner, so it must have sounded like BS. The EMT guys turned up and suggested I go to the hospital for observation, but I refused, so they wrapped my ribs and slipped me the Vicodin. Danielle put me to bed, and I woke early. My head was clearer, but my back felt like I'd been in a bomb blast. The cracked ribs only hurt when I breathed. Danielle stayed with me, kept me from taking more painkillers than I should and away from the booze cabinet, and generally did what she did regularly, which was make me wonder how I got so lucky in the first place. It was the following morning before she left, having confirmed that the worst of the pain was gone and my head was clear enough to not suffer an aneurysm or OD on painkillers and scotch. She slipped into her uniform and kissed my forehead and headed off to her shift. I slept for a while and then got up. It was quite a process, like I'd aged fifty years in a day. I was stooped and shuffled into the kitchen for a glass of water and to call Ron.

"I'm glad you're still with us," he said.

"Only just."

"I dropped by yesterday, but you were out of it."

I had no recollection of his visit.

"I wanted to let you know I got some info back on the Lawry boy, Sean," said Ron.

I had a vague recollection of meeting the kid. "Aha."

"Turns out Alice Chang's gossip vine is good. I went through back channels and wound up with a copy of the arrest report. Seems Sean was at a frat party in Georgia, and a girl got doped."

"Rohypnol?"

"No, Alice Chang was right again. She called it liquid ecstasy. The arresting officer called it Liquid X. From what they told me, it dissolves like Rohypnol, and it's salty. But they got a toxicology report says the girl was also full of tequila."

"Isn't ecstasy an upper rather than something you'd dope someone with?"

"Not my area," said Ron.

"So what happened?"

"Apparently Sean planned to have his way but got interrupted by some of the girl's friends. Long story short, cops come, arrest Sean, but since he was interrupted nothing illegal happened, just the drugs charge. And the cops up there figure it was slipped into her drink, but they can't trace the drink or the glass back to Sean. So when Senator Lawry turns up, he promises that he's taking the kid back to Florida, so they put it into the too-hard basket and let Sean go."

"So he's a wannabe rapist. What a quality DNA line that is."

"Quite right. But since getting back to Florida, the kid seems to have flown under the radar. No trouble I can find."

"Maybe his uncle put the fear of God in him. Either way, we got more immediate issues. I need to get a bead on this Pistachio guy. Where he goes, what his movements are."

"I'll see what I can find. Was it the same guys you ran into in the office parking lot?"

"No, I doubt those guys will be up and at 'em just yet. These guys were Brooklyn locals. I guess they've given up on the stuff I flushed. They were making a point."

"I wonder if their advice might be worth heeding. This job at the university isn't paying enough to make it worth getting dead."

"And if they'd just beat me up, I might agree. But they trashed my car, Ron. Now I'm just really annoyed."

"I get it," he said. "Let me get back to you. Get some rest."

I sat on the sofa and stared for the longest time at the space in my living room where a normal person might keep the television. I was concerned that Pistachio not only knew where I lived, but had the *cojones* to do what he'd done, so far from his turf in Miami. My cell phone rang. It was Sally. He'd heard the news through his extensive vine, and wanted to make sure I was still ticking. He said he'd send over a fruit basket and assist with any retribution that needed handing out. I told him I was too sore and he was too old for that kind of silliness, and he told me to keep my head down and enjoy the fruit. Shortly after Ron called back. I put him on speaker because it hurt too much to hold the phone to my ear.

"Pistachio, aka Alexander Montgomery, seems to be attempting to ingratiate himself into South Florida society. He attends the opening of a champagne bottle apparently, mostly in

Miami. One contact at a club for the well-heeled down there told me *there's a difference between getting in and being welcomed*. But you'll never guess what guest list he's on tonight."

"I'm having trouble spelling cat right now."

"Then I'll guess for you. He'll be at The Breakers."

"Slumming it in Palm Beach? What's the do?"

"You'll love this. It's a fundraiser for the governor. Word is he's considering a presidential run."

"Save us. So how do we get in?"

"Whoa, boy. You're not in any condition to leave home, let alone hobnob with the hoi polloi."

"I'll be fine. More or less. But I can't let this rest. I need to get in this guy's face."

"Sometimes you really are a macho moron, you know that, right?"

"And sometimes I'm a teddy bear. How do we get in?"

"Best way I can think of, take a room at the hotel. Then wing it."

"Make it so. What time's check in?"

"Usually about four o'clock."

"Pick me up at three thirty."

CHAPTER THIRTY–SEVEN

The Breakers is Palm Beach wrapped up in a building. It's old money, expensive and stuffy. It has views to die for, and the walls ooze old-fashioned class. That class showed in the security guard at the gatehouse who never even batted an eyelid at Ron's beat-up, '88 Corolla, or the fact its inhabitants claimed to be checking in to a room that cost over a thousand bucks a night. He checked us off on his computer and directed us to the valet. The room was on the low end of the scale for the establishment, with a queen bed and a view over the pool and cabanas. If one stuck one's head out the window one could catch a glimpse of the Atlantic Ocean. I lay on the bed and took two more Vicodin while Ron did a recon tour of the building. He must have found a bar or some nice ladies, or both, because he took his sweet time coming back, and when he did, he had that look in his eye.

"I can't believe I don't get here more often," he said, grinning like a kid in FAO Schwarz.

"Keep your kit on for five minutes and tell me."

"Killjoy. So the governor's function is in the Mediterranean ballroom and courtyard. There's the usual gubernatorial security, but I just had a drink at the bar with a lovely filly who can get us access to the courtyard. Getting into the ballroom will set us back two thousand apiece."

"I don't think I want to get that close to the governor, and I'm sure the feeling's mutual."

"We might catch Pistachio on his way in or out."

"Which would be fine if we knew what he looked like."

"I think I can help with that," said Ron.

We wandered into the Mediterranean courtyard in our tuxedos, looking a million dollars. I felt like James Bond, except I wasn't carrying a gun or a license to kill. A tux was about as far away from my usual shorts and shirt as I could get, but my mentor, Lenny Cox, had insisted that a tux was mandatory for our line of work. Lenny always said there wasn't a room in Palm Beach you couldn't get into in a tuxedo. It didn't hurt that Ron had a socialite on his arm. He had introduced her as Lady Cassandra and offered no further explanation, but her elegant blue dress and shoulder-length bottle blonde hair pegged her as a wealthy divorcee or widow. It didn't seem prudent to ask which. But a simple *they're with me* from her and we were in. I ordered two champagnes and a martini. The Vicodin and martini did the trick so I could stand up straight without pain. I let Ron wander the courtyard with Lady Cassandra, and I took a chair in the corner and watched the party. There was a light breeze coming in off the ocean, keeping the night brisk. A hint of grilled chicken satay hung on the air. As tempting as the martini was, and as much as it put me in character with my sweet tux, I hung off it. Ron and his escort sauntered back to me.

"That's your man, there," she said in a voice dripping of Georgia plantations and summers in Europe. I followed her eyes. Alexander Montgomery was holding court with four other men by a tiki lamp. They were all in penguin suits and puffing on fat cigars. Even with the rich and fabulous, Florida's laws drove the smokers outside. Montgomery was average height, with sandy white hair and the beginnings of a good set of jowls. From the way the gathering hung on his words I could see he held the power in the group, as well as a fair measure of charisma. I turned to Lady Cassandra.

"I trust this won't get you in any trouble."

She smiled. "Young man, at my age I could do with some trouble. Besides, I don't believe the society of our little island is improved by the likes of him."

I smiled and nodded and crossed the room at pace. I headed straight for Alexander Montgomery but had two other guys in my peripheral vision. They were vaguely the same, in the ways that a person would notice straight off the bat. Like their regular suits, conservative ties and stony expressions. They were the same except for the focus of their attention. One stood by the entrance to the ballroom, watching the gathering in the courtyard from the top of the stairs. The other guy stood in the corner of the courtyard next to a large palm, not taking his eyes off Alexander Montgomery. I hit Montgomery's gaggle of chums and squeezed in between two shoulders. They all held shot glasses, and I could smell tequila. As expected the group fell silent and I felt all eyes on me, but I didn't take mine off Montgomery. He frowned in a way that suggested he was trying to place me but failing. I nodded like we were old buddies.

"Pistachio," I said.

The frown deepened. "What?"

"I think the phrase you are looking for is *I beg your pardon*."

He grinned. "Have we met?"

"No. But I did meet the guys you sent around to my house the other night to beat me up and smash my car to pieces. Thanks for that, by the way. I've been looking at a new car, and now my insurance is going to pay for it."

"I'm afraid I don't have the foggiest what you're talking about," he said in his English accent.

"Sure you do. You recall two of your limey brothers you sent round to my office. They didn't come away so well. No? Well, surely you remember the drugs you're peddling on the university campus? And Jake Turner? He was the kid who refused to sell your drugs and then died of a suspicious overdose."

Montgomery's jaw clenched, and he glanced over his shoulder. The hired help in the corner stepped out from his post as the circle of men spread to leave me as a group of one. Pistachio's security guy strode to me and put a hand on my elbow.

"Let's go," he said.

"No, I'm good," I said. "You go on without me." The grip on my elbow tightened, but it was still the only part of my body that didn't hurt.

"Excuse me," said the other security guy, who had stepped down from the ballroom entrance. I noted Ron and Lady Cassandra just beyond him.

"Get lost," said the guy holding my elbow.

"I'm afraid I can't do that, sir," said the other guy. "I'm with the governor's security detail. I have reason to believe you are carrying a firearm." He believed that because Ron had told him, on my instruction. There was no way a hood like Pistachio would go anywhere without a bodyguard and no way that bodyguard wouldn't be armed. But there was also no way that the FDLE team tasked with the governor's security would be happy with a concealed weapon in the room that wasn't one of theirs.

"I've got a permit," said the guy, dropping the grip on my elbow.

"I'm sure you do, but I can't allow an uncleared firearm inside the security cordon." He turned to Montgomery. "And we don't want a scene, do we?"

Montgomery grinned again, and then threw back the shot of tequila he had in his hand and thumped the glass on the cocktail table beside him. He smacked his lips and grinned.

"We were just heading inside anyway." He looked at the bodyguard. "Why don't you wait out with the car, Nigel." The other men in Montgomery's posse downed their shots, puffed their chests and followed their guy into the ballroom. The two security men stared each other down, and I could smell the testosterone in the air. Finally the governor's man spoke.

"Let's take a look at that concealed carry permit then," he said, leading Montgomery's man away from the courtyard. I watched them go, planted to the spot by pain and adrenaline and martini. Ron came over to me.

"I think you got his attention," he said.

"You think?"

"Question is, do you really want it?"

"That's a big fat no," I said, rolling my shoulders and wincing at the pain. I stepped to the cocktail table and slipped a tequila glass into a freezer bag in my pocket. "But the only way to catch a weasel is to draw him out of his hole."

"What happened to the grouse?"

"I am nothing if not a mixed metaphor."

"Well, let's hope he's not more patient than we give him credit for."

I shrugged my eyebrows in response and patted his arm. He looked good in the penguin suit, almost distinguished. I slipped my key card into his jacket pocket.

"The room is all yours."

"What will you do?"

"Head to the bar for one more of those martinis, then Danielle's coming to pick me up."

"You'll be okay?" he said.

"Time will tell, my friend. Time will tell."

CHAPTER THIRTY—EIGHT

When I woke the next morning I was alone and the Vicodin and martinis had worn off. I lay still in bed. There was a swarm of bees in my gut, but none of my muscles hurt as long as I didn't move. My head was clearer than it deserved to be, but I put that down to my ever-vigilant girlfriend who had collected me from the Seafood Bar at The Breakers and deposited me in bed before returning to her shift. I gave her the rundown of my *tête-à-tête* with Alexander Montgomery. She gave me an *I hope you know what you are doing* look and a goodnight kiss. Lying in bed with the bees reminded me that maybe I didn't know as much as I thought I did. Driving Pistachio out from under his rock was a risky strategy, but I figured I had no hope of playing on his turf, so I had to get him out in the open. Besides, the visits from his henchmen had the potential to grow tired very quickly. I rolled with a groan onto my side and pushed myself to sit up. The vertigo had gone, but the pain still bit into my shoulders. I took a deep breath and grimaced and stood up. I found that I was dressed in a pair of boxer shorts that I recalled neither buying nor putting on the previous evening, but as they would save me bending over I decided to go with them.

I padded out to the kitchen, put some coffee on and took a couple of ibuprofen. The coffee machine was giving its final gurgle and splatter when the doorbell rang. My shoulders tensed at the sound. I really wasn't in the mood for another beating just yet. I didn't move immediately, as I had visions of my Glock handgun sitting in the gun safe in my office. My car was in pieces in a wrecking yard, so if I were quiet, perhaps they'd figure I wasn't home. The coffee machine finished coughing up the last of its brew, and I vigorously pursued my strategy of keeping quiet, until I was interrupted by someone banging on the rear sliding door of my house. My open-plan living room and kitchen exposed me to the patio and Intracoastal beyond, which was normally the best thing about the place, but proved to be a bummer when I was trying to hide. I turned to the patio and saw the sly grin of Detective Ronzoni. He wore his stock JC Penney suit, gray on gray, with a yellow tie featuring a large-mouth bass. The bass sat on top of Ronzoni's belly, making it look like it was staring up at the sky. Ronzoni resembled a tulip bulb in a cheap suit. I padded over and slid the door open.

"Go right, then right again, left at Route 1, then left over the Flagler Memorial Bridge and you'll find Palm Beach."

"I know where Palm Beach is, smart guy."

"So I wonder to myself how a Palm Beach detective finds himself in Riviera Beach? We have a police department here you know."

"I've had a complaint." He smiled.

"If you insist on wearing fish ties, that's gonna happen."

He glanced at the largemouth on his belly. "I happen to have won this tie."

"What was second prize, two ties?"

He took a second to mull that comment over, and then gave me an ironic grin.

"Hilarious. We've received a complaint against you."

"Well, you better come in then, before the neighbors start talking." I turned and wandered back into the kitchen. Ronzoni pulled the door closed and followed.

"You want some water, Zamboni?"

"Ronzoni. And yes."

I poured Ronzoni some water from the door of the fridge, dropped in some ice cubes and handed him a glass. Word around the traps was that Ronzoni didn't have sweat glands or saliva glands or some such thing, so he had to regularly drink water. Either way I didn't offer coffee despite the fresh pot.

"Let me get a shirt on," I said.

"Please," said Ronzoni, sipping his water.

I grabbed a tee from my bedroom and with considerable effort pulled on a pair of chinos, and then returned to the kitchen to pour myself a coffee.

"So tell me about this complaint," I said, sipping the black brew and feeling it course into my bloodstream.

"We received a complaint regarding malicious vehicular damage."

"And this was so important you couldn't use the phone?"

"This was an important resident."

"Aren't they all important in Palm Beach?"

"They are."

"So who was this resident?"

"I'm not at liberty to say at this stage."

I sipped my coffee. "So what's the beef, in English."

"You smashed the taillight of the complainant's Mercedes."

"And how did I do that?"

"You threw a rock, or some similar projectile."

"And there is a witness to that?"

"Yes."

I sipped my coffee. "All right, Detective, what's the deal? I haven't smashed any taillights with a…" I stared into Ronzoni's dark eyes as I realized that I had smashed a Mercedes taillight with a rock, shortly after Montgomery's men had smashed me and my Mustang into pulp.

"Montgomery? You're following up a complaint from Alexander Montgomery?"

"I don't know who you are talking about."

"Doesn't he live in Miami? What's that got to do with the Palm Beach PD?"

"Who are you talking about, Jones?"

I slammed my coffee mug onto the counter. "So he got his goons to file a complaint. But they sure as hell don't live in Palm Beach."

"Jones, how many people have you annoyed this week?"

I frowned at Ronzoni. "What the hell is going on?"

Ronzoni hoisted himself onto one of my barstools. "Who is Alexander Montgomery and what have you done to him?"

I looked at my coffee and then back at Ronzoni. He wasn't always the brightest bulb, and sarcasm went by him like a small town two miles from the interstate, but he was a good cop, determined and mostly honest. I had no intention of sharing everything with him, but I figured it couldn't hurt to bring him a little into the loop, especially while the promise of further injury to property and person lingered over me. I gave him the overview of my retention by the university, the overdose death of Jake Turner and my uncovering of the drug chain led by Alexander Montgomery, aka Pistachio.

"But that's a nut," said Ronzoni.

"Tell me something I don't know."

"Why would you call yourself after a nut?"

"I'm told it's all about branding."

"If you say so. How'd you find the guy? You're not exactly Mr. Collegiate."

"I found a source on campus. A student. She got me in."

"Her name?"

"Nope."

"She deal?"

"Nope."

"Okay." He leaned back in his stool and smiled.

"You really are a trouble magnet, aren't you," he said.

"It comes with the territory. Not everyone appreciates being investigated."

"Don't I know it. But you've got a talent. You've annoyed someone not even related to your case."

"How so?"

Ronzoni finished his water and gestured for another. I took his glass to the fridge and poured some more. When I brought it back to him he wore a look on his face like he was enjoying knowing something I didn't and he wasn't sure if he wanted to break the magic by sharing. I watched him sip the water, and then look at me.

"So?" I said.

"Does the name Rinti mean anything to you?"

"Senior or Junior?"

"So it does."

"I've met Bruno once or twice, years ago. But not the son."

"Gino. Well, it turns out it was his Mercedes you damaged."

"Allegedly. But he doesn't live in Palm Beach, does he?"

"No, he's based in Miami. But Senior now lives on the island."

"That's just great. First he ruins the Miami skyline, then he bugs out to Palm Beach." I went to sip my coffee but I'd lost interest in it.

"So how did you become the messenger boy for the Rintis?"

"I would question the direction you are taking this conversation, Jones. I am here as a courtesy, both to a resident of Palm Beach and to you. So don't push it."

"Okay. But I wouldn't have thought Rinti was Palm Beach material."

"Anyone with money is Palm Beach material. But there is welcomed and there is tolerated."

"I'm hearing that a lot."

"I'm sure Rinti is the latter."

"So what happens now?"

Ronzoni slipped off his stool and polished off his water in one long gulp, like a camel filling its hump.

"Now, I go back to my desk and write up my report. I assume you can verify that you were not in Palm Beach during the incident?"

"Paramedics can confirm I was unconscious on my front lawn, and Riviera Beach PD can confirm my car was smashed to pieces. By Rinti's men, it turns out."

"If you want to file a complaint, talk to the local boys. That's not my concern."

"Not worth the trouble."

"Fine. Then case closed. Rinti will have to take civil action, which I doubt he will." Ronzoni walked back to the sliding door. "I think he was sending a message. You sure you don't know why he's got a beef with you?"

"Nothing comes to mind."

Ronzoni shrugged and slipped through the door and wandered away across the patio and around my house. I stood with the door open, the soft breeze sending briny air to me, and pondered the idea that it had been Rinti's men who had beaten me and my Mustang, and consequently I had beaten Pistachio's bushes somewhat unnecessarily. And instead of having one lunatic criminal after my hide, I had two. And Rinti clearly had more to gain from the university development than I anticipated.

Or more to lose. Either way, a vacation to the Australian outback was starting to look like a good option.

I closed and locked the door and returned to the kitchen. I poured the rest of my coffee down the sink and mulled over whether another visit to the campus was the dumbest thing I could do. Clearly *El Presidente* Millet had passed on my news to Rinti. That made me like the good doctor even less, and he wasn't exactly on my Christmas card list to begin with. I was considering a shower and a leisurely drive down to Lauderdale when I was startled by another bang on my sliding door. I looked up to see Detective Ronzoni again standing on my back patio. His grin was gone.

"Let me guess, Colombo, one last question."

"What was the name of the student, your source at the university?"

"I'm not giving you a name, Detective."

"Let me put it this way then. Does the name Angela Cassidy mean anything to you?"

I felt all the blood in me sink to my feet. I must have lost color because Ronzoni lurched forward as if I were about to faint.

"Get your shoes on," he said. "I'll drive."

CHAPTER THIRTY–NINE

Ronzoni didn't drive fast. That was a bad sign. Cops like to drive fast, just because they can. Except when they really don't want to get to where they're going. He told me he had heard a call across the radio from the PBSO regarding a college student and it had caught his attention because we'd just been talking about the college. He then told me he'd requested a name and the name that came back was Angela Cassidy. That's all he told me. We got in the car, and Ronzoni called in that Palm Beach PD was en route to the scene with relevant intel. *Roger that*, was the reply.

We didn't speak for the next ninety minutes. Ronzoni headed down I-95 to Broward County, and then cut west along I-595 and turned in a big U back north along Route 25. He pulled off the main road on to a service road, where we could see a fleet of Palm Beach County Sheriff's vehicles about a mile down. The area was as flat as a griddle pan and sticky hot. There wasn't a building our side of the horizon, at least not one big enough to see. A channel of water ran parallel to the service road. The whole area was essentially a managed swamp, part of the Everglades that had been tamed to provide irrigation. Ronzoni parked at a haphazard angle on the side of the road and we stepped from the car. The sky was cloudless, and I wished I'd brought sunglasses. Ronzoni flashed his badge and asked for the detective in charge. A deputy I didn't recognize pointed us down the bank. We ducked under the yellow tape marking the scene and edged our way toward the water. Half a dozen people were standing around. Three uniformed deputies, a woman in a skirt and rubber boots, a guy with a camera and another guy in a suit. We headed for the suit. He saw Ronzoni and nodded.

"Burke," said Ronzoni.

"Ronzoni." Burke looked at me. His suit was blue but came from the same collection as Ronzoni's, and his hair was balding and close-cropped.

"Miami," he said.

I just nodded. I wasn't feeling very chatty. I'd met Burke before, at PBSO functions and barbecues that Danielle had dragged me along to. I found him to be an earnest but competent guy. Burke looked back to Ronzoni.

"You got something for me?" said Burke. There was often flow across jurisdictions and departments, between the police who focused on the incorporated towns that paid for them and the sheriff's office who patrolled the unincorporated parts of the county. Crime was rarely so easily pigeonholed.

"Not sure. Jones here might have something. What's the story?"

"Homicide. Caucasian female. Age twenty. Single shot to the side of the head. This is a stormwater treatment area. One of their guys found the body this morning."

"You got a name already?"

"She had ID in her jeans. Student card. Name's Angela Cassidy. Ring any bells?"

Both detectives looked at me. I nodded.

"I know an Angela Cassidy."

"Friend or client?" said Burke.

"Source."

The woman in the rubber boots marched up to us and spoke to Burke.

"Can we get her out of here now before she heats up like a hot pocket?"

"One sec," said Burke. "You want to see, or no?" he said to me.

I nodded.

We trudged across damp grass to the black canvas sheet that covered the body.

"We haven't met," said the woman, extending her hand. I took it and she gripped hard. Not at all feminine. A woman in a man's domain, walking the fine line that Danielle trod every day.

"Lorraine Catchitt, like what you do with a baseball, not what a cat does in the litter tray." She smiled. She had soft features hardened by too much time in the Florida sun.

"Miami Jones."

She flopped her head to one side, and I noticed her short ponytail was tied by a rubber band.

"Ah, I thought I recognized you. You're Danielle Castle's squeeze."

I nodded without enthusiasm. I didn't hang around dead bodies enough to appreciate gallows humor.

"I'm a forensic investigator with the ME's office." She bent over and pulled the sheet back with a flourish, like a magician. I fought the compulsion to throw up. Angela Cassidy lay on her back, staring at the sky. One side of her head was matted black, thick strands of hair braided together by congealed blood. Her face was unmarked. But it was not peaceful. It was twisted into a frozen, angry pose, like a photo snapped in the midst of an argument.

"That's Angel," I said.

I sat on my haunches, looking at her. She was an intelligent, beautiful, young kid. And had she never met me, she still would be. I pushed up on my knees and stood.

"One shot to the head on the left side," said Catchitt. "From above and slightly behind, so the shooter was possibly left-handed."

"Did it happen here?" I asked.

She nodded. "We got the bullet from the grass. ME will make the call, but it looks like it all happened here."

"What do you mean, it all happened here?"

Catchitt looked at Burke, then Ronzoni, then me.

"There is considerable evidence of trauma."

I sucked in a deep breath and looked at the green water in the canal. I heard Angel's laugh in my mind, from the house party, and I pictured her scowl, from the last time I saw her. "What sort of trauma?"

"I don't know," said Catchitt.

"What do you mean, you don't know?" I stared at her, trying my best not to kill the messenger.

"The ME will make the call."

"This isn't your first day. Best guess."

Catchitt shuffled her boots in the damp grass. "Best guess? Something like a baseball bat."

Acid rose in my throat, and I turned and charged up the bank. I put my hands on the side of the ME's van, bent over and sucked in big gobs of steaming air. Ronzoni and Burke stepped up but kept their distance. I pulled myself together and joined them.

"Now what?" I said.

"Tell me what you know," said Burke. This time I held nothing back. Ronzoni didn't flinch or make a fuss when I mentioned things I hadn't told him earlier, like my run-in with

Montgomery at The Breakers function. He was a pro and he knew how the game was played. When I was done Burke pulled a stick of gum out and popped it in his mouth.

"So this Montgomery, he's in Miami then."

"Brickell Avenue."

I looked around the flat expanse, grids of canals feeding the agricultural area that sat between Lake Okeechobee and Big Cypress National Park.

"How come this is your deal, anyway?" I said. "Shouldn't this be Broward County's file?"

Burke shook his head. "Couple miles south, it would be, but we're just across the county line."

We watched as two ME officers hauled the gurney now holding Angela Cassidy up into the van. Catchitt plodded along behind in her boots.

"Any idea how long she's been out here?" I asked.

"Sometime early this morning," said Catchitt.

"You sure? Not earlier?"

Catchitt shook her head. "This morning. Any earlier, the gators would've got her." She gave a muted smile and wandered over to her sedan to change out of her boots. The van pulled out, and we watched it head back to the main road.

"I'll let you know what comes up," said Burke. "Just don't do anything without my knowing. Got it?"

I nodded.

"I'm serious. You fly off the handle, Danielle's the one who's going to be left holding the bag."

"I got it," I said.

Burke looked at Ronzoni. "You want in the loop?"

Ronzoni shook his head. "All yours. Just let me know if I can help."

Burke nodded and ambled back to his car. Ronzoni and I followed suit. Ronzoni drove fast on the way home. We didn't speak. I watched the landscape change from the flats of the glades to the heights of the towers on the coast. I was standing on a tight rope, high above everything. On one side, power and anger and strength, and the determination to put Pistachio into a deep, deep hole. And on the other side, wasteland, the blood sucked from my veins, listless and staring full on at the knowledge that by taunting Montgomery at The Breakers the previous night, I had put the first, the last and every other nail into Angela Cassidy's coffin.

CHAPTER FORTY

Burke must have put in the call because when Ronzoni dropped me at home Danielle was waiting. She opened the door and I walked in, and she closed it and then wrapped her arms around me. She smelled of soap and cucumber shampoo. I put my arms around her and she pulled me in. This was the toughest person I knew, a woman who worked the mean streets every day, who could beat me in almost every physical endeavor short of an arm wrestle. And all I could think of at that moment was how fragile she felt, brittle like a small cardinal I once held in my hand as a boy in Connecticut. I wasn't sure what to do. So I buried my head into Danielle's shoulder and cried. Not great gasps of anger, but quiet tears of pure sorrow. For a young girl trying to find herself but who now never would. For myself, for my lunkheaded actions that condemned an innocent. For God knows what else.

Eventually my tears stopped, but we stayed holding each other for the longest time. When we separated she wiped her thumb under my eyes, then kissed me gently and led me to the sofa. I kicked off my wet shoes and sat. Danielle made tea with milk and brought me a mug. I wasn't even aware I had tea in the house. I'm not a hot tea drinker. Florida is too warm for it. But I held onto it because it was solid and comforting. Danielle brought her mug over, and we sat at opposite ends of the sofa, backs against the armrests, feet touching. I sipped tea, and looked from Danielle to the blue sky outside, the breeze picking up, the *tink-tink* of rigging against masts on the air. I was at the end of my mug before Danielle spoke.

"It wasn't your fault MJ, you know." It was a sweet thing to say, but the lack of conviction betrayed her.

"It wasn't my doing, but I'm not sure I can be absolved of fault." We fell into silence again, and Danielle went and poured more tea. This time I held the mug but didn't drink it.

"What are you going to do?" she asked, across her steaming tea.

"I don't know. Yet."

"Burke's a good investigator. Let him work."

"I will."

"And don't go off reservation yourself."

I looked at her. Her eyes were focused on mine. "You don't think this guy lives off reservation?"

"You said you'd let Burke handle it."

"No, I said I'd let Burke investigate it."

She dropped her mug down on the coffee table. "What do you think is going on here? This isn't the Wild West. We have laws, ways of doing things."

"People like Montgomery laugh at your ways of doing things."

"And your methods are working so well."

I had nothing to say to that. I looked at the tan liquid in my cup.

"I'm sorry," said Danielle. "I didn't mean that."

"Yes, you did. Because you're right. I knew I couldn't take on Montgomery on his turf, and I've been proven right. But my mistake was thinking if I beat the bushes with a stick he'd come flying out like a flock of grouse. What I didn't think of was that these grouse have guns, and they could stay in their bushes and shoot." I looked at Danielle. Her eyebrows were down and her forehead crinkled.

"What I should've done is blow the whole damn bush apart."

"You can't do that," she cried.

"Why? Because of your laws?"

"No. Because you're all I've got." She flipped her feet onto the floor and marched out the back door. I watched her standing on the patio, arms wrapped around herself, holding on tight. She was staring at the water, or the houses on the mainland, or maybe the horizon. I watched her for a good few minutes, this woman who had come to me at my lowest point, shone her life light on me and then for reasons I still didn't comprehend, decided to stay. And bit by bit, ever so slowly, right under my keen eye, we had become two halves of one whole. Such observations were never my strong point, but watching Danielle hold herself, the realization crashed upon me like the waves breaking on the eastern side of Singer Island. Here I was at a new low, and the one person who would save me was herself in need of saving.

I flopped off the sofa and padded out to the patio. Afternoon clouds were drifting in off the Atlantic, but it was still bright. I slipped in behind Danielle and wrapped my arms around hers. Holding on to her holding herself. She intertwined her fingers with mine and pressed her head into my shoulder. A Catalina yacht drifted by under motor, and we watched it for longer than was necessary.

"We'll see what Burke says," I said.

She tightened her grip on my hands, and we stood in place, watching the pelicans dive, from great heights, into the water, time and time again, until they got the fish they were after.

CHAPTER FORTY—ONE

The following day was one of those wishy-washy days where it's not bright but not dark, not sunny but not cloudy, and not warm but not cold. Wisps of foam threaded across the sky like fake spiderwebs from Halloween, and I couldn't decide on chinos or shorts. One thing I knew was that hanging around in my house was going to drive me stir-crazy. Danielle left for her shift with a kiss and the words *be safe*. I decided on shorts, threw a satchel over my shoulder and I headed out for the office on foot. My car was a wreck, and my motorbike seemed to prefer the company of a mechanic.

Two hours later I arrived at my office, sweating like I just consumed a handful of habanero peppers. Lizzy, handed me a towel with a smile that disarmed me. It wasn't that she never smiled, but she rarely did it to me. Our working relationship was cordial and professional, but we differed on one major point. Namely, that she was convinced my soul was going to burn in hell. It wasn't personal. It was just she thought my life choices, drinking habits and occasional taking of her Lord's name in vain had me destined for an eternity in purgatory. I was starting to wonder if my stint had started early. But Lizzy had her best Christian charity on. She ushered me, *ushered me*, to my desk, then disappeared and returned with a cup of real espresso from one of the bars down on Clematis Street.

"Real coffee?" I asked.

She nodded and I detected a modicum of a smile on her vermilion-painted lips.

"You not having one?" I asked, putting the thick rich coffee to my mouth.

"I don't get paid enough that I can go splurging on fancy coffee. I'll just have from our coffee machine." That dented the impact a little, but it was still good coffee.

"So calls," she said, licking her finger and turning a page on her notepad, and then another page, like there had been so much note taking done in my absence.

"Kimberly Rose, asking how the case was going and had you heard about Angela Cassidy. I told her that you had. Then State Attorney Edwards called—he always has such pleasant manners."

"He's elected."

"Still."

"And he slept with his secretary while he was married to Danielle."

"I would've thought you'd be happy about that," she said, lifting her chin.

"I'm ecstatic about that, but I'm just saying let's not go all overboard with the good manners thing."

"I'm just saying that he has a pleasant phone manner, that's all. I'll leave judgment to our Lord."

"Awesome. What did he want?"

"He said he was waiting to hear from you. Didn't say about what."

"Okay. Anything else?"

"Detective Ronzoni." She looked at me as if she were peering over invisible glasses. "His phone manner could do with some work."

"I'm sure."

"He wanted to let you know that Rinti was declining to take the matter further. And that you were lucky for that."

"I'm feeling very lucky right now."

"He also said you should keep your head."

"I'm trying."

"And that's it for now. Can I get you anything?"

I thought about a smart remark but figured her charity deserved some in return. She closed the door gently and returned to her desk, and I kicked my shoes off, and put my feet up onto my desk and leaned back into thinking mode.

I had promised Danielle, more or less, that I would let Burke do some digging on Montgomery, and I intended to keep that promise. So short of his guys turning up with knuckle dusters in my office, that situation was in a holding pattern. So I thought about Rinti. Two points stuck out for me. One, that having his guys come to beat me up and smash my Mustang into my favorite royal palm, he had shown his hand somewhat. All I had done was talk with President Millet, but the comeback had been swift and savage. That meant the deal was worth a great deal of money, but it also meant it was being put together in a less than kosher fashion. The second point was that I needed to handle the Rinti situation in a much more discreet manner than the Montgomery incident. For Danielle's sake, if not my own. While publicity was a good thing, my business depended on a level of discretion. The boring cases that law firms and insurance companies fed us, which were Ron's specialty and our bread and butter, might dry up if we became just that little too notorious. So subtle pressure was what was called for. On President Millet, on Senator Lawry, the politician pushing the deal through the state house and county commissions, and on Rinti himself.

Each had their own unique pressure points. Millet was in the deal for prestige, to build his dream campus and give the bird to some supposed competitor in New England, who probably never gave him a second thought. So his soft spot was losing that prestige, or worse, getting shamed. And there would be no greater shame than being investigated by the state attorney's office and facing jail time. I picked up my phone and dialed Eric's office. Truth was I could have leaned out my window and yelled to him in the courthouse complex across the parking lot. It wouldn't have done any good as he was in court and unavailable, so I left a message that I'd returned his call and went back to my thinking position to ponder soft spot number two.

State Senator Lawry. He'd lived with the moniker *Boondoggle* for two decades, and that told me two things. He could be bought, but he was careful. Payola, nepotism and fast-tracked deals were all in a day's work for Boondoggle. But he had a nemesis. The media. And one reporter in particular. Maggie Nettles of the *Palm Beach Post*. Maggie had recently exposed Lawry's role in a deal to bring a movie studio to Palm Beach County. Lawry had fast-tracked the deal, thrown a hundred million in taxpayers' money at the project, convinced another fifty million out of county and city coffers, then stood back with a *who me?* look on his face as the whole thing was mismanaged into a giant flame ball of broken promises, bad debts and unemployed staff within a year of opening. Maggie Nettles had questioned the fast-tracking and use of public money from the start but was shouted down by the mantra of jobs and progress. Her post-debacle reporting was decried by Lawry as a personal vendetta by a small-minded staff writer. But the fact was he had put himself on the line and was smarting from the whole episode. I was hoping that some appropriately applied pressure from the media might bring out Boondoggle Lawry's pragmatic side and see him pass over this project. I dialed the *Palm Beach Post* and asked for Maggie Nettles. I was put through and the phone rang for close on a minute. I waited for a voicemail that never came. Just as I was about to hang up someone picked up the phone.

"Maggie Nettles." There was a hint of New England in her voice, like she'd grown up in Eastern Connecticut or maybe Rhode Island.

"Maggie, this is Miami Jones."

"Of course it is."

"I'm a private investigator here in Palm Beach County."

"Of course you are."

"And if you prefer, I'll take what I know about Senator Lawry to the *Miami Herald*."

Silence, then: "Alright, I'll play." Not exactly an apology, but I was just thankful I hadn't asked Lizzy to put the call through for me. She would have torn Ms. Nettles and her phone manner a new one.

"First, I don't want to be quoted. I'll give you info, but you'll have to get your quotes elsewhere."

"If the info is good enough."

"Oh, it's good enough. So no quotes."

"Because quotes from the local private Joe always spice up a story. Fine. No quotes. You are sources unnamed."

"And one more thing."

"Would you like me to send over a courier to collect your list of demands?"

"Drop the attitude. I don't have time for it."

Silence, then: "Alright. Tell me your story."

So I did. Everything about the college and President Millet and the super campus and Rinti Developments and Senator Lawry. I even added in the bit about his nephew getting an internship with Rinti. The *Post's* readers love a good nepotism angle as much as anyone. I didn't tell her anything about Kim

Rose, the late Jake Turner, the late Angela Cassidy or Alexander Montgomery, aka Pistachio. These were irrelevant details to her story, and I had no desire to have poor Angel's lasting memory be a news story about corrupt Florida politics. There was every chance Maggie Nettles would come across the deaths, if she hadn't already, and she might use them to color her story, as the journos liked to say, but they would not be central to it if I could help it. When I was done she asked no questions.

"I'll check all this out. If it's kosher, I'll want to get more detail from you. Off the record, of course."

"I would expect nothing less." I gave her my number and hung up. I felt pretty good. I was removed from the fray, so to speak, but could help engineer a result that would get some element of revenge on Rinti, help Kim Rose out of her pickle, do a public service for the good people of Florida and save them some more misspent cash, and stick Doctor Millet and his tweed pretensions back down the ivy-crusted hole he came out of. I was still basking in my cleverness when Lizzy beeped on the intercom.

"Sorry to disturb," she said, which was a first. "Ron is on the line. Says it's most urgent."

"Thanks, Lizzy." I punched the flashing button on my phone.

"Ron."

"Miami. Something's happened. It's Cassandra. When can you get to Palm Beach?"

"I'll get a cab right now. Be there in twenty."

CHAPTER FORTY–TWO

Lady Cassandra was doing hard time in a penthouse apartment on South Ocean Boulevard, just a decent four iron away from Worth Avenue. The doorman looked have been joined by an armed security guard, neither of whom was keen to let me up until Ron came down to collect me. They searched my daypack regardless, found no weapons but gave no smiles. They were going to do just fine.

"Tell me," I said as we got into the elevator.

"She was shopping at 150 Worth," said Ron, swiping a card and hitting the button for the top floor.

"So not stocking up on canned goods then." 150 Worth Avenue was one of the ritziest shopping precincts in the country.

Ron looked at me with bloodshot eyes. He didn't frown, but he didn't laugh either. He just looked tired and stressed. If I didn't know better, I'd say he looked scared.

"Go on," I said.

"The guy had a knife. He grabbed her in Neiman Marcus. Told her she'd end up like the college girl. Gator bait."

The elevator dinged, and the door opened into a bright foyer of Italian tile. Beyond was an open living room that was the work of a high-cost designer, and beyond that a bank of windows that looked out onto the boiling gray of the Atlantic Ocean. I grabbed Ron's arm before stepping out of the elevator.

"Where is she?" I said.

"Laying down."

We stepped out into the apartment. It was filled with light even on a gray day. The kitchen was hidden through another door. It was the kind of place one didn't have an open plan kitchen because one didn't want the party disturbed by the caterers. We sat on stools at a stone island the size of a pool table. Ron didn't offer drinks, which told me everything, but I asked how he was anyway.

"Don't worry about me—I'm not the one who was attacked."

"She okay?"

"Shaken, mostly. She's a tough old duck. She's got a small cut on her neck, more from pressure than intention, I think."

"Did she get a description?"

"The usual. You know how it goes when people are under stress."

"Sure."

"This guy's the real deal, isn't he?" said Ron.

I nodded.

"Who's the real deal?" came the voice from behind us. We spun in our seats to see Cassandra standing in a bathrobe that looked like it had been stolen from the Four Seasons. Her hair was only marginally tousled for someone who had been taking a nap, but then it occurred to me that she probably hadn't done too much sleeping.

"Just the new backup quarterback for the Dolphins," said Ron.

Cassandra glided into the room with a soft smile and put her hand on Ron's shoulder.

"You're a terrible liar, Ronnie." She moved to the fridge and took out some Perrier.

"Would you care for something, Mr. Jones?" she said.

"No, thank you. Are you up to telling me what happened?"

"Not much to tell. I had just crossed over from 150 Worth to the Neiman Marcus building. I hadn't been in there for more than a few minutes. I'd gone to purchase a new scarf to take up north for Thanksgiving." She paused and took a sip of water. "He grabbed me from behind. I should have been more aware." She shook her head, disappointment writ across her face. "He pulled me down into a rack of garments. Ponchos, capes, I'm not quite sure."

"What did he do?"

"He held a knife to my throat. He smelled of cigar smoke. He said that my boyfriend . . . Really, boyfriend?" She looked at Ron. "I prefer consort, but nevertheless . . . He said Ron should drop it. No, leave it, he said. Leave it, in an English accent, like it was one word. *Leavit.* Then he said he'd be watching, said I'd lose a finger for every day Ron kept on the case."

"And then?"

"Then he dropped me. I fell back into the apparel and he dashed away, and I just lay there until one of the floor staff found me. It wasn't long—they are very good at Neiman Marcus, you know." She fingered a white gauze that was taped to the side of her throat.

"I'm sure," I said and turned to Ron. "Any security video?"

Ron nodded. "Tall, well built, ball cap, sunglasses. Needle in a haystack. The store has already beefed up security, but the Palm Beach PD doesn't think there'll be another victim, given the circumstances."

"I'll call Ronzoni, get him to put some extra patrols around the building, just in case." I looked at Cassandra. I wasn't sure if she really was a lady, in the nobility sense of the word, but right now she looked like I imagined those noble types look in these situations. Tired, confused as to how such a thing could happen in their world, but at the same time resolute.

"Are you okay?"

"No, I'm damned annoyed, if you'll pardon my French. These people think they can do anything. Now I'm afraid to go out my own front door without Ron." She began to weep, and Ron slipped off his stool to comfort her. He suggested she lay down, and headed back toward her bedroom. As she got to the door I spoke.

"I'm sorry I got you into this."

"You are not responsible for this man's choices, Mr. Jones." She turned to leave but stopped and glanced back over her shoulder.

"But you are responsible for putting an end to it." Ron put his arm around her waist and helped her out. I wandered out to the balcony, a large space with an outdoor dining setting of what I guessed to be walnut. I leaned on the railing. The view was breathtaking. The sky was washed-out gray, like a watercolor, and the ocean was a thrashing melange of ash and caps of white. It was the kind of day that could turn either way and bring sparkling sunshine or a hurricane. The kind of day that held in its bosom the darkest of thoughts. I waited on the balcony until I heard the glass slide behind me.

"Is she alright, really?" I said to the ocean.

"She's embarrassed as much as scared."

"That's how it goes. The victims end up thinking it was their fault."

We both stared off at the horizon for a time.

"This place secure?"

"You saw it. The elevator's keycoded, armed guards downstairs, so yeah, it's secure."

I nodded. "You guys seem serious."

"She likes me," shrugged Ron.

"Lots of ladies like you, Ron."

"This one more than most."

"And you?"

"Ditto."

I turned to Ron. He was flushed red, even more than normal. Ron was the kind of guy who wore his heart on his sleeve, and worry was not a cloth that suited him.

"What do we do?" he said.

"Way I see it, two options. One, we do what he wants. We walk away. Leave the whole thing to the PBSO and wash our hands of it. Upside, we're all theoretically safe, and the pros are still on it. Downside . . ."

"Two kids are dead, and he'll probably get away with it. They are calling Jake an accident, and they have nothing to go on for Angela."

"Option two, we go forward. Straight into the lion's den."

"Exactly."

"Walking away is a smart option, Ron. Taking Montgomery on won't bring Jake or Angela back."

Ron turned from the rail and faced me. His eyes were moist.

"Miami, all that is necessary for evil to triumph is that good men do nothing."

I stared back at the ocean. It was a good point well made. But it unsettled me. I had promised Danielle I would stay out of it and let Burke investigate. And I wasn't even sure I could take Montgomery down. And taking him down was the only option. He'd proven that half measures would lead to carnage.

"I promised Danielle I'd let the sheriff's office do their thing."

"And how is their thing going?" said Ron.

"Good question. Let's find out."

"You gonna call the detective?"

"Burke? No, he'll want to know why I'm asking."

I took out my phone and called the medical examiner's office, waited on the line for a silent minute, then I heard a voice.

"Lorraine," she said. It was odd for a law enforcement professional to use her first name, but maybe she got tired of telling the whole catch-it/cat shit story.

"This is Miami Jones."

"Ah, Miami. How goes it this fine Florida day?"

"Wondered if you had an update on the Angela Cassidy case?"

"Not much one for small talk are you, Jones? Well, I'm afraid there's not much good news. Cause of death and injuries suffered were confirmed as I outlined at the scene. No DNA. Only physical evidence is a boot print near the body."

"Can you match it?"

"You'd like to think so, wouldn't you. But the guy who found the body wore the exact same size and model boot."

"You're kidding."

"I wish. He swears he didn't go within ten feet of the body, and I'm inclined to believe him, but it makes the boot print more or less inadmissible without further evidence, which we don't have. Burke's keeping the file open, for now at least, but your guy—Montgomery was it? He has an alibi, as does his bodyguard. So does the guy who found the body, as it happens."

"So it's cold?"

"Cooling, rapidly. Sorry I don't have anything better for you."

"Not your fault. You just read the tea leaves you're given. It's not like you can make evidence appear."

I thanked Lorraine and she rang off. I put the phone to my chin and looked at Ron.

"They've got nothing have they?" he said.

I shook my head and gazed into the middle distance.

"But you've got something haven't you?"

I nodded.

"We have to go off reservation," said Ron.

I nodded again, and then pulled my sight back into focus.

"We can't tell Danielle," I said.

"We can't tell anyone. Just tell me what you want from me."

"Get Cassandra protected."

"Done. The family has a chalet in Vail. I'll take her to the airport myself."

I reached into my satchel and pulled out a shot glass in a plastic bag. The glass I had taken from The Breakers after my little chat with Montgomery.

"What's that?" said Ron.

"Alexander Montgomery's fingerprints."

"A plant?" said Ron. "But what will you plant? It can't be any old stuff, not to stick."

"No, it needs to be his stuff."

"How do we pull that off?"

"I know a way." I pushed myself away from the rail and turned to the apartment. Ron walked me to the elevator.

"You get her taken care of, you hear?"

"What about you? You can't pull this off alone."

I shook my head. "I know some cops in Miami-Dade."

Ron nodded.

"How well?"

"They were in Desert Storm with Lenny."

Ron nodded. "Good."

We hit the ground floor and walked out of the dark lobby into gathering clouds. The winds were picking up, suggesting a storm.

"I appreciate this," said Ron.

I shrugged. "Let's not kid ourselves we're doing a good thing here."

"After thirty years dealing with the dark side of our society, I'm not so sure."

We didn't shake hands. Ron turned and walked back into the apartment building. I wandered down to Worth Avenue, wondering how much a cab was going to nail me for a ride out west of the turnpike. I had to visit Sally. I needed to borrow a car.

CHAPTER FORTY-THREE

Fortunately the cab ride was a short one. I called Sally as I walked, and he directed me to a small used car dealership just south of Clear Lake. As I got out of the taxi a young guy in an Adidas tracksuit wandered out from a small shed at the back of the lot. He dropped a set of keys in my hand and pointed me to an old rust-red Dodge Caravan. The minivan didn't cruise the freeway like my Mustang, and it handled like a wet cat on an ice pond, but it did offer one thing my Mustang didn't. It was invisible. Which proved to be a bonus as I sat on the fringe of the university campus watching the early evening comings and goings of the students. I was as confident that Officer Steele would miss the Caravan as I was he would have picked up the Mustang within five minutes of my arrival. The building I was watching was a small apartment block set to the side of the main residential halls on the edge of campus. It was smaller and newer than the other blocks, like it had been an afterthought. Which I suspected it was. The university had seen the opportunity to cash in on the thousands of international students who desperately wanted to spend their parents' hard-earned money on four years of partying in the United States. A concrete and shell mosaic sign that read *International House* sat before a cluster of palm trees.

I was working on a plan: if I wanted to find a queen bee, I wouldn't spend all my time looking for a beehive—I'd just go to the flower garden and follow the worker bees home. Joseph, or Jo Jo, as he had called himself when he was selling drugs, might be a hard guy to find. I wasn't even sure he was a student. But he had told me his brutish-looking bodyguard, Carlos, was an exchange student from Haiti. So I put two and two together and came up with an evening sitting in a twenty-year-old family van, watching teens wandering in from class or out to dinner or drinks or study at the library. Too young to know what they didn't know, full of promise and hope and the belief that they would determine their lives, not the other way round. I had felt like that once, and for a time, when I played baseball and had a hope of making The Show, it was true. But then, as it does, life enveloped me. And although I could have chosen other paths, even gone into coaching and maybe made it to the Bigs as a pitching coach, I knew it was time on that part of my life, and I embarked upon this part. And despite everything, I had few regrets. I enjoyed my friends, my job and where I did it, and I had the eye of the most wonderful woman in the world. And I had reached the age where I knew that was enough. My trip down memory lane made me pick up my phone and make a call. A late dinner, since I was in the area, since we had stuff to discuss.

I was starting to flag, wishing I had brought a coffee or a bag of pretzels along, when I saw the giant pink-gummed, yellow-toothed Haitian duck out from the front entrance of the apartments. He set off on foot away from the campus, and I felt conspicuous following in a car, even a minivan, so I jumped out and took off after him. He lumbered along for five minutes, until he got to a single-family home with three cars in the front yard. All recent models, all domestic. It was the Trans Am that caught my eye. It wasn't five minutes before Carlos came lumbering out after Jo Jo. Joseph wore a pink polo with a yellow cable knit tied across his shoulders. He carried a day pack in his hand, which he tossed onto the back seat of the Trans Am. He slipped into the car and Carlos folded himself into the passenger seat. I pushed in behind a palm and watched them scream out of the driveway and tear off into the night. Two salesmen, out to serve their clientele. They wouldn't be back for hours, maybe even dawn. But I knew what I needed to know. I ambled back to my car, careful not to get picked up by the campus cops. Maybe they knew about Rinti's men beating me up and figured I wouldn't be back, but either way I didn't see anything of concern.

I got back to the Caravan and headed east to Fort Lauderdale. I pulled into a gravel parking lot off one of the canals. They called Fort Lauderdale the Venice of the Southeast, mostly because they were morons and had never set foot in Italy. But as contrived as Lauderdale's canals were, they made for a pleasant spot to sit and enjoy a frosty beer and some stone crab. *Chip's Place* served both, in an old Florida environment of plastic tablecloths and bug screens. I only eat stone crab in season, starting in the late fall, but I drink beer all year round. I was sipping a Yuengling from a frosty mug when Kim Rose walked in. She must have known the place because she was dressed down, in a plain blue T-shirt and blue jeans. She ordered a beer, and I ordered another and some smoked fish dip.

"It's good to see you," she said, clinking glasses.

"How you doing?"

"It's been a tough few days. Police, counselors for the students. Everyone's pretty shaken up over Angela." She shook her head. "Such a waste."

Our server arrived, and I ordered the stone crab and Kim the dolphinfish. When the server bounded away a melancholy look swept over Kim's face.

"I blame myself," she said. "I could've done more."

It was the thing people say in such circumstances, a throwaway line. Absolution in a sentence.

"It's not your fault," I said. "There are bad people in the world. And the university isn't a walled garden. Sometimes those people get in."

She half-smiled and sipped her beer. "Thanks, Miami. I appreciate it. I don't have anyone there I can talk to, you know. Confide in."

"Don't mention it. But I must warn you, it isn't going to get any easier in the short term."

"How so?"

"Well, you weren't responsible for Angel's death. But there are things you are responsible for."

She frowned. "Such as?"

"Such as the rampant use of performance-enhancing drugs in your sports teams."

"That's just not true. There may be isolated cases, but—"

I put my palm up to her. "Don't, Kim. We go way back. I know you. And you know me. So you know I wouldn't leave a stone unturned on this, and I wouldn't be saying it based on hearsay. Jake Turner sold PEDs. He sold them to his teammates to make them better, because they couldn't keep up with him. You turned a blind eye because that's what you do. You wouldn't take PEDs yourself, or at least you never had to, but you tolerate others who do in the name of the team. I have student-athletes, I have coaches. They all admit it. In private at least."

Kim put her beer down. She couldn't have drunk it anyway, because her mouth was open like the entrance to a mine.

"I thought you were on my side. But Millet's got to you."

"Save the histrionics, Kim. Millet's a pretentious fool, and you were right about him. He wants you gone, and the athletics program with you. But that's not happening. He's going down."

"Good. That's good. With him gone, we can really do some things."

"Kim, you're not listening. Millet might be on his way out, but that's about him, not you. Look, we're old friends, and I care about you. That's why I'm here. I think you need to reconsider whether the college path is for you."

"You don't think I can do this job? Of all the people."

"Kim, I don't think—I know. I know you can do anything you set your mind to. You could be an AD—hell, you could run programs at any school. Florida, USC, Notre Dame. You could do it."

"But?"

"But, you're not part of the solution, you're part of the problem. You're focused and driven and determined, and you're the biggest believer in the concept of team this side of Pete Carroll, but that's not enough."

"Not enough?"

"No. These kids aren't your teammates—they're your students. They're not yet adults, despite what we all think when we get our driver's licenses. See, you owe them a greater duty of care. And for all your strengths, you just don't get that. You're like Joe Paterno. He was a great coach and a good man, but he forgot that first and foremost he was a guardian. Parents trusted their children to him. He owed them a duty of care beyond his understanding of the job profile. As do you."

Kim moved her lips like she wanted to respond but no words came out. She was saved by the arrival of our food. Chip had the stone crab shipped over from the Gulf, fresh off his cousin's boat, or so he claimed. Regardless it was sensational. I'm no animal rights activist, but there's something karmically good about eating a crab that doesn't have to die to give up its delicious bounty. I'm sure losing your claw is no picnic, but it beats being boiled alive in a pot with a handful of Old Bay seasoning. Kim ate her dolphinfish with a fork and without enthusiasm. We ate most of our meal in silence, until Kim put her fork down and looked at me.

"Do you think people can change?" she said.

"I think people do. But if you're asking can you take this knowledge on board and run a better athletics program, then I'd say no. There is a culture here, and it's not a good one. A clean sweep is needed, and if necessary I'll be holding the broom."

She glared at me with shark-eyed focus.

"Look, I'm not perfect, far from it," I said. "I told you about my PED use. I got lucky. In a system full of people turning blind eyes, I was guided by someone who was prepared to face his responsibilities and help me see the error of my ways." I leaned back in my chair and held Kim's gaze.

"Maybe you need some time under the wing of someone like that. I don't know, maybe your skills will be better utilized at the pro level, where at least the athletes are adults and theoretically old enough to make decisions for themselves. And there are a lot of good pro teams out there that care about running a clean program. I'm sure you could help them out. Maybe they could help you too."

She blinked but didn't take her eyes off me. I could see the cogs ticking over. Her brain, which was capable of seeing gaps open on a soccer field well before the opposition ever did, churning over the options.

"With your so-called rampant drug use on my resume? I won't even get an interview."

"Right now there's nothing on your resume. And there doesn't have to be."

We didn't order dessert or coffee, and I paid the check as Kim stood, looking out over the dark canal outside. We wandered out into the parking lot. The night was cool, and gravel crunched underfoot. I walked Kim to her car and she fumbled for her keys, unlocked the door, and then turned to me.

"This is not going to beat me, Miami."

"I would be awfully disappointed if it did."

I smiled and leaned in and kissed her cheek. Then she got in her car and drove away. I watched the taillights turn out of the lot, and I shivered. I had the coldest sensation that we would never see each other again. I ambled to the minivan and turned the engine over. Sometimes people are like the Roman Coliseum, permanent fixtures in an ever-changing world. And sometimes, people are like the fuel modules on the Saturn V rockets. For a time, they are crucial. Life-defining even. But then they fall away, their job done, their role played. And the rocket flies on.

CHAPTER FORTY—FOUR

I woke early to a quacking noise coming from my phone. I hit the screen, and the duck stopped and I rubbed my face awake. I had set my phone's alarm because there was no alarm clock in the room. Perhaps there never was, or perhaps the last guest had made off with it. I wouldn't have trusted it even if it were there. My expectations are not high when I pay nineteen dollars for a motel room. I had left Chip's Place with every intention of spending the night reclined back as far as possible in the seats of the Dodge Caravan. But after I passed under I-95 I hit a motel with a lit sign offering free HBO and clean sheets, and the certainty that Jo Jo and Carlos would not return until daybreak, or resurface for hours after that, piqued my interest in a motel that would actually proclaim clean sheets as a selling point rather than a bare necessity of business.

In the end it was worth every penny. The bed was soft but no more so than a hammock, and the noise from the next room died down after one fiery bout of orgasmic screaming. I splashed some water on my face and headed into the predawn morning. I stopped at a gas station to fill the car and grab some coffee and breakfast sandwiches, and then I cruised to Jo Jo's street. I parked three houses down on the opposite side. The Trans Am was already home. Maybe a slow night, or maybe Joseph had a test today. I drank my coffee and ate a soggy bacon and egg sandwich and watched the street wake. Some people worked for a living, and headed out in their sedans and SUVs. A few small groups appeared, casually dressed, satchels and backpacks and books. The more conscientious students heading off to early lectures. Jo Jo's house didn't stir until after ten. First one car, then another, until only the Trans Am was left. Around eleven thirty Joseph appeared in a white polo and Nantucket red trousers. He got in the Trans Am, revved it so the folks in Miami could hear, and then pulled out toward campus, covering a five-minute walk in under a minute.

I waited for half an hour to make sure no one returned, and then I wandered over to the house and did the tour. I circled the house once. No movement, no pets, no surprises. Three good ways in: pick the front door, break a side window, put a patio chair through the back sliding door. None were necessary. The back patio was a concrete pad under a bug screen canopy. Beer bottles and swimwear littered the plastic patio furniture. A college room share. Which meant kids who thought they were invincible. Which meant kids who thought their house was invincible. I slipped on a pair of latex gloves and stepped inside through the unlocked sliding door.

The house smelled of cheese corn chips, but the kitchen looked spotless. Not even an errant beer can. Whoever did KP wasn't tasked with the patio. I paced through the house to check it was clear. Then I returned to the first bedroom. A mattress on the floor, or what I assumed to be a floor since it was covered in at least one layer of discarded clothing. The second room was the exact opposite. Even the bed was made. I slid open the wardrobe to reveal a selection of pressed polos that would have made Macy's proud. I checked the bottom of the wardrobe and drew a blank. Then I thought about what Angel had said about Jake's drug stash. I lay on the floor and looked under the bed. A suitcase. I pulled it out. It was a brown leather job that may have once been used by Bing Crosby. It had gold latches that I could pull open with my fingers. I opened the case to reveal an apothecary store. Pills of every color, a brick of white and a selection of bags of green. Then there were the three large bags of Maxx tablets. Enough to supply an entire outdoor music festival, or get a guy sent down for distribution. I snatched the Maxx bags out and pushed the suitcase back under the bed. Then I stood. I looked at the space under the bed, and then I got back on my knees and pulled the case open again.

I dashed back to the kitchen. Such a clean kitchen had cleaning products. I pulled open the sink cupboard and smiled at the options. I could have started a cleaning business. At the back was a large bottle of bleach. I grabbed it, and a paring knife from the drawer, and strode back to the bedroom. There I slashed at every bag like I was in a horror film, and then when I was done, I poured the bleach over all the drugs until the bottom of the case was a bleachy, druggy swamp. I snapped the suitcase closed and pushed it back under the bed, then I returned the empty bleach bottle and the knife to where I'd found them. I pulled a used plastic grocery bag from the collection under the sink, dropped the three bags of Maxx in it and retraced my steps out of the house through the rear patio, and back to the minivan. The street was still. Fewer people home now than any other time of day. I started the car and punched in a call on my phone.

"I'm good," I said.

"We're expecting you."

I clicked off without further word, and I pushed the selector into gear and pulled out toward the freeway with an obnoxious New York voice ringing in my head. *I want to go to Miami!*

CHAPTER FORTY-FIVE

It was James Bond time again. I stopped in a service plaza on the turnpike and changed into my tuxedo. I had Lenny Cox's mantra on my mind: there isn't a room in Palm Beach you can't get into wearing a tux. I hoped the same was true in Miami. More to the point, it was about hiding in plain sight. People see a uniform, and nothing more. I pulled out some latex gloves and took out my satchel. The tequila glass I had taken from The Breakers was in its freezer bag. I took a fingerprint dusting kit we kept in the office and some tape. I dusted the glass and found some nice fat prints belonging to Alexander Montgomery. I transferred the prints onto the bags holding the Maxx tablets I had taken from Jo Jo's room.

Once I was happy with my work, I packed up and headed into Miami. The restaurant was a pub cum grill, specializing in English food and beer, which in my experience meant sausages and tepid ale. It was a smallish place with faux brickwork and gas lanterns, and neon in the window promoting *Worthington's*. A skinny kid with bad skin sat on a collapsible chair in an alcove at the entrance. A small cabinet was fixed to the wall behind him, where I assumed he kept the keys to cars he valeted. I sat in a lot further down, where the cheapskates who didn't want to tip a valet would park and I watched the kid at work. I noted three things. One, he worked alone. Two, he parked the valeted cars in a two-tiered parking structure behind the restaurant. Three, when he got busy, he flipped the key box shut but didn't lock it.

I pulled the Caravan around to the rear parking structure and waited. My contacts in the Miami-Dade PD had surveillance on Montgomery's office and had reported that someone had made a reservation for dinner at this restaurant, the lazily named Peasant's Rest. I figured Montgomery, being a Brit, was homesick for some offal and onions or some such delicacy. I sat back in the minivan to wait. Time would tell if my assumption was right. It did, and I was. Another win for first-class investigation masquerading as following a hunch. The pock-faced valet pulled the green Jaguar registered to Montgomery's company into the structure and parked halfway down a row from where I watched. He hit the security button and spun the keys around his finger like a gunslinger, and then dashed away to his post. I smiled at the Jag, then stepped out of the Caravan and strode away.

The evening was mild but it felt sticky in the parking garage. I marched around the back of the restaurant, past cigarette butts and the smell of old cooking oil, so I came at the front of the restaurant from the side where I could see the alcove and front door best. I waited for a car, another Mercedes, to pull up out front. Perhaps I had underestimated the clientele of the pub. That or there were a ton of Brits walking among us who were making out like bandits. The valet pulled the Merc forward, and I strode out from my hiding spot. I made a point of walking with purpose, like I had a reason for being where I was, important and unstoppable. It was easy. Wearing a tux has that effect on me. I walk tall and stand straight. The valet pulled away and I got to the alcove as the couple from the Merc stepped in the stain glass-windowed door. I held the door for them and got a smile in return. I wasn't worried about being recognized later. No one would remember anything but the tux, unless it was worn by George Clooney. But holding the door gave me a second to scope the room and see if Montgomery or his bodyguard driver Nigel were near the window. They were not, so I patted my breast pocket like I'd forgotten something, and then let the door go. As I turned I flicked open the key box with my other hand. I glanced at the keys and was glad Montgomery didn't drive a Merc or a Bimmer. The Jag tag stuck out like a hunting green beacon. I snatched it out and pushed the door closed, and headed around the restaurant's other side, back to the parking garage.

I strode along the exterior wall so as to avoid the valet dashing back to his post, and came in from the side beyond the Dodge Caravan. I stopped and grabbed my latex gloves and the Maxx tablets. Then I took a deep breath. I knew I was about to cross a line. The concept of rule of law was one I truly believed in. It was, of course, also central to Danielle's value system. But in the end we all have our own moral code. Most of us agree on the central principles—that's what made the whole thing work. It was the fringes where the fabric frayed. I didn't believe in capital punishment, but I had taken a human life. I thought diplomacy was always preferable to violence, but I had beaten an errant husband who wouldn't stop using his wife for a punching bag. No system was perfect. And for those times, I was prepared to step outside the system. My gut churned at the thought of what I was doing, but I used the sleep test. How many people would lose sleep over Montgomery's going to jail, whatever the means? None that counted was the answer, and that was enough.

I clicked the button and pulled open the rear door. The interior smelled of soft leather. I lay across the back and felt under the passenger's seat. It was a tangle of wires. Electric positioning, seat warmers, maybe some audio. Not a lot of room, but enough. I shoved two bags of Maxx under the driver's seat and one bag under the passenger's seat. Then I leaned back to evaluate how easy they were to see. Not very, I decided. I was about to slip out when I heard a car pull into the garage. I leaped back in and pulled the door shut with my foot. The interior light stayed on. I held my breath and listened to the tires screech on the polished concrete as the car turned into a slot. I heard the door open. If the valet saw the light on in the Jag he would surely investigate, and my plan would be a bust. Or worse.

The door on the other car slammed closed, a deep, expensive thud. I still held my breath. It felt like the thing to do. Then the interior light in the Jag gave up, assumed it was alone and faded to black. I heard the beep-beep of a security system being set, and the soft pad, pad, pad of cheap shoes running back toward the restaurant. I let out a long slow breath, waited fifteen seconds, then flipped the door open and slid out. I pushed the door closed and stood tall, brushing my lapels like I was 007 himself and had every reason in the world to have been lying on the backseat of a stranger's car. I slipped my hand inside my jacket and pulled out a jewelers hammer. A quick look around the vacant garage and a swift tap, and I cracked the taillight. My second taillight inside of a week. It was becoming a thing. I gave the light a second crack to make the hole in the red plastic a good size then I flipped the hammer around and used the pointy side of the head to crack the bulb. The damage was noticeable enough, but on the opposite side from where the valet would appear, so with some luck he wouldn't notice.

I slipped the hammer back inside my jacket pocket, hit the key fob to engage the security system and walked out of the parking garage and back around the rear of the restaurant. I waited until the valet had driven the next car away toward the garage, and then strode over to the alcove. An elderly couple was standing half in, half out of the alcove, right in front of the key box. I marched up, stepped in behind them, flicked the box open, dropped the key on a hook, and then tapped the door shut. The couple didn't move, but they didn't protest either. I gave them a smile and a good evening.

"Good evening," they replied in unison. Perhaps they thought I was a valet too.   The sharpest dressed valet in all

Miami-Dade. I walked away, to where I had come from, but instead of looping back behind the restaurant, I kept walking, across a ribbon of grass and into the strip mall next door, to put my future into the hands of two guys I had never met in my life.

CHAPTER FORTY—SIX

The cops' names were Dorsey and Stoat. After five minutes of sitting in the back of a patrol car, I forgot which was which. The car was an older Crown Vic that had done more miles than a New York taxicab, and smelled of stale coffee and dander. After introductions, and having given my tuxedo a good look and a perfunctory smirk, we fell into an easy silence. Our only common ground was Lenny, and he was dead. But I knew they had all served in the Gulf together, and somehow the two detectives came out owing Lenny Cox a debt of gratitude. A lot of people owed that kind of debt to Lenny Cox. But the debt bound us and there was very little work involved in talking them into helping me. It was a good ninety minutes before we saw the valet dash off and return with Montgomery's Jaguar. I hoped he got a good tip, because he must have run a half marathon over the course of the night, and he wasn't going to be popular once Montgomery figured out what had happened.

We followed the Jaguar along surface streets, keeping one or two cars between us as cover. It wasn't Dorsey or Stoat's first day on the job. We reached up onto I-95 and hit a sixty-five zone and the Jag pulled away. We were doing seventy-five when we neared downtown and the zone dropped to fifty-five. The Jag didn't slow. Neither did anyone else. We pulled to within one car and Dorsey or Stoat flashed the headlights. The car in front touched his brakes, and then pulled out of the fast lane. Then we pulled in close to the Jag. Whichever of Dorsey or Stoat was driving flipped on the flashing blues, while the other logged the speed, all official like. The Jag wasn't keen to pull over. We sounded our siren, a deep *roop* sound, and finally Montgomery's driver got the hint.

I watched the whole thing go down from the back seat of the patrol car. Dorsey or Stoat punched the button and a video monitor on the console came to life, along with audio. Both officers approached the Jaguar from opposite sides. The one on the driver's side spoke to Montgomery's bodyguard about speeding in a fifty-five zone, and his busted taillight. He asked for license and registration. The bodyguard protested innocence and ignorance of all wrongdoing. Then the cop snapped to attention, flicked open the safety latch on his holster and put his hand on his gun. He didn't immediately pull it.

"Sir, do you have a weapon?" I heard him say through the audio.

"What?"

"Is that a gun under your jacket?"

"I have a permit."

"Sir, step out of the car."

"I said, I have a permit."

"Put your hands on the steering wheel and slowly step out of the car."

The bodyguard did as he was told. I knew from our meeting at The Breakers that his permit was good.

"Is there someone else in the car?" said the cop, glancing at the tinted rear window. His hand was still on the butt of his gun.

"Yes, my boss."

The other cop, Dorsey or Stoat, opened the rear door on the other side and asked Montgomery to step out. As he did I heard the cop say, *what is that*, and then he pushed Montgomery against the car.

"Spread 'em," he said, as he patted Montgomery down. Montgomery's face held an arrogant grin, like he didn't just know something you didn't know, he knew a thousand things you didn't know.

"Dorsey, you need to see this," said the cop with his hand in the middle of Montgomery's back. Dorsey kept the bodyguard in front and marched him around the car. Stoat pulled his firearm and kept it on Montgomery and his man. Dorsey looked, then leaned in the car and came up holding a bag of Maxx tablets.

"What are these?" said Dorsey.

Montgomery lost his arrogant face. Now he just looked angry.

"Those are not mine," he said.

"They're in your car."

"I have nothing to say. I wish to speak to my attorney." He glanced at his bodyguard. "Say nothing."

Dorsey handcuffed the two men while Stoat stood guard, and then he came back to the patrol car. He got in and looked at me through the cage wire.

"You wouldn't believe it—I see the guy has a gun, under his right arm. He's a lefty. If he were a righty, I'd never have seen it. Then the other guy, he's getting out and he hooks his foot under the front seat and kicks out the drugs. It couldn't have been easier."

"What now?"

"Now I get back up. I figure you don't want them sitting in the back there with you."

"Got that right."

The video recorded Stoat mirandizing Montgomery and his guy, and then a second patrol car arrived and took them away. Dorsey collected the three bags and brought them to his car, and then we waited for a truck to carry the Jag to the impound yard. The truck pulled out into freeway traffic, and Dorsey and Stoat ambled back to the patrol car.

"All done?" I said.

"Yeah," said Dorsey. "We'll drop you back at your car, then we got a report to write."

"And those guys? The drugs?"

"The drugs will go into evidence as soon as we get back. The case will go to Vice."

"Okay," I said, and sat back for the ride to the parking garage. We got there with no further talk, until I got out of the Crown Vic.

"Thanks for your help," I said through the window.

"He's a feisty one," said Stoat. "He's just been caught red-handed with a good-sized stash, enough for jail time. And you know what he says as I'm stuffing him in the car? He says do I got a family?"

I frowned. I wasn't sure what Montgomery could do from jail. Maybe it was just talk.

"Do you have a family?"

Stoat smiled. "Yeah, that's what I tell him. I gotta ex-wife. And he's welcome to her. You know what he does? He smiles. Just smiles."

CHAPTER FORTY-SEVEN

A little ray of sunshine entered my life when I got the call the following morning that my insurance company had okayed my claim and I could go and choose another car. With my bike in the shop and the Dodge Caravan making me feel like I'd descended into nineties suburban hell, I decided there was no time like the present. There was enough cloud to cast shadows, but the sun was bright and full, and I was having an easy time convincing myself that what I had done the previous evening was the right thing to do. Ron had deposited Cassandra at Palm Beach International en route to Vail, and was looking for something to take his mind off it, so he agreed to chauffeur me to a few car lots. I had liked the sweet smell and soft touch of the leather in the Jaguar that I had found myself facedown in the previous night. But Ron had convinced me that not only was a Jag not really my style, but it would probably stick out at least as much as the Mustang had, which we had previously agreed was not a good quality in a car commonly used for stakeouts, following suspects and other sneaky purposes.

"What about a Camry?" said Ron. "Plenty of room, and it blends in everywhere."

"You were saying something about the Jag not being my style?"

Ron glanced at me as he drove. "You're no spring chicken, Miami."

"I'm no granddaddy either. No Camry—keep driving."

Ron smiled. He was enjoying himself a little too much. We approached a Subaru dealership.

"What about an Outback?"

"Am I pregnant with twins?"

"They're not just for moms."

"Check out the library parking lot at story time. The place is thick with them."

"They're very sporty."

"So they're yummy mommies."

"Like Danielle," he said.

"Except she's not a mommy, which is pretty central to the whole concept."

"More's the pity."

"What are you saying, Ron?"

"Nothing. I just think she'd be a good mom. That's all. She has a very kind heart."

"And killer abs. There's plenty of time to ruin them later."

"If you think so."

"Did she say something?"

"Not to me. But I got eyes. Great women like that don't wait forever."

"Wait for what?"

"And she had lunch with Eric."

"That was nothing."

"It wasn't lunch with you."

"You think Danielle's going to leave me if I don't get a boring car?"

"I didn't say that."

"Then what are you saying?"

He glanced at me and back to the road. "You're no spring chicken."

We pulled into a dealership and a short test-drive, a couple calls to the insurance company and some faxed paperwork later, I drove off the lot in a new black Jeep Wrangler.

I was following Ron back to the office, the wind blowing through my hair, when my phone rang.

"Miami Jones."

"Mr. Jones, this is Senator Marshall Lawry. Would you have a few minutes for me this morning?"

Senator Lawry was on the on the back nine of the Palmer course at PGA National when I caught up with him. Despite the nature of the game, I was the only person on the course traveling on foot. The senator's foursome was surrounded by a posse of golf carts. There were so many I expected to see a carpool lane in effect. Lawry's security guy took my name on approach, and after a drive that was short but straight, the Senator waved me over to his cart. He was a big man, broad in the chest and long in the chin, with thinning hair that struggled to cover a sweat-glistened pate. His handshake was strong and his smile warm. If one were to design a politician from scratch, Senator Lawry could provide a fair dose of the blueprint.

"Mr. Jones, thank you for making time for me on such short notice." His accent had a hint of the south in it. The fact that Tallahassee and the panhandle were part of Florida was simply an historical aberration, for the northern parts of the state had much in common with their northern neighbors in Georgia and Alabama, and almost nothing in common with the Miami end.

"Any opportunity to take a walk around PGA National."

"You golf?"

"Not these days, but I enjoy a good walk as much as anyone."

Lawry pushed the accelerator, and we zoomed along the path toward the senator's ball.

"I've heard some good things about your practice," he said.

"We aim to please."

"Can't be easy in your line of work."

"Or yours."

Lawry smiled. It made me think of an alligator. "Indeed, Mr Jones, indeed."

Lawry stopped the cart and stepped out. I figured I should follow suit. We met behind the cart as the Senator selected a club from his bag.

"Do you do much corporate work, Mr. Jones?"

"Some. We have a decent business community in the Palm Beaches."

"Indeed." He smiled again. Lawry took out a five iron and trotted out to his ball. Although I told Lawry I didn't play golf these days, that didn't mean I had never played. I just didn't do it regularly anymore. But I had been a professional baseball player, and there were few things most baseball players liked to do more with their time off than play golf. So I had done it enough to know that based on the length of his drive, the senator had a snowball's chance in hell of reaching the green with a five iron. He hit the ball crisply, but he failed to take advantage of his size, and he decelerated through his swing rather than accelerating into the ball. I'd seen the same thing in baseball hitters who had lost their confidence and were overthinking things. As it was Lawry's ball flew straight and true and dropped a good thirty yards short of the green. He strode back to me looking neither pleased nor perturbed by the shot.

"I have no doubt there are companies that could use your expertise," he said slipping his club back into his bag.

"We're doing okay," I said. We got back in the cart, and he drove us down the fairway.

"Fortune 500 companies, Mr. Jones. I know a lot of people."

"People like Gino Rinti?" It was true I'd shown my hand, but I just wasn't as good at tiptoeing around the mulberry bush as a politician. Lawry just smiled.

"You have an interesting way of making friends, Mr. Jones."

"I have all the friends I need."

"We can always use more friends."

"Gino Rinti's boys beat me up and smashed my car."

"That's my point. Friends wouldn't do such a thing to each other. But I think we can overcome all that. Everyone can win."

"Not Jake Turner."

Lawry stopped the cart at the edge of the green.

"Terrible loss, Mr. Jones, terrible. But these things happen. We must do all we can to ensure they don't, but occasionally, inevitably, they do."

"Like your nephew?"

"Who?"

"Sean. Didn't you help your nephew out of a drug arrest and have him shipped to a new college?"

"There were no charges. Sean never took anything."

"No, he gave it, is what I heard. Doped a girl to take advantage of her."

"There were no charges."

"But you hushed it up and even got him a job with your friend Rinti."

"Like I told you Mr. Jones, friends help each other."

"Then you must be great buddies with your nephew."

"I never speak to the boy. He's had all the chances he's going to get. But he's making a go of it, I hear. His father got him a nice apartment, a cleaning lady and the whole nine yards, so he can focus on his study. Look Mr. Jones, you've met him. The boy's young and he's stupid, I'll admit, but he's family. You do things for your family, don't you, Mr. Jones?"

In a way, that was what I was doing that very moment.

"What is it you want, Senator?"

We repeated our dance to his bag where he selected a pitching wedge.

"I want you to know you have friends. Mr. Rinti is prepared to let bygones be just that. I think you'd do well to do the same. There is a lot of upside. Powerful friends could do you a lot of good."

"I already have powerful friends."

"Not this kind of power. And the downside of not having friends? Well, I understand that a private investigator license, once lost, is almost impossible to regain."

"I don't see much danger of that."

"I'd hate for someone to have a word to the governor, telling him you are standing in the way of Florida jobs. No telling what he might do."

"Go ahead and tell the governor. I think you'll find he'll take my side."

Lawry smiled. "Aah, I see. You have a marker there. Good, good. You keep it close, but remember, governors come and go."

"So do development projects."

"That they do, son, that they do." He took a couple steps toward his ball and then he looked over his shoulder.

"This could be a great opportunity for you. Or not. Your choice. But I urge you to choose wisely." He smiled and waved his club in the air. "I'm sure you know the way back to the clubhouse." The senator turned away to his ball, and I watched him take two practice swings at his chip, and then scuff the shot with the bottom of his club. The ball never left the grass and scooted across the green, hitting the flag stick, bouncing up and dropping into the hole. I didn't wait to see Lawry's reaction. I just turned and began my long trudge back toward the clubhouse. Sometimes this game truly was a good walk ruined.

CHAPTER FORTY–EIGHT

Boondoggle Lawry left a sour taste in my mouth, one that only a cleansing ale could wash away. I stopped by the office to rouse Ron from his slumber, and had just pulled into the parking lot when my phone rang.

"Jones, it's Stoat, Miami PD. You driving?"

"No, what's up?"

"He's out."

"Who?" The word popped out before my brain played catch-up.

"Montgomery, Pistachio. Whatever you want to call him."

I flopped back heavily into my seat. "What happened?"

"He didn't even spend the night."

"What happened!"

"We booked him, and his lawyer turns up, which is par for the course. Me and Dorsey drop off the evidence, then we clock off. When we get in this morning we find out the lawyer called the state attorney. All hell broke loose, and the SA wants to know what we've got on him, and the answer is nothing."

"Nothing? What the hell you talking about?"

"He checked the evidence room. There was none."

"What happened to the stuff?"

"We signed for it, and logged the case file in the system. But the SA calls, and there's no evidence logged and no case file."

"How is this possible?"

"Vice. Montgomery owns someone, or someones, in Vice. They did it early, and they did it clean."

"But there was video. I saw it." I slipped out of the car and rubbed my face.

"Dorsey checked after we heard about the SA. Our patrol car went in for refurb last night. The whole video unit was replaced. The whole thing. There was a postdated rec order, but no one knows who did the work. Or they're not saying."

"What kind of a show are you guys running down there?"

"This guy has some serious pull. That was your mistake. Doing it in Miami-Dade. This is his turf. If he's got bent cops anywhere, it's here. You should've done it in Broward. Or up in Palm Beach. Or we should've involved the feds."

"I just don't believe this crap goes on."

"Miami, it doesn't go on. Not like this. This guy is seriously connected."

I stopped and looked up at my office.

"If he's that connected, I don't know how we touch him." I took a deep breath and paced a couple of circuits of the length of the Jeep.

"It's worse than that. He's got to know he was set up," said Stoat.

"He'll know that. But there's no reason to think it was you."

"Not us," said Stoat. "We've been taken care of. Other cops are involved now, crooked but still cops. This morning Dorsey and I both found, shall we say, a brown paper bag in our locker. An incentive to keep quiet. No doubt it came from Vice, not Montgomery. They'll tell him they've handled it. And I'm sorry about your situation, but we'll keep quiet because there's no upside in doing anything else."

"So what do I do?" I said.

"Watch your back, that's what. Montgomery overreacted by approaching your partner's woman. But now there are cops involved, there's a chance they advise him to cool his jets. No one wants bloodshed, eventually it attracts too many eyes. If you let it lie, I think he will too. It's in his interests."

"I hope you're right."

"Sorry it went down like this."

We ended the call, and I leaned against the fender and looked back to the office. Stoat's theory was logical, but I lacked confidence in it. Logic was not the domain of those who believed themselves untouchable.

I heard a car pull in behind me and tensed.

"Hey, you," I heard Danielle say. I spun around. I tried to muster a smile but it didn't come.

"You okay?" she said.

"Montgomery was arrested last night. But the state attorney in Miami dropped all charges and let him out."

"Why?"

I gave a humorless laugh. "Long story."

"Let's go for a run."

"I'd kill for a beer."

"First we run." She winked. "Then a beer."

We got in our cars and headed for Singer Island. The clouds had pulled together and then pushed apart leaving the sky postcard azure. I drove the Jeep in a funk, wanting to believe that Montgomery would leave us be if we left him. Which meant that Angel would not be avenged, and my guilt would fester. It wasn't a great feeling. I really longed for that beer, but I had already broken one promise to Danielle in the past twenty-four hours, and I'd lost. So if she wanted to run, she'd get a run.

CHAPTER FORTY—NINE

We ambled past the bars and restaurants at City Beach, and quickened our pace as we crossed the concrete path that acted like a drawbridge across the sand moat between the beach and the promenade. As we came up over the grassy dunes I saw the lounges and umbrellas set out for rental, looking barren and vacant, the beachgoers turned off by the mild day and earlier cloud. Now the ocean sparkled and soft white foam played on the hard sand, just short of our feet, which didn't suit my mood. Our normal running positions were reversed. I took the lead and pushed hard. My lungs burned before my muscles did, but then my muscles did too. I still ached from the beating I got from Rinti's boys, so now everything hurt equally. I ran an extra half mile from our usual turnaround point, and waited, hands on knees, for Danielle to arrive. She was a better runner than me, lighter on her feet and technically proficient. She moved like a gazelle. When she got to me she was breathing hard, and she frowned.

"Working some stuff out there?" she puffed.

I nodded. "Good to go?"

She returned the nod, and we headed back, footprints deep in the wet sand. I negative split the run back, and it hurt. Everything burned by the time I reached the lifeguard tower nestled on the dunes, and that was the point. Danielle came in at her regular pace. I was still grimacing when she arrived.

"You okay?" she said.

I shrugged as we jogged up the back and over the dunes. We walked toward the falling sun in silence for a time, and then Danielle touched my arm.

"You worried about this guy, this Montgomery?"

"Not really. I just think he should be in jail."

"Did he get out on bail or something technical?"

"He got out because all the evidence disappeared."

"Are you kidding?"

"The drugs, video, officer's report, the whole shebang. Within hours."

"I can't believe it. You hear of things like that, but I've never seen it. I mean the odd traffic citation, or rich guy's DUI sure, but not drugs."

"Conceptually the same. Just more drugs in Miami."

"I guess you're right. But it doesn't give him a get out of jail free card. The system still works."

"You think?"

"It's like water in a barrel, isn't it? There might be a few rusty holes, and a little water might escape, but most of the water gets captured most of the time."

I didn't respond. We crossed North Ocean Drive and headed down to my house. I was tossing Danielle's words around in my head, but I wasn't thinking about the water captured in the barrel. I was more concerned with the stuff that had spilled out, and who was going to clean it up. And if no one did, what kind of damage it would do.

Danielle showered and then switched out with me. I turned the water down cold and let it ice my muscles until they ached. When I got out I was blue and Danielle was leaning against the door jamb. She watched me toweling off.

"What aren't you telling me?" she said. There's a certain unfair advantage to interrogating someone when they're naked, which may not have been Danielle's point, but with her being a deputy I couldn't rule it out.

"Probably a lot, but what are you referring to?"

"It's more than just this girl, Angela."

"I'm struggling to get her off my mind."

"You're naked in front of me and you have another woman on your mind? I'd tread carefully if I were you." She raised an eyebrow, which didn't tell me anything. She might be playful or she might be about to slug me in the chops for the wrong answer. I wrapped my towel around my waist and faced her.

"Ron's friend Cassandra received threats."

Danielle's eyebrow lift turned to frown. "Montgomery?"

"Not enough to take to a judge, but yes, Montgomery."

"So you told Palm Beach PD."

"They don't think it will happen again. We got Cassandra out of town just in case until Burke gets somewhere." I left out the part about going well outside normal operating procedure. I didn't think after the barrel-of-water speech Danielle was up to hearing about our attempt to plant evidence.

"I spoke to the forensic investigator on Angela's case," I said. "She said the case will go on the back burner. Says they have no evidence, and no probable cause to work over Montgomery." I padded out into the bedroom and slipped on some chinos and a St. Lucie Mets tee. The shirt always stirred up a few passions at Longboard's, and I was in a combative kind of mood.

"So why has Ron's friend got you so agitated?" Danielle had turned 180 degrees and leaned the other shoulder on the jamb.

I looked at her, wet hair clinging to her neck. Doing to a plain T-shirt and jeans what Audrey Hepburn did to a little black dress. And I realized why Stoat's call had me so agitated. I thought it was because I'd messed up and been made to look like a fool, and there was a good dose of that in my anger. But there was more.

"Is it what I said the other night? About losing you?" she said. "Because if it is, I'm sorry. I shouldn't have put that on you. It wasn't fair. If I can trust Ron to handle himself, I should be able to trust you."

"Ron's not worried about himself. He's worried about his loved ones. And I'm worried about mine."

Danielle stepped to me and gave me a light kiss, and then hugged me. I wrapped my arms around her, and was reminded again for all her toughness, how fragile she felt. She pulled back and gave me that half smile that made my old blood pumper do back flips.

"Let's go get that beer," she said.

CHAPTER FIFTY

All's right with the world when I walk into Longboard Kelly's on a mild fall evening and see the party lights emitting their multicolored glow across the courtyard, and I find Ron sitting at the bar, beer in hand. The courtyard tables were half full, and Muriel was leaning on the back of the indoor bar, chest out, chatting with Ron. We arrived at the bar as Muriel bumped her hips and stood to the taps, and poured me a beer.

"Vodka tonic?" she asked Danielle.

"Sounds good." Danielle touched my shoulder. "I'm just going to give Burke a call." I nodded, and Danielle headed for the rear of the courtyard, next to the surfboard with a bite out of it, where the noise was lowest and the phone reception was best. Ron and I watched her go, and then clinked beers. I took a long gulp and a deep sigh. I wasn't sure if it was the drink or just being in a place that often felt more like home than home that gave me relief.

"You look strung-out my friend," said Ron.

"Nothing a few beers with you won't fix."

"I can't stay too long. I have a hot date."

"That's moving on quick, even for you."

"The Lady Cassandra has asked me to join her in Colorado."

"Well, good for you." We clinked glasses again. Ron looked happy, and that made me happy. I realized that I looked at Ron like the kids on the college campus looked at me. That somehow each of us must have reached an age where we no longer yearned for a full heart. But seeing Ron now, I realized the truth was that hope sprung eternal in all of us.

"What about you then," he said.

"Same old stuff."

"I heard Montgomery got nabbed by Miami PD. Not saying you had anything to do with it, but it's good news."

"He got out."

"What?"

"He was released. Didn't even spend the night. All the evidence went *poof*. Gone."

"I don't believe it," said Ron.

"Believe it. He's got serious pull down there."

"I *don't* believe it."

"What, you think every cop in the world is golden? Come on, even Danielle doesn't believe that."

"No," he said, grabbing my shoulder and turning me toward the parking lot entrance. "I don't believe that."

Standing just inside the courtyard, surveying the scene for a vacant table like a regular Joe, was Alexander Montgomery. He wore a cream linen suit and white fedora, and looked like he just rolled in from his Carolina plantation. He spotted a table to his liking and strode over to it with his bodyguard/driver in his wake. They shifted their chairs so they faced the entrance to the courtyard and sat down.

"He didn't seem to notice us," said Ron.

"Oh, he knows we're here, all right." I put my beer on the bar.

"Maybe you should just leave it," said Ron.

"Is that what you think? I should leave it?"

"Or call the cops."

"Is he breaking the law by being here?"

Ron shrugged. "Perhaps you should just go and smash him over the head with a hockey stick. Get him back for your car."

"Thanks, Ron, helpful. But the car was Rinti's guys."

"My mistake. I'm struggling to keep up with all the people who want to bonk you on the head."

"You and me both."

"So what are you going to do?"

I looked across the courtyard at Danielle, who was pacing back and forth, head down, phone to her ear.

"I think I'll go say hello."

I edged my way between tables, ducking between umbrellas emblazoned with beer logos, over to Montgomery. He looked relaxed, like a wealthy gent summering on the Cote d'Azur. He glanced up at the last minute, giving me a grin that I might have read too much into, but felt like the smile of a serial killer. Either way it wasn't pleasant.

"Why, if it isn't *the* Miami Jones. Listen, Jones, what does one have to do to get a drink in his place?" He grinned.

"You have to get off your lazy backside and go to the bar." I looked at his gut. "You look like you could do with the walk." He dropped the smile. No man likes being called fat, and don't let anyone tell you different.

"What are you doing here, Peanut?" I said. I thought butchering his marketing name might bring a response, but all I got was a clenching of the jaw, and then he relaxed again.

"Nice evening, so Nigel and I thought we might down a few bevvies." The plummy accent was grating on me.

"You want to be careful," I said. "I hear the staff spit in your drinks."

"So why do you drink here?"

"They don't spit in my drinks."

Montgomery leaned back in his chair. The grin returned. He really did think he was the ant's pajamas.

"What do you want, Montgomery?"

He leaned forward and gestured me closer, like he was going to pass me a state secret. I put my hands on the table and looked him in the eye.

"If there's one thing I learned growing up on the mean streets of London, it was respect."

"Mean streets? I heard you went to private school and then your daddy got you a job for an oil company."

"He did no such thing," he hissed. He took a breath to calm himself, and his grin morphed into a snarl.

"You could well do to learn some respect."

"I have respect," I said. Now it was my turn to grin. "I respect the sanctity of the locker room. I respect the winning and whatever superstition you believe keeps it going. I respect the batter who's two and oh in the count with the winning run on base and still has the guts to swing for the bleachers. I respect a man who treats a lady like a lady, and a lady's right to be treated like a man. I respect war monuments, minutes of silence and Old Glory. But I do not respect junior oil salesman with delusions of grandeur and nasty streaks."

Montgomery's snarl turned so hard he looked like Billy Idol.

"You think you're so clever, you Americans. But we all found out last night who's clever and who's not. So I'm going to tell you what I think. I think when a man comes onto my turf and messes with my business, I have a right—nay, a duty—to come onto his turf and mess with his business."

"You're going to mess with my business? It's really not that lucrative."

"I'm going to mess with you," he hissed through clenched teeth. "I'm gonna smash up your car."

"Someone already beat you to that."

"Then I'll burn your house to the ground. I'll burn your office to the ground, with your grandpa of a sidekick in it. Then what? Maybe I'll start on that fine filly I saw you walk in here with. She looks a real goer, hey, Nigel?" Nigel nodded.

I stiffened and Montgomery's snarl grew wider. "Yeah, why don't you take a shot at me? Get yourself an assault charge. Bet you can't get out before tomorrow. And while you're away, we'll keep her company, won't we, Nigel. *Nige* has a special bat and everything."

I pushed at the table, and it scraped a few inches, squeezing Montgomery into his chair and causing all the eyes in the courtyard to turn to us. I could feel blood pumping in my temples, and it made it hard to think. The idea occurred that I should take some breaths in through my nose, like I did on the mound, but I wasn't convinced I wanted to calm down. What I wanted was to break Montgomery's neck. Snap it in half and worry about the eyewitnesses later. But I didn't. Montgomery pushed his chair back and brushed his shirt with his hand.

"On second thoughts, they probably only have that pish American beer here anyway. I'd rather drink dishwater." He stood and Nigel followed him.

"Say, Jones, you have a pet? A dog or something."

"No."

"Don't get one. Ever." He smiled at his wit and patted Nigel on the shoulder, and they sauntered out of the courtyard. I watched them go, and then I did some deep breathing to relieve the thumping in my head. I turned to look at Ron, who was looking at me with a frown. So was Danielle, standing next to him.

"Who was that?" she said as I got to the bar. I picked up my beer and finished it in one long gulp.

"How's Burke?" I said.

"You're right. They don't have anything to go on. But who was that?"

"That," I said, thumping my empty glass on the bar, "was Alexander Montgomery, aka Pistachio."

"That's him? What was he doing here?"

"Ruffling feathers."

"Yours?"

"Everyone's. I think we all need to keep our wits about us."

"I'm going to call the office," said Danielle. "There's got to be something we can do."

"There's not. This is one bit of water that seeped out of your rusty barrel. Now he's all over the floor, wreaking havoc. We've got to figure out another way to mop him up."

"You're getting good value out of that metaphor. Or is it a simile?" said Ron.

"Simile. I think."

"You want me to stay?" he said.

"No, go see your lady."

"You need something, just yell."

"Keep your eyes open, pal. Seriously."

"Always do. You never know when the boom is going to swing across the deck." Ron finished his beer, slipped off his stool and winked at Danielle.

"Are you two serious?" she said. "This guy is a murder suspect. And I don't care if he's out of the barrel. I'm calling the sheriff on this one. And I've got lunch tomorrow with Eric. I'm going to get him in the loop too."

"You have lunch tomorrow with Eric?"

"He called. I was going to blow it off, but now, no way." She frowned. "You said it didn't bother you."

"It doesn't. I didn't know it was a regular thing, but whatever. It doesn't bother me."

"Too bad if it does. I'm meeting him because I want everyone possible to know about this Montgomery guy. And Eric might be able to help."

I nodded to Muriel for another beer. "You know, I think you're right. He can help."

CHAPTER FIFTY—ONE

I was right. State Attorney Eric Edwards could help. Just not
with Montgomery. He wasn't about to do anything that might
get his tie dirty, let alone bloody. Sure, he'd swoop in once the
cops had done the hard yards and arrested the guy, claiming he
was the crime-fighting prosecutor. But that didn't mean Edwards
wouldn't do some investigating. His version of down and dirty
work was political in nature, and as such he could be very
helpful. Especially with my pressure points, and one Dr. Millet.

I decided to get the hop on Danielle and her lunch with
Eric, so I tapped his office for an urgent midmorning
appointment. While I waited I looked over some documents for
Ron regarding an insurance fraud case he was working. We had
corporate clients, Boondoggle Lawry be damned. Lizzy didn't
offer to get me coffee from down the street, so I was comforted
that some things were getting back to normal.

I wandered across to the state attorney building in bright
sunshine. Although confident that Montgomery wouldn't do
anything in broad daylight, I kept my eyes moving and my ears
open. I got there without incident. Eric made me wait ten
minutes in his lobby, which was fine with me. Eric didn't hire
ugly paralegals. It was a character trait. Or a character flaw,
depending on your point of view. So I enjoyed the scenery,
young and bouncy as it was, and then Edwards buzzed me
through. He was shuffling papers on his desk, which I had

always imagined was what lawyers did, and was overjoyed to see it confirmed. He barely looked up at me.

"Make it quick—I've got a busy day."

I was tempted to say something about his day being filled with lunch dates with my girlfriend and his ex-wife, but I decided to keep that in my pocket.

"I've news about the college investigation."

Edwards stopped shuffling and looked at me. "Oh, you're here about that."

"What else?"

"Nothing." He gave me his *I know something you don't know* look, as if lunch with Danielle was their little secret. I wondered if Yale law had a class to perfect that facial expression.

"So my sources tell me that the president of the school is about to crack. He's not good with political shenanigans, and I think a call from the state attorney's office might push him over the edge. I think a skilled orator like you could turn him."

"You want me to threaten him?"

"A gentle reminder of the implications of corruption charges for one's career, that sort of thing."

"And you think he'll roll?"

"I do." Actually I didn't. My guess was he was the kind of ferret that would close up like a clam, and destroy all the evidence. But the net effect would be the same for my purposes.

"Is he around?"

"I have reason to believe he will be in his office at four o'clock this afternoon." I believed that because I had left a message with Millet's secretary, pretending to be from Senator Lawry's office, telling her that the senator would be calling at four. I was pretty confident that was a call Millet would cancel his own funeral for.

Edwards picked up his phone and hit a button. "Maisie, what do I have on at four this afternoon? Office time? Fine, book me in for a call." He hung up the phone and began his shuffling again.

"Was there anything else?" he said.

"No, nothing. You have a nice day."

He looked at me and smiled his winningest politician's smile.

"I intend to," he said, as I walked out the door.

CHAPTER FIFTY-TWO

Since my girlfriend was lunching with her ex-husband, and
Ron was swanning it up in Vail, I dined on a tilapia sandwich at
Longboard's. Mick was his usual chatty self, delivering the plate
with a thud and responding to my request for some lemon with a
mumbled *don't need it*. He was right. The fish had a hint of smoke
from the grill, and needed no further assistance. I took my time
getting down to Lauderdale, and the top of my Jeep flapped
loudly on the freeway, giving me pause to consider my choice
again. One does a lot of freeway miles in South Florida. I parked
in the visitors' lot next to the administration building. None of
the campus rent-a-cops knew my Jeep, so I didn't expect trouble.
Besides, I wasn't planning on staying long, or coming back
anytime soon. I waited in the car, considered a visit to the
athletic department and dismissed it, and then when I was ready
I strode up the steps of the glass-fronted building, took the
elevator to the third floor and marched my way to Millet's office.

His receptionist saw me coming around the atrium but
stood mouth agape as I swooshed past with a wink. She was an
aloof thing but had clearly given up on stopping the likes of me
from barging into her boss's office. Which is what I did. Millet
was at his desk, staring at his phone like it was a freshly delivered
parcel with a radioactive materials sticker on it. He looked small
and tired behind the large desk, and the space took on the
proportions of the reading room in the New York Public

Library because of it. Millet glanced up at me and gave a sigh of resignation. This was not how he had envisioned his academic career. Murder, drugs, crooked developers, self-interested politicians and pushy PI's.

"I hear you're going to be on the front page of the *Post*," I said as I strode up to his desk.

"What are you talking about?"

"The corruption charges. Federal investigation. You using donations and federal Department of Education funding to pay organized crime figures like Gino Rinti, who then used said funding to bribe Florida state senators to fast-track your little project."

"Don't be ridiculous," he said. "If you repeat any of that . . ."

"Not me. *Palm Beach Post*."

"That woman?"

"Maggie Nettles. Good, I'm glad she got hold of you. I wouldn't want you to miss the opportunity to present your side of the story."

"She's muckraking, and so are you. I happen to be waiting on a call from a state senator right now. I can assure you this project is above board and full steam ahead." I almost expected him to say rah-rah!

"Senator Lawry, yeah. I wouldn't expect to hear from him today, or ever again. Not now the state attorney's office has launched a corruption investigation and the good senator is blaming you for everything."

Millet's mouth dropped. The thought that he could be left holding the dead duck had not occurred to him, given the white pallor that washed across his face. I could see his mind ticking over, hoping against hope that I was wrong, but having a hard time dealing with that pesky reality. Then the phone rang. On cue, as expected. Millet looked at me and almost smiled. Almost. He let it ring a second time. The phone was Schrödinger's cat. Until he answered it, it could equally be his salvation or his demise. Senator Lawry, as expected, stiff upper, everything's fine, let's get this thing done, blow the naysayers. Or not Senator Lawry. It rang again, the sound swallowed by the leather-bound tomes encasing the room. Millet put his hand on the receiver and lifted it.

"Yes? It's who?" His eyes looked in my direction, but not at me. More like he was staring into another dimension of space and time. The corners of his mouth dropped. "All right. Put him through." Millet's body shrank in his natty suit. He listened for a moment. "Yes, Mr. Edwards, this is he." More listening, then: "I'm afraid I don't have the particulars in front of me . . . Yes, Rinti Developments are involved in the feasibility study, but it really hasn't progressed from there . . . I believe some members from Tallahassee have visited, but I can't specifically recall who . . . Senator Lawry? No, I don't recall him either way . . . A formal time to answer your questions? I suppose I could . . . Monday next? Fine, that's fine . . . Until then. Goodbye." Millet slowly placed the receiver down. His vision focused back into the room.

"Not Senator Lawry, then," I said.

Millet shook his head. "State attorney's office. Somebody Edwards."

"Ooh, Edwards. He's a real Elliot Ness type."

"But I've done nothing wrong." Millet looked at me, pleading. I'm not sure if he was trying to convince me or himself.

"Yeah, look—it's just me, but I think you might want to give yourself five or ten minutes to reassess that position, then get cracking on putting the kibosh on this whole mega-campus deal.

Then you might consider jumping on Craigslist and checking out some middle school engineering teaching positions. Just a thought." I turned and left him openmouthed, and ambled back out to the atrium. I apologized to the receptionist for barging in, and then danced my way down the fire stairs two at a time. I got across the lobby and my cell phone rang. I thought it was Eric Edwards. It wasn't.

"Jones? This is Maggie Nettles. I checked out your story. Looks like your info's good."

"Tell me something I don't know."

"Lawry has a bank account in Nassau."

"Figures."

"I have a copy of the wire transfer note, from another Bahamas account that I can link back to Rinti Developments."

"Nice."

"And the transfer note. It's from one of those old-fashioned printers. Dot matrix? All the little dots. Anyway, the comments field is interesting."

"Because it says . . ."

"1132 College," she said.

"Which means?"

"The university admin office, Millet's office, is at 1132 College Drive."

"Thin."

"I don't need to follow the rules of evidence, Jones. I just need to sway the jury of public opinion."

"So what do you want?"

"More background. And don't worry, you are unnamed sources."

So I sat on the steps of the administration building, right under Millet's window, and outlined the story in more detail. Maggie was good. She had already connected most of the dots. I left out my personal interludes again, but left her with a pretty meaty story.

"And you might want to hit up Millet one more time," I said. "See if he wants to get anything off his chest."

I rang off and wandered to my Jeep. Pink blankets of cloud sat on the horizon, giving the sky a good dose of character. I felt pretty good, considering a very nasty guy wanted me and my as yet unobtained pet dead. I may not have been a rocket scientist, but I had good days. And this was turning out to be one of them. I got in the Jeep and fired it up. I was tossing up between the turnpike and I-95 at rush hour when my phone rang again.

"Jones? Ronzoni."

"Detective Ronzoni." I felt so good I didn't even consider messing with his name for once. "How goes it?"

"Plaza Lakes. Mean anything to you?"

"Danielle has a townhouse in that community."

"That's what I thought. I just heard a call on the radio. Plaza Lakes."

"What call?"

"Officer down."

CHAPTER FIFTY—THREE

Hospitals get busy at the strangest hours. Accidents and sickness don't follow the sundial. Wellington Regional was a smaller facility than Broward General, but it was still a tangle of humanity. I parked in the lot out front of the new building that looked like an office complex, and asked a nurse at the front desk for directions. For all I knew she may have been the same nurse I got directions from at Broward General when I visited Jake Turner. Those pink or blue pajamas they wear make them all look the same.

Danielle's colleague Burke stood in the hallway outside the room. He was on a call, but when he saw me he cut it off and walked to me.

"She's okay," he said.

"Define okay."

"GSW to the arm and lower torso. She's just out of OR. The doc says stable. Nothing major hit. She'll be okay."

"I need to see her."

"You can stick your head in the door. But she's still drugged up."

We walked to the room, where a nurse protested without energy. Burke gave her a look and she relented. I stepped into the room. I was struck by the silence. There were no beeps and machines whirring. I couldn't even hear Danielle breathe. She was tight under crisp sheets, her arms on top, punctured by IV drips. Her hair was matted back like she'd been swimming or had used too much gel, and her skin lacked the color of life. I bent down to check she was breathing and heard the steady one-two, in-out, that I had grown to love waking up to. It was solid, not raspy or gurgling, and it gave me confidence. It was the only thing about the room that did. A monitor on the other side of the bed showed her pulse on a graph, and her BPM. Peaks and troughs. I kissed her on the forehead, and she felt cool and clammy on my lips. Then I slipped back out of the room. Burke was waiting.

"We got a partial witness, a neighbor. He didn't see the event, but he heard the shots. He hunts, so he knew the sound. He saw a guy, dark and solid, get into a car he described as green and sporty, but not that sporty."

"A Jaguar?"

"Maybe. He did say as the car peeled away toward the community exit, it braked hard and he noticed only one brake light worked."

The other one being busted by yours truly, but I kept that to myself.

"How did they get into a gated community?"

"We're looking into that. It seems the security guy at the front gate might have stepped away for moment."

"Stepped away? I'll step him away."

"Cool yourself, Miami. We don't need you flying off the handle."

"What do you need, Burke? Two dead kids, a woman threatened at knife point and now a deputy shot. And you're oh for four. Zippo, zilch."

"Right now it's not about what I need—it's about what Danielle needs."

I took a deep breath. What I really wanted was to put my fist through a wall. Which would hurt both my bones and my wallet. Burke gave me a moment. He was clearly used to waiting for angry people to collect themselves. And technically Jake and Cassandra weren't PBSO cases, but he had the good grace to not defend himself. I guess oh for two wasn't really any better.

"You going after him?"

Burke nodded. "Miami PD got stakeouts covering the car, the apartment, a house in Coral Gables and his office on Brickell."

"Miami PD let him walk, so I won't hold my breath waiting for them to sneak up on him."

"Not much we can do about that. We can't go down there ourselves. Anywhere else we need to add?"

"Not that I know of. My office manager was checking him out. I'll ask her."

"We need to get the weapon."

"So that means they'll get rid of it."

"Where?"

"Hell, could be anywhere."

"How many perps just choose anywhere?"

"You're the cop—you tell me."

"Almost none. Half toss it on a direct path from the crime scene to wherever they're going. The other half choose somewhere known to them. It's rarely random."

"So you're checking around Plaza Lakes."

"Needle in a haystack, but yeah."

"Or somewhere they know."

"Like I say, Miami PD are staking the locales in case they show up. But where aren't we looking?"

I thought on it for a moment, and one face leaped into my mind.

"Alligator Alley, where they left Angel."

"Maybe. I'll get a patrol out there." Burke stepped away to make his call. I felt like I should do something too, so I called the office. Lizzy was still there.

"I'm glad you didn't leave yet," I said.

"Detective Ronzoni said I should stay until he came to get me."

"Ronzoni's coming to get you?"

"He said he would drive me home to get some things, then take me somewhere safe. He told me about Danielle. Is she okay?"

"Stable. Listen, you checked on Montgomery's property, was there anything we didn't know?"

I heard paper shuffling, and then Lizzy came back. "An apartment, house, the office, the Jag. There is another car, a Land Rover, registered to the company. And another house in Nassau, also registered to the company, and a boat."

"A boat? Where?"

"Registered and berthed in Miami."

"Lizzy, thanks. You keep the door locked until Ronzoni gets there, and make sure it's him before you let him in."

"It's under control. And you. You be safe. I'll be praying for you both."

"I never thought I'd say this, but I appreciate that. I need all the help I can get right now."

I rang off and looked at Burke, still busy on a call. I figured it made him feel better to be doing something, but also figured whatever he was doing to be pointless. If Miami PD were covering Montgomery's hideouts, then Montgomery had any number of outs, because there was no way to know who we could trust down there. And as Burke had said, we couldn't go down there ourselves. Which got me thinking. About trust and location. We couldn't know who to trust in Vice down in Miami, but that didn't mean we couldn't trust anyone. And the fact was Burke couldn't go down there. Didn't mean no one could. I made another couple of calls. In baseball parlance, I was positioning my field. If it came to it, I needed to be able to maneuver the batter to where I wanted him. Then I made a third call, to set the sucker pitch into play. Stoat answered.

"It's Miami. You guys are watching Montgomery."

"It's all plainclothes, coordinated by Vice."

"That's what I thought. Do you have uniformed guys you trust?"

"Of course."

"I need you to do drive-bys. Constantly. At all his properties and office."

"We'll be in patrol cars. If he doesn't see us, someone he owns will."

"I'm counting on it."

Burke wandered over, and I rang off with Stoat, who promised to have patrol cars doing laps of Montgomery's hangouts.

"Anything?" said Burke.

"Lizzy found a house on Nassau."

"I can alert Homeland Security to watch all ports, in case he tries to slip out of the country. Anything else?"

"No. Call Homeland Security."

Burke went to place his call, and I stepped back into Danielle's room. To hell with visiting hours. The nurses bent the rules for law enforcement. It might not have been fair to the regular folks with loved ones lying in the wards, but things were different for those who put themselves in harm's way every day. If you didn't look after the warriors, then who would defend the city walls? I sat with Danielle for what seemed like forever. The human mind has an amazing capacity to process thoughts in such a short time. I thought the Jake Turner case through from beginning to end, Kim Rose and President Millet, internships and Rinti and Senator Lawry, Officer Steele and Angel and an English petroleum executive by the name of Pistachio. I thought about my career, ups and downs, cold winters in Connecticut and hot summers in Florida, and a baseball career of sorts in between. I thought about meeting Danielle, and her kicking my backside in sit-up competitions, and sultry, quiet nights on my back patio, and the smell of her on my pillows when she didn't stay, and the joy of seeing her wander out of the bedroom in the morning to the smell of fresh brewed coffee, wearing nothing but a threadbare Modesto A's T-shirt. I did a lifetime's thinking in an hour as I watched her sleep. And I thought about hitting the streets, doing something, anything, to find this guy and right this wrong. And then I watched Danielle breathing delicately, and figured that was all macho ego and vanity. What I needed to do right now was be the face she saw when she woke.

And then her eyes opened. Slow and deliberate, like an old animatronic figure at Disneyland years ago. She blinked a few times to clear her vision, get used to the light. Then she saw me. She didn't smile. I don't think she had it in her. I held her hand tight and smiled for both of us. Then she opened her parched lips and whispered. I couldn't hear, so I leaned closer.

"Pistachio," she said, and then she gulped a dry swallow that hurt. She closed her eyes, and I moved to get some water but she didn't let go of my hand. She held on tighter than I thought she could, and she pulled me in. Danielle fixed her eyes on me and licked her lips.

"MJ, the water is out of the barrel," she said.

"I know, sweetie, I know. Everyone's on it. Burke, the PBSO, Miami PD."

She squeezed my hand tighter so it hurt, and ever so slightly shook her head. She gulped again, and then whispered to me.

"End it."

CHAPTER FIFTY—FOUR

I made my way to the ER waiting room. Sal Mondavi was sitting in the corner doing just that. He looked like a patient waiting on a bed. Despite living in Florida longer than I'd known him, he still carried the gray pallor of someone with a terminal disease, which to my knowledge he did not have. He pushed himself up from his chair as I approached.

"Thanks for coming, Sally. I didn't know who else to call."

He shrugged. "How is she?"

"She woke up, so that's something."

"Waking up is everything. So, kid, what's the plan?"

"Everything about this guy is in Miami."

"Let's go."

"I appreciate this, Sally. I owe you big time."

He gave me a stern look. "You owe nothing, and you mention that again I'll make you sit through my Superbowl III video."

"Cast me into hell, Sal."

Sally picked up his leather bag, the sort of thing a doctor would have carried on house calls in Sally's day. We retrieved the Jeep and headed south. I updated him on the latest goings-on as we headed down I-95.

"Sounds like this putz needs to learn some respect."

"Funny, that's what he said to me."

"In my experience it's always the ones that lack respect that complain loudest about not having it."

"So what do you think?"

"Seems to me that the guy thinks he's untouchable. But if you've ever heard of the grassy knoll, you should know that no one is untouchable. And he's not from a family, so he doesn't know the business. He doesn't follow the rules, such as they are. So I've got no doubt that he's treading on all kinds of toes. No one likes someone making a lot of noise, flashing his cash and connections. These things are done quietly and sparingly."

"Well, he certainly got the attention of the South Florida law enforcement community. Especially those he doesn't own."

"That's my point. You shoot a deputy, you better have a damn good reason, because it's going to bring some heat. And not just for you, for everyone. The other organizations aren't going to like it. I remember back in the seventies, a kid called Jonny Cassini gets to thinking he's the new godfather of the Bronx. He kills a cop he couldn't buy, just to prove a point. Only point he proved is how quick an up-and-coming crime boss can be disappeared."

"You think that might happen? The other organizations take Montgomery out?"

"I know these families. Most of them are from or at least connected to New York, even the Latinos. If this guy becomes too hot, he'll end up on a one-way flight to the Bermuda triangle. But they're smart. They'll wait and see if he learns his lesson, keeps his head down. No one wants a war."

"But he's not going to keep his head down. He's arrogant beyond belief."

"Which is bad news for you. Because the families don't know that, so they'll wait. If they knew him, they'd act fast."

"So someone could end up dead before they act."

"Exactly. Let's make sure it's not you, kid."

I burned through Fort Lauderdale and looked west as I did, toward the stillness of the Everglades, and I heard the voice of Lorraine Catchitt, the forensic investigator at Angel's murder scene: *any earlier and the gators would've got her.* It added an extra bind in my twisted gut. As we got to the first of the Miami exits my cell phone rang. I glanced at the screen, which read *Lucas.* I had placed my field by making two calls from the hospital. One was to Sally, the other to Lucas.

"Lucas," I said.

"G'day mate," he said in his slow drawl. "You must be a flamin' psychic. That boat you asked about? Sure enough, the guy just called. I'm to fuel it up and have it prepped in an hour."

"Thanks, Lucas."

"No worries. See ya shortly."

Sal looked at me. "Something?"

"Montgomery's running. So I figured I'd limit his options. Patrol guys are making a lot of noise around his hangouts in Miami, so his bent cops won't be able to secret him away. I left one obvious option open to him, to see if he'd take the bait. Looks like he has."

CHAPTER FIFTY—FIVE

The parking lot by the Miami Beach marina was dark with shadows from the mangroves. I parked the Jeep in the far corner, where it was all but invisible. The lot was still and silent as the mangroves absorbed wind and sound. The dock master's office was lit by a solitary spotlight over a glass sliding door. A cheap plastic chair sat by the door.

"So who is this guy?" said Sally, as we walked toward the light. He limped with the weight of his doctor's bag, but I knew better than to ask if he needed help.

"Lucas? He's an old friend of Lenny's. Ex-Australian SAS or something. Lenny saved Lucas's family back in the day, and Lucas sees it as a debt he owes for life. Somehow that debt got transferred to me."

I tried the sliding door and found it locked, so we skirted the building and came around to the dockside. The promenade was lit like it was ready for a parade, and each of the docks fed out like fingers, lit by small safety lights into the wood. We stopped and looked around. There was no movement but the tinking of rigging on a handful of masts, but there weren't many of those. Most of the boats were motor yachts, and most of them were large. I didn't see Lucas, but he saw me.

"How's it going?" came the voice from the shadows behind us.

"Jesus, Lucas," I said. He morphed out of the shadows, his beaming white teeth the first thing I picked up. He stepped forward, tanned, leathery skin darker than the night.

"You boys alright?"

"Been better." I introduced Lucas to Sally.

"How are ya?" he said to Sally, who shrugged his answer, and then Lucas looked at me. His eyes shone like beacons from his dark features, and he carried the sweet scent of cigar smoke.

"You visited Lenny lately?" he said.

"Not for a while," I replied.

"I got up there last week, shared a six-pack with him."

"I need to make some time."

Lucas nodded. "Well, let's see this boat." He ambled away, the clap-clap of flip-flops smacking on the wooden boardwalk. Sally fell in beside me and whispered.

"You were talking about Lenny Cox then?"

"Aha."

"And he's still dead, right?"

"Oh, yeah."

"So is this guy all there?" Sally tapped his head.

"Completely. He likes to visit the cemetery, drink to old times."

Sally nodded and fell silent.

Lucas used a key card to get through the gate, and then walked us to a boat that must have been a hundred feet long. The name scrawled across the transom was *El Jefe*.

"El Jefe? Really?" I said.

"Your man Montgomery just bought it a few months back. The last owner called it that, and I guess he likes it."

"Can we get in?"

"Sure. These guys who want full service have to leave their keys so I can fill 'er up, get 'er cleaned and all that."

"They don't have a crew? It's a big boat."

"Some do, but not this guy. We supply crew with a bit of notice, but most of them pay us to do the maintenance. So who is this joker?"

I gave Lucas the rundown on Angel and Danielle and Jake Turner. He listened and the furrows in his brow deepened.

"Sounds like a nasty piece of work. And a Pom, too. So what's the plan, mate?"

"I'm going to get on, stow away until they get where they're going, then if I can get the gun that killed Angel and shot Danielle, I will."

"And if you can't?" said Sally. "You need to know how far you're willing to go before you start. You do not want to be making this up on the fly."

"I know, Sally. I know what I have to do. I'm just trying not to think about how my life will be different."

"Kid, every morning when you wake up, you're a different person, based on the choices you made yesterday. It's inevitable. But today, your choice is about whether you or your loved ones wake up tomorrow at all. So it's not a choice. You're crossing a line, no doubt, and it's a line best not crossed, but given you have no real option, then the only question is, do you believe that crossing the line is the right thing to do?"

"I do."

"Then suck it up, and get it done."

I took a deep breath and nodded. I had taken a life before, that of the person who had killed Lenny Cox. But that had been instantaneous, reflex. This was a considered action. But Sally was right. I may not have to take it all the way, but if I did, I couldn't flinch.

"Let's do this," I said. I pulled on a pair of latex gloves and stepped on to the swimming platform at the rear of the boat.

"You planning on driving this boat back?" said Sally. "Even if things go pear-shaped?"

"That's a good point," I said.

"I think I can help you there," said Lucas. He outlined his proposal and Sally and I listened, and then agreed it was the way to go.

"Is it rough out there?" I said.

"Nah, mate, light onshore breeze, a little chop is all."

I looked at Sal. "You know where this place is?"

"I'll be there," said Sally.

"Take my truck, mate," said Lucas, pulling keys out of his pocket. "The old red Tacoma in the lot. There's one of them GPS thingies in the glove box, and behind the seat you'll find some bolt cutters and a .22."

"Speaking of which, my gun is in the safe in my office," I said.

"Are you sure you've thought this through?" said Sally. He dropped his bag to the dock, bent down and snapped it open, and then fished out a gun and handed it to me.

"Nine millimeter, and here's a spare clip. It's untraceable, but if you use it, don't bring it home with you."

"Thanks, Sal. I'll see you guys later."

I watched Sally lumber back down the dock toward the parking lot, and Lucas take off in the opposite direction, toward the water. I double-checked the safety on the gun lest I blow part of myself off, then tucked it into my chinos and climbed on board Pistachio's boat.

CHAPTER FIFTY—SIX

The boat had two levels above deck, and I was guessing two below. One of those would be the engine room, and I figured a guy who called ahead to get fueled didn't spend much time down there. The aft deck on the main level was small but led through glass doors to an impressive lounge. I stepped inside and closed the door behind. The lounge had a bar of solid marble that ran its length. In Jane Austen's day they could have held a ball in the space. Montgomery, or perhaps the doofus who had christened the vessel *El Jefe*, had filled the space with a pool table, and still had room to disco. At the aft end of the bar was a door of gleaming rosewood that looked like a pantry but led down to the lower level.

At the bottom of the steps I found a small coffee service area with a large box that read *PG Tips tea*. On the opposite side, reading chairs sat in two groups of four. Beyond the chairs a hallway ran down the side of the boat toward staterooms. There were two that were smaller but still the size of hotel rooms, and at the front a massive master stateroom with private en suite and a walk-in closet. I figured they weren't going to be having friends over, so I hid inside the stateroom closest to the lounge, and waited.

I waited longer than I wanted, because I could feel my nerve slipping away with every tick of the clock. I closed my eyes and saw Angel, running on a floodlit soccer field, doing sprints and dribbling exercises, breathing hard but full of life. Then I saw Danielle, lying on a stainless steel table under cold light, her lips pale, eyes closed, the life snuffed out of her. I opened my eyes with a start because what I heard was the sound of footsteps on the deck. I stood behind the door and listened but heard nothing. No voices, no more footsteps. The soundproofing in the room was good. But not good enough to mask the sound of the engines starting. A deep rumble came from below my feet. It idled for a few moments, and then I felt a jolt as we pulled away from the dock.

I crossed the room and looked out the window. It was much more than a porthole and offered a panoramic view of the bay and Miami skyline as we motored from the marina. I looked up and saw the MacArthur Causeway, which we left behind as we moved east from the marina, out past Fisher Island. We banked south and kept a slow, steady pace until I saw the lights on Key Biscayne. Then the engines growled and we picked up speed, and I saw the lights along the beaches on Key Biscayne give way to darkness as we headed out to sea.

I wasn't too sure how far we'd go. If they were just tossing evidence, we might not go much further at all. On the other hand, they might be headed for the Bahamas. The boat was certainly big enough, and it was one way to avoid apprehension at the airport. I cracked the door open and slid out, and then I retraced my steps and checked that the other two staterooms were still empty. I edged back along the hallway and up to the lounge. The light bounced off the polished hardwood floors, but there was no one on them. A spiral staircase shot up onto the upper deck, where I guessed the cockpit to be. If Montgomery was up there he may be standing right at the top of the stairs, and that felt like a rabbit sticking its head up out of its warren, so I strode through the lounge, slid the glass back and stepped out to the small deck I had come in on. There was a set of steps leading up to the next deck. There were no lights on up there. I figured it made navigating easier with all the upper deck in darkness. It definitely made me feel better about sticking my little rabbit head up.

The upper deck was large. A bank of sun loungers sat in the moonlight before a hot tub under a canopy. Opposite the hot tub was another small bar. I pressed against the sliding glass that led to the cabin and saw nothing. No movement, no people. A kaleidoscope of light played on the ceiling, shooting up through the spiral stairs from the lounge below. I crept inside to where a long dining table waited naked for plates and forks and food. Another smaller lounge, with a sofa opposite a flatscreen television. The television hung on a birch paneled wall that looked to separate the living space from the cockpit. On the side of the wall was a glass door, through which glowed a green light. Night light. I pressed myself against the wall and peered through the glass door.

At the helm I could see Nigel, Montgomery's bodyguard cum driver cum ship captain. He was certainly a very useful guy. His face glowed in the green light being thrown by the instrument panels before him. He stood firm, hands on the wheel, staring out into darkness. Between him and me was a built-in mahogany chart table, and running the length of the back wall of the space was a long bench seat. I saw nothing of Montgomery. It occurred to me that he was not on board, having sent his minion to dispense of the evidence, while Montgomery himself hid somewhere. I figured there was one way to find out. I slid in the door and trained Sally's gun on Nigel. Two hands, firm footing.

"Don't move," I said, which was ridiculous because I startled him and he jerked around. "Hands on the wheel." He looked at the gun and then did as he was told. I stepped a pace toward him, past the chart table.

"The gun in your holster. Slowly use your right hand. Pull it out by the fingers and drop it." He moved his right hand off the wheel and tucked it under his right armpit where his holster sat. Where you would house a gun if you were left-handed. Like the shooter that killed Angel. Nigel pulled the gun out between his thumb and forefinger.

"Drop it," I said, encouraging him not to do anything stupid. He held the gun out and spread his thumb and finger dramatically and let the weapon fall to the floor. He put his hand on the throttle and made to slow the boat down.

"Don't," I said. He lifted his hand and placed it back on the wheel. I had him kick the gun toward me, and I picked it up.

"Where's Montgomery?"

Nigel glanced at me blankly, hesitated, and then gave me a crooked grin.

"In Miami," he said. I wasn't going to believe his first answer under any circumstances, but I knew he was lying. The hesitation was enough, but the grin was too much.

"Don't mess around with me, *Nigel*." I said his name in my best *Downton Abbey* accent. "I am just itching to shoot you. Now be a good fellow, and tell me, where the hell is Alexander Montgomery?"

"He's standing right behind you." Nigel grinned again, and I heard the metallic slide of a pistol being cocked.

CHAPTER FIFTY—SEVEN

I slowly turned I and saw Montgomery, pointing a Glock at me.
He held it sideways with one hand, like some gangbanger from
Harlem, and high up, such that he almost had to point it down at
me. His other hand held two soda cans.

"Thank you, Jones," he said.

"For what?"

"For being so daft. And for making my life that little bit
easier. Now we can kill two birds with one stone. Get rid of the
gun, and you." He smiled like he'd just thought of something
clever.

"It's ironic, really. You getting offed by the same gun that did
that stupid little girl at the college."

I looked at the weapon in Montgomery's hand, and he
waved it about.

"Not this one, dunce. That one. In your hand."

My head dropped to look at the gun I had taken off Nigel. I
hadn't realized that I had dropped both hands so I had a gun by
each thigh. The one belonging to Nigel suddenly felt heavy.

"Don't forget, guv—that gun also done his missus," said
Nigel.

"Of course it did. Good memory, Nige. So there you are,
Jones. Both your little tarts and you." He gave me a vicious
smirk.

"Danielle's not dead."

I had hoped to wipe the smile off his face, but it didn't
work.

"Well, that is good news. I felt that whole thing was rushed. Now we can go back and take our time over it. Give her a right proper send-off."

Montgomery laughed a mirthless chuckle. "You should have listened and left it alone, but you had to push it. My boys told you to leave it, but you put them in the hospital. Now this is all on you."

I grimaced at the thought that the weasel spoke the truth. It was on me. All except for the inciting incident.

"Why did you kill Jake? Surely there are plenty of kids to sell your crap."

"The boy done himself wrong, not me. He was a good little marketer, moved a lot of EPO, steroids, you name it. But he got all high and mighty over our designer party products. We gave him a bunch of Maxx, but he refused to shift it. Even the Liquid X, he wouldn't do it."

"So you filled him full of Maxx."

"You don't get it, do you, Jones? You couldn't give Maxx to Jake, he would never take it. Besides, doping is really not our style."

I stood between them, side on so I could see both their evil grins in my field of vision. I felt sick.

"Now, enough chitchat. Do yourself a favor and drop the guns, nice and easy."

I let my grip go so Sally's gun slipped down my hand and I could grab it by the butt between my thumb and forefinger, just as I had instructed Nigel to do. Then I lifted it out toward Montgomery and the Glock he had pointed at me.

"Drop it," said Montgomery.

So I did.

Everyone who has ever played golf knows how hard it is to not look at a moving ball. It takes a lot of training to perfect the practice of keeping your head down and focusing on the spot where the ball was, rather than the natural inclination to look up and focus on a moving object. Montgomery didn't play golf, or at least he wasn't very good at it. His focus was on the gun as I cocked my wrist and flicked it into space between us, rather than focusing on me. So while he was watching my gun gently arc its way to the floor, I fell too. I just let the weight in my hips drop and my knees collapse and my feet push out and I fell like a tree with a mission, down behind the mahogany chart table. As best I knew, Montgomery had a gun but Nigel no longer did, so I wanted to be on Nigel's side of the table.

I hit the floor a fraction of a second after the gun I had dropped, and simultaneously with Montgomery's first shot. I wasn't too concerned about getting shot by Montgomery. Holding the gun the way he did, he would be lucky to hit Yankee Stadium if he was standing at the main gate. So he got his shot away, but I wasn't there anymore. It was a good shot though, for after passing through vacant space where I had been, the bullet exploded into Nigel's thigh, halfway between the knee and the hip. Nigel howled and Montgomery kept shooting. His second shot was better. At least it didn't hit Nigel. Montgomery reacted and aimed his shots where I was going. I lay on the floor and said a prayer for good, thick, expensive mahogany. Montgomery exploded his magazine into the base of the chart desk, pock-marking the beautiful wood but not getting through to me a single time. Once I heard the *click-click* of an empty clip, it was my turn. I sat up from behind the desk, two hands on the gun that had killed Angel. I pointed it at Montgomery's head. And I thought about crossing lines and leaking barrels. I took a deep breath, in through the nose, out through the mouth.

Montgomery laughed. "You haven't got the—"

I pulled the trigger. He hadn't gone for the gun that lay on the floor between us, though I was sure he would have, if given the chance. And I could convince myself on that basis that shooting a now unarmed man was self-defense. But the truth was, I was sick of him. Sick of what he had done, sick of the cancer he was on our paradise. But mostly I was sick of his voice. I didn't want to hear anything more he had to say. So I shot him. Full on in the face, right smack-bang in the middle of the target. The bullet and the majority of the rear of Montgomery's head plastered itself all over the wood-paneled wall and the rest of him dropped like an empty suit.

Then I picked up Sally's gun from the floor and turned my attention on Nigel. He was backed up against the console, whimpering, holding his leg like a smashed chicken wing. Montgomery's shot had hit something significant because Nigel was spurting a pool of blood across the floor. He was holding his thigh at the top, where the bullet had entered, but the blood seemed to be coming from below, at the back of his leg.

I stood over him. He was in a lot of pain. It was writ across his face, but he was trying not to let it show. He was a tough guy, in every sense of the phrase. He was also an animal. An injured animal. The humane thing to do was to put him down. But I had a question first.

"Tell me about the boy. Jake. No point lying now."

Nigel's head dropped, like it was heavy, then he picked it up again and looked at me. "He told ya, that's not our style. Only reason to finish someone slow is for it to hurt, and you can't hurt him if he's out of it." Nigel coughed and winced. "And that boy would have had to have been out of it already for him to ever take Maxx, he was such a princess. You'd have to knock him out with roofies or GHB or something first, and that's amateur date rape stuff."

"Or Liquid X," I said to myself.

"GHB and Liquid X are the same stuff, you moron." He shifted slightly and a bolt of pain must have shot up from his leg. By rights the leg should have been elevated to lessen the blood loss, but that wasn't going to happen. "The last guy we had dealing resigned, he graduated college, and Jake should have took his place. He was such a princess. But we didn't off him. The kid moved a lot of PEDs."

Something about what he said set all sorts of synapses firing off in my brain.

"Why the baseball bat? With the girl? That wasn't about pain," I said.

He groaned. "All work and no play make Nigel a dull boy."

I felt bile burn my throat. I pointed Sally's gun at Nigel's face. He looked at Montgomery lying on the floor, the rest if him dripping down the wall. He sucked in a breath to control himself, then through gritted teeth he spat.

"Aim true, scumbag."

"This is for Angel," I said. And I dropped my aim, held the gun by my thigh. It was the line that Sally had talked about, and Nigel and I had both left it behind. I stood over him and waited, his bloody hands on his leg wound. At first he didn't understand, wondering if I were giving him a reprieve. Then, as he felt his heart beating, the understanding swept across his face and he scowled, unable to move, weeping first with pain, then with the realization that life was slowly leaving him, and I held his gaze for the longest time, until the blood had all pumped out onto the floor and his last dirty breath had left him.

CHAPTER FIFTY–EIGHT

Sometimes things happen for a reason. I hadn't expected Montgomery to shoot his bodyguard in the leg, but he had. So I figured rather than leave two bodies and a crime scene to solve, I'd leave two bodies and a solved crime. There may have been flaws in my plan, but I was banking on the Miami PD not knocking themselves out over this one. I left the empty Glock in Montgomery's hand. Then I picked up the gun Sally had given me and put it back in my trousers. I wiped down and then placed the gun that had killed Angel, shot Danielle and then killed Montgomery into the dead hand of his bodyguard. The Miami PD would run ballistics as a matter of course and find that this gun was the one used in all of those cases. The scene looked like a servant-master relationship gone wrong. Maybe Nigel wants a piece of the action, Montgomery taunts him, guns are pulled, guns are fired, voilà. I'd leave Miami PD to create the best story. But the deaths of two drug dealers responsible for murder and the shooting of a law enforcement officer would be wrapped up as cleanly and quickly as possible, so they could move on to some crimes that mattered.

I pulled the throttle back on the console to bring the huge boat to a stop. It coasted for a long while, and as it did, I carefully stepped around the blood and bodies and out of the cockpit. I waited in a dark corner of the small upper deck lounge in case there was anyone else on board, alerted by my stopping of the boat. No one came. After several minutes I crept back out the glass doors, which I closed behind me, and then down the external stairs to the main deck. I jumped over the transom and landed on the swimming platform that was wet from the backwash of the slowing boat. Leaning against the transom, right on the words *El Jefe*, I waited. The engines rumbled against my back, even in neutral. The smell of marine diesel filled the salty air.

Then I heard the high-pitched buzz coming from the darkness between me and the distant lights on Key Biscayne. I watched the lights bobbing up and down, and the buzzing continued long before I saw the rubber ducky motor into the halo of light spilling from the lounge on board *El Jefe*. The boat was a red inflatable, and at the helm was the heavy silhouette of Lucas. He looked like a retired Navy SEAL, all sinew and muscle and wind-burned skin, out in a vast, dark ocean in a little tender, but looking completely at home doing it.

"Jesus, mate, could you have gone a little further out? I think I can see the Biminis from here." He came astern and edged the rubber bow into the swimming platform.

"Stay low—you don't wanna fall in the drink."

I did as I was told and got in a crouch and stepped across onto the bow and then down into the tender. There was a wooden plank for a seat, and I sat facing Lucas. He came off the throttle, and we drifted for a moment, both looking at the big motor yacht, its engine still grumbling but making no headway.

"All done?" said Lucas.

I nodded.

"Righto, let's get home. Just watch out, could get a bit wet." He hit the throttle and the whiny engine burst to life, and we screamed southwest, bouncing across the water past the beaches on Key Biscayne. Lucas skirted Bill Baggs Cape at the southern end of the island, and then turned inland past the lights of Gables by the Sea, and into Deering Bay. As we neared the country club to the north I felt sea grasses lapping at the boat, and Lucas tilted the motor up a touch and pulled back on the throttle. Over the buzz of the motor I called to Lucas.

"You know anything about the Greek alphabet?" I yelled.

He nodded. "Used it for signals back in the service."

"You know gamma?"

He nodded again, took his hand off the tiller and made a sign with two hands.

I nodded to him, and he dropped his hand back to control the boat. The shore loomed before us, dark and uninhabited, and I had visions of us ending this whole sorry episode run aground on a sandbank. But Lucas puttered his way in, until finally I saw a small light, flashing on and off. Lucas headed for the light and brought us into a small beach, surrounded by mangrove and brush. Sally stood on the beach with a flashlight in hand. Lucas motored the boat at Sally and pushed us up onto the sand. He killed the motor and in a well-practiced move collapsed the small motor on itself and pulled it free of the boat. He pulled out the fuel line, and launched himself over the side and into the knee-high water, and then he flung the motor on his shoulder and carried it up the beach. I stepped out of the inflatable and pulled it further onto land, and then Lucas returned and together we carried it up to his Tacoma and slid the boat into the flatbed. The truck sat at the end of a dirt track on the tiny beach.

I turned to Sally.

"You got a cell phone on you?"

"Yeah. You planning on ordering a pizza?" he said, handing me his phone.

"Sorry, pal, no. I gotta call the cops."

"Are you serious?"

"Very. But don't worry, not Miami cops."

Sal frowned.

"Best get in the truck," said Lucas. "Crocs like hanging out here."

"You neglected to mention that earlier," said Sally, scrambling up into the cab. The three of us squeezed onto the bench seat of the old truck. Lucas put his hand on the key in the ignition and turned to me.

"We good?"

"Define good," I said.

"Are we going to have to go out into the Atlantic Ocean in a rubber ducky in the dead of night again anytime soon?"

"No."

"Then we're good," he said, kicking the truck to life and driving us out of the darkness and back to civilization.

CHAPTER FIFTY—NINE

I arrived at the townhouse in the early morning, when most folks were either sleeping or munching on their granola. The disheveled face at the door didn't look happy to see me.

"What do you want?" he said.

"Your uncle sent me," I said, stepping around Sean Lawry into the townhouse. Sean eyed me as I passed. He might have been unimpressed by my moxie, but I had every reason to believe he was assessing my excuse for visiting. I got to the kitchen island before he finished his thinking.

"Why don't you just come in?"

"Thanks."

"My uncle didn't call you. You shouldn't be here." He opened the door a little wider. I chose to miss the hint.

"He didn't tell you about our round of golf?"

He frowned and let the door ease itself closed.

"What round of golf?"

"He didn't tell you?" I said. "Gee, I thought you said you guys spoke all the time."

"We speak enough."

"Enough to get you out of trouble but no more."

"Look, what do you want?"

I glanced around the room. "Your roommate about?"

"No, she's at class."

"This early? Could it be she's having breakfast at her own home?"

"What?"

"Where were you, Sean? The night Jake OD'ed?"

"Here. I told you that. My roommate backed it up." Sean strode around the island and took a soda from the fridge. He didn't offer me one.

"You got a real clean place here, for a college guy."

"What's your point, man?"

"My point is, Sean, you don't got a roommate. Sure as hell not a female one. You give women the creeps. I asked Alice Chang about you—when she heard your name, she went and put on a rape whistle. She didn't even realize she was doing it."

"You're talking trash."

"Who is she, Sean? This Elissa who's pretending to be your roommate. Looking at this place, I'm guessing she's your cleaning lady."

"You are seriously annoying me, man."

"Like the girl at your last college? The one you hit up with Liquid X? You tried to have your way but her friends turned up, right? What a bummer."

"You repeat any of that, you're finished."

"Your uncle fixed it, kept everything quiet and got you out of town. But it was the last straw, wasn't it, Sean? He thinks you're a waste of good Florida oxygen. He told me as much. You mess up one more time, you're on your own, right? Cut out of Camelot, so to speak."

"What have wizards got to do with anything?"

I shook my head. "But you did mess up again, didn't you. Big time. You were interning with Jake Turner, the big man on campus. Popular, star athlete, going places. Even Rinti could see he was a smart kid, a fast thinker, a team player. You said he was finishing the best years of his life, but that wasn't Jake, that was you. He was leaving you in the dust and it drove you crazy."

"Turner was nothing."

"Oh, but that's not true, is it. Did he wave it in your face, Sean? How he was self-made and going places, and you were a worthless piece of nothing living off the last of your uncle's coattails?"

"That's crap, man. Jake was a loser, like you."

"Jake was like me, in a lot of ways. Probably too cocky for his own good, just like me. And he didn't like you one bit."

"The feeling was mutual."

"No doubt. So he taunted you with his achievements until it drove you nuts. Which is when you let slip something you knew but he didn't. The Rinti deal on campus. You shouldn't have known either—your uncle doesn't trust you. But you overheard."

"Just because he and my dad think I'm invisible doesn't mean I am."

"But once you blurted it out at Jake, the cat was out of the bag. The big jock, about to lose his beloved athletics. You figured he was going to tell tales and blow the whole deal. Your uncle, Rinti, the school, they'd all blame you. The coattails were about to be severed. You'd lose this natty pad and your housekeeper."

"None of this means squat."

"Oh, but it does, Sean. It means you had motive to kill Jake Turner."

"Turner OD'ed, moron."

"Yes, he did. With a little help from you."

Sean gave a look of shock that was right up there in the acting stakes with that kid from the *Home Alone* movie.

"You repeat that, I'll own you. You got no proof."

"I got plenty of proof, Sean. Like your MO. You have a history of using Liquid X on other people."

"Liquid X didn't kill him."

"How do you know that?" I tapped my fingers on the counter and let him stew for a bit. "You're right, of course, it didn't. But you knew what it would do. It would effectively make him fall down drunk, isn't that right? Make it easy to get something more powerful into him. Like Maxx. Which you and pretty much every other kid on campus knew he had been tasked to sell, since the previous dealer graduated, or resigned as they preferred to say at Maxx HQ. You knew he had it, and you could use it."

"Listen, Miss Marple, I've had enough of you and your Spanish Inquisition. You got no proof, so get lost and don't come back."

I was going to say something clever, but a knock at the door stopped me. I had to smile. The timing couldn't have been better if we had synchronized watches. On a brand-new townhouse with a spiffy new door bell, very few people knock on the door. Let alone knock again, harder.

Sean scowled at me. "Who the hell?" He strode to the door and wrenched it open.

"Mr. Sean Lawry?" came the clipped tone of Officer Steele.

"What the?"

"May we come in? Thank you." Steele entered not by stepping around Sean Lawry but by herding him into the middle of the lounge room like a sheep dog. Steele was in his crisp police uniform. As was his rotund partner Harris, who shut the door. Steele nodded to me.

"Jones."

"Officer Steele."

"Listen, you guys can't just bust in here—I know my rights. You need a warrant or something."

"Sir, I asked if we could come in."

"Well, he's trespassing," said Sean, pointing at me.

"You invited me in."

"That was before you started going on about Jake. That has nothing to do with me."

"We all know that's not true, Sean," I said. "When we found out about your history, I admit I didn't make the connection, other than you being a good for nothing dirtbag."

"You can't talk to me like that."

"It was my ignorance. When I heard Liquid X, I assumed it was ecstasy, or MDMA. I was wrong, wasn't I, Officer Steele?"

"You were. Liquid X is a street name for GHB, which is a depressant, not an activity-inducing amphetamine, like ecstasy."

"Exactly. And Jake's doctor told my partner that Jake had high levels of a hormone in his body when he OD'ed. She wrote the name down but Ron misread it. He confused a Y for the Greek letter Gamma. As in gamma hydroxybutyric acid."

"Or GHB," said Steele.

"Otherwise known as Liquid X. The same stuff you drugged the girl in Georgia with."

"There were no charges laid, so you're going nowhere."

"In my own meandering way I am indeed going somewhere. The reason no charges were laid, apart from your uncle, was that you got interrupted before you did anything to the girl. So there was only the drug charge. They took blood from the girl and found GHB, or Liquid X, and large amounts of tequila in her system. But at a party, the cops couldn't pin the exact glass with the drug residue down to you, even if they had found it. And that's how you delivered it, isn't it, Sean? One of the signature properties of GHB is that it dissolves in liquid, but is very salty-tasting. Hard to slip into a daiquiri, but easily masked by tequila. And perfect for an electrolyte sports drink."

"What sports drink?" said Sean.

"The one you doctored at lacrosse training. Each player had their own bottle on a table at training and games. I thought for health reasons, but it seems it depended on which PEDs they were using. I saw the bottles when I went to a game myself. Just there, out in the open. You saw them too, when you followed Jake. You also knew that he usually went to the baseball diamond after training to chill out and stretch. So you doped his drink and followed him to the diamond."

"I doctored a sports drink? Good luck proving that, moron."

"Officer Steele?" I said.

Steele turned his eye to Harris, who held up an evidence bag with a sports drink bottle in it."

"Right where you said it would be," said Harris. "Under the home team bleachers."

"That could be anyone's," said Sean.

"Except it has two sets of fingerprints on it," said Steele. "Jake Turner's, which we had on file, and another set we matched to an arrest record in Georgia."

I smiled a big wide grin. "That would be you, Sean."

"That's not . . . that's nothing."

"No, it's something, as I am sure the lab tests of the contents will show. After Jake drank the drink his friend Angel described him as being out of it. You didn't realize she was there, did you? You followed Jake to the stadium entrance, but Angel's habit was to climb up the fire escape at the back of the bleachers. And she was there. She said he was clumsy, that he knocked his drink bottle off the bleacher. She left, then he tried to do the same, but you met him on the walkway between the two stands." I turned my gaze to Steele. "And this was the bit that felt off kilter from the get-go," I said. "Underneath a bleacher was certainly a place you would find a kid doing drugs."

I looked back to Sean, "You had that bit right. But when I went under, the wooden home bleacher was way more likely. It was darker, creepier. The aluminum bleachers let in more light; it was practically a sunroom in comparison. It didn't feel like a drug haven. Until I realized it wasn't. Had Jake done this to himself he would have been under the home bleacher, but you needed to see what you were doing. So you chose the side with the best light."

"I've never been near those bleachers, let alone under them."

Steele nodded at Harris, who left the room, toward what I assumed was the garage.

"He can't just wander around in here," said Sean.

"Actually, he can," said Steele.

"I want my lawyer," said Sean, standing upright like he'd taken a shot of resolve.

"You got a lawyer?" I said.

"My uncle . . ."

"He's washing his hands of you as we speak."

"I've got an alibi, dammit."

"About that," said Steele, looking to his notepad. "Miss Elissa Cartwright, freshman at the university. She decided she didn't want to go to jail for you or your five hundred dollars. She confirmed her residence on campus in freshman halls, and her employ by your father's real estate holding company, owner of this dwelling, as a cleaner. She also confirmed that she was on campus the night Jake overdosed, not with you."

Harris wobbled back into the room, holding another evidence bag, this one containing a pair of Nikes.

Steele continued. "She further confirmed that the next day you gave her a pair of mud-covered running shoes to clean, which she left in the laundry, a room you clearly do not frequent."

"She didn't clean my stuff? That cow."

"She said, and I quote"—Steele referred to his notes—"'I'm paid by his daddy to keep the place from looking like a dump, but that don't make me his personal slave.'"

"Ouch," I said. "Damn hard luck that. No alibi, prints on the bottle that contained the drug that knocked Jake out, and shoes covered in the same mud that is under the bleachers."

"Our lab will check that out," said Steele.

"Look for a footprint under that bleacher, too. That ground felt like potter's clay."

"Will do."

"And no doubt the Maxx that killed Jake came from his own stash. Check for Sean's prints at Jake's place, especially on the trunk that's probably still under his bed."

"I have a team there now."

"What say you, Sean?" I smiled.

His lip curled and he spat. "You can't do this without a warrant or something!"

Steele stepped forward and pulled a document from his pocket. "You're right, Mr. Lawry," he said, tapping his chest with the paper as Harris pulled Sean's arms back and cuffed him.

"A warrant, for your arrest. You have the right to remain silent. Anything you do or say may be used against you in a court of law."

CHAPTER SIXTY

That night I slept fitfully but I didn't dream. The following day I took a long shower and then stopped at a grocery store to pick up some flowers. I went and saw Danielle, who was on the mend, and then I drove to her house, went in under the yellow police tape and collected a bunch of her things. Then I drove home and cleaned the kitchen, made my bed, sorted my wardrobe and scrubbed down the bathroom. You might say I did anything to keep busy. Later I picked Ron and Cassandra up from Palm Beach International and dropped Cassandra back at her penthouse. They both looked refreshed and relieved.

"Just reading the paper on the plane," said Ron. "Lots going on."

"Indeed," I said.

"*USA Today* has a puff piece about women working in the front office at NFL clubs."

"You don't say."

"Yeah. Seems the Minnesota Vikings have just hired a new assistant GM, and it's a woman no less."

"They are very progressive, those Nords. And they have a good, strong work ethic too. I think Kim will do just fine there."

We left Lady Cassandra to unpack her case, and Ron came with me to the car dealership to return the Jeep. When something just doesn't feel right, it probably isn't, so you should take your licks and move on. I wore a hefty off-the-lot surcharge and then walked to the dealership next door, owned by the same guy, and rolled out of the showroom with a beige Ford Escape, for full sticker price. Ron suggested it was an all-round more suitable car for stakeouts and trips to big-box stores. When we got back to the office Lizzy was at the door.

"What did you get?" she said.

"A Ford Escape."

She looked at Ron, her face scrunched beneath her black bangs. "An SUV?"

Ron nodded. "A small SUV." He smiled.

"Wow," said Lizzy, turning back to me. "Not another dumb macho car."

"No. You underestimate me."

"Usually. But perhaps there's some growth. Now, you might like to know you have a visitor."

I frowned.

"State Attorney Edwards."

I smiled and walked into my office. Eric was sitting in a visitor's chair with his legs crossed, pressing a sea-green tie with his hands. He jumped to attention when the door flew open.

"At ease, Edwards," I said, walking to my desk.

"You're just a card, Jones. Really. Now I have a bone to pick with you."

"Gee, and I thought you were here to invite me to lunch."

"Why would I do that?"

"Seems you've been having a lot of lunches lately."

Edwards grinned, his *I know something* grin. "Says whom?"

"Never mind. What you want, Eric?"

He smoothed his tie and lifted his chin. "You owe me an explanation. Stephen Millet has resigned to take a post as director of an online university in New Mexico."

"Nevada," I said.

"Whatever. And Senator Lawry held a press conference this morning to confirm that the planning committee has not approved, nor will they approve, any state funds for a private college, as was suggested in this morning's *Palm Beach Post*."

"Good news."

"Not good. You've been talking to Maggie Nettles. Her article claims there is an ongoing investigation into the senator's dealings with Gino Rinti. An investigation spearheaded by the state attorney's office."

"You have an investigation going?"

"No, Jones, you imbecile. I just did what you told me."

"So say there's no investigation."

"You really don't understand politics do you?"

"Nup. Now, is there anything else, I have to get to the hospital to collect Danielle."

"How is she?"

"She got shot, so not great."

"Yes, well," he said, smoothing his tie one last time. "You haven't heard the end of this, Jones."

"Great seeing you, Eric. Thanks for stopping by."

Edwards opened the door.

"And Eric, if you feel the need to eat with Danielle, go ahead. She's a big girl. But don't make a bigger fool of yourself by thinking you're going to get her back."

"Eric smiled. "Who says I want her back?"

"Not Danielle. She said watching you eat reminded her why she was so happy to get a divorce."

Edwards growled and slammed the door so hard the pebbled glass shook. Ron sat down on his sofa and kicked his feet up.

"Danielle said that?"

"Come on, Ron, she'd never say something like that."

Ron smiled. "And he thinks you're no good at politics."

I shrugged. "You think it's safe to go to the hospital now?"

The intercom buzzed. "There's a call for you," said Lizzy. "Gino Rinti on line one."

I shook my head. "Did I win the lottery and someone forgot to tell me?" I picked the phone up. "Rinti, good of you to call."

"I don't think so," he said, sounding like he had just smoked a pack of *Galoise*.

"Yeah it is—you just bought me a new car."

"I don't think so."

"But sorry about the whole college development thing collapsing. Those politicians can be fickle."

"You're just hilarious, Jones. And you think you won. But you won nothing. There's plenty more deals left in this state. Plenty more beaches. You won nothing."

And he was right. Nothing had changed. Florida was still Florida, and the fact Senator Lawry was killing a deal today didn't mean he wouldn't make another happen tomorrow, for the right price. And the fact was, Millet's plan wasn't the worst. I had no bone to pick with someone who wanted to build a world-class university in Florida. None at all. But when people start dying, you have to ask yourself whether you're going about it in the right way.

"Hey, Gino, how's your dad?"

"What do you care? He's got cancer."

"Couldn't happen to a nicer guy," I said, and I dropped the phone back into the cradle.

CHAPTER SIXTY—ONE

I parked the Escape in the parking lot that had become way too familiar, ignored the same nurse and got the elevator to Danielle's hospital room. She was dressed and sitting on her bed, watching the local news.

"You see this?" she said. "Coast Guard found a boat floating north of Miami Beach. Two dead guys inside, looks like a drug transaction gone wrong."

"That's Miami for you."

"Reports are suggesting Miami PD think my shooter may have been involved."

"That is good news." I smiled.

Danielle frowned. "Where were you the night before last?"

"Here."

"Then?"

"I guess I went for a beer with Ron."

"I thought Ron was in Colorado?"

"He's back."

"When?"

"I don't recall. I'll have to call him and confirm that."

"What does that mean?"

Now it was my turn to frown. "Do you remember anything from that night?"

"I was shot, then drugged."

"Don't remember saying anything?"

"No. Why, what did I say?"

I looked at her, still pale and in pain.

"What did I say?" she said again.

I shook my head. "Nothing. You wanted to go home. So let's do that."

She winced as she stood.

"Are you sure you don't want to stay another night? The doc seemed to think you should."

"It's pain. It'll hurt here, it'll hurt at home. I'd rather be at home."

"Got some pain meds?"

She held up a prescription.

"Let's get out of here then."

Danielle didn't comment on the new car, and nodded off as I took the freeway. I woke her up when I stopped in front of my garage. She blinked hard to acclimatize, and then I helped her to step down from the Escape.

"Whose car is this?"

"It's mine."

She frowned like she'd been dropped into the twilight zone. As I helped her through the front door, she looked at me.

"I'm sorry, but I think I'd rather be at home. My home. It's just all my stuff. You know?"

"Your place is a crime scene right now. Besides, all your stuff is here." Danielle shuffled into the bedroom, and I went to the kitchen to make her tea. After a few minutes she reappeared.

"You made the bed."

I nodded.

"And there's a whole wardrobe of my clothes in there."

"Yeah, I was thinking we needed to consolidate."

"Consolidate?"

"Yeah. You need your stuff here, while you get better, and I want you close so I can look after you. But then I was thinking, you have a place and I have a place, so we have a big carbon footprint."

"Carbon footprint."

"That's right. So I thought we should reduce our footprint. Consolidate."

"Are you asking me to move in with you?"

"Well, yes. I guess I am. I mean, if this whole thing has shown me anything, it's that we're not going to be here forever. And I'd like to spend more of what time I have with you in it. Not just nearby. Really in it." I stirred the tea and pushed it across the counter.

"What do you think?" I said.

Danielle gave me that half smile, gulped two pain tabs and sipped some tea. Then she shuffled around the counter and kissed me.

"I'm going to lie down for a bit," she said, as she took her tea and padded toward the bedroom. When she got to the door she stopped and looked back to me.

"And MJ, call Ron." She smiled. "Get your stories straight."

GET YOUR NEXT BOOK FREE

Hearing from you, my readers, is one of the the best things about being a writer. If you want to join my Readers' Group, we'll not only be able to keep in touch, but you can also get an exclusive Miami Jones ebook novel, as well as occasional pre-release reads, and other goodies that are only available to my Readers' Group friends.

Join Now:
http://www.ajstewartbooks.com/reader

ACKNOWLEDGEMENTS

Thanks, as always, to all my readers who send me feedback. A huge thanks to Marianne Fox for the editorial smarts; all the beta readers, especially Heather and Andrew; and the folks at The Breakers in Palm Beach, which is, as the story says, a true Palm Beach institution. Any and all errors are mine, especially but not limited to the third bottle of wine. That's just poor judgement, right there.

ABOUT THE AUTHOR

A.J. Stewart wrote marketing copy for Fortune 500 companies and tech start-ups for 20 years, until his head nearly exploded from all the stories bursting to get out. Stiff Arm Steal was his fifth novel, but the first to make it into print.

He has lived and worked in Australia, Japan, UK, Norway, and South Africa, as well as San Francisco, Connecticut and of course Florida. He currently resides in Los Angeles with his two favorite people, his wife and son.

AJ is working on a screenplay that he never plans to produce, but it gives him something to talk about at parties in LA.

You can find AJ online at www.ajstewartbooks.com, connect on Twitter @The_AJStewart or Facebook facebook.com/TheAJStewart.